JANE HAYES

# Winning the Nightcap

Editing by Paisley McNab, Perfectly Write Editing Services (Copyediting)
Editing by E&A Editing Services (Beta Reading Service)
Cover art by Acacia of Ever After Cover Design (Cover Design)

This book was professionally typeset on Reedsy.
Find out more at reedsy.com

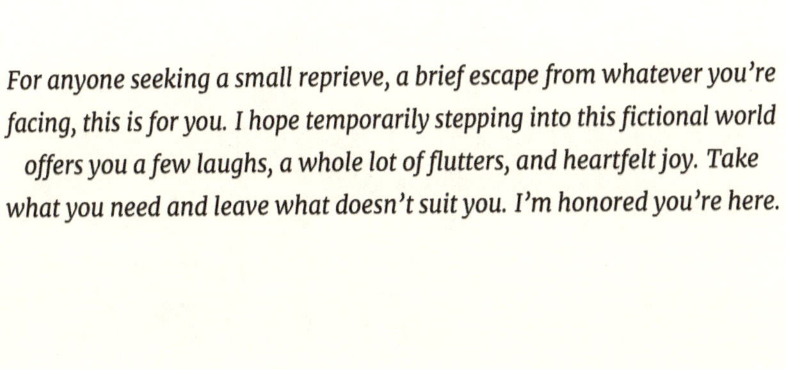
For anyone seeking a small reprieve, a brief escape from whatever you're facing, this is for you. I hope temporarily stepping into this fictional world offers you a few laughs, a whole lot of flutters, and heartfelt joy. Take what you need and leave what doesn't suit you. I'm honored you're here.

# Contents

# Author's Note

The following page contains a list of content warnings. If you have triggers, I encourage you to take a look before reading this novel. Your health and wellness are important to me and should absolutely always come first. If you don't have any triggers and prefer to be surprised, please skip ahead.

# Content Warning

Content Warning includes:

On-page sex descriptions (intended for 18+ years of age, or legal age of adulthood);

Mentions and brief descriptions of birth trauma and postpartum mental health conditions (not main character);

Descriptions of Alzheimer's disease, the progression of the condition, and caring for a loved one living with Alzheimer's;

Discussion of pet loss (historical) and grief; and

Mentions of emotional and verbal abuse (historical).

# Chapter One

## Bec

"Holy shit, *your boobs*. I mean...uh, look at you, Momma! You look incredible." I walk into Ellie's living room to give her a squeeze hello, while she sits on the couch holding sweet baby Luca. "But seriously, what happened to your boobs?"

I know I should be looking at my best friend's face, sincerely looking into her eyes and telling her that she looks radiant—a true rock star for birthing the most beautiful newborn baby I've ever seen. But I can't, not when her nipples are staring at me like that.

"Apparently, my milk coming in means I get a natural lift before they drop to the ground forever. Too bad this gift is ruined by the fact that I'm so sore I could just about cry every time this little potato latches on. Who the hell knew breastfeeding was the least natural thing I'd ever try to do," she explains.

I don't have it in my heart to mention that there is spit-up in her hair and on her shirt. *Is it on the couch too?* She probably already knows; best to just let that go, since I assume there will be more any minute.

"Oh my god, is that for me?"

"Of course, I come bearing gifts. Some caffeine for you, supermom. Let's see your body work miracles and turn this sugar fest into liquid gold for little Luca here." I hand over her favorite chai latte from the local coffee shop and a blueberry muffin the size of my face.

I grab my coffee, throw my purse onto the floor, and get comfortable next to Ellie on the sofa. Have you ever seen a sectional from Costco before? Those couches look normal in a store the size of a warehouse. You bring that bad boy home, and it'll devour half of your living room. It's the best thing in the world. I've crashed over here plenty of nights, and I choose this couch over the guest bed. Every. Damn. Time.

"Hey, Bec. Good to see you. You guys want pizza or burgers for lunch? I was just about to order for delivery, so I can wash up a few dishes while it's on the way." He looks around, scratches his head, then rests his hands on his hips. "We somehow don't have a single clean plate in the house, so I need to wash a few before we can eat."

Dom, Ellie's husband, looks like he's seen a ghost. Or he is a ghost. I've never seen a more exhausted person in my life. His shirt is rumpled, and he almost looks lost. His restless eyes scan their home like there are a million things to do and he is just managing to keep it together with one small task at a time. I can see the dishes piled high in the kitchen sink from here. Day five and this kid has given my put-together friends a true shake-up to their routine. What a force of nature.

Dom walks over and gives Ellie a kiss on her forehead while brushing a hand over Luca's head. He's the only guy I trust with my best friend, and this is why. He looks like he's about to fall asleep standing up, frazzled beyond belief, and still trying to take care of Ellie and his son with a look of pure adoration on his face.

Ellie perks up. "My vote is pizza. Dom, can you please bring me some water?"

"Yeah, sure. Here, just take mine." He hands her his coffee mug.

She stares down at it, not taking it just yet, and gives it a sniff. "Uh, Dom, is that coffee with Baileys?"

"Yeah, there's water in coffee, right? I didn't realize I grabbed Baileys instead of coffee creamer. I'm calling it a happy, sleep-deprived accident." He is talking so fast; I can barely make out what he's saying.

I should have come sooner.

Best friend stepping up to bat in three, two..."Hey Dom, why don't you go rest for a bit. I'll get Ellie some water and order us some food. We'll wake you when it gets here."

"Seriously?!" He half screams at me. I swear he's tearing up. Shit, this dude is acting like I'm about to hand him a check for ten million dollars. I guess sleep is more valuable around here right now.

"Yeah, I got it. Tag me in, man."

Ellie pipes in. "That's a great idea. Babe, go rest now so at least one of us can function later. You crash now, then it's my turn."

Dom kisses Ellie again and sprints upstairs to hopefully fit in a very needed power nap. I grab Ellie some water and call in our order for delivery. When I'm done, I sit and turn to Ellie. "Seriously, I'm so proud of you. How are you feeling, little momma?"

Ellie's been with me through everything. An all the way back to preschool–type friendship. Finish each other's sentences–type friendship. Don't speak for two weeks and then pick up like it's been five minutes–type friendship. Held my hair back on my twenty-first birthday–type friendship. Spiritually, the girl's my twin. My soul mate. But we couldn't be living more different lives right now. That fact is staring me in the face in the form of an eight-pound slobber monster. God, that thing is cute. Terrifying...but cute.

"I think I'm in shock. The birth was so fast and not what we were expecting at all with the emergency C-section. I'm relieved to be home and safe with Luca. We barely slept at all while we were recovering in the hospital. Everything feels confusing, and I'm unsure how to do anything confidently anymore. The only thing I'm sure of is how much I love this little guy."

She's staring at the slobber monster like I've never seen anyone look at anything before. It's incredible to see her becoming a mom right in front of me. I can feel the shift in her. Like when you see a kid watching fireworks for the first time, true wonder behind their eyes, not quite believing what they're seeing. Magic.

"Well, pizza will be here in an hour. What can I do to help? Put me to work." I stand and she looks at me with gratitude.

"You don't have to do anything. I just appreciate you for being here."

"Anytime you need me, I'll come running, you know that. Let me switch dishes, throw in a load of laundry, and get the trash out while you pick out today's Netflix binge, sound good?"

She switches the baby from the right side of her body to the left side, using a mountain of pillows to prop him closer to her, and starts nursing. "I'll browse, but you know what it's going to be. Season four is out next month, we have to get ready." *Stranger Things* is one of Ellie's favorite comfort shows, and mine too. Time to get to work and then introduce Luca to the city of Hawkins.

* * *

"Tell me you saw it! Right there, there's a ladder right there! I know he got out, and that's how he does it," Ellie yells. We're wrapping up the season three finale, and Ellie is worked up. She hands Luca over to Dom to burp. Seriously, how often does she have to feed him? I say a silent prayer for her milk makers. They look angry, and I don't blame them. They're working over time and not in the fun way.

"I don't know, I think he goes through the gate into the Upside Down to survive the explosion," Dom says. We've had this debate a million times. We know we can't lose Hopper. But the *how* is a source of controversy. "Bec, do you want to hold Luca again?"

"Oh no, you go ahead and have some dad and son bonding time. I don't want to interrupt." I know how this works. Post-nurse burping time means you volunteer to be a human spit-up rag. I was already fooled once while we were watching episode six. Not again.

"Hey, did you see in the group chat that Dee has a date tomorrow?" Ellie asks.

"Please tell me she didn't agree to go out with that guy she works with…what's his name? John?"

"Not a chance. She asked Sarah out again, the engineer. I'm shocked she's giving Dee another chance after how their first date ended," Ellie says, her voice heavy with disbelief.

"From what Dee described, Sarah seems sweet and funny. Maybe she'll just laugh the whole thing off." Our friend Dee is single like me, and I swear, she rivals me for most embarrassing first date stories. You'd think we were competing. I would've kept this story to myself, but Dee has absolutely no shame. She can't help but laugh at herself.

"She threw up on Sarah's shoes! I couldn't show my face again if I did that on a date." Poor Dee. Bad time for food poisoning to hit. I guess they were on the highest level of Topgolf. She said her options were to either vomit on her date's shoes or over the edge of the building and watch it fly three stories down. In her state of panic, she chose the shoes. It seemed like the better option to me too.

"But what a good story to tell the grandkids someday, right? I'd rather my introduction to my soul mate be something hilariously embarrassing than something boring," I say, finishing my chips. I'll need to restock Ellie's snack stash tomorrow. I helped her do some serious damage to her supply tonight.

"Speaking of, who's on your radar lately? Anyone promising?" Ellie asks.

"God no. Everyone I'm matching with online has been nice enough, but there's no spark, no connection. I haven't checked any of my messages recently, come to think of it. Besides, it hasn't been that long since Josh and I broke up."

"It's been three months. I bet meeting someone fun will help you close the door on all that drama. Humor me, and pull up the app. Let's see if you have any matches waiting and show Luca his first love story."

I reluctantly find my phone. I haven't checked my messages lately. I've been busy at work and tired of putting in the effort just to find myself on another lackluster date. But I have a feeling that Ellie and Dom are going to be busy while they adapt to being a family of three, and unless I want to spend all my free time working or volunteering, I need to find a way to occupy my time. So, Ellie helps me swipe, and I wish I could say I was excited about any of the possibilities.

* * *

The next day, I pull into Ellie's driveway with another chai latte, supersized blueberry muffin, and a few grocery bags. I woke up early, threw my hair in a messy bun, unwilling to tame the frizz, put on some sweats, and ran to the store to stock up on her favorite snacks. I texted her from her driveway to make sure I wasn't waking her, in case she was lucky enough to be napping, but she gave me the all clear to storm into their home because, in her words, Everyone in this house is always awake for the rest of time.

Sounds like it's time for Mom to get some sleep.

Ellie is pretty much right where I left her last night, cozy on the couch with Luca all scrunched up and asleep on her chest. Her straight blonde hair hangs around her face and over one shoulder in a messy braid. The dark circles under her eyes contrast with her ivory skin. She has to be running on next to no sleep right now.

"You're a lifesaver," she whispers. "Not just for the snacks, but because I have to pee. Can you take Luca so I can go?" Ellie's physical recovery seems more difficult than I imagined it'd be. She has to move really slowly and getting up and down seems really painful for her.

"Of course, hun. I feel bad you were stuck all this time having to go. Can't you put Luca down and run to the bathroom since he doesn't move without you?"

Ellie is patient. Ellie is understanding. Ellie is not the person to bite your head off. But oh my god, I'm afraid right now. She's looking at me like she's going to grow claws and rip me to shreds.

"I've tried. I've tried to put him down, but every time I do, his tiny little voice box turns into a megaphone, and he wails louder than an ambulance. It takes me so long to get to and from the bathroom and on and off the seat, and I *cannot* listen to him screech the whole time. It takes so long to get him calm afterward. Trust me, this is better."

"Yes, ma'am. Fully trusting you." I take Luca into my arms, avoid direct eye contact, and lend her a hand to help her off the couch.

"Sorry." She stands and winces while tears begin to stream down her face. "My mood is so crazy, and I'm just so tired and uncomfortable."

I feel my shoulders and spine relax. She's not going to kill me. "Ellie, it's going to get easier, don't worry. You're doing an amazing job with this huge transition. Go to the bathroom, and then why don't you lie down? I'll watch Luca while you rest. Does he need to nurse soon, or can you sleep for a while?"

"He just ate, are you sure? That would be incredible." Now the tears are really rolling.

"Yes, my best friend in the world just birthed the best baby in the world, and she needs to rest. I'm so happy to be able to spend some time with him. Now you go." She hugs me tight and slowly and carefully makes her way upstairs to nap after I agree to wake her for the next feeding. She also mentioned that Dom ran out to get diapers right before I got here, so it may be a bit before he gets home.

I set up on the couch with Luca on my chest and start up *Parks and Rec* where Ellie left off. "Hey, bud, Aunt Bec here," I whisper. "Time to introduce you to April and Andy. The best two of the crew. What do you say?"

I've interacted with babies before, but I wouldn't say I'm a confident babysitter. I'm happy to wave at babies from afar, to say hi to babies, and to hold them while they're happy. But if Luca starts crying, I might panic a little. Maybe I'll start singing "Baby Got Back" like Ross and Rachel do for Emma when she cries. That'll be plan A.

While brainstorming a plan B, I realize that Luca is starting to wriggle around on my chest. "Oh crap," I whisper. "Are you waking up already? Back to bed, little man. Mom needs to rest, so you need to stay calm and quiet."

The kid must immediately know that I am not Mom or Dad because the fussing is getting louder. *Shit.* And...now, he's crying. Okay, two minutes into my shift, and I am already screwed.

I stand and start bouncing my knees, swaying from side to side, and gently patting his back, trying to mimic what I saw Dom do last night to soothe Luca. I start to half sing, half whisper the lyrics to "Baby Got Back," but before I make it to the chorus, I feel something warm sliding down my front. And my arm? *What is that?*

I look down to find spit-up all over my shirt. But that's so far from my arm....Why does my arm feel wet? I switch my arms around so that my right arm is now on Luca's back and I can pull my left arm away.

I freeze. "Oh fuck." Yep...that's poop running down my arm. Then it hits me. The smell. I cannot do this. Time to panic. "Oh shit, oh shit, oh shit," I hiss while walking around with my arm in the air, at a loss. Dom better be buying some better diapers because these ones suck ass.

I walk to the area in the living room where Dom and Ellie keep the diapers and wipes, all the while trying to soothe Luca. Maybe I'm trying to calm myself, too, and give the pep talk I need to survive until Ellie wakes up or until Dom gets home to take his spawn away from me so I can shower. Dom changed all the poopy diapers last night. I knew I should have practiced at least once before I went solo.

With Luca lying on the mat, I can fully assess the damage and...wow. *How* is Luca capable of this absolute destruction? My shirt and arm are covered, and there is no saving his outfit. Wonderful. Since I know Dom won't be home for a while, I go ahead and take off my shirt, using it to try to wipe myself clean. I'll grab Ellie's sweater off the couch in a second.

I get the diaper and wipes ready, but then I make a critical mistake. One that will haunt me. I take off his diaper too soon, and Luca isn't done. He isn't done *at all.* "Sweet baby Jesus, no!"

Full on explosion. I am the target. Direct hit.

And because my life is a mess, I hear the front door open at this exact moment. "Don't come in here, Dom! Run, save yourself!" I whisper-shout because my best friend is sleeping and I don't know if I'm more scared of the poop machine in front of me or the sleep-deprived best friend snuggled away upstairs.

"Dom?" I hear an unfamiliar voice call out.

*Shit, what the actual fuck?* Who is that? Were Ellie or Dom's parents coming over and they forgot to tell me?

My brain isn't working fast enough, and before I can form any kind of reasonable way to say, *Hey, there's baby poop everywhere, and I'm in a bra; please don't come around the corner,* the most gorgeous man walks into the living room. I haven't spoken to him for over three years, but I've given him plenty of thought since then, and dammit, he looks good.

*Fuck me.*

# Chapter Two

## Aiden

I freeze and divert my eyes, turning back to the front hallway, "Holy tits...fuck, Bec. I'm sorry," I yell. The last thing I expected walking into Dom's house was to see Bec in a sports bra, her beige skin covered in what I hope is baby food or something. Based on the smell and color, that seems unlikely. "Dom invited me over. The door was unlocked, so I came in when no one answered. I knocked; I swear."

I feel like an idiot. I should run so far away that this memory can't even find me. I typically welcome all of my memories with Bec when they flood my mind, more often than I care to admit, but this one, this one I want to burn.

"Uh...yeah, just, uh, give me one second to clean up and grab a sweater," she says.

I wait. Thinking silently about all the decisions I made to get me here, to the most awkward moment in my twenty-eight years of life.

"You can turn around, I'm dressed now. Just getting Luca changed." I turn slowly, trying to decide whether I want to face this moment or disappear and never return. "So, uh, what are you doing here, Aiden?"

Bec is working quickly with what looks like a million buttons. She glances at me over her shoulder and then turns away again.

God, I want her to look at me. She's even more beautiful than I remember. Despite whatever the fuck is going on right now.

"I'm here to meet Luca and congratulate the new parents."

"Oh yeah, right, of course. Dom mentioned last night that you moved back to Columbus. He ran out for diapers and should be back soon. Ellie is upstairs resting." After she puts Luca into a clean outfit, she faces me with him in her arms. "I would say it's nice to see you again, but I'm sure this is by far the worst way to run into someone in the history of humankind," she says, smiling at me. Her cheeks pink from embarrassment.

I chuckle. Okay, so she's still funny. At least we can joke about this. We'll go with that. I scratch the back of my head. "Yeah, can't say I've ever walked into a situation like this before, but it's nice to see you all the same."

I hear the front door open behind me and turn to see Dom walking in, his hands full with boxes of diapers. "Oh shit, Aiden, I completely forgot what time you were coming today. Sorry about that. Hey, Bec," he calls out.

"Mind trading me? I'll take the diapers to the nursery if you take Luca. I need a minute to clean up," Bec says.

"Sure thing, come here, little man."

I never considered how surreal it would be to watch the friends I made when I was fresh out of high school grow into responsible adults, husbands, and fathers. I mean, this guy used to hold the keg stand record in our group. A fun fact I'm sure I'll be sharing with Luca someday. Ellie will love that.

Dom's one of the best guys I know. I have no doubt he'll be an amazing dad. It's something he's always talked about, even when we were both acting like immature assholes in college. Then he met Ellie and everything became real. He's living his dream, building his family.

*Shit, what am I doing?*

"So, this is the newest member of the crew. Congratulations, Dom. I'm really happy for you and Ellie." I clap him on the shoulder as I follow him into the living room of their suburban home and we sit on their massive couch while Dom flips on SportsCenter. Their home is comfortable and inviting, bright and colorful, well loved and lived in. There are small blankets, tiny teethers, and packs of baby wipes everywhere I look.

Lush green plants are scattered throughout the space, and several paintings hang on the vibrantly painted walls. The look is bold, but the style works. There are pictures of family and friends in the mix, and I even spot one of Dom, Ellie, Bec, and me with the rest of the wedding party at their ceremony from a few years back.

I live downtown, about twenty minutes away, closer to the stadium and training facility. My new space feels cold and impersonal compared to this.

"Holy shit, what happened here?" Dom is staring at the baby's outfit, which I assume was ruined during Bec and Luca's diaper battle.

"I may have underestimated Luca's ability to blow out a diaper and two outfits at once; his and mine," Bec answers as she walks back into the room, avoiding eye contact with me entirely. "Long story, but all you need to know is Luca is now clean, but his pajamas from earlier are *not*. They'll need to be washed ASAP. Want me to throw them in the laundry?"

"No, that's okay. I assume you took over so Ellie could rest?" Bec nods. "I really appreciate it. Last night was a rough one, I know she needs it."

"And I was fully committed to staying until she woke up for the next feeding, but now I desperately want to go home and shower. You need anything else before I head out? I brought some snacks for Ellie and some paper plates too. I left them on the kitchen counter."

"No, really, you've been a huge help. Don't let this diaper disaster drive you away for too long. We'll see you soon, right?"

"Yep, I'll text Ellie later. See ya." She turns to leave, moving as fast as she possibly can.

"Nice to see you again," I call out.

Bec raises her hand quickly to wave over her shoulder but doesn't turn around. "Yep, sorry for the...uh...nakedness. Welcome back to town." And then she bolts—no chance for me to get another word in. Disappointment washes over me as I watch her leave. I've given a lot of thought to what it'd be like to see Bec again over the years. Safe to say I never pictured this.

Dom looks over at me, eyebrows raised. "Nakedness?"

* * *

"Damn, I'm going to owe Bec until Christmas for this." Dom laughs and runs his hand through his hair. "Sounds like a train wreck."

We're sitting on Dom and Ellie's patio while he holds a sleeping Luca in his arms. It's surprisingly warm for an October afternoon in Ohio. I'm eager to soak up the last few days of nice weather before the bitter chill of fall finally settles over the city.

I take a sip of my beer. "I feel terrible. I just stumbled into the house assuming I'd find you and Ellie around, not...you know. That is the first and last time I'll do that."

"Ellie is going to crack up when she hears about this. She'll never let Bec live it down." He can barely restrain his chuckle, clearly trying not to wake Luca. "So how are you feeling being back in town? Seems like things went well with the new team."

"It's okay. Despite not making the playoffs, it felt like we found a good rhythm by the end of the season. I'll be more comfortable next year. It'll help going to Spring Training with the team."

I know how lucky I am to play baseball professionally. I've loved the sport for as long as I can remember. It's always been my escape. When the rest of my life feels like it's falling apart, I know I can always find a quiet space in my mind, turn it all off, and focus on the game.

My four years as second baseman with the Detroit Lightning came to an abrupt end this past June when I was traded to the Columbus Aviators. "It's good to be back in Columbus too. I've missed this city ever since we graduated, even if the move complicated things a bit."

"With your mom?" Dom asks.

I let out a sigh and take another drink, feeling my shoulders cave slightly with the heaviness the topic always brings. "Yeah, things are settled for now, but it's not getting any easier with the distance. Eventually, we'll have to make the move." My gut drops thinking of what that time will bring. What that'll mean for my family.

"I'm really sorry. You know Ellie and I are here for you. Whatever you need."

"Thanks, man. All good for now. But I want to hear about you guys and this future MLB star in your arms. He'll take after me, right? When can he start T-ball? Like a year or so?" I grin, and Dom laughs.

"I don't know shit about babies. I started reading a book about the different milestones and I got so fucking stressed. Ellie had to talk me down. I was so nervous, man. She told me to put the book down, trust my instincts, and we'd learn together as we go. As if I have instincts on this. I'm keeping to the basics for now. Feedings, diaper changes, and naps. I'll let you know when we get to T-ball."

He might claim to be nervous, but Dom already seems like he's settling into his new role as a dad. "You've got a really special family, man."

Dom takes a deep breath and stares down at Luca. "Yeah, I really do."

"Aiden! When did you get here?" I turn to see Ellie step out onto the deck barefoot and holding onto the railing. Dom mentioned her physical recovery from the birth has been slow, so I stand and walk over to give her a hug before she can trouble herself walking down the few steps to greet me.

"Maybe two...two and half hours or so ago? We didn't want to wake you, so we came outside. Congratulations, Ellie. You made a cute kid."

She smiles wide. "Thanks, it's been a wild ride already. I know he'll keep us on our toes. I can't tell you how much better I feel after just a few uninterrupted hours of sleep. Hey, where's Bec?"

"She fell victim to an epic diaper blowout and headed home to shower," Dom explains. "I'll give you the full story later." He winks at Ellie.

"Shit, was it bad?" Ellie cringes. I'd rather not be here to listen to Dom animatedly share my humiliation with his wife.

"Well, it wasn't great, but I'll let Dom explain. I should let you two get back to Luca. I'll get out of your hair. Oh, and here." I reach for my wallet and hand Ellie a gift card for their favorite Italian restaurant. "I had no idea what to get a baby, but I figured you two would probably enjoy a night of not having to cook."

"That's so thoughtful, Aiden. Thank you. We've been surviving on snacks and takeout, and I don't see that changing anytime soon. Here, Dom, I'll take Luca to nurse. Come back over soon, Aiden. We're so happy you're back in town. It's been too long." I smile and nod as Ellie gently takes Luca from Dom and goes back into the house.

I make my way to the front yard toward my car and hug Dom with a pat on the back. "Congrats again on the baby. It's wild to see you as a parent, but you and Ellie are knocking it out of the park. I'll be sure to send *multiple* text messages before I come back over here."

Dom laughs and rocks back on his heels, slipping his hands into his pockets. "Yeah, I'm blaming the lack of sleep for that slipup. I promise I'll write it down next time. I can't trust myself to remember shit anymore. Not until Luca decides to sleep for more than two hours at a time."

"And hey, next time you talk to Bec, apologize again for me," I say. I'm still rattled by our run-in. I wish she hadn't sprinted out of here and I had time to give her a real apology. And maybe a minute to catch up with her...find out what she's been up to since I last saw her. Maybe casually ask if she's single.

*What the fuck is wrong with me?* There's a better time to ask than when she's changing a diaper.

Now that the season is over, I'll finally have time for a social life. I'd love to be able to visit friends without making an ass out of myself. And maybe even consider going on a date. Jesus, how long has it been?

Today was...not a great start.

Dom sighs. "Trust me, I'll be apologizing for both of us for a long, long time."

# Chapter Three

## Bec

The girls and I rotate hosting responsibilities for our book club, and this month is Dee's turn. We sometimes end up staying the night after a few drinks, but since Luca was just born, Ellie will get picked up by Dom since she's not ready to be away from him overnight. Tonight, Carissa is my snuggle buddy.

We're sitting around Dee's glass coffee table, littered with take-out containers. I'm in her oversized, plush velvet, green chair with my back against one arm and my knees hooked over the other, feet dangling off the side. Her apartment is comfortable and stylish with rich, earthy fabrics and colors and soft lighting. Her incredible view of downtown is framed by huge floor-to-ceiling windows, the entire exterior-facing wall of her living room giving us a picturesque view of the twinkling city lights. I live just a few blocks away, but my view has nothing on Dee's.

"I need a new vibrator, who has a good recommendation?" Dee surveys the group. "Bec, didn't you say you found one that was panty melting? Help a girl out."

Yes, I did say that, and yes, I meant it. My new not-so-little friend has kept me company for three glorious months now, and I couldn't gatekeep. I'm a better friend than that. "Let me send the link in the group chat. Everyone, and I mean *everyone*, needs one of these." I wiggle my eyebrows at Carissa, who laughs, looking down, her auburn hair falling over her face, shielding her from my targeted stare.

Her ex, Sir-douche-a-lot—sorry, I mean Damien—constantly put her down when they were dating, including when it came to expressing any type of sensuality. In my experience, only the most insecure men feel the need to shit all over women like that, claiming they're doing it to "protect them." I watched as my strong, confident, bubbly friend retreated into herself until that relationship ended. We were all relieved and trying to help any way we could when she began to share the painful truths as their entire relationship broke down. If anyone needs to find her confidence and feel sexy again, it's Carissa. And I guess maybe myself, too, if I'm being honest.

Dee squeals when she gets the link, already getting out her credit card. "This book was so hot. My vibe finally kicked it, but we had an amazing run. He went out in a blaze of glory two chapters before the epilogue." She stares at the ceiling wistfully, like her last vibrator and she had a sentimental relationship.

I mean, I guess my vibrators outlasted the only serious relationship I had in the last few years. Holy shit, my human relationships have been outdone by my vibrators. When was the last time I had sex? I need to go on a date...immediately.

"Chapter twenty-five...wow. I may be operating on zero sleep and have next to no energy or sex drive, but that was just unreal. I almost wished I could wake Dom for some fun." Ellie is expecting to be cleared for sex by her OB at an upcoming appointment but shared that she and Dom are going to wait a while longer.

Another reason I love their relationship is how comfortable and understanding they are with each other. I guess when she told him she didn't feel ready physically or emotionally, he was incredibly supportive and reassured her that there's no rush. When she's ready, he'll be ready too. Ellie and Dom are over here making it seem impossible for anyone on my dating apps to stand a chance at reaching the bar they're setting sky high, but my book boyfriends certainly rise above all expectations, so for now, they'll have to do.

"I'm still not over the shower scene. Something about crazy, hot shower sex does it for me. And the mouth on that guy, I swear I replayed that part on my audiobook at least ten times for the dirty talk," I say, reaching for my margarita.

We run a very sophisticated book club, choosing a new romance novel every month and then regrouping to rehash all our favorite smutty moments while eating too much takeout. We're real scholars here, all bibliophiles.

I can devour a good read in a day if I'm not working—so long as it has a healthy dose of spice. I consider it critical to debrief in a meeting of the minds with plenty of time for serious plot analysis. Like, would the heroine really be able to straddle the mafia boss and bounce on his dick, coming three times while he drove his hot rod car on the highway at ninety-plus miles per hour? You know...purely intellectual debates. The answer is clearly yes...if she's flexible.

"Seriously, when it's done right, the dirty talk alone can get me there. I about screamed when he grabbed her chin and told her to look him in his eyes and ride him until she felt him bottom out." Dee grabs the pitcher to top off everyone's drinks.

"Oh god, I forgot about that part. I wish it was a duology. Another book with that man? Yes, please," Ellie adds.

"We could choose another book by this author for next month if we want," Carissa proposes. "We don't have the November book picked out yet."

"I love that idea. I checked out the author's website after I finished this book, and she has another stand-alone novel that came out last

May. And best of all, there's an audiobook version," I share, downright giddy at the thought of reading another book by this author. I was planning to anyway, but it's more fun to share it with the girls.

"I do not understand your obsession with audiobooks. Don't you get worried your phone will start playing the book out loud when you're out in public?" Carissa looks like she wants to crawl out of her skin just imagining the embarrassment.

"No way I'd ever get busted, I always use my old, wired headphones when I listen to my audiobooks in public. Extra precautions, you know? No Bluetooth issues. Plus, it only makes it hotter. Walking down the street listening to how the main character is getting railed by the six-foot-three, muscled hottie against the edge of his penthouse balcony? Just my dirty little secret on a Wednesday afternoon stroll that no one needs to know about."

It's true, I love that extra little kink of being in line at the coffee shop around the corner from my apartment, surrounded by unsuspecting people going about their day while the voice artists paint me the smuttiest picture of my wildest dreams.

"Speaking of dirty little secrets, would you like to share with the rest of the class what happened last week? Ellie wouldn't spill the details, and that means it's too good not to share." Dee, being the queen bee of living brazenly and unapologetically, would never let me bury this story no matter how much I wish I could.

"It's not that good," I counter. "I just accidentally saw Dom's friend from college last week, and I might have been missing my shirt. While covered in baby poop. And having a small breakdown. You know, normal Saturday afternoon type stuff. Okay, who wants to compare favorite characters..."

"Stop deflecting, Bec, and give us the details. How the hell did this happen?" Carissa pipes in, and I know there's no escaping their interrogation. I sigh and recount my humiliation at the tiny hands of baby Luca. By the end of my story, Carissa is cackling, wiping away the tears streaming down her face, while Dee is lying flat on her back, hysterically laughing. At least Ellie has the decency to pretend to look apologetic and hide her giggling, since her baby caused this whole damn mess in the first place.

"Please tell me we'll meet this guy, Ellie. I have so many questions for him," Dee schemes.

"Oh god, take it easy on him, Dee," Ellie pleads. "And you already met him. Aiden was in our wedding party, one of the groomsmen. He's a great guy. He keeps telling Dom how bad he feels about the whole thing. Now when he comes over to hang out, he texts us three times to confirm the plans, including one text from our driveway before he'll get out of his car. He's scarred for life."

"Wow, I didn't know my shirtless form was scarring. Better call my exes and offer compensation for their trauma." I sip my drink and I can feel my blush creep in, remembering how gorgeous Aiden looked despite the shock written on his face and how much I wanted to crawl into a hole when he saw me covered in literal shit. I didn't stick around long enough to talk, but the guy is still hot.

*So fucking hot.*

"Oh please, your cleavage probably rendered the poor guy speech-less. You know your curves could kill. He's scarred because your body was covered in *poop*. Not exactly a fantasy brought to life; that's a goddamn nightmare," Dee says.

"Yeah, well. It wasn't a dream for me either. Who just walks into your house unannounced like that anyway?" I shout.

"*You do*, Bec," Ellie shrieks with a laugh. "You always just roll into our house. The only times you don't are when you think we might be banging. Or these days, napping, which by the way, you're the best for that." Ellie smiles warmly. "Though, I would recommend that you avoid stripping in public spaces in the future, especially since the season is over. I'm sure we'll be seeing Aiden more often."

"I'd hardly call leggings and a sports bra stripping," I mutter under my breath.

"What do you mean now that the season is over?" Carissa asks.

"The regular baseball season is over. The Aviators didn't make the playoffs, so I assume Aiden and Dom will hang out more often in the off-season." Ellie casually snacks from the table while Carissa and Dee stare at each other, confused. "You know, because Aiden is a pro baseball player. Remember, he and Dom went to school together, and after college Aiden played for the Detroit Lightning? He was traded to Columbus this past Spring. Dom was ecstatic when Aiden called to tell him he was coming home."

"Holy shit," Dee says, snapping her head in my direction as her short, dark brown, wavy hair skims across her shoulders as her eyes find mine. I look away, immediately gulping my drink. She fucking promised...she better keep her big mouth shut. "Oh, *Aiden*...I remember that fine piece of man candy now." She sips her drink and stares at me, goading me.

Nope, not looking at her. I can avoid her stare for the rest of time if I have to. If she wants me to confess, she'll have to wait a lifetime.

"I need to see a picture to jog my memory," Carissa pipes in. She probably didn't even have a chance to meet Aiden with her stupid ex clinging to her at Ellie and Dom's wedding. Ellie pulls up her phone and shows Carissa a picture of Aiden sitting in their living room holding Luca. It's not fair that years later he's only become more attractive. His perfect lips show off his bright smile, his jaw is still peppered with the perfect amount of scruff, and he keeps his brown hair a little longer on top, giving him that just-out-of-bed disheveled look. "Oh wow. Maybe we need to go to a few baseball games next year."

"That's a great idea! I'm sure Aiden would love to have a few extra fans in the stands. You won't have to wait that long to see him, though.

He's invited to Friendsgiving at our house next month."

I knew I'd see Aiden around now that he lives in town. I go back and forth between dreading our next interaction and craving it. I wish I could sever this connection, or at least silence it so I could just focus on anything but the way he makes my desire flare.

I'm fairly confident my battery boyfriend is going to be busy this fall, helping to take the edge off. If there's one thing I know, I need to avoid any one-on-one interactions with him given the way we met.

*Come on, Bec. You can do this...right?*

# Chapter Four

Bec

## The Wedding

I still have a few hours to kill before the other girls make it to the hotel. This is what I get for volunteering to decorate for Ellie's bachelorette party tonight. I have to admit, I killed it. I went balls to the walls, or rather, dicks to the bricks, dutifully hanging paper penises all over the suite. When you've known Ellie as long as I have, it's basically required that I go overboard here.

Ellie and the rest of the girls will arrive soon, presumably loaded up with even more gaudy décor, sashes, and supplies for her single-life send-off. Until then, here I am, killing time at the hotel bar alone. At least I know in a few hours, I'll be pleasantly tipsy and heavily tipping a hot stripper.

I sip on my Moscow mule, mindlessly skimming through my phone, when I feel someone approach. I could go the rest of my life without awkward small talk at a hotel bar, but here we are. As if he can hear my thoughts, he asks, "Sorry, do you mind if I sit here? The place is pretty packed, and I don't see any other seats."

I look over and warm brown eyes lock with mine. I can't seem to remember how to find my words. Shit, this guy is hot. Tousled dark brown hair effortlessly achieving that imperfectly perfect look. He towers over me as he stands behind the bar stool next to me. His shoulders are broad, and his stance is casual, confident. The trimmed stubble on his strong jaw gives him a gruff edge that I inexplicably want to run my fingers along.

Down, girl.

"Uh, yeah. Sure. Go ahead," I say.

He mutters out a thank-you and orders a bourbon neat from the bartender, who basically trips over herself to talk to him. Understandable.

I turn back to my phone and say a silent prayer that my whole face isn't red from our three second interaction. God, this dry spell of mine needs to end. I need to find a man this weekend and have some uncomplicated, no-strings-attached fun. Preferably with a man that gives my lady bits butterflies just like this.

A couple burst into laughter on the other end of the bar, and I involuntarily look up to see them cackling, seemingly tangled up and soon to be even more so. At least someone is getting lucky tonight.

"What's the punchline?" my hot, bar neighbor asks. At least, I think he's asking me. I turn to see him watching me intently.

"Excuse me?" I barely manage to whisper, but he must hear me.

"What do you think the punchline is?" He lifts his head, nodding to the couple who is still hysterically laughing. "It's a game I like to play. See an interaction, ask a question, use your imagination to fill in the blanks."

I stare at him, confused, not understanding why he's talking to me. He isn't deterred. "I'll go first," he says. "Those two are here for their twenty-year high school reunion. Never managed to make it past the friend stage as teenagers, yet here they are, single and finally ready to take the leap. They're laughing as they reminisce about their most embarrassing stories from their senior prom. You know, the awkward bumping and grinding, and fumbling make-out sessions getting broken up by grumbling chaperones." He smiles crookedly, softening his appearance. "Your turn.

You pick the customers, and I'll pick the question."

I can't help but smile back. "Okay, um, the two women by the door."

He sips his drink and I watch his lips with blatant interest. What's the harm, right? I'm here for a fun weekend, and he is clearly too hot to hang onto for longer than that. He hums thoughtfully and gives me an obvious once-over in return. "All right, do they have any tattoos?" he asks.

Now this, I can do. Will I come across as original and intriguing or weird and terrifying? Only time will tell. "They both do. The taller girl has a lioness on her shoulder. She's strutting around with obvious Leo energy. Fierce, creative, confident. Now her friend is giving me more earthy vibes. Practical, grounded. She has a tree for each season down her spine. And of course, they have matching best friend tattoos that they drunkenly got together in college. They thought it'd be hilarious to get each other's handprint on their ass. It signifies endless ass slaps of encouragement. A permanent go get 'em, girl, if you will."

I hold his stare as his eyes flit back and forth between my own, and he finally chuckles. "Well, shit, you're good at this. What about you, any tattoos?"

I shrug, taking another sip of my drink. "Afraid I can't answer that. Tattoos are way too personal. I don't give away my secrets so easily." I giggle at his bemused expression.

"Fair enough. I think I may have met my match here, but just to be sure..." He scans the crowd in the bar. "Okay, the two men in suits in front of the far window."

I light up, his enthusiasm is magnetic. "What was their last fight about?"

He doesn't miss a beat, immediately diving into an animated explanation. "What kind of pet to adopt. Blue Suit is clearly a cat person and Black Suit is a dog person. Obviously, the dog person will win, and they'll end up getting a dog now and a cat later on, who will hate that dog."

"Woah, woah, pump the brakes. How do you know he's a dog person, and why does that mean he will obviously win?"

*He rolls his eyes playfully as if I should already know, like it's common knowledge or something. "You can tell he's a dog person by his energy and affection. He wears it on his sleeve. His partner is the complete opposite, playing it cool, stoic. They'll end up with the dog because dog people are impulsive and ruled by emotions, big bleeding hearts. Mr. Black Suit over there will see one sad pet-rescue commercial then claim he accidentally wandered into a shelter and had to bring home a senior dog with no bladder control and five expensive monthly medications. A cat person will be more methodical and sensible. Poor Blue Suit will have to wait a while longer to find the perfect cat who will inevitably train the dog to stay ten feet away with its hiss and sharp claws."*

*I nod, biting my lips trying to contain my amusement as I consider the ridiculous assumptions he's making. "Hm...and what about me, am I a dog person or a cat person?"*

*He scoffs, not taking any time to consider the question. "Dog," he says. "It's written all over you. Playful, trusting, outgoing, bubbly, uninhibited, loyal. If you were a cat person, you probably would have told me to fuck off when I first walked over."*

*"You think you've got me figured out after five minutes of conversation?"*

*"I'm right, aren't I?" He winks and takes a sip of his drink, and dammit, my body likes that way too much.*

*I break eye contact and shrug, taking a long pull from my straw. "Maybe. I'm going to guess you love cats. You give off this tough exterior but are secretly all mush on the inside. Hiding your sensitive side that just wants to curl up and cuddle, masking all your vulnerabilities behind a broody, mysterious exterior."*

*"I like to think I can occasionally be cat-presenting, but I'm a dog person through and through. I need the validation only a dog can give. That happy go lucky, leans in when you do–type affection." His expression turns diabolical. "I can't help the vibe I give off. But I haven't gotten any complaints yet on my cuddling skills." He raises an eyebrow at me and*

doesn't break eye contact while he finishes his drink. He places his empty tumbler on the bar and I watch his gaze roam from my eyes to my mouth, all the way down to my cleavage with interest.

Well, shit. That'll do it. *My lady bits are awake and reporting for duty. Maybe he could be my weekend fling. I didn't RSVP for a plus one to the wedding on Saturday, but if we're both staying in the same hotel, maybe we could...*

"Your turn to pick." His voice brings me back to the present moment. *Right, maybe I should continue with this not-so-normal small talk rather than proposition a complete stranger.*

"Okay, uh, that couple, booth near the hall."

He glances over to the couple and turns back to me. Trouble written all over his face. "What's their kink?"

"Excuse me?" I half shriek, choking on my drink.

"You heard me, what's their kink?"

"Um..." I can feel myself blushing. He waits, seemingly amused at how flustered I am. "Okay, well, I'm going to go with exhibitionists. Same siders in a booth? Undoubtedly, they're into some serious PDA."

"Interesting." His attentive stare has me melting. My body is frozen in place and simultaneously burning from the inside out. The contrast is exhilarating, and I feel like every nerve ending is coming alive. "Aren't you going to ask me? What's my kink?"

I exhale in a nervous laugh. "I don't even know your name. I don't typically go around asking strangers how they spend their time in the bedroom."

"I'm Aiden. And I'm thinking my newest kink is flirting with a certain gorgeous brunette with quick wit at this hotel bar."

He's into me, I'm going for it. What the hell. "I'm Bec, and I'm here until Sunday."

"Well, that's some good luck for me. I check out on Sunday too."

Game on, Aiden.

# Chapter Five

## Aiden

"Hopper, sit. Down. Stay. Dammit, come on, man." I sigh in defeat. Hop prances around my feet, ignoring every cue I try. He wags his tail, sniffing everything he can, pulling on his leash with excitement, which used to not be a big deal, but at eight months old, he is rapidly gaining weight and strength.

I've always loved dogs. A house has always felt more like home with a dog there too. Despite the lack of training, having Hopper has been a comfort in my quiet apartment since I moved.

But looking around this puppy training class, I realize how the last few months have really gotten away from me. I managed to scramble to find dog sitters while I wrapped up the season.  But with Hop growing quickly and adapting to his inconsistent environment, any effort I made at training, even the most basic signals, completely fell apart.

I know it's my fault for adopting a puppy right before my season started, and I need to give him the attention and consistency he needs. Now that the season is over, I can finally offer him that.

There are seven other puppies here with their families spaced throughout the room, and I'm wondering if Hop and I might be in the wrong class. The other dogs are calm and quiet while Hop is on his back making fake puppy snow angels on the tile flooring. The wiggles have taken over, and I know what comes next—tail-chasing zoomies.

A man around my age looks over at me with sympathy while his puppy sits calmly on the other side of his wife. This is the beginners' class, right? I know we're joining this class late, but could we really have missed that much in three weeks?

Then the guy does a double take, looking back in my direction. "Hey, you're Aiden Price?" I nod. "Wow, glad to have you in Columbus. You guys really looked great at the end of the season, man."

"Thanks," I say with a nod. "Hoping we get in the playoffs and make a run next year."

The Center for Faithful Companions was the highest-rated dog training facility in the city when I researched my options online. Countless inspiring trainee testimonies flooded their website. Enough to make me hopeful that maybe Hop and I aren't a lost cause trying too little too late. The receptionist assured me we could catch up despite being unable to make it to the first few sessions. She even mentioned that our trainer is a favorite among their clients.

The room is large enough to fit eight large-breed puppies and their families. Some people are here with their dogs alone, like me, with a few couples thrown in, and one family including kids. I'm sitting in a folding chair in the corner with Hop, who is now trying to climb my leg into my lap, all fifty-plus pounds of him.

"Good morning," I hear from the doorway to my right.

*Holy shit, Bec?*

She walks to the center of the square room, clipboard tucked to her side.

I haven't seen her since our run-in at Dom's house three weeks ago. It might have been one of the most awkward moments I've ever experienced walking in on her fighting for her life in what I can only assume is the worst blowout in diaper history. I barely got the chance to appreciate her perfect body. It's been years since I've seen her, admittedly never that much of her. Her sun-kissed skin is glowing, and her toned legs carry her around the room in skintight leggings, showing off her thick thighs. Her ass looks incredible, just like I remember, and her simple *Center for Faithful Companions* black T-shirt hugs tight enough for me to see her full chest.

*What am I doing?*

*Stop staring.*

She scans the room, speaking to the different groups getting ready for class. She's obviously our trainer today, which answers the years-long question of what Bec does for a living.

"Welcome back, everyone, let's start by running through last week's lesson. I'll make my rounds to each of you to see how everything is going before we jump into a few new skills."

She scans her clipboard. "We also have a new pup joining us today, uh...Hopper?" She calls out, quickly looking around the room to finally spot my dog, and then locking eyes with me.

If *horrifyingly stunned* was in the dictionary, I think I'd see a picture of Bec right now. I watch her jaw drop, the color drain from her face, quickly followed by an unmistakable blush rushing to her cheeks. She licks then bites her lower lip, seemingly frozen, standing in the middle of the room as the other trainees stand and space out to begin working through whatever skills they covered in the previous class.

I stand, deciding it's better to push past the weirdness, and head to the center of the room with Hop chomping at my heels. "Uh, hey, Bec. So, about the last time I saw you, uh...shirtless, and I turned, and uh, I didn't see anything, I swear..."

*Shit, I'm rambling.*

"I remember," she quickly interjects. "No need to revisit it. Happens all the time. Wait, no." She closes her eyes and shakes her head.

"It definitely doesn't happen all the time. I mean it happened and now it's over."

Flustered, she breaks eye contact, studying her clipboard as if the answers to life's greatest questions are written there. She sighs and looks up at me. Those blue eyes I remember so clearly staring up at me, sending a pulse of electricity through my chest, and her lip pales as she bites it again. How did I not notice she's even more beautiful now than she was years ago? Oh right, the baby poop.

So much baby poop.

"Listen, I'm really sorry about all that. I'm embarrassed that I walked in like that, and I hope it isn't too weird that I'm taking this class. I didn't realize you taught here. Come to think of it, I didn't know what you did until now." I explain, hoping she doesn't think I'm the world's biggest creep.

"No worries, really. If anything, I learned a valuable lesson. Always wait to clean yourself up until *after* the diaper change is done. And if you think Luca's done pooping, he's not. Little man faked me out once, but never again." She laughs, and I swear the sound alone has my mood soaring, transporting me back in time.

"Seems like you took one for the team. Of course, Dom arrived home just in time to miss diaper duty. I hope he pays you back for that one."

"Oh, trust me, I plan to exploit his guilt for as long as I can." Her posture softens as she seems to get more comfortable. Weird how much I like that she's doing that around me again. "Well, anyway, tell me about this cutie you got here." She bends down to one knee to get Hop's attention, interrupting him as he paws excitedly, nipping at my shoelaces.

"This is Hopper and as you can see, we are in need of serious help."

She looks up at me, beaming. "You mean to tell me I am in the presence of one Chief Jim Hopper?" She pets Hop, who immediately surrenders and flops over to show his belly, which she rewards with scratches.

I chuckle and scratch the back of my neck. "Yeah, I was binging *Stranger Things* when I brought him home, and obviously he has the seriousness of his namesake." The contrast in personalities is exaggerated as Hopper's tongue flops out onto the tile. "Honestly, he may be the biggest goof I've ever met."

"Well, we can get him ready for Hawkins in no time, I'm sure. Though, I have to agree with you. He seems more like a Dustin to me." She stands and winks at me. "You're looking at a fellow fan."

*Damn, she's cute.*

*Seriously, what is wrong with me?*

*Stop staring at her.*

Since Dom got married, I often find my thoughts drifting back to memories of meeting Bec. They'd pop up randomly, unprompted but always welcome. The pang of lust and longing that would run through me when I remembered the way Bec felt in my arms always left me feeling empty. The bold confidence and carefree attitude she exuded were contagious, and even in my memories, they held me captive.

I shouldn't be surprised, but it's catching me off guard that Bec can still make me feel like a fresh breath of life is running through me. Like waking up because the sunshine crosses over your face, suddenly blinding you, making you realize how dark it was before.

Bec snaps my focus back to her. "Since you missed the first few classes, we can schedule a makeup session to catch you two up if you'd like. I usually offer those to clients on Sundays. I have an opening at nine tomorrow morning. I realize that's short notice, so if you're not free, we can find another time."

"Sure, yeah. I'm free if you are." *Do I sound too eager to be alone with her?*

"Great," she says, smiling and looking down. "Time to get to work, Hop. Hawkins needs you in top shape." His tail wags as he zooms around her feet, my heart racing as fast as he is.

# Chapter Six

Aiden

## The Wedding

"Dream vacation. Go," I challenge. The hotel bar is still packed, but Bec and I moved to a booth a while ago and I barely notice anyone around us. We've been talking for what feels like minutes, but my watch tells me it's been a couple of hours. Bec mentioned she's waiting on a few friends to arrive, and I have to meet the guys soon for the bachelor party. My gut twists under the pressure of time encroaching on us. Bec seems unfazed, but I'm already trying to think of ways I can see her again.

The conversation has been light and fun. When was the last time I felt this relaxed around a woman?

"Hm...money's not a factor?" she asks. I shake my head. "I guess, I don't know...somewhere remote. Give me wooded forests, hidden waterfalls, active volcanoes, sprawling mountains." Her gaze is distant, a content smile overtaking her, like she's there already.

"Volcanoes? So, you're a thrill seeker."

"Not really. But when my typical day-to-day routine starts to feel monotonous, I like to imagine experiencing the world in a simpler way.

Exploring a corner of the world that's undisturbed. Wandering through the natural beauty.  It fills me with a sense of calm I can't seem to replicate anywhere else. When I get in my own head, and my problems feel larger than life, it's nice to imagine being somewhere like that instead, just breathing in the silence. Appreciating my small place in a massive universe."

"Is it safe to assume you live out in the country somewhere?"

"Ha, nope. Not a country girl. Don't get me wrong, city life suits me. I live here in Columbus, but when I need a break, I like to get away and try to remind myself that whatever I'm worrying about doesn't really matter. Sometimes I get the itch to get away to remind myself how just being here, being myself is a gift. I am enough right now, exactly as I am."

Bec looks at me and startles a little, as if she forgot I was listening. She stirs her drink, fidgeting with the napkin underneath.

"Sorry, that was a lot of rambling for a pretty standard question."

I reach across the table to take her restless hand into mine.  "It was a good answer, Bec."

"You're a good listener.  Makes it a little too easy for me to run my mouth and embarrass myself. All right, next question. What's your favorite memory?"

"My eighth birthday," I blurt out, not thinking. Here I go bringing down the mood with a fucking memory like that. It's true, but complicated to explain.

"Great party? Awesome present? Why is it the best?" Bec sips her drink and gazes at me with a relaxed smile.

Do I drag all my shit out in the open? I don't talk about this with anyone except my family or maybe Dom, but there's something about Bec. I don't understand what it is, but I know I need more. She has this dangerous air about her. Like if she asked me for the impossible, I'd find a way to make it happen. My instinct is to tell her anything she wants to know, give her anything she wants, and do anything she asks. I have no idea how she has *this hold on me, but she does. I answer honestly.*

*"My mom left my dad the week before and moved my little sister and me into an apartment. It was small. My sister and I shared a room. We had barely unpacked. Most of our stuff was still in boxes. Mom made macaroni and cheese for dinner because it was my favorite. And a homemade box cake, chocolate with chocolate frosting. To this day, you can't convince me that any cake tastes better than those box mixes. We didn't have any furniture in the living room other than an old TV, so Mom used a couple of moving boxes to form a makeshift backing to a "couch" and threw all our blankets on the floor. The three of us spent the night watching my favorite movies. My sister complained that she didn't get a pick and then proceeded to quote almost every line. The two of us acted out our favorite scenes together, which made Mom laugh and give us a standing ovation."*

*Bec stares at me pensively. I haven't talked about that time in my life in a long time. It feels like she's looking straight into my memory, reaching into my thoughts, and digging into the root of all that lingering, stale pain. It's unsettling, leaving me feeling raw and vulnerable.*

*"Clearly there's more going on outside the frame of that picture-perfect memory." I can feel my shoulders tighten, hesitant to share more, but knowing I would if she asked me to. Because I can't picture myself saying no to her, even though we're practically strangers to each other.*

*Bec reaches across the table, wrapping her warm hand over mine. "I'm not going to pry, Aiden. I want you to share what you want, and stop when you need to. Thank you for telling me. I can picture it all so clearly. It's obvious your mom and sister are important to you. Plus, you have good taste. Mac and cheese and double chocolate cake? That's a menu I can get behind. But I gotta know...did you have good taste in movies too? What was the lineup?"*

*I chuckle, feeling the tension release from my body. "I had too many favorites when I was eight. I think I chose The Sandlot, Rookie of the Year, and Angels in the Outfield."*

*"You were quite the baseball fan, huh," she says.*

I had a feeling she didn't recognize me. Good.

*"But you're missing the best one. Ever seen* A League of Their Own?*"* *she asks. When I shake my head, her jaw drops. "You've got to be kidding me? You better go to your room and pay to stream that movie right the fuck now! Sorry, Aiden, no hotel porn for you until you watch the best baseball movie of all time!"*

*Her outrage is amusing, and I throw a smirk her way, settling farther into the booth, getting comfortable. "How can you say that so confidently? Have you seen any of my favorites?"*

*"No, but trust me, I don't need to. You'll understand when you tell me—in about two hours—how right I was. Go on, I'll wait here." She sits tall, crossing her arms across her chest, and even though she's trying to act serious, she can't hold in her laugh. The sound shakes the shadows from my thoughts. It's impossible to linger in the past when her entire personality radiates sunshine.*

*"I think it'll confuse the staff here if I pay for that movie when I've already rented two adult films."*

*Her mouth drops open as she stares incredulously at me, her eyes full of intrigue, whispering, "Seriously?"*

*"No."*

*She laughs and shrugs. "Your loss."*

*"Okay, it's my turn. What's your biggest fear?" I ask.*

*"Straight for the jugular on this one. Okay, I guess I'd say...losing myself? I feel like I'm finally starting to figure out who I am. I'd do anything to hang onto it."*

*"You seem pretty confident to me."*

*"Showing confidence and feeling confident are two very different things. I've always been able to turn it on when I need it. But when shit hits the fan and I'm put in a position where I have to either force myself into the mold someone else wants or say fuck that and just be myself, I have a record of*

*doing what will cause the least amount of conflict. I used to think it was a strength. Keeping the peace, playing mediator, making sure everyone else gets what they need. Until I realized the cost is too high. It'd be so easy to lose track of who I'm becoming, because I'm just starting to figure it out for myself, you know? I don't want to sacrifice who I am or who I want to be."*

It makes sense what she's saying. While she's exuded strength and self-assurance tonight, there's also a vulnerability lingering right below the surface. Our conversation has been mostly joking with each other back and forth, trying to outdo one another with quick wit and a heavy dose of sarcasm, but when I share something personal, her empathy and ability to say the right thing without asking me to share more than I want tells me just how compassionate she is. Anyone can take advantage of that, and it pains me to hear people she's trusted in the past have hurt her and made her feel like she has to be someone she's not.

"People who care about you wouldn't ask you to sacrifice any part of yourself." She looks at me thoughtfully, and I can tell she's absorbing what I've said. "And tonight? Do you feel like you can be yourself with me?"

"Oddly, yes." The admission seems to be difficult for her, a shy smile on her face as she looks back and forth between the drink in her hands and me. "Normally, I feel like I need to keep people at a distance until I have a better feel for them. Until I know I can trust them. For some reason, I don't feel the need to do that with you."

"Strange, I was just thinking the same thing about you. Be yourself with me, Bec. I won't ask you to change. I'd never want that." I mean it. There's something incredibly special about Bec, and the way she's looking at me makes me feel like maybe the connection isn't one sided.

* * *

*We're walking down the hallway, toward my hotel room, when Bec's hand* wraps behind my neck, nails scratching along the base, fingers tangling in my hair. She pulls me closer like she needs my lips on hers more than she needs air. I can't wait any longer. I find an alcove and push her against the wall beside the ice machine, hidden from anyone walking past us. My hands roam to her ass, and I pull her against me. She gasps, her soft lips parting, and her body melts. She tilts her hips to meet mine, staring at me with those piercing eyes.

Bec is a vision. Long brown hair curling down her back, a graceful sway to the way she moves, and a carefree energy radiating off her. I want to get tangled up with her and dig my fingers into her soft curves.

Physically Bec is stunning, but there's also something intriguing about the way she thinks. Her big blue eyes lock with mine, and the heat between us grows. Her hungry gaze only fuels the fire building in me.

I slide my hands under her ass, and she wraps her legs around my waist. I lean in, pressing her against the wall. "What do you like, Bec? What do you need?" I murmur in her ear before gently biting at the lobe.

I press my lips to her neck and trail soft kisses down her bare shoulder, finally letting my tongue slip out to taste her skin. Her black dress hugs her curves, and it begins to ride up her thighs. She shivers in my arms and her fingers tighten in my hair. "I need you to kiss me, Aiden. Now."

"I am kissing you," I mumble against her jaw, pressing another teasingly soft kiss along the edge. Bec pulls my hair hard, and I chuckle, lifting my gaze to meet her heated stare.

"Is that the best you can do? Such a shame. You had so much promise—" I cut her off, swallowing her words in a frenzied kiss, both overwhelming and heightening my senses. I'm consumed by her soft lips, my need driven even higher when a quiet moan spills from her into our working tongues. Bec shifts, gripping my shoulders tightly, her fingernails pressing into my skin. She writhes in my arms, and I harden in response. She smells like summer rain with a hint of something floral that I can't quite place. She tastes like mint and ginger, spicy and sweet.

Who the fuck is this woman?

"Where's your room?" Bec pants into our shared breath, holding me tighter, and I grip her just as fiercely. A mess of hands and limbs and desire. Before I can answer, her phone rings. "Shit," she hisses. I lower her to the ground as she fumbles with her phone.

I don't give her space. I lean my body into hers, peppering her neck with kisses while she answers the call. "Hey, girl. What's up? What? No, I'm fine, why?" Her voice is breathy, and I can hear her need coursing through her, reflecting my own.

I run my hand over her stomach and turn her around until she's facing the wall, her back flush against my chest. Bec presses her free hand against the wall for support, and I trail my hands along her sides before gripping her hips and tasting her neck, gently biting.

She struggles to stifle a quiet moan and presses her ass into my groin. She leans her head to the side to give me more space to ravish her neck and shoulders with my tongue.

Holy shit. I love the feel of her full, lush curves. Her body is fucking perfect. I can't wait to wreck it.

"You're here already?" she asks.

Well damn, this doesn't bode well for the plans I've been making in my mind. They all involved Bec. Bec in my bed, in my shower, on my face, on her knees.

I pause, lifting my head, and Bec turns to face me. Disappointment on her face, I'm sure a mirror to my own. "Awesome, I'm glad you were able to head out early. Yeah, I'm here. Just finished getting ready in my room. I'll head to the suite in a few. Yep, I'll see you there. Okay, bye." She doesn't break eye contact as she disconnects the call and lowers her phone to her side.

I'm not done with Bec yet, and she sure as shit doesn't look done with me.

"I'm sorry. My friends are parking. I probably only have fifteen minutes *or so."*

*Fifteen minutes...well, that would be plenty of time for—*

*Her palms come up to my chest, pushing me back playfully with a smile. "And before you even think about it, the plans I had required much more time than that." Her gaze rolls down my tall frame and back up. She tilts her head, taking her time giving me another once-over, further emphasizing her point, and damn if I don't want to know what the fuck she would do if I gave her all my time.*

*"Lucky for me, it seems we have all weekend. It's only Thursday," I say. Hopefully, I don't sound like an overconfident asshole. I don't do cocky. I normally do aloof and levelheaded, but I really do want to see her again.*

*"Yep, lucky you." She pops up on her toes, kissing my jaw before smacking my ass as she passes me, gliding gracefully back into the hallway. I'm stunned for a second, watching her stride away from me. Coming to my senses, I jog to catch up with her while unlocking my phone.*

*"Hey, in all seriousness, I promise not to blow up your phone. I would love to see you again. Can I get your number?" There is something about our connection that I don't quite understand. Is she attractive? Fuck yeah. But this feels like more. An unfamiliar pull drawing me in. A restlessness settling in my bones at the thought of separating from her. An electric current lighting me up from the inside at the thought of keeping her close.*

*She turns, walking backward toward the elevator with her arms held out to her side. "Shouldn't we leave it up to chance? See if the universe pushes us together again? Then we'll know we were destined to do the no pants dance." She gives me a shimmy. I'm sure she thinks her exaggerated wiggle is silly and not seductive, but shit, it's doing it for me.*

*"No, fuck the universe." I wrap my hand around her bicep and tug her close, mere inches separating us. "I'll show you stars myself."*

*Definitely over-the-top cheesy, but I can't help myself.*

*For once, I'm not second-guessing everything I say to a woman. I'm not worried about making an impression. Bec has me acting on impulse and intuition. She doesn't know who I am. No preconceived notions, no pressure. It's freeing. I can be myself and not worry about being exploited or judged. All unfortunate side effects of my career.*

*She barks a laugh and pushes the button for the elevator. "You were so close to coming off so smoothly. But wow, that line is unforgettable in the worst way possible. Aiden, what am I going to do with you?"*

*"Give me your number, and we'll find out. How about it, Bec? Take a chance on me." The elevator rings as it opens, but I hold her attention, staring into those beautiful eyes. She takes my phone, dials her number, and presses the Call button before handing it back to me. She steps backward into the elevator, holding up her phone to show my number coming through on her end.*

*"I like the sound of that, Aiden. Don't keep me waiting long." She smirks as the doors close.*

*Holy fuck. I think it's going to be an unforgettable weekend.*

# Chapter Seven

## Bec

I'm running late. Of course I'm running late.

I could lie to myself and say it was because I lost track of time, but I can admit to myself that I've been a bit of a wreck this morning thinking about seeing Aiden for his one-on-one makeup class. Well, one-on-one, plus an overzealous puppy.

I changed my outfit three times before finally throwing on leggings and a T-shirt with the Center's logo. It's my usual look for class, so I'm keeping it simple and comfortable since I'm up and moving all day and eventually covered in dog hair anyway. Do I normally wear this much makeup and curl my hair for class? No, but what the fuck ever. I need a confidence boost to walk into work today. Well, to run in, since all the fuss made me late.

"Morning, Abby!" I call over my shoulder, hearing our newest trainer return the greeting. I jog past the front desk into the employee office where I drop my bag and grab my clipboard and treat pouch, clipping it to my leggings above my hip. All the trainers share a small office, since we never spend much time there anyway. It's mostly used for storage.

"Uh, Bec? There's a beautiful man with an adorable lab asking for you. I'm assuming you have a makeup class this morning? I let him into Training Room Four to wait," Abby says while tucking her braids behind her ear and leaning against the door to the office.

"Shit. Yeah, I'm running late this morning. Has he been here long?"

"Not too long. He didn't seem bothered, so I wouldn't worry," Abby says.

"Awesome, thanks for getting them set up. Oh, and remind me to send you the name of the book the girls and I are reading next month. That is, if you still want to join us and dirty up your pristine book collection with some certified filth."

"After seeing your face while you were reading at the front desk yesterday, I absolutely need to know what I'm missing. Consider me ready and waiting to be scandalized."

"Please...I kept my cool. I'm a professional smut reader. My poker face is unshakable."

"Bec, you sat with your jaw on the floor for two minutes straight, followed by a fit of nervous giggling and borderline squealing. Not even the phone ringing snapped you out of it. I don't even think you were blinking."

"It's not my fault! That was my first monster romance. I'm not sure how to recover from it. The main character had...let's just say they had some anatomy *enhancements* that were...intriguing." That book had me questioning things about myself, mostly how I can find myself my own monster. Thank god for my e-reader. The cover was anything but discrete and I fucking loved it. But I don't need our clients at the Center knowing anything about my books.

"Okay, well maybe don't start me off with monster romance," Abby says with a laugh. "Let me dip my toe in the water before you throw me into the deep end."

"I promise, I won't start you with monsters. But I'm not taking it easy on you. The mouth on this next guy is sure to be downright sinful."

Abby shakes her head. "I don't know why I agreed to this, but I'm in. Oh, and I'm heading over to New Hope this afternoon for a meeting on the adoption fair if you want to join. We have a new sponsor, and we're running through updates on other potential donors."

New Hope is the animal shelter where a lot of the Center's employees volunteer. We've had a close working partnership between our organizations for years. I try to make it there a few times each month to work with the dogs waiting to find families, especially those with more difficult behaviors that could potentially ward off an adoption. There's a ton of work to do before the adoption fair in February. It takes months of preparation, so we all try to help out when we can.

"Of course I'll be there," I say.

Abby nods and returns to the front desk. I smooth my clammy hands over my waist and walk down the hall to room four, where I find Aiden waiting with Hop. The mischievous lab is biting and tugging on his leash, shaking his head back and forth with vigor.

"Hey, I'm so sorry I'm late. I'm normally early, I swear," I rush out, trying to catch my breath. He turns toward me and, ugh, it's painful how handsome I find his seemingly effortless self-assurance to be. He doesn't even seem real. He must think I'm a mess.

"Don't worry about it. Hop and I were just getting a jump start on things." Hop looks up at him at that moment, wags his tail, and tugs hard on his leash. Aiden sighs and looks up at me with pleading eyes. "We may be a tough case, so I thought I'd try my hand at some bribery to make sure we don't get kicked out of class." He gestures to the table underneath the windows where two to-go cups sit. "I didn't know what you like, so I got a dark roast with sugar and cream and a pumpkin spice latte. Figured you could pick, and I'll take the other."

"You...brought me coffee?" He nods, looking shy and uncertain. "Well, that was really sweet of you. You sure you don't mind me choosing? Because I would love the dark roast."

"I was hoping you'd say that. I'm not ashamed to say I look forward to the pumpkin flavors coming out in the fall. The woman at the coffee shop said she was surprised to learn that I'm *basic.* Whatever that means. Here." He hands me the cup with a smile so genuine, my stomach gives a little flip. "So, what do you think? Can we stay or should Hopper and I give up now?"

"Nah, Hop seems like way too much fun to kick out of class before we teach him how to give you more trouble."

"See, I had a feeling you'd use your powers for evil." He smirks and takes a sip of his drink, and I can't hold back my laugh.

I perch against the table's edge, hugging my clipboard to my chest. "I've worked with dogs much more challenging than him. To get started, I want to learn more about your history. I mean...not *your* history. Your history with Hop." I feel my cheeks heat and I look down at my clipboard, avoiding eye contact. "What kind of training you've tried, if any. What his usual routine is. Who else is involved in day-to-day training. We'll want to use consistent techniques with him moving forward. Anyone you live with, or you know...anyone who is over at your place regularly will need to use the same commands."

"It's just me that'll be training him. I acted a little impulsively and adopted Hopper right as my last season started. I was away pretty often, traveling for work. I tried to train him while I was home, but given how often I was on the road, I had to piece together help from a few friends and hire local dog sitters to watch him. There was next to no consistency as far as training. I was scrambling to find anyone who could take him for a few days at a time. I didn't want to be any more of an inconvenience by asking them to take on training too. As far as a routine, we haven't had one. I guess that's probably part of our problem."

It strikes me that maybe Hopper isn't the only one struggling with all of the changes over the last few months. It's understandable, anyone would be expected to have a tough time having to relocate their entire life for work while attempting to train a puppy.

"All things considered, you're not as far behind as you think. One benefit to all the changes you've had is that Hop seems really well socialized.  Based on what I've observed so far, he's friendly with both dogs and people, which is great.  Let's focus on using cues. We'll introduce a few today, and I'll show you how to apply them consistently. You'll also want to work on establishing a routine for him, including plenty of exercise. He's gotta get that puppy energy out, otherwise it won't matter what you say, he won't hear you over the sound of his zoomies. How does that sound?"

He seems to take a moment to ponder what I've shared. "I think finding a new routine could be good for both of us. A little shake-up might be exactly what we need."

It might just be my imagination, or call it wishful thinking, but a small voice in my mind reminds me that I wouldn't mind being a part of a little shake-up with Aiden. I push the thought away immediately. There's no point going down that road again. He doesn't need me gawking at him and mulling over missed opportunities. No, we'll keep this professional, friendly at most, given our joined social circles. I'm sure that's all he's looking for from me anyway.

I take a peek at Hop, who is sprawled out on his side, his eyes wide and staring up at me. The dog is completely still, except his wild tail, giving away how excited he is.

When I glance up at Aiden, I find his eyes locked on me. His posture is tense, hesitancy radiating off him. "Bec," he starts, then sighs, briefly closing his eyes before looking back at me. "Can I be honest with you?"

"Uh...sure, what's up?" I say cautiously.

*Please don't bring up the baby shit again.  This might be the time humiliation actually kills me.*

"I wasn't sure if you wanted to talk about, you know, the wedding and us? I know we were in really different places back then, and I..." he trails off, pulling his hand over the back of his neck. I wish I could say the movement didn't immediately draw my attention to the muscles twitching in his powerful arms and shoulders, but that'd be a huge fucking lie. His damn T-shirt is too tight. His arms are undeniable eye candy. I can't help but stare.

"Um, sure, it's probably not a bad idea to clear the air, I guess." I wrap my arms around my clipboard, holding it to my chest like a shield. Maybe the barricade will quiet the butterflies fluttering around my insides, making my heart race.

Are we really talking about this? I figured, given some time, we'd make a few jokes and just let it lie. But nope, we are doing this. Half of me is dying to hear what he has to say, while the other part of me is dreading it.

He takes a step closer to me. Hopper eyes his movement, then winds his way between us. He rolls over dramatically, taking his shot that one of us will lean down to reward him with belly scratches. But I'm paralyzed, the breath knocked out of me, waiting to see where this goes and hear where Aiden's head is at. I've wondered ever since he stumbled back into my orbit.

"I don't want to make you uncomfortable. I know it was a long time ago, but I wanted to make sure you are all right with me being around. Since the season is over, I hope to hang out with Dom and everyone more often, but I didn't know if that would be weird for you."

I can't help the wave of disappointment that washes over me. He doesn't want to talk about us, not really. Just enough to make sure that he can be around, hang with his friends without me making it awkward. It was dumb to think he might still think about me that way.

*Stupid, Bec. You're being stupid.*

That weekend was nothing.

I can feel my face flush, recalling how often I'd mull over memories of that weekend in the past few years. Especially when I needed a reminder of who I am or who I used to be before Josh and I broke up. Before I started questioning myself. Have I wondered if Aiden ever thought about that weekend too? Of course. But obviously we were just a fleeting moment. I need to recognize it for what it was and let it go.

"Of course not. Nope. No weirdness here." I shake my head quickly, pursing my lips, and I can't seem to stop. Looking back down at my notes, I huff a laugh. "Zero weirdness. In fact," I say, shoving my hand out between us. "Friends?"

*Wow, smooth, Bec.*

I'm doing a wonderful job making this weird as shit and it hasn't even been two seconds.

He slowly reaches for my hand and gently shakes it, like he's afraid any firm contact might break me. His confused expression morphs into a polite smile. "Sure. Yeah, okay. Friends," he agrees.

I feel my heart sink. I don't know what exactly I want from Aiden, but when the word leaves his mouth, I know being his friend isn't it. None of this sits well with me. I tell myself the discomfort settling over me will fade, and I really hope I'm right.

# Chapter Eight

## Bec

"I can't believe you convinced me to do this. I'm three seconds away from staging a scene so I can leave." Dee lies on the ground and lets her arms flop lazily to her sides.

I glance at her and giggle while I finish my reps. "Stop, you're fine. We only have the leg press after this, and then we can cool down on the StairMaster."

Her head snaps up and she glares at me incredulously. "Cool down on the StairMaster? That is not possible. No one *cools down* while climbing stairs."

I grab a pair of dumbbells and start my next set while Dee rolls to her side, dragging herself up to sit and wrapping her arms around her bent knees. She's the most dramatic gym partner in our group, but she's usually always willing to go. It helps that she and I both live downtown, separated by only a few blocks, our gym conveniently located between us. There's also an incredible brunch spot next door with bottomless mimosas on Thursdays. It would take next to no effort to convince Dee to abandon our workout and wander over there, but for some reason I feel restless, like I need to keep moving.

We're almost done with our workout, and I still feel on edge. Dee's noticed. She's fun and free-spirited, but she's also observant, fiercely loyal, and knows me well.

"You good, girl? You look like you've got something on your mind." She takes a drink from her water bottle and starts stretching.

"Yeah, I'm fine." I grab the spray bottle and clean the mats and weights we've been using before moving on to the next exercise. "Just a little restless lately. Work has been busy."

Truthfully, work is great. I love what I do, and I feel fulfilled every day I get to work with dogs. I'm not sure I even know how to put into words what's bothering me, but I don't need to. Dee sees right through my facade.

"Come on, we both know you love your job. I've seen you when work is stressing you out and this isn't that. Let me guess...guy trouble? Did you swipe right and now you're fielding unsolicited dick pics from some asshole? Give me his name, I'll give him hell. Oh, or did you run into that pro-ball hottie and take off your shirt again? Please say yes," Dee says as she helps me rack the equipment, and we head to the leg press machine.

"God no, don't remind me." I adjust the weight settings and start my reps. "But I did run into him again. Fully clothed this time, hallelujah. He joined one of my training classes this week with his adorable lab puppy."

"Stop it." Dee laughs and holds the side of the machine while she throws her head back. "Oh my god, *he's in your class*? That's amazing. You should totally ask him out. Teacher-student romance? Yes, Ms. Miller. Tell me, is there still lingering chemistry?" she asks with a little shimmy and a gleam in her eye. Fucking ridiculous. I love her.

"What? No. He's a nice guy, but he's not interested in me like that." I finish my set and Dee sets up for hers. She might be short, but damn, Dee can push a lot of weight around.

She eyes me skeptically before asking, "How do you know? Did you ask him out?"

Dee's the only one who knows how Aiden and I met, and I swore her to secrecy years ago. I still feel bad for not telling Ellie, Carissa, and Dom, too, since Aiden is one of his best friends, but I didn't want to pull any focus away from the wedding festivities at the time and now it just seems stupid to bring up since it really wasn't a big deal.

"Not a chance, come on, Dee. He's a professional baseball player and I'm a dog trainer. In what world does that ever work? Don't get me wrong, he's unfairly attractive, but we agreed to be friends. It's better this way. I'm not trying to be a random hookup for someone who could date anyone he wants. Besides, I'll have to see him at all of Ellie and Dom's big moments. I don't want it to be any weirder than it already is."

"Hey." Dee stops, giving me her full attention. "Who the fuck are you and what have you done with Bec? Because my Bec doesn't self-deprecate. Don't say you're a dog trainer, like that's not fucking awesome. You're a badass professional who helps countless dogs and families. Plus, you've got an ass so tight, you can play quarters off it. You really need to put that on your dating profile."

Okay, I let Dee drunkenly play quarters off my butt *once* in college and she'll never let me live it down. Her aim was surprisingly accurate, I'll give her that.

"*Anyone*, professional athlete or not, would be fucking lucky if you looked their way," she continues. "You're a ten, Bec. Inside and out. Now, be nice to my friend...or I'll kick your ass." She continues her set, glaring at me.

I don't know what I did to deserve my friends, but I'm grateful for them more than they could ever know. "Thanks. I think I needed to hear that. I'm not sure why I feel so insecure lately. I think Aiden got in my head." *Wouldn't be the first time.*

"We both know why you're feeling that way, babe. Your relationship with Josh might have been fucked, but you can't project that onto Aiden, or anyone else you might be interested in."

"I don't know. I just feel like I'm not the same person I was when I first met him. I don't even know how to be that person anymore."

"Who says you need to go backward? You live, you learn, you grow. The best of Bec is yet to come," Dee says as she pushes through another set. Jesus, she's as strong as her personality.

"The best of Bec lately is just me embarrassing myself in front of Mister Fine. And despite how horrified and humiliated I felt seeing him at Ellie's, he was really nice about the whole thing, which almost makes it worse. If he wanted to try something more, I would consider it, but we talked about it last weekend, and he just wants to be friends. Clean slate. It's better this way, though. You know me, relationships aren't really my thing anymore. Besides, I've got a few new matches online that look promising enough to keep me busy without tying me down. That's what I want right now, I swear. Nothing more."

A pang of longing steals my breath when I picture that night for a moment. Meeting Aiden, his hands on my hips, my hands in his hair, and his lips on mine. I know I'm lying to myself. I don't want to be friends, but distance between me and Aiden Price is the safer option.

"Bec, anyone who could meet you and think you weren't worth a shot is an idiot. If he's too stuck up to realize you're a damn catch, then he's not worth another thought. Fuck that hotshot and his giant man muscles."

I appreciate the sentiment, but with the way Aiden somehow keeps sneaking into my thoughts, it's easier said than done. I sigh. "Enough of my drama, why don't we skip the stairs and hit up next door for some mimosas instead? You could help me look through my matches? I could use a date."

Dee practically leaps out of the machine. "Yes, fuck, yes. Let's get out of this hellhole."

The thought of going on a date makes my stomach clench with hesitation and nerves, but I need to do something to get over these borderline obsessive thoughts centering around Aiden and one mean-ingless weekend.  There are plenty of other great guys in this city, anyway.

# Chapter Nine



## Bec

I lied; this city is full of douchebaggery to the highest degree. I'm a heartbeat away from faking an "emergency" text to get me out of this horrific date. I can't believe I'm wasting my Friday night on this guy.

"And then my boss goes, Doug, you can't just walk out of the meeting. I looked her up and down and reminded her, I'm the CEO's nephew, and he signs her paychecks. I don't have to do anything. *Psssh*, her face, I wish you could have seen it. She was practically purple; she was so pissed."

*What...the actual...fuck?*

This is the last time I swipe right for anyone whose career is listed as *finance* in their profile. I should have known after how things worked out—or didn't work out—with Josh to just avoid the entire financial-man species.

Doug is hot, arrogant, and repulsive. Sounds a little contradictory? Well shit, I have eyes. I can't deny he's gorgeous, but if he opens his mouth one more time, I may vomit all over the table.

He's been talking about work for fifteen minutes straight and how he acts like an entitled prick, shitting all over his coworkers. All this after he asked me to take a picture of him for his online content because he looks "too hot to ignore." Not a picture of the two of us. A picture of him, alone, giving me a smoldering look and then several of him looking off into the distance all moody, like I was the fucking paparazzi catching him candidly for his fans. Yes, he called his social media followers his fans.

Okay, maybe I should have faked that text already.

"So, Beckett…" *Yeah, not my name, buddy. But nice try.* I'm not going to waste my time correcting him. With any luck, I'll never see him again after tonight. "What do you do?" he asks.

I don't know whether I should be impressed that he stopped talking about himself long enough to ask a question about me or if I should be even more irritated that he didn't at least skim over my profile before our date to see that I very clearly listed that I'm a dog trainer. Why am I not surprised by the lack of effort?

At this point, we've eaten, split a bottle of wine, and declined dessert. All I have to do is get through the split-the-check dance I insist on playing at the end of a date to avoid the people-pleasers guilt syndrome, and then I can run home and throw on my baggiest pajamas and fall asleep watching the cheesiest rom-com I can find. I need a quick reminder that there are men out there who are the complete opposite of Doug. Even if those men are fictional and most likely written by women, but whatever.

I can't believe I bothered buying a new dress for this date. What a waste. I got caught up in the excitement of it all. I've gone on a handful of terrible dates since the breakup, but it's been a while since I matched with someone who seemed cool. I feel like I'm being catfished, or this guy paid someone to answer the questions for him. Not one part of his profile screamed asshole, but the facts are right in front of me.

"I'm a dog trainer. I work with families, service dogs, therapy dogs, and one of the local shelters," I say before draining the rest of my wine glass.

I'll have to come back here with the girls sometime. This restaurant has a chill vibe with natural wood tables, dark forest green walls, black ceiling, gold sconces with intricate, vintage detail, giving off low amber lighting, and there's some indie folk melody humming in the background. Perfect ambience for a night out, current company excluded.

"Oh, really? Well, that sounds like a fun job. What do you plan to do next? Are you still in school?" He's scrolling through his phone, not even looking at me.

*Seriously, what a dick.*

"What do you mean?" I close my hands into tight fists in my lap, digging my nails into my palm before letting go.  I can feel blood rushing to my head and my face getting hot.

Is he seriously suggesting that my career isn't legitimate?

"Well, I assume that's not the long-term plan. Not much money in that, I figure." He sips at his wine, still scrolling through his phone. I want to scream but manage to stay levelheaded. I'll be pissed if he gets me worked up enough to embarrass myself. Who is he to make me feel like I have to defend myself for choosing a career I love?

"I didn't choose my career for the *money*, Doug. I love what I do and I'm damn good at it."

"Yeah, sure. You won't need to worry about all that once you have a husband and a family anyway. Makes sense."

*Oh. Fuck. No.*

There's nothing wrong with wanting a spouse and a family and making that the priority, but for him to just assume that I'd want that in place of my career...yeah, I'm done.

"Okay, well, that's enough for me. This should cover my half of the meal." I toss down some cash because—fuck this guy. I don't want anything from him, not even a free meal.

"What do you mean? Aren't you going to invite me over to your place?"

Never in a million years would I be that desperate.

I was right to ignore the dating apps if this is what's waiting for me. I'm deleting them as soon as I get home. I'd rather spend my entire adult life without a partner than share a meal with another Doug.

"No, this isn't going anywhere. Tonight was…well, it was something." God, I wish I had Dee's fire for thirty seconds so I could tell this guy exactly what I thought of this date. But the people pleaser in me makes her final appearance for the night and convinces me to ignore him. She's a stubborn bitch.

It's beyond time to leave and be done with this night. He's not worth any more of my time or energy, and my words would bounce right off his skull anyway.

I grab my purse, slinging it over my shoulder, and go to stand, my chair sliding back along the wood floors with a creaky whine. I feel my chair catch as it runs right into someone as they pass by our table.

"Oh, I'm so sorry. Excuse me." I turn around and find a familiar face staring back at me. "Aiden, hey. What are you doing here?" He's standing just a few inches away from me as I look up at him. He hasn't stepped back, and I'm still wedged between my chair and the table. His presence commands every bit of my attention, the scent of him and his cologne mixed together is intoxicating. The intensity of his stare has a way of lighting a fire in me, feeling way more than friendly. A quick perusal of his outfit only confirms that this man is too fine for his own good. It's not fair for him to make normal clothes—white sneakers; fitted, dark jeans; a gray T-shirt; and a black bomber jacket—look *that* good.

"Bec, wow, you look…you look incredible." I like hearing that from Aiden far more than I should. I can't help but smile in response.

I don't fully understand the relief I feel now that he's here. Maybe it's because I've spent the night counting down the uncomfortable minutes left of my date with Doug. Or maybe it's just Aiden. When I'm not psyching myself out over our weird history, or eye-fucking his bangin' bod, it's easy to remember how soothing his presence is. Calm, confident, steady, safe. It's both a comfort and a thrill being near him.

"Beckett, if you want to split it evenly, you owe me five more bucks." I hear Doug call out distractedly from behind me. I glance back at him to see he has the check in front of him, and yet he's still scanning through his phone. God, he's such a tool. "Bye, Doug."

I feel Aiden lean in and place his hand on the small of my back. "Hey, you have a few minutes? My table is over here. Come sit for a second?" he asks.

I nod, letting him guide me to a booth with high walls, giving the space a private feel. I sit down and he leans in close, caging me in, one hand behind me on the back of the booth, the other grabbing my hand in my lap for just a second and squeezing it. "Hang tight," he says. "I'll be right back, yeah?" I nod again, unsure of why he wants me to sit here, trying to ignore the flutter in my stomach from the close contact. But having him near, looking at me like that makes me want to stay and find out.

I watch Aiden walk away, my eyes going wide when I see him stop at my table with Doug. He leans over, wearing a neutral expression, speaking calmly. But Doug...Doug puts his phone down, and as they talk, I see him lift his hands up, seemingly growing more heated by the second. He exchanges words with Aiden and then abruptly storms out.

Aiden watches him leave, then strides back over and sits across from me. "You okay?" he asks.

"Uh, yeah. I'm fine. What did you say to Doug?"

He doesn't answer me. He studies me. The familiar flicker of embarrassment strikes me in my gut. Did he hear the way Doug was talking about my job? About how much money I make?

It's one thing to be humiliated by a date I'll never see again. It's another thing entirely to have Aiden witness it.

Dee is never going to believe what an asshole that guy was after we both vetted several matches for a date. Sometimes you need a second opinion to see if you're missing any red flags. Jesus, Dee and I must have either missed a giant one or a million small ones.

"Aiden!" I hear a woman exclaim behind me. A flurry of blonde hair whips by me as a tall, willowy knockout of a woman walks up to Aiden, sits next to him, and pulls him in for a hug. Holy shit, Aiden's on a date—one that I'm now crashing—with a model, from the looks of it. *Kill me, now.*

"I better get going. Thanks for checking on me." I grab my purse and run out of there as fast as I can, not looking back when I hear Aiden call my name. I thought tonight couldn't get worse, but then I remember I have to see Aiden in class tomorrow. And I'll have to pretend this clusterfuck of a night never happened.

# Chapter Ten

Aiden

Bec's been avoiding me this entire class. Which is damn impressive, given that Hopper is dressed up as a Demogorgon. Pretty fucking distracting if you ask me. Hop's been a ball of chaos at home, destroying two pairs of cleats and one of my gloves in the last week, so it felt like a fitting costume.

The Center for Faithful Companions encouraged everyone to dress their dogs for Halloween. Looking around, there's an Ewok, a Ghostbuster, a classic pumpkin, the works. I was hoping the costumes would give me and Bec something to joke about and help diffuse any tension between us, but she hasn't made eye contact with me since we walked in. She's definitely committed to ignoring us. She's kept her instructions general to the entire class or to other families.

The last few interactions we've shared outside of class have left a lot unsaid between us. She was quick to shut down conversation about the past before we really even had a chance to talk much about it. Conversation flowed easily when we met years ago, but now it feels stilted. I don't know how to fix it, but I know I want to.

During Hop's makeup class, I could feel Bec's walls going up, strong and sturdy around her. I could almost see her shutting down in front of me when I brought up the wedding. I don't know what I said to upset her. I didn't want to push her further and say anything wrong, so I shut my mouth.

I didn't want to look like the idiot I clearly am by asking her if she'd thought about us at all over the past few years. Of course she hasn't. She made it abundantly clear she wasn't interested when we met, and I should have known that would stand today. Did I really think living in the same city would change anything?

I wanted to tell her that after all this time, I still feel an irresistible, magnetic pull toward her. I wanted to tell her I can't stop looking at her and waiting for her to look at me because for some reason I can't explain, I want her to see me. I wanted to tell her that her smile, her laugh, they light up the fucking room and I don't want to miss a minute of it. I wanted to tell her that even though we don't know each other well, I sure as shit want to. I want to know everything there is to know about her.

I couldn't. I couldn't say any of this to her. Not with the way she looked at me with guarded apprehension. So instead, I walked out of there officially friend-zoned. Obviously, I'll respect it. Bec clearly doesn't feel the same way I do, which sucks.

Am I making a mistake not being honest with Bec about how I'm feeling? No. I don't want to ruin a shot at friendship with her by telling her I'd be interested in a fuck of a lot more than that. At least as her friend, I'll get some kind of relationship with her.

When I spotted Bec out last night with that asshole, jealousy tore through my gut. Hearing him talk shit about her job, not even getting her goddamn name right, the condescending tone of his voice...it all made me see fucking red. I try to never jump straight to anger. I've done everything in my power to avoid behaving like that. I won't allow it, but fuck, I couldn't stop the feeling from consuming me. It took everything I had to get Bec away from him so I could deal with it. I know she doesn't need me to defend her. She's more than capable. But a rush of possessiveness overtook me, and I just wanted her away from him. Bec is a beacon of light in the dark, and anyone who wants to dull her shine can go to hell. She doesn't deserve to be spoken to like that.

Afterward, she ran out of the restaurant so quickly, I didn't have a chance to make sure she was all right. I can't imagine his words didn't sting, no matter the type of confidence she exuded when we first met. I know firsthand that the image you project to the world doesn't necessarily match what's happening inside your mind, and I haven't seen that same confidence since I moved back to town. Not yet, anyway. And while I'm proud of her for not letting that asshole see her shaken, for not wasting energy on someone so beneath her, I want to make sure that the soundtrack playing in her mind didn't absorb any of his idiotic opinions. I don't want his misogynistic bullshit poisoning her sense of self-worth.

Fuck, I need to stop thinking about it, I'm getting pissed all over again.

"Okay, everyone, that's it for today. Have a safe and happy Halloween! Don't forget to take a family photo at reception to show off your pets' costumes. We have a photo booth set up and treats for your furry trick-or-treaters." She walks to the dry-erase board on the far wall and starts erasing her notes from today's lesson.

I want to talk with her about last night, but as she wipes the board clean, her hips sway from side to side and I can't take my eyes off her perfect ass. Fuck, probably not the best way to show her that I respect her wishes to be friends and friends only.

Dom and Ellie invited me to a party around Thanksgiving, and I assume Bec will be there too. I need to clear the air, if not to make these weekly training classes less awkward, then at least to make sure we can hang out in the same group of friends without making each other uncomfortable. All I want to do is spend my time getting to know her, but she's clearly not on the same page.

I stroll to the board, where it looks like Bec's starting to jot notes for the next class, tugging Hopper along gently by his leash. "Hey, uh, Happy Halloween, Bec."

*Smooth, Aiden.*

"Happy Halloween," she says. When she turns around to look at me, I see a flash of her smile from the hotel bar where we met. God, what I wouldn't give for a second chance right now. We were different people then, but does that really mean that there isn't a chance of us being good for each other now? Lost in my thoughts, she pulls me back. "About last night. I'm so sorry. God, that was embarrassing. I hope I didn't ruin your date. She is absolutely gorgeous, Aiden. I'm really happy for you."

"Uh...huh? Oh shit, you mean Evie?" I chuckle. "I promise you weren't interrupting anything, she's..."

"No seriously, it's great that you're getting out there after your move and everything. I hope I didn't make it too weird and you both enjoyed your night together. If she's going to be spending more time with you and Hop, you can even bring her to classes with you if you want. It's important for everyone in the household to be on the same page and using the same training techniques to give Hop the best chance to catch on..."

Holy shit, she is going off in a whirlwind and not even remotely close to seeing what really happened last night. I'm fucking dumb, *of course* she'd assume I was on a date. I've got to stop her before she spirals.

"Bec, wait, wait, stop." I cut her off, pulling her hand into mine to get her attention. When she falls silent, I drop her hand, reminding myself to keep my distance like she wants, even though it goes against my instincts. "Are you talking about Evie? The blonde woman who arrived right before you left? That was my sister. She's a graduate student at the University of Columbus. We try to catch up a few times a month."

"Oh, uh...well, that's not what I expected." Her face scrunches up, and I can't help but notice how cute she is when she's embarrassed around me. Seems to be a trend with us lately. "And somehow, I'm even more embarrassed now, knowing I ran like that. Ugh, sorry, you obviously caught me at a really bad time, I was a little frazzled. Please apologize to her for me, I was so rude. My date turned out to be a nightmare, and I was trying to make a clean exit, and I wasn't expecting to see you."

"I think 'nightmare' might be a bit too generous," I reply. "The guy was a fucking idiot, Bec. I'm sorry he couldn't appreciate how lucky he was to be sharing a table with you." She lets a smirk slip by and, god, I want to bite that lip.

"Damn...I was really hoping you hadn't heard just how terrible the whole date ended. That's humiliating." She tucks a stray curl behind her ear, looking down.

"Bec, look at me." I wait for her to slowly give me her attention. When she does, I swear the room blurs into nothing. It's just her and me. Well, her, me, and Hop, who won't stop chewing on my shoelace. "Don't be sorry, not for one second. His arrogance and stupidity are a reflection of him, not you. He couldn't possibly understand that he made the biggest mistake of his life treating you like that."

I can feel a heavy weight lift off my chest as I watch her absorb my words, her face slowly breaking into a shy but stunning smile. I hope with everything I have she doesn't give that fucker another thought. She's worth more than he could ever imagine, and the dumbass let her slip right through his fingers. Then again, so did I.

# Chapter Eleven

Bec

The Wedding

"**B**itch, is that a hickey? You kicked off the weekend without me, didn't you?" Dee screams, leaning closer to inspect my skin. The club music is so loud I can barely hear her.

We played several pervy games in the hotel room, had dinner tipping heavily to compensate for our obnoxious enthusiasm, and went to the strip club. We finally made it to our last stop of the night, dancing at one of the local clubs, and Ellie looks one shot away from needing me to hold her hair back. I leave the dance floor to grab her a glass of water from the bar. Dee follows me while the rest of the group continues grinding to the pulsing beat.

"Can you really see one?" I dip my chin, trying to catch a glimpse.

"Right here under your sash." Her eyes sparkle with deviancy as she eyes the evidence of my time with Aiden. "Gimme. The details. Now." She turns to the bartender and orders two shots.

"Dee, what are you doing? Ellie clearly doesn't need any more. Three waters, please." I smile at the bartender, adding to Dee's order.

"The shots are for us. Now loosen those lips and tell me who was between those hips.”

"Ew, what? No, no one was between these hips." Unfortunately.

I am fully on board with the idea of a carefree weekend with Aiden. A carefree, naked weekend, preferably. There's no way that's happening tonight. I'm on maid-of-honor duty, with overtime. Ellie is going to need food before she crashes, and it's already two in the morning. I have no idea what Aiden is doing this weekend—huh, weird that never came up—but I can't imagine he'd welcome a booty call at this hour.

Ellie and Dom are both out tonight for their respective bachelorette and bachelor parties. They're sharing their hotel suite together all weekend, not caring about tradition. The message Dom's brother sent me a few minutes ago let me know they're already back at the hotel with pizza. I text him back, asking him to save Ellie a few slices to make sure she gets some food in her stomach before bed. We have to be up and at the spa by nine for a full morning of pampering tomorrow before the rehearsal dinner.

"Mark my words, Bec. I will get it out of you." She winks at me, shoots her shot, grabs two of the waters, and heads back to Ellie and the girls.

I stand at the bar for a second longer, questioning my sanity because all I can think about is Aiden. His gaze, intense and focused. His stare lingering on my curves. His grip firm as he pressed me to the wall. I've never felt that turned on or desired in my life.

There is something captivating about him, and I feel like he could easily pull me under his influence. I hope his weekend plans are more flexible than mine because I don't want to miss out on getting to know him better. Or at least getting under him.

After taking my shot, I rejoin my friends. Ellie screams, throws the water from Dee onto the dance floor, flings her arms around my neck, and slams into my chest. "Holy shit, I'm getting married, B," she screams before pulling back and grabbing me by the shoulders with a serious look. "But first I need to sit on Dom's face." She giggles and wobbles, her eyelids *slowly drooping down, and she lets out a small hiccup.*

*Yep, it's time to wrap this up and get to the hotel. I guarantee she'll pass out within the hour, fully dressed with a slice of pizza in her hand. I'd bet a hundred bucks there's no face sitting tonight, but I laugh and smile back at my best friend. Knowing she found a love that makes her happy fills my heart with joy. She deserves the best, and I know Dom will give that to her. Turns out some people really do get their happily ever after.*

* * *

**Aiden**: *Hey stranger, can I see you tonight?*

**Bec**: *Who is this?*

**Aiden**: *Am I so easily forgettable?*

**Bec**: *I'd have to remember you to confirm if I've forgotten you.*

**Aiden**: *Let me jog your memory. 6'3", mysterious smile, charming personality, witty as fuck, great butt.*

**Bec**: *And modest as hell. Good morning, Aiden.*

**Aiden**: *Ah, so not easily forgotten then.*

**Bec**: *All the alcohol in Columbus leaving my system is slowing my mind today. Give me a few hours...maybe my brain cells will return. What time?*

**Aiden**: *Meet for drinks in our spot at 10?*

**Bec**: *By our spot, do you mean the hotel bar or behind the ice machine on the 14th floor?*

**Aiden**: *I do have fond memories of the 14th floor, but let me buy you a drink and get my fill of you before you get your fill of me.*

**Bec**: *Promises, promises. See you at 10, stranger.*

* * *

*My stomach has been doing flips since Aiden messaged me, and it flips again as I reread our text conversation for the millionth time. It could be* the hangover, but most likely it's him and the thought of where tonight might lead.

"I'm going to assume the dopey smile on your face has something to do with the mysterious Mister Hickey. I've waited long enough. Who are you hooking up with this weekend and do they have a friend for me?" Dee is relentless. I surrender rather than prolong the inevitable. She'll get it out of me eventually.

We're waiting in the ceremony space for the rest of the party to arrive so the wedding planner can start the rehearsal. Everything about this hotel is beautiful. Tomorrow, Ellie and Dom will get married in the rooftop garden courtyard. The atmosphere is perfect; twinkling string lights cascade around the space, casting it with a golden glow. The sky above is painted with streaks of a rose-hued sunset. The floral arrangements are heavy with rich purple blooms and greenery, offering a refreshing spring fragrance. The picturesque view of the city skyline is an awe-inspiring backdrop.

I share the details of how I met Aiden—no last name—with Dee while we wait. To say her face is glowing with amusement is an understatement. She's practically steepling her fingers, grinning like I imagine a tiny devil on my shoulder would.

"Well, well, well. Bec came to this wedding ready for some fun. I'm happy for you. You deserve a romp with a hottie, and this Aiden sounds like he could deliver. Plus, he'll be starving for you when he sees you in this dress tonight."

That's the idea. I brought a few options for the rehearsal but opted for the bolder choice. A satin, cap-sleeved, red wrap dress with a plunging neckline and the hem falling just below my knees with a less than modest glimpse of my thigh peeking through the slit with every step.

"So...does he have any friends or what?" She playfully bumps my hip with hers. I hear Dom's boisterous voice echoing through the space as he greets a few others from the wedding party who must have joined the group.

*"Dee, I literally know nothing about this guy other than he's hot as fuck, knows how to kiss, and he's here until Sunday." He's the perfect candidate for my weekend fling. No drama, no attachments, no pressure. And if his kiss is on par with his other...skills, then I'm in for the ride of my life.*

# Chapter Twelve

## Aiden

## The Wedding

*After the bachelor party last night, I considered texting Bec. I don't want to assume anything, but in case we continued what we started, I didn't want us hooking up while I was drunk.*

*The brutal hangover this morning was a reminder of how hard Dom's family and the other groomsmen can party. Dom's older brother, Jake, and his husband, Chris, were passing shots around like they were water. The thought of whatever the fuck the last shot was makes my stomach uneasy.*

*"Aiden, man, glad to see you looking better." Jake reaches out and claps me on the shoulder.*

*"I can't be the only one hurting after last night. You were all drinking the same shit as me." I shoot a pointed look toward him and Chris. They both plaster on guilty smiles.*

*"Oh please, we took it easy on you." Chris laughs. "It's not our fault your tolerance is shit. I bet your body is just in shock since you don't let loose like that during the season. I'm surprised you could even get away for the wedding."*

*When Dom asked me to be a groomsman, I assumed I'd only be able to make it to the ceremony. I was surprised I was able to make it for the bachelor party and rehearsal, too, given my schedule for the season.*

*My eye catches movement to my right, a flit of red dancing at the edge of my vision. When I focus on the woman who's approaching Dom with her arms stretched wide and a beaming smile on her face, my heart starts pounding out of my chest.*

No. Fucking. Way.

*No fucking way is Bec here. Hugging Dom like...they're close.*

*I would have heard her name by now if she knew Ellie and Dom, right? Shit, is she family?*

*Come to think of it, I don't think Dom's mentioned any of the bridesmaids by name. Or maybe Bec is a nickname, and I wouldn't have recognized it if he had mentioned her anyway.*

*I feel my jaw hanging in the air, looking like a dumbass. I work quickly to fix my face into a mask of indifference. Was I expecting and hoping to see Bec tonight? Yeah. Did I assume it would be much later and with a lot less clothing? Also, yeah. Seeing her wrapped in red silk might just kill me. With her cleavage prominently on display and the peek of her thigh when she walks, I can't take my eyes off her.*

*Regardless of the shock I feel seeing her here, the draw I felt to her last night resurfaces, catching me off balance. The pull to reach out to her, be near her, and feel her skin against mine is stronger now.*

*I'm going to follow her lead and leave it up to her to decide if she wants everyone to know we met last night. I don't want to fuck this up. Something tells me I'll regret it if I do.*

*Introductions are made as the group confers together, a blending of Dom and Ellie's closest family and friends. I barely hear any of it. Bec turns to one of her friends and laughs.*

*I freeze, anxiously waiting for her to realize I'm here, curious to see what her reaction will be. When her eyes finally lock with mine, I'm not disappointed. Her lips part and her entire body freezes, interrupting the fluid movement she always seems to convey, her skirt floating, wrapping around her as her body stills. She pauses for a moment before I see, more than hear, a puff of breath fall from her lips, her shoulders briefly dipping and then she smiles.*

*My chest constricts. Everything inside me lights up. This woman feels different, and I barely know her—clearly, given the last place I expected to see her was Dom's wedding rehearsal. Maybe Bec was right and the universe is forcing our paths to cross again. We could have left this all to chance, like she suggested. I've never believed in fate or bigger forces at play, but it's hard to deny this is a twist I didn't expect.*

*"Well, hey, stranger. You wedding crashing?" She approaches me but keeps a few feet of polite distance.*

*Dom looks at me, confused. "Bec, you know Aiden?"*

*"We met briefly last night at the hotel bar. Nice to see you again." She effortlessly offers up a safe answer. I'll try to avoid blurting out that I most definitely gave her that hickey she tried to cover with makeup— unsuccessfully, but still, a nice effort.*

*"Yeah, you too. Didn't realize I'd be seeing you again so soon, but it's a welcome surprise." I shoot off a smirk in her direction, hoping this unexpected connection doesn't scare her off. If anything, it makes me more curious to get to know her better. The chances that I'd find someone who already gets along with one of my best friends and makes me feel this way seems too good to be true. "So how do you two know each other?" I gesture to Dom and Bec with my finger, lifting it slightly off the tumbler in my hand.*

*"Dom is the lucky bastard who stole my best girl's heart. After careful consideration, I've decided to allow him to marry Ellie." She shoves Dom playfully in the arm, and he answers back with a booming laugh.*

*"The vetting process in your group is unmatched. I don't know who made me work harder; Ellie, Dee, Carissa, or you."*

*"You rang?" A woman, looking to be about Bec's age but several inches*

shorter, comes up and slaps Bec on the ass.

"Dee, this is Aiden," Bec says, giving her a pointed look that I don't quite understand until I see Dee's mouth drop open. She stares at me with a look in her eyes so wicked it honestly scares me.

"I went to college with Dom, nice to meet you." I offer my hand to Dee.

Dee takes my hand, slowly sizing me up with her eyes, and I feel my gut shrivel under her shrewd stare. "Oh, it's wonderful to meet you, too, Aiden." Bec sharply bumps Dee with her hip and glares at her. Dee completely ignores her, a wild grin on her face. "I've seen your handiwork, gotta say, I'm a big fan."

Yeah, I think it's safe to say she knows who gave Bec that hickey.

"You a baseball fan, Dee?" Dom asks, oblivious to Dee's innuendo.

"Not especially, but I enjoy the uniforms. Does that count?"

"I know I've mentioned it before. Aiden plays pro baseball. About to start his next season with the Detroit Lightning. Can't wait for you to play in town sometime so Ellie and I can catch a game."

Bec looks over at Dom, her jaw dropping slightly before she quickly closes it, confirming what I suspected last night. She has no idea who I am. Well, not until now.

Normally, my job helps me gain attention from women who are curious about the lifestyle of a professional athlete, but I can see Bec withdrawing. Almost like this fact changed something in her perception of me, and not for the better. Shit.

# Chapter Thirteen

## Aiden

"Where's your head at, Price? A little light conditioning looks like it might kill you." My pain-in-the-ass first baseman, Pete Matthews, goads me. This month, our infielders are meeting a few times a week for off-season training, and I'm relieved with the reprieve from our hectic schedule.

"Yeah, you tired, old man? Past your nap time already?" Roman chimes in like the smart-ass he is.

"Not you, too, Rivera. Talking an awful lot of shit for a guy only two years younger than me," I snap back. Roman Rivera, the best shortstop in the league and one of the first to welcome me when I was traded, scoffs in response as he cycles through his set.

"You may only be two years older, but you're acting a fuck of a lot older than that. Come out with us tonight. You haven't made it out since the season ended. Maybe find someone in town to help you relax. I'm sure someone would love to give the new guy a shot." Roman winks at me.

He means well, and yeah, I might have turned down a few offers to go out to a bar with the guys after our season wrapped. Unfortunately, I have no desire to meet anyone when I can't stop thinking about Bec.

"Nah, man. I'm not looking to dive into anything new right now." It's not like I'm not trying. But every time I think I've cleared Bec from my mind, I'll come across something so small that my brain works in overdrive, making a million tiny thought connections that I don't even fully register, until her face pops up crystal clear in my mind. The other day, I was eating cereal in my kitchen and before I knew it, I was down the weirdest rabbit hole in my mind and imagining Bec naked and bent over my kitchen counter, gripping the edge, moaning while I...

"Jesus, Price, you don't have to marry the next girl you sleep with, just get out there," Pete pipes in, wiping his forehead with a towel. "Get in and get out."

"Aw, now that's just sad." Roman grabs him in a headlock, ruffling his hair. "Who hurt you, Petey?"

I may have joined the team midseason, but Pete and Roman were quick to offer their help to get me up to speed. So, while they both love to give me a hard time, I'm grateful to share the infield with them. They made the transition easier than I expected it to be.

It helps that we've gotten to know each other outside the game too. We met up a couple times to grab a few beers after our away games while we were on the road. I even shared a bit about the situation with Mom. It's not something I talk about often, especially since I don't want my family's personal business to end up in any headlines. The media is always clawing for personal stories to drum up interest.

But things are easier when my team is aware of what's going on, in case something ever comes up unexpectedly. Like today, when Evie texts me, asking me to call her as soon as possible.

Not lifting my eyes off my phone, I mumble to Matthews and Rivera, "I need to get in touch with my sister. Be right back." I give a heads-up to the assistant coach and step into the empty hallway, dialing Evie's number without hesitation.

"Hey, big brother, what's up?"

"What do you mean, what's up? Evie, you asked me to call ASAP. What's going on?" Irritation flows through me like a tidal wave, audibly lacing my every word. She knows I always assume the worst, and when she sends me a text like that, I inevitably anticipate getting bad news. I can't avoid the way it kicks my protectiveness into overdrive.

Why does anyone communicate like that anyway? Getting a *call me as soon as you can* text might as well mean *pause everything you're doing and prepare for emotional trauma.* If everyone is safe and healthy, those types of texts should be illegal.

"Woah...chill, bud. Just throwing out a casual greeting. You know, like humans do from time to time? I can hear you're clearly not in the mood, so let me just add that Mom and I are fine. Relax before you get all worked up. The staff from the assisted living facility called me this morning and gave me an update. I thought I'd keep you in the loop."

My entire body relaxes and guilt ebbs at me. Evie doesn't deserve my attitude, but after everything, I can't keep the stress out of my voice. I'm usually better at masking it. Keeping my communication calm. Listening first, acting second. The stress of the last few months is catching up to me.

"Fuck, I'm sorry, Evie. Thanks for calling, what'd they say?"

"Well, they're starting to notice her symptoms worsening. Nothing too concerning. Nothing they can't help her manage for now, but they wanted to make sure we were aware. They don't think she's there yet, but they suggested we consider what we want her living situation to look like in the next few months, because they anticipate she'll need a higher level of care." I can hear the unease in her tone.

"How was she the last time you saw her?" I run my fingers through my hair in frustration, trying to remember the last time I was able to visit Mom. I make a mental note to look at my calendar when

I get home to see when I can make the trip to Detroit in between conditioning sessions.

"I drove up there two weeks ago and have been FaceTiming with her every day. She seems like her normal self, though come to think of it, she may have been repeating her questions a bit more often than usual. But you know, it's hard to tell if it's happening consistently when she's so far away," Evie replies, the regret in her voice heavy and unmistakable.

"Yeah, it would be better to have her closer to us. I know we talked a lot about the location change in June when I was traded, weighed the pros and cons. Want to catch up this weekend and we can regroup, maybe look up a few local places to check out, like they mentioned?"

"Way ahead of you. I emailed you a list of places to get us started. I found a few online, plus a few of the other graduate students from my program were able to recommend several reputable places. Wanna grab coffee on Saturday at the corner spot? We can go through the list and come up with a game plan."

"Sounds great, except Hopper and I have our puppy training class. Want to meet for lunch afterward instead?" I ask.

"This wouldn't happen to be the same class taught by the stunning brunette from that cute restaurant last Friday? God, she ran faster than I've ever seen you manage in all of your time as a professional athlete." I ignore her dig, picturing the shit-eating grin that I know is on her face right now. It's always accompanied by a dramatically raised eyebrow, shooting sky high on her forehead. The way she used to practice that single eyebrow raise when we were younger used to drive me nuts, but the way she can practically reach her hairline with that look is signature Evie. I don't even question it anymore. Under the right circumstances, that look would have you assuming she can see straight through any bullshit you throw at her. Which is why I go with honesty; she'll make it worse if I try to hide anything.

"Yes, Evie. Bec is the teacher. Happy?"

"Ah, dear brother. The question is, are *you* happy? Because the way you absolutely sank into your sad little booth, picking at your dinner after she bolted, makes me think that we're looking at a classic case of unrequited love. What'd you do to piss her off, dummy?"

That's just it. I have no fucking clue with Bec. I never know if what I say to her makes her want to avoid me, befriend me, or if she couldn't care less. I can't get a read on her to save my life. I know the chemistry I felt for her hasn't faded. If anything, being around her again has only intensified what I felt when we met. Despite the confusion I feel about what's on her mind, I find myself counting down the days until I can see her again.

I lean against the wall, pinching the bridge of my nose between my fingers. "Nothing, Eves. Shit. There's nothing going on between Bec and I." *Unfortunately.* "We're just friends."

"Uh-huh, and whose idea was that? I'm guessing not yours. A little salty over there?"

I fall silent, not quite sure what to say.

"Hey…Aiden," her tone softens, picking up on my hesitation. "You really like her? Fuck, I'm sorry I didn't mean to push…"

"No, really, it's fine. I don't know her that well. It's just…"

"But you want to, don't you?"

I sigh. "I don't know, but she's made it clear that friendship is all she's looking for." There's a lull and I know Evie is about to hit me in the gut. I can practically hear her contemplating her next words. Growing up in our house, all we had was each other and Mom. There were no secrets. Not after everything we went through. Evie knows me well. Which makes it easier for me. She can read me without me having to put what's in my head into words. That's why I wait, preparing for her to hit home with her always on point intuition.

"You know, Aiden, you could try being honest with her. Telling her that you want something more. See where it goes? You won't know unless you put yourself out there and say what you're thinking, what you're feeling. She might want the same thing. You deserve to be with someone that makes you happy. That takes care of you like you take care of the people you care about. It's okay to let other people see you, you know. There's nothing to hide."

"Yeah, thanks, Eves. I'll think about it. Don't worry about me," I say, even though I'm not sure I agree with her.

# Chapter Fourteen

## Bec

Is my best friend an extraordinary person?  Yes.  Is she overambitious to the point that I'm questioning her decision-making? Also, yes.

How Ellie convinced Dom to host their annual Friendsgiving dinner this year, I'll never know.  They have so much going on with the baby, and they always go above and beyond for this get-together; I'm amazed they found the energy, especially since they always host the dinner the Saturday after the holiday. Part of me wonders if Ellie felt like she needed this piece of her pre-baby life to stay the same. A connection to her previous self, maybe.

Dom and I have talked with Ellie about how we can best support her and help her to stay in a good place. She's talked with both of us about how her transition to motherhood has been more difficult mentally than she expected. I know she's been trying to find a professional to help her work through it, but she hasn't found the right fit yet. Dom, Dee, Carissa, and I are on the official mommy support team, along with both of their families. She's the most incredible person I know, and I want her to feel all the love around her. Making sure she gets rest and keeps doing things that make her feel fulfilled can only help,

I hope.

Thankfully, the dinner has always been potluck style, alleviating the preparation work significantly. I offered to come over early to help, which is how I end up in the dining room laying out place settings and stacks of clean dishes on the table while Luca babbles and slobbers happily on Ellie's chest in a baby wrap.

Like every other year, there's no formal sit-down meal. Food will cover the kitchen counters in crock pots and serving dishes, and everyone will eat as they please, mingling throughout the night. Ellie and Dom have a fairly large, modern home with an open floor plan, and while they invite a lot of friends to get together, it never feels crowded.

Call me cliché, but it's my favorite time of the year. Don't get me wrong, I love warm weather as much as anyone, but the nostalgia that hits during the holiday season warms my soul. And Ellie always goes all out, even this year with a newborn. The girls and I came over last weekend to help decorate for Christmas because Ellie likes to have the house full of holiday cheer for Thanksgiving too. She insists we watch Christmas movies the entire time, drink champagne or seasonal craft beer, and make cookies. It takes all day and I love it.

Being single with a small, one-bedroom apartment, I never decorate quite like Ellie does. I can barely fit my skinny artificial tree in the corner. It's basically a Charlie Brown–style tree that I overdress in an abundance of lights, overwhelming the sparse branches.

When Ellie and Dom first moved in together, he tried to implement a rule that Christmas decorations couldn't go up until after Thanksgiving. Obviously, he was overruled. He also tried to claim that Christmas was over before New Year's Eve, so the decorations should come down before then too. I'm sure you can guess how that worked out. Ellie's tree won't come down until *maybe* the second week of January, if he's lucky.

But this year, Dom hasn't been a Grinch at all. He even offered to get new outdoor lights and already has them up, including a huge Christmas wreath on the front of the house, a focal point highlighted in green and red flood lights. It's like after having a son, he finally got on board with the festivities. Not sure how much Luca will get out of the holidays this year since he's a newborn, but I would never say anything. I love watching my friends put their hearts and souls into making the season magical for their baby. I have to imagine that seeing it all through the eyes of your child, especially when it's your first, is a special kind of magic for them to experience as parents.

Christmas carols play softly throughout their home, which smells heavenly; a mix of the gingerbread cookies in the oven and the orange, cranberry, cinnamon mixture that's simmering on the stove for cocktails. The lights are set low complimented by garland and twinkling lights scattered throughout the space. The fire crackles softly in the living room encased in the glow from their large Christmas tree.

"Bec, you have to give me this recipe. I'm going to eat this entire thing before anyone even gets here." Ellie is perched at the kitchen island, scarfing down my potluck contribution, buffalo chicken dip and pita chips.

"El, it's all yours. Oh, and I almost forgot, wait until you see the cute marshmallows I found for the hot chocolate bar." I find my bag and pull out a bottle of chocolate liquor and candy. "They're frickin' snowmen...with top hats. I had to get them. And I also grabbed the candy canes you asked for."

"Stop it, those are perfect. Do we need another dish to set them out?" she mumbles through another bite of dip.

"I'll grab one." I get to work putting everything on the counter next to the insulated drink dispenser full of hot chocolate. Like I said, Ellie and Dom go all out. "The house looks amazing. You and Dom still feeling up for all this? How'd you sleep last night? You can rest until people start to arrive if you want. I can take Luca."

*Please, god, no repeats of last time.*

She gives me a sweet smile as she brushes her hands off on her skirt. "Luca had a good night, thank god. I'm feeling surprisingly human today, and I'm excited for tonight. You're sweet to offer. What would I do without you, babe?" Her smile softens a bit, a hint of concern written on her face. "But I don't want you worrying about me. What about you? It feels like you've been going above and beyond lately for me, the girls, your family, your job. Are you doin' okay?"

"You know me. I prefer to be busy and in everyone's business. I don't have much going on outside of work. Besides, I love being here with you and your family. You trying to say I'm cramping your style hanging out all the time?" I smile, tossing a marshmallow at her playfully, which bounces off her forehead and lands on the countertop.

She laughs, picks the candy up, and pops it into her mouth, chewing thoughtfully. "I would argue that you are letting *me* cramp *your* style. Dom has a bunch of single friends stopping by tonight. Want me to introduce you? I promise nothing embarrassing. I'll be subtle."

I believe her. If Ellie gives me her word, she stays true to it. I know she just wants me to find my piece of happiness like she did with Dom. The problem is, I don't think everyone gets a happily ever after, even when they're looking for it. I'm not going to drive myself crazy looking for Mr. Right. Why stress about something that may never happen for me? And if I do find someone, what are the chances it lasts? What are the chances that someone sees all of you, and still loves you for it? It seems unlikely that I'll ever find someone to love me, flaws and all. Flaws that Josh has made sure to highlight for me. If he taught me anything, it's that I don't want to be with someone who loves me in spite of my flaws. I want someone that doesn't see them as flaws at all but as a part of me, fractured and still beautiful. Imperfect, but perfect for them. I know the chances of finding something like that are one in a million. Sure, it can get lonely at times, but I'd rather be alone than risk having to deal with the painful fallout of learning my forever person wasn't meant to be mine forever after all. With family and friends like mine, why would I need anything more?

At least that's what I tell myself in those moments, few and far between, when I find myself wishing I had someone to share things with. And maybe it's not even that. Most of the time, I feel fine during the big, special moments. It's the boring, day-to-day, little moments that get to me. Sometimes I wish I had someone to get coffee with in the morning or binge-watch a new show with at night. Someone to kiss my forehead in the last moments of the day before we both fall asleep wrapped in each other's arms, finding a sense of safety and security together, away from the world. Someone to make the little moments feel like the special moments too. Someone to look out for me, the same way I want to take care of the people I love. But like I said, I'm fine. *Totally fine.*

Ellie knows me. Knows I don't put a lot of faith in finding my happily ever after as easily as she did. I know she won't push me past what I say I'm comfortable with. "If fate throws me a soul mate, then I'll happily give them a chance. Until then, I'm afraid I'm all yours. You can't get rid of me that easily." I wink, biting the head off a snowman marshmallow.

She rolls her eyes at me. "Then consider me an agent of fate tonight, Bec. I'll throw ten soul mates at you if I find them deserving of your greatness."

"Ah, then I'm sure you won't be able to find *anyone*." I flip my hair over my shoulder dramatically while I spew false confidence.

"Keep your heart open, Bec. You never know when your match will find you. Could be while you're out grabbing coffee, could be while you're inhaling Christmas cookies at our party. I like to think every moment is a chance for love to strike." She cradles Luca gently, rubs her palm over his back, and kisses the top of his head.

"Love you, momma bear, thanks for always looking out for me." Knowing Ellie always has my back means everything. The way my loved ones make my heart full, I can almost convince myself there isn't room for anyone else anyway...almost.

* * *

"So, how'd it go? Did you hit it off with Travis?" Ellie asks.

I plop down next to her on the couch, where she's nursing Luca with a soft muslin blanket draped over her shoulder. Most of the guests are congregated in the kitchen and dining room, offering her a bit of privacy. Not that she cares. I've seen Ellie's tits more than I've seen my own at this point, whipping them out like clockwork whenever Luca needs to eat.

"Ellie, you have outdone yourself. I appreciate the *supreme* matchmaking effort, but I'm tapping out. I'm exhausted from small talk." I've met more of Dom's friends tonight than I can count, but I'm calling it quits. Sure, they're all plenty attractive and polite. But it's the same as always. There's no spark.

Maybe I have unrealistic expectations. Is it wrong to hold out for those movie-worthy fireworks? That's only happened to me once before, and that definitely didn't work out.

*Don't look at him.*

Aiden and I have been circling each other from opposite ends of the party all night. I'm trying to keep it that way to avoid embarrassing myself again, which seems to keep happening every time I'm around him. But I swear, in those weak moments when I can't help glancing in his direction, I find his eyes already on me. I might be imagining it, but it still warms a piece of me each time it happens, and I have to turn away to hide my smile.

Dom glides past me and sits in the chair catty-corner to the couch. "Did I hear you giving up on my friends so easily? You haven't even met Tanner yet. I could really see you two getting along." He takes a drink from his beer and offers to get Ellie and me one, too, which she declines, gesturing to her hot chocolate on the coffee table, and I pass as well, since I'm driving home tonight. I have an early training session at the shelter in the morning. Normally, I'd just crash on Ellie and Dom's couch, but I want to avoid an early commute downtown. I know myself; I'll inevitably snooze my alarm a million times until I'm late, thinking I can make the drive in half the time it'll take. Morning Bec is an unreasonable bitch, always convincing me that ten more minutes of terrible sleep is worth any consequence of being late.

"Tempting, but no thanks. My social battery is empty. At this point, I'd bore anyone you put in front of me straight into a coma. Don't let me waste their time."

"Aw, come on, Bec. Haven't you heard that most people meet through mutual friends? You're not even giving my guys a chance," Dom whines.

"Excuse me, Grandpa, most people meet online nowadays. I know it must be hard to understand, since online dating didn't exist when you were single. I'll show you how to increase the font size on your phone whenever you're ready," I say with mirth, fully prepared for his rebuttal. Even Ellie can't hold in her giggle.

Dom gives me an unimpressed look. "Yeah. Ha, ha. Laugh all you want. I'm ready to fully embrace old dad life. I even got myself some New Balances to wear when I mow the lawn next summer, right, sweetie?" He looks to Ellie for confirmation, as if this is something I would ever doubt. As if this is something to brag about.

"Uh-huh, hottest thing I've ever seen. Love me some grass-stained sneakers. Can't wait to eat up all that daddy eye candy from the porch." Ellie gives him a wink, which he returns. I can't stifle the stroke of jealousy that flares in my gut witnessing their effortless love.

"Ugh, Mom and Dad are so gross, aren't they, Luca? Just flaunting their love in the open like this, throwing names like *Daddy* around in public. Tell them to get a room." I tickle Luca's toes, and he scrunches them up so cute, I melt a little.

"What about Aiden?" Dom asks. Heat creeps up my neck to my cheeks. I have no idea if Aiden told Dom...well, anything, but I'm going to assume he has no idea. He isn't acting like he knows any better, and I'm not going to be the one to explain to him what's going on...or what isn't going on.

"Yeah, I'm going to have to pass on anyone that has seen me covered in baby poop. Kind of kills the romance, don't you think?" I shrug, hoping Dom drops it. Because while it kills me to remind anyone of that embarrassing moment, it's better than Dom insisting on setting me up with Aiden.

"Okay, that's fair." He holds both hands up in defeat, relaxing back into his seat. "Can't blame a guy for trying. He's a great friend. I'd like to see him end up with someone cool, is all. I want to see you both happy, you know?"

Any lingering annoyance I felt about their attempts to set me up evaporates instantly. Tonight is another reminder of how lucky I am that when Ellie married Dom, I gained another brother. While I don't expect it to, his sentiment thaws a few of the frozen edges I surround myself with, knowing that I have friends in my corner who want the best for me. Good people who care about me and my happiness. I know that's hard to come by, and I couldn't imagine anything I value more.

# Chapter Fifteen

Aiden

Bec looks fucking hot tonight in a dress that hugs her full hips and thick thighs. Her bold lipstick makes me want to run my thumb between her lips. I want to kiss it off her.

I've avoided her all night, doing my best to not gawk at her. I don't know how well I'm doing, since I'm pretty sure she caught me staring a few times.

I peek in her direction again to spot her catching up with Ellie and Dom as the party begins to wind down. All I can assume is my awkward stolen glances, without even saying hi, have probably made Bec feel even more uncomfortable around me than she did before tonight.

It doesn't help that Ellie and Dom keep introducing her to what looks like every single guy here. Jealousy shoots through me every time I see her laugh and smile at men who are undoubtedly interested in her.

I have no right to be jealous, I know that. Bec's single and can do what she likes. I just...I don't know what to think about it, to be honest.

"Could you be more hung up?" Turning, I see Jake, Dom's older brother, approach, handing me a new beer. He raises his glass to mine, tapping lightly before taking a sip but it's not enough time for me to think of a subtle response.

"Don't play dumb, Price. You couldn't be more obvious if you were ringing a bell and wearing a sandwich board with Bec's face on it covered in hearts," Chris, Jake's husband, says as he looks at me over Jake's shoulder, wrapping both arms around his waist.

"Go easy on him, he's got a crush, gentlemen. I think it's best we give him a few minutes to write a note asking Bec to the homecoming dance. Which one of us should deliver it for you, Aiden? Don't forget to include 'yes,' 'no,' and 'maybe' check boxes for her to choose from," Dylan chimes in, slinging an arm around my shoulders and roughly pulling me toward him.

I shove Dylan off me. "Ha, ha. Very funny. Tell me, who did you harass before I moved back? Must have been awfully boring here without me."

"Dom," they all say in unison.

"But he's a new dad, so he's off limits right now," Chris says.

"Exactly. So lucky for you, our schedule has completely cleared up. We are free to insert ourselves in your love life and offer you some crucial advice." Before I can interrupt him, Dylan goes on, "Number one, if you're interested in someone, you should speak to them. This requires you to be within a five-foot radius and to use your words like a grown-up," he says like the unbearable smart-ass that he is.

"Number two, you cannot stare at your love interest from across the room all night like a serial killer. That's grounds for an intervention. The longer you creep, the more lecturing you'll have to suffer through," Jake taunts. "You've already earned about three hours of lecturing, at least. It's going to be brutal; I promise."

"Number three, if you find yourself incapable of following rules one and two, you have to confess the truth to your friends, who care enough to ask for it so that they can help you." Chris leans in close to whisper loudly, "That's us, we're the friends. Now, spill."

Sighing, I drag my free hand over my face. Dylan knows what happened when I met Bec, but do I want to confess to harboring this likely unhealthy infatuation with Bec in the years since? No fucking way. Could I use some advice? Abso-fucking-lutely. I'm confused as shit about what to do. I don't know how to be friends with someone I can't stop thinking about in a *not*-so-friendly way. Every moment I spend with her embeds curiosity further into my skin, leaving me wanting to know more about her. Shouldn't I keep my distance, since I can't pretend I don't want more with her? It doesn't seem like I'm hiding it very well if these three can call it out after only one night.

"There's not much to tell. Bec's cool. We met when Dom and Ellie got married, and I'm taking my dog to one of her training classes. We're friends." I rush out, trying to be honest and give as few details as possible.

"Uh-huh...and was it your idea to be 'friends?'" Chris asks, hitting me with air quotes.

"No way, not with the way you're blatantly pining for her. I'd bet money on it. You just moved back. How'd you manage to end up friend-zoned so quickly?" Dylan asks.

"Fuck...I don't even know," I say, deciding that the risk of over-sharing is worth it if I can get some solid advice. "I don't want to risk losing her friendship, but I think there's a chance we could be good together."

"Just come out with it and ask, Aiden. See if she's on the same page. If she's not interested, no harm. You'll probably feel awkward around each other for a bit, but then it'll be forgotten and you guys can stay friends," Jake suggests.

"I agree. And imagine it does work out...you two would make a really fun couple. Then you can thank us for your successful relationship and give us a shout-out in your wedding invitations. You're welcome." Chris laughs at his own joke. He has one of those contagious laughs that captures the attention of the room and makes you want to laugh too.

"I know just how to give you two the chance to talk it out. Bec, where are you off to? Leaving so soon?" Dylan asks, pulling my attention to Bec as she pauses in the hallway, seemingly attempting to slip out of the party unnoticed.

"Yeah, I have a training session scheduled tomorrow morning. Sorry we didn't really get the chance to catch up." She looks from Dylan to Jake and Chris, notably ignoring me completely.

Not a great sign.

*Fuck, abort the plan.*

"No worries, we'll catch up some other time. Hey, you're headed downtown, right? Aiden was just about to order a ride since his car is in the shop. Think you could give him a lift?" Dylan asks. "Better to carpool. Go green and all that."

*Jesus, could he make this more awkward?* I mean, he's not lying. I was going to call a ride home, but still.

"You don't have to..." I start to say, trying to give her an out.

"Oh, sure," she says at the same time. Her face falls. "Oh, unless you'd rather not..."

*Fuck, I just made it worse.*

Trying to salvage the moment, I hurry and say, "That'd be great. If you don't mind the extra stop, I'd appreciate it." She offers a meek smile in return.

I think it's safe to assume any discussions of being more than friends are off the table. Avoidance is easier than the disappointment I'll face when Bec says no to me...again.

# Chapter Sixteen

## Aiden

"Thanks again. I could have called for a ride to save you the trouble." I close the door behind us as Bec and I leave Dom and Ellie's house.

"No worries. It sounds like your building isn't too far from mine anyway." She pulls her keys from her purse and unlocks her car. We walk down the driveway in awkward silence. When she starts the car and begins to adjust the heat, I hear a podcast come on.

*"That's it, baby. You take it like such a good fucking girl. Look at you on your knees for me, sucking me, tasting me."*

Wait...what the fuck?

What kind of podcast is this?

"Holy mother-trucker shitballs," Bec shrieks, scrambling to find her phone, I assume to stop playing...whatever it is that's playing in her car right now. The way her hand is flailing around in her bag, I assume it's bottomless, making it impossible for Bec to find her phone and stop whatever the fuck is happening right now.

*"Come on, Delilah. Finger your cunt. I know you're dripping for me."*

She freezes, all efforts to retrieve her phone stopping completely. She slowly raises her gaze to meet mine. Her eyes are wide with horror as we both listen to what might be the most erotic thing I've heard in my life. Is she listening to porn? While driving? I file this information away for later...I don't have time to process it right now.

*"Oh...oh god! Oh fuck!"* A woman screams, followed by a series of moans and grunts.

*"That's right, come for me. Then, I'll make you come again on my cock. I'm aching for your hot, wet pussy, Delilah."*

I think I'm having an out-of-body experience. A first for me.

I'm staring at Bec, while her entire face flames a deep shade of pink and her mouth drops open. It's not well lit in the car, only the light from her dashboard controls and the faint glow from the light above Dom and Ellie's garage, so I know she's truly mortified if I can see her blushing. I don't know whether or not to look away as we both listen to a woman completely coming apart, screaming and moaning.

Holy shit, I've got to look away from Bec. Hearing this...and looking at her. I can feel myself getting hard and that is the last thing I need right now.

I turn away, focusing my eyes forward, which must snap Bec out of it because out of the corner of my eye, I see her slowly reach over to the knob on her console and simply turn the volume all the way down.

Silence. The loudest silence in history fills the space between us.

"Wish I had thought to just turn down the volume," she whispers.

"Hm." I nod, my head bobbing like one of those dashboard bobble heads they carry in the team's shop of all of the players.

What the fuck am I supposed to say right now? I'm half-hard, my mind racing to make sense of what just happened, but all I can think about is if Bec would sound like that coming for me. Would she want me to talk to her like that? If I told her all the things I want to do to her, would she let me?

"So, um, I like smutty romance books. The girls and I have a book club. That's this month's book I was listening to earlier."

"Sounds like educational stuff. A lot, uh, a lot of good stuff there. Sounds like...a nice time." I inwardly cringe.

Did I just say that sounded educational? I mean, yeah, I might feel a little enlightened, but only because I just discovered a side of Bec that I am *too* happy to meet.

"It's very educational," she replies.

*Huh?*

Bec's looking down in her lap, her hands braced on the steering wheel. She pauses and lets out an audible breath. "I'm going to drive now. But later, when I get home and I'm alone in my bed, I'm going to listen to that again. I'm going to think about this moment and pretend that it's happening to me," she says, meeting my eyes. "Are you going to think about it too?"

I'm stunned speechless. Fuck yes, I'm going to be thinking about what I just heard...most likely it'll play in my mind on repeat for the rest of time. But is she asking me if I'm going to be thinking about her thinking about it, and maybe thinking about me too? What is she going to be doing while she thinks about it? Is she flirting with me? Am I losing my mind? I think my brain just melted.

A flash of confidence strikes, surprising me, and I decide to take a risk. "Bec, there is no way I could think about anything else for the rest of the night. But now that you've told me that you'll be thinking about it, too, there won't be any Delilah in the version I replay for myself later."

*It'll be you, Bec.*

I let the implication speak for me.

Her eyes flash to my mouth. She licks her bottom lip and bites it. A habit of hers I continue to notice and now find myself watching and waiting for glimpses of. I want to bite it too. "What else happens in your version?" It's practically a whisper, but I hear every word reverberating in my mind.

I don't know if it's the tension that I've felt between us since I moved back to town, or if it's the safety of darkness lowering inhibitions and reservations for us both, but all of a sudden, I feel like the Bec from years ago is sitting next to me, turning my insides into liquid fire. I want to reach over, wrap one hand around the back of her neck, and pull her close. Grip her thigh and run my palm up her leg to find her center warm and wet for me.

*Holy fuck. I gotta get out of this car.*

My thoughts are going from rational, reasonable, and respectful to fucking filth.

"I wanted to show you when we met. I like to think it would have sounded a lot like your book. I would have taken my time with you. There isn't an inch of you I wouldn't have worshipped. We would have made a mess of things. Made a mess of each other. We would have gotten a noise complaint in that hotel and deserved it. I would have left your body feeling weak, thoroughly used up from the inside out. You would have begged me to carry you out of the room when we finally had to leave, because I wouldn't waste a minute we had together, wringing every ounce of pleasure out of you that I possibly could."

She gives me a wicked smile and simply states, "I think I like your version better than my book." She shifts her car into gear and drives us to the city in silence, leaving my mind to wander through thoughts of what could have been and what could possibly still be.

* * *

**Aiden**: Hey Dom, can you do me a solid?

**Dom**: Sure, what's up?

**Aiden**: Can you text me the name of the book Ellie's reading right now?

**Dom**: Um, why are you asking what book my wife is reading?

**Aiden**: Don't make it weird, man. Bec mentioned their book club, and I've been trying to get back into reading. Can you just send me the title?

**Dom**: Did she mention the types of books they read? Because if you're looking for a thriller or classic, the girls can't help you.

**Aiden**: Okay, Bec may not have meant to tell me about the book club, but yeah. I know the types of books they're reading.

**Dom**: What do you mean?

**Aiden**: Her audiobook may have started playing when she drove me home last night.

**Dom**: Holy shit...what did you hear?

**Aiden**: Let's just say it was eye opening. I need to do a little more research.

**Dom**: Understood. Let me go find her book. I'm sure this goes without saying, but I'm going to need more details later.

**Aiden**: I'll need a drink first.

**Dom**: Consider it done.

* * *

"Ow, oh shit, my side hurts," Dom says, laughing his ass off. He slaps me on the back and flags down the waitress for a beer. "I can't breathe, man. That is hilarious."

I join him, letting out a reluctant laugh as I recall everything that happened in Bec's car last weekend. Thankfully, Dom was able to meet me after work for a quick drink downtown before heading home to take over for Ellie with Luca.

I needed to tell someone about what happened, and not just the revelation about Bec's books. I finally came clean and told Dom about how Bec and I initially met and how I still think about the possibility of more between us. It was a relief to tell him. I asked him not to share with Ellie for now, since I'm pretty sure Bec hasn't told her either. He didn't love that, but he understood. He also said that if she's pissed at him for not telling her, that he gets to throw me under the bus. Not sure Ellie will let him get away with that, but I agreed anyway.

"It really was...something. I'm nervous to see her this weekend for Hop's training class. I can't imagine she wants to see me."

"Nah, don't worry about it. Bec's chill as fuck with a great sense of humor. She'll shake it off. Besides, it kind of sounds like you two still have some kind of attraction going on. Why don't you go for it and ask her out?"

"Bec already told me we should be friends. Don't get me wrong, I was disappointed she didn't want to talk about exploring anything more than that. She really is cool as hell."

*And hot as fuck.* I immediately went to rub one out in the shower after Bec dropped me off at my place after Dom's party. I thought of her the entire time, guilt-free since she said she'd be doing the same thing, but I'll keep that part to myself.

"Huh, she didn't mention that at the party when I mentioned trying to hook you two up," Dom says.

"What'd she say about me?"

"Got it bad, huh? A little eager?" He looks down at his shoulder where I've gripped him roughly, turning him to me in demand of an answer. Okay, so maybe I got my hopes up a little. I release my hold on him and try to calm down.

"I don't want to sound desperate, but I sort of can't get her outta my head."

"Could have guessed. Listen, I've known Bec for years. Her last relationship didn't end on great terms, from what I know. If she feels something for you, she'll probably keep that locked down and wait for you to make the first move. All she said at the party was that you seeing her covered in baby shit probably killed any shot at romance. I didn't realize what had already happened between the two of you, or that you were still interested, otherwise I could have put in a good word for you. Sorry, man."

Before I can respond, I get a call from Evie. When I answer, the urgency in her voice tells me everything I need to know. I'll be making a trip to Detroit this weekend. I thought maybe we had more time to figure things out, but I guess not.

# Chapter Seventeen

## Bec

## The Wedding

**M**y mind is reeling. This is too complicated. My fun, carefree weekend just turned into me trying to sex up one of Dom's best friends.

Ellie is my chosen family, my sister. After this weekend, Dom will be family too. I can't risk my relationship with Ellie by having a casual fling with Aiden. He doesn't live in Columbus, so I doubt we'll run into each other often, but I'm sure we'll see each other again eventually.

If we do hook up, will he expect me to want a relationship just because our friends are married? I don't want commitment, especially long distance. I want fun and freedom with no strings attached. Anything serious between us would never last, and the inevitable fallout with someone this close to my friends is asking for a headache. Besides, a fucking pro baseball player, are you kidding me? No wonder his body felt rock solid.

There's also a voice inside telling me to run because things with him feel too perfect. Call me a realist, but there's no way something that feels like this could last. Anything that burns this brightly, this quickly, will extinguish just as fast.

*The wedding coordinator is a no-nonsense woman in a sharp suit. She calls for everyone's attention and runs us through the logistics for the ceremony quickly.*

*When the rehearsal wraps up, Ellie, Dee, and I gather around a corner of the bar, champagne in hand. Ellie and Dom's wedding party and closest family members are here for cocktail hour before dinner is served in the private party room adjacent to the bar.*

*I gape at Ellie. "You and Dom never thought to mention that one of his groomsmen is a professional baseball player?" I thought Dom was exaggerating when he told me one of his friends was an athlete. I figured if Dom was telling the truth, I would have met the guy by now since I'm basically their permanent third wheel. Dom had to have mentioned Aiden by name before...why didn't I recognize him?*

*Oh, who am I kidding? I don't know anything about sports. I don't think I could name five professional athletes if I tried. Well, I guess I can name at least one now.*

Shit, no, I can't. What the fuck is this guy's last name?

*"Yeah, and are any of his teammates coming tomorrow? I think I'm officially into baseball players," Dee interjects like the horndog she is. She's been egging me on since we learned about Aiden's profession, talking about how a baseball butt is the absolute only butt she can imagine is better to play quarters off of than my own. Goddammit, I'll never live that stupid weekend down.*

*Ellie sips her champagne before responding. "Why is it a big deal? Are you interested? Oooo, come to think of it, you and Aiden would be a supercute couple. Want me to put in a good word for you?"*

*"What? No, I'm just shocked Dom wasn't lying." I don't know why I don't own up to my almost-hookup with Aiden. It's not like Ellie would be upset or judge me. Apparently, she's even willing to set us up together. But when Aiden was a stranger, there was no pressure. No implications beyond Sunday night. Him being one of Dom's friends, not to mention close*

*enough to be in his wedding, makes it feel like something more serious.*

*"I know, right? I thought the same thing when he first told me too. I'm hoping we can go to a few of Aiden's games when his team is in town. You guys want to come with?" Ellie asks.*

*"Fuck yeah," Dee rushes out before glaring at me. "You're coming with us, no excuses. Think we'll be able to drag Carissa along, or will Damien ruin everything?"*

*I spot Carissa through the windows leading to the large balcony. She's tucked away under Damien's arm. They just started dating a few months ago, but none of us have a good feeling about it.*

*"Who knows?" Ellie replies. "Have either of you heard how he's been this weekend?"*

*"No word yet," I say while Dee shakes her head.*

*"I'll check in with her tonight. Make sure she's doing okay," Dee offers, to which Ellie and I both agree.*

*"What about you, Ellie? You're getting married in less than twenty-four hours. You ready to commit to Dom's dick for the rest of your life?" I ask.*

*Ellie smirks, glancing over at Dom with mischief in her eyes. "I'm good, trust me." She leans in close, lowering her voice. "I can barely walk straight. Dom wrecked me this morning. The wedding has him so fucking hard, every time I turn around, he's basically humping my leg."*

*"You need some training advice? I've seen this problem tons of times. Most dogs grow out of it by his age, though...maybe we should take him to the vet. See if there's a medical issue." I joke.*

*"You brat." She giggles, and I know I'm forgiven. It's her own fault for always bragging about Dom's dick. I mean, good for them, but I'd rather not hear the girthy details.*

*"You're practically green with envy, Bec. You need to get laid," Dee proclaims.*

*"Oh please, I'm fine. It hasn't even been that long."*

*"Are you kidding, hasn't it been like ten months or something? I think*

I'd die." A little dramatic, but she has a point. It has been way too long.

"I can take care of myself, don't worry. I don't need anyone intervening. I'm talking to you, Dee." She huffs out a sigh, annoyed by my usual stubbornness.

I had what I can only assume was a sure thing lined up for the weekend with Aiden when life decided to play a prank on me instead. I keep weighing my options, going back and forth on if I want to pursue something with him, assuming he's still interested. Part of me just wants to say fuck it, ignore my anxious brain, and see where things go. Have a spontaneous weekend of fun and hope we're on the same page, walking away without attachment after the wedding is over. The other part of me is screaming to walk away and pretend last night never happened. The impulse to play it safe and keep him at a distance is reverberating through my mind. The urge to withdraw is so strong I feel it down to my toes.

Of course, at this moment I peek over to find Aiden's eyes already locked on me. His presence almost overwhelming me even at a distance. I don't understand why my body is reacting to him like this when I barely know him. It's enough to draw me in and terrify me all at once. I can't let this go any further. He's the type of person I could lose myself in, and I promised I wouldn't risk that when I'm just starting to figure my life out. I don't intend to go back on that promise now.

# Chapter Eighteen

## Bec

"Okay, everyone, thanks for a great lesson today. For our next class, focus on the cues *drop it* and *leave it*. We'll regroup at the start of class next Saturday to see how the pups are doing with these. See you all then."

As everyone packs up and files out of the classroom, I focus on my clipboard and begin to note the progress I observed for each of the families and their pets today. I briefly note that I need to revisit leash walking with the Johnson family to make sure that their pup, Bailey, is showing improvement before my thoughts are interrupted.

"Hey, Bec, you got a second?" Aiden looks at me with defeat in his eyes. I don't know him that well, all things considered, but he's obviously stressed. His posture is tense, and his hands are tucked in his pockets. Hop seems oblivious to Aiden's mood as he sits next to him, his tail wagging happily, beaming up at us.

It's been a week since Ellie's party where I was outed in front of an unsuspecting Aiden as the romance novel addict I love to be. Poor guy seemed completely stunned by what he heard, though I've got to say, he recovered from the surprise...very well. When he described what he wanted to do to me when we met? Well, his words stuck with me all night. I immediately grabbed my vibrator when I got home, thinking of everything Aiden promised we would have done in that hotel years ago. No regrets here. Best orgasm I've had in months.

*Fuck, Bec, stop thinking about masturbating right now. Focus on what Aiden's saying.*

"Of course. How can I help? Hopper seems to be doing well with the skills we've covered so far," I say, not sure where his apparent discomfort might be coming from.

"Yeah, he always seems to respond better to you in class than he does when it's just me and him at home, but I have seen an improvement. He only ignores me the first few times I ask for something instead of altogether." He smiles, and I can't help but smile back.

Aiden is acting shy, which is unexpected. I assumed a professional athlete like him with the big career, the fame, the income, and the insanely good looks would be unbearably confident, borderline arrogant at all times. Instead, he seems humble and refreshingly authentic. Is he normally this shy? Well, I guess not all the time considering what he said to me in the car. This month's book is great...but Aiden's dirty talk is better.

Over the last week, I've convinced myself that we both got caught up in the moment. I don't want to read any further into the mishap and risk embarrassing myself all over again. There's no way he meant what he said. He agreed to being friends, so I have to believe that's all he wants. I'm not getting stuck again with someone who doesn't want me as much as I want them.

"I was wondering if you had any local recommendations for dog boarding. I have to go out of town, and I figured you'd know someone reputable who could take care of Hopper."

"Oh, sure. I know a few places. I can give you their info." I pull out my phone to find the contact information for the local boarders I know and trust. "When are you traveling?" I ask.

"Uh, that's the thing, it's all sort of unexpected, and I need to leave tomorrow morning. Not sure how much advance notice is needed. I'd ask Dom, but it'd be too much to take that on with the new baby and everything. My sister is working crazy hours the next few days, otherwise I'd ask her." He releases a heavy sigh and looks up at the ceiling. Realizing this is why he's so stressed, so unlike his usual self, I instantly want to help.

Not wanting to pry about why he has to travel on such short notice, I look back to my phone. "I think you might have a hard time locking down a place by tomorrow, but here are a few numbers for you to try. These are the places I work with regularly and recommend for grooming and boarding."

I hand over the contact information, knowing the chances of him securing a spot with one of the local borders before he has to leave town is slim to none. These places often book up weeks in advance. I offer the only other thing I can. "If none of them can take Hop because they're fully booked or whatever, I can always watch him for you."

He looks at me, shocked. "You'd do that? I mean, I'm sure you have plenty going on."

"Well, I don't have any classes scheduled tomorrow here or at the shelter. If I get called in for any reason, I can bring Hopper with me, and he can be my assistant." I smile down at Hop, who nudges my leg affectionately like he knows he just got promoted from being my student to my right-hand man. I give him a scratch under his ear, and he leans into my hand. "We can even get some extra training sessions in. I did promise to host the girls tomorrow night for our...uh, book club. So as long as you don't mind him hanging with all of us, I can watch him. How long are you out of town for?" I look back to Aiden who looks incredibly relieved, his entire demeanor relaxing.

"I leave tomorrow morning and hope to get back Monday night."

"Well, let me know either way. I'd be happy to have Hop stay with me.  I haven't had a dog around since I lost my girl, Lucy.  It's just me at home.  I'd love the company." Aiden looks at me, not saying anything. His expression unreadable.

"Well, I should warn you that I let Hopper sleep in my bed. And he's a blanket hog."

"Well, as it turns out, I am too. Thankfully, I have plenty of blankets to share."  I wink at him, and he chuckles. Something in me warms knowing I can make him smile like that.

"Noted, Bec."

My imagination gets carried away, reading too much into his tone and trying to find an innuendo there. I picture Aiden letting me steal all his blankets. I don't think I'd give them back.

# Chapter Nineteen

## Bec

**A**iden: Bec? It's Aiden. I'm not sure if your number is still the same.

**Bec**: Yeah, it's me. Everything okay?

**Aiden**: I wanted to see if your offer to watch Hopper still stands. All of the places I called are fully booked. I would pay you, of course, and owe you a huge favor.

**Bec**: You don't need to pay me. I'd be happy to watch him and have him steal all of my blankets. Any other quirks I need to watch out for?

**Aiden**: Well, he basically does the opposite of everything I say. Is that a quirk?

**Bec**: I'd say that's an opportunity.

**Aiden**: He also enjoys eating trash, shoes, socks, pillows, and basically anything on the floor is fair game.

**Bec**: This dog trainer sponsored vacation will serve dual purposes. You won't recognize his behavior when you pick him up.

**Aiden**: Seriously, I'll think of a way to pay you back for this. I can't tell you how much of a relief it is to have a safe place to leave Hop. And to have someone I trust watching out for him.

**Bec**: Wow...that's sweet. Promise I'll take good care of him. Now, what time do I need to have my place puppy proofed by? I need to hide my shoes.

* * *

"Come on up," I call into the intercom, buzzing Aiden and Hopper into the building. I've been a mess of nerves all morning. Having Aiden in my apartment feels intimate, not that anything is going to happen, since he isn't interested in me like that anymore.

Part of me feels wary about him seeing where I live because, while I find it comfortable, I can only imagine the type of place his salary affords him. I don't think he'd judge me for the small, modest space, but I'm in my head about it all the same. Josh used to give me shit for how average my apartment is. *Not the only thing about me he found to be just average.*

I can't keep my plants alive, so the windowsill is flooded with decrepit plant remains in mismatched pots. I'm not good at putting different pieces together cohesively. I don't have an "aesthetic" or theme. I have a collection of well-loved, hand-me-down furniture, thrift store finds, discount pieces, and a hodgepodge of gifts people have given me that I can't bring myself to ever part with because at some point someone thought of me when they saw it.

I don't know why I ever cared what Josh thought of my space, because even if no one else in the world appreciates my style, fuck them, right? I like it and I've decided that's what matters. It's not perfect, but it's mine.

I give the living room and kitchen a final once-over before Aiden knocks on my door. I can hear the patter of paws on the hallway tile.

A freshly showered Aiden greets me as I open the door. His hair has that whole...tousled and curling slightly at the ends, effortlessly perfect thing going on. Goddamn him.

"Morning. I brought you breakfast, but I wasn't sure what you liked, so I got a few different things." He hands me a massive to-go bag and coffee from the nearby bakery as Hop excitedly prances into my apartment and starts sniffing his way around.

I walk into the kitchen, following Hop and placing the bag of greasy food on the island. The smell makes my mouth water. "A few things? From the looks of it, you got me *everything* they have." I tease. "That was really thoughtful, but you didn't have to do that. Thank you." I turn around, catching him taking me in with his eyes, but I can't quite read his expression.

He shoves his hands into the pockets of his joggers. Wow, they certainly hug his muscular thighs...and okay, the way his biceps are stretching the sleeves of his fitted shirt...I wonder what he looks like in his baseball uniform. Maybe I can do a quick google search later...

*Stop, Bec. That's fucking creepy.*

"You're really helping me out here. It's the least I can do. I know how important it is to have people in your circle you can count on, and I haven't always had that. I appreciate you taking on Hop for me." He looks sincere, almost sad.

His vulnerable admission catches me off guard, disarming me and making me feel like I've caught a glimpse of a side of him I haven't seen before.

"That sounds lonely, Aiden. I hope your circle grows a little bigger here in Columbus." I sip at the coffee he brought me. "Besides, you're doing me a favor. I miss having a dog around to cuddle. This is what friends are for."

We fall silent, and I think back to when we met. When I thought I'd get to cuddle with *him*. Okay, maybe more than cuddling. I shake the thought from my mind. I need to forget about our *almost* moments if this friend thing is going to work.

Aiden hesitates, then takes a few quick strides toward me, towering over me, backing me against my kitchen counter but not touching me, mere inches separating my chest from his. I tilt my head back to look at him, caught off guard by his sudden approach. My heart starts racing and I wish like hell that he'd put his hands on me and pull me closer.

"Is that still what you want...to be friends?" Aiden asks, almost in a whisper.

"I...uh, I...yeah? Why not?" I lie with a shrug, feeling my cheeks heat, my face flush, and my breath quicken. I'm confident he can hear how unsure I sound. It's not that I don't want to be his friend, I'm the one who suggested it. *Like an idiot.* But we've already talked about this, so why is he bringing it up again?

Aiden has been my "what if" man for over three years. I've only been in one relationship since the wedding, and it was messy. Ever since, I've avoided dating anyone seriously. I blame one thing or another, usually work, pouring all of my free time into doing what I love. In truth, I haven't met anyone who can quiet the insecurities Josh left behind. And when I try to give someone new a chance, I end up thinking about Aiden, comparing everyone to him and the feelings that he ignited in me when we first met. If meeting someone new doesn't do enough to beat the memory of Aiden in a single weekend, then why bother?

For the briefest moment, I imagine seeing a ripple of disappointment wash over Aiden's face, quickly replaced by a neutral expression. I need to end this conversation before I try to fill the silence with nonsensical rambling, or worse, embarrass myself by rehashing our past to see if he still thinks about me too. "So...Hopper, you up for joining girls' night tonight?" I call out to diffuse the tension. Aiden still hasn't taken his eyes off me.

It's at this exact moment I realize I fucked up. I've been so distracted by Aiden—memories of him and his consuming presence in my apartment—that I'm just now realizing how quiet it is. And that a certain puppy is nowhere to be found. "Uh, Aiden...did you see where Hop went?"

Aiden looks around and calls for Hopper with no luck. My apartment isn't that big, so after quickly scanning the living room, coming up empty, I walk over to the doorway of my bedroom. I find Hopper rolling around on my bed, making himself quite the cozy spot in the middle of my oversized, fluffy comforter. I might have a modest income, but if I'm splurging on something, it's comfortable fucking bedding. My priorities on this are set and I regret nothing.

Aiden comes up behind me and leans on the door frame, my back inches from his front. His proximity has my insides racing. Why does he have to smell so damn good?

"Huh, I don't remember buying that toy. Come to think of it, I didn't unpack any of his toys yet. They're still in the bag I brought over with his food. Did you have some lying around for him?" Aiden's question pulls me out of my stupor as I realize I have no idea what he's talking about.

I see Hopper lying on my bed, chewing on something pink. Then, I hear a familiar buzzing. It hits me like a slap in the face, and I feel my stomach fall to the floor.

*Why? Why is the universe doing this to me?*

I mentally wave goodbye to my last shred of dignity that's about to evaporate into thin air. I'm going to title this next chapter in my embarrassing life story "The dog is chewing on my fucking hot-pink vibrator."

*Bury me here. I cannot go on.*

I thought I stashed it away earlier this morning after cleaning it, but I must have left it on my bed. I have no idea if Aiden realizes what Hop is chewing on, but maybe I can play it off. "Oh yeah, I had a few old toys lying around."

*It's not old. It's new, dammit, and it cost me a hundred and fifty bucks.*

"But come to think of it, I'm pretty sure that one is broken, I better take it from him so he doesn't rip the squeaker or stuffing out or anything. Hopper, drop it." I say, using the cue that we just introduced in yesterday's class. While I don't expect miracles, I sure am hoping for one. Can Hop pick up this skill in less than twenty-four hours? Please say yes.

Holy shit. Hopper drops the vibrator on the bed and stares at me. He adjusts the toy under his paws, and yep, there's the clit stimulator poking out, taunting me. I slowly, calmly approach the bed. "Hopper, leave it." Maybe I can just sneak in and grab it before Aiden realizes.

Aiden leans a little farther into my bedroom, probably noticing that this toy is *not* the dog kind. Well, not unless you prefer doggie style.

*Focus, Bec...this is not the time.*

"Uh, Bec? What kind of dog toy is that?" Aiden asks.

A few things happen at once. Aiden takes a step forward toward Hopper, who instantly switches into play mode. He thinks this just turned into a game of chase, and the prize is my pink, vibrating boyfriend. Hopper leaps off my bed and runs past Aiden and me like a flash of lightning into the living room.

I didn't think I could be any more mortified, but yep, I sure can. Aiden and I chase Hop around my living room and kitchen, calling out commands that he completely ignores. During the chaos, he must bite down on one of the buttons to switch the settings. I can see the ribbed shaft spinning and rotating. I'll never be able to think about it the same way ever again.

Aiden finally grabs Hopper by the collar and calls out for him to drop it. Hop listens, but at this point, all that's left to spit out is a mangled remnant of my phallic friend. Taken too soon. Dee will be devastated to hear we're no longer vibe twins. She claims the two had a spiritual connection and responsibility to make each other proud.

The shaft is bent sharply to the side, and the clit stimulator is hanging on by a thread. Somehow, the vibration is still going strong. I've got to say, I'm impressed. The motor on this thing is clearly built to last. I might have to replace this one with the same model since it's proven to be tough as fuck.

"Holy shit, is that…" Aiden goes still, releasing Hop and staring down at the dancing silicone wand.

I rest my hands on my hips, eyes squeezed shut, my head bobbing, biting the inside of my cheek so hard I think I'll bleed.

"Yep. Yep. Sure is." Because what the fuck am I going to say? There is no denying what we're looking at here.

I bend down, grabbing the remains off the floor, and hold the power button to stop the fucking madness. How the hell was it still able to rotate like that? Once again, I find myself in one of the loudest silences of my life with Aiden.

"Pretty sure Hop may have destroyed…that…beyond repair." I look at Aiden, who can't stop staring at the vibrator. I'm pretty sure this whole ordeal broke him too.

"Yep." I pop my lips on the *P*.

"Obliterated."

"Got it."

"Completely wrecked."

"Aiden."

"Sorry."

I squeeze my eyes shut, unable to keep looking at Aiden while holding my fucking vibrator in my hand. "Can we please pretend this whole thing never happened? I cannot handle one more embarrassing thing going wrong in front of you, Aiden. I swear, it's like ever since you moved back, the universe has it out for me." I turn and make my way over to the trash, tossing my friend away. *Godspeed. Thanks for the memories.*

"Listen, it's nothing to be embarrassed about. That's healthy, you know," Aiden says, and I cringe. The last thing I want Aiden to know about me is how I...take care of myself, healthy habit or not.

"Aiden, this may be even more embarrassing than you finding me covered in baby poop or you hearing my smutty audiobook. Both of those combined are probably still less embarrassing than this moment."

"Bec, it's hot." That catches me by surprise. Aiden reaches his hand up to his neck and pulls toward his shoulder with his head down. The shithead is smirking, peeking up at me from under his dark lashes.

"Uh, wh-what now?" My face is on fire and my palms are clamming up.

*What the fuck is he talking about?*

Hop strides away to get comfortable on my couch, while Aiden walks over to me, stopping inches away. I can feel the heat radiating off his chest. He stares down at me, his voice going low. "I said, it's hot as fuck. I'm going to have a hard time focusing on driving while I think about that vibrator between your thighs, making you pant and squirm in your sheets." His gaze hoods and I'm pretty sure my jaw is on the floor. The Aiden I met years ago just showed up, and my downstairs is fucking thrilled.

"Oh. Well, I mostly used it in the shower."

"Jesus fuck," he mutters, closing his eyes, head tilted up to the ceiling. When he looks at me again, his stare is blazing. "Are you sure you want to be friends?"

"Is there another option?" I practically whisper back.

"Yeah, I can think of quite a few other options I'd like more than just friends." He pauses, looking down at my lips. "Promise me you'll think about it, hm?"

I nod, unable to find my voice. He steps back, walks over to Hop to scratch his ear, kisses the top of his head, and makes his way back to me. He reaches out and tucks a curl back behind my ear. "I'll see you soon, Bec." I catch a hint of a smile as he turns and walks out of my apartment.

*What the fuck just happened?*

When we met, it was never meant to be anything serious. Just a night of fun.

But if we got together now...a part of me knows it could be explosive between us. Moments like this remind me of the potential chemistry. We're simmering, at risk of boiling over if we allow the heat to turn a bit higher.

I sigh, knowing not even Hopper's company is going to keep my mind from mulling this over the entire time Aiden is gone. But for now, I need to double-check that all my shoes are out of reach. Aiden wasn't kidding. Hop is in his *fuck around and find out* stage.

Aiden's asking me to think about what I want. It's been hard not to since he crashed back into my life two months ago. In my gut, I know that I want him, but my head is screaming, demanding that I let him go. I never felt this way with Josh. If that breakup hurt, what would a breakup with Aiden do to me?

Despite the risk, maybe trying something a little bit more with Aiden wouldn't be a horrible idea. It doesn't have to be anything serious. Friends with benefits maybe. Or a casual date here and there, just to test the waters. That way, if it doesn't work out, it'd be easy to default back to being just friends.

Maybe we need to fuck around, too, consequences be damned. I think I want to finish what we started, to see where it leads, but does he? Will Aiden expect more from me, or is what I have to offer enough? Is it enough for anyone?

# Chapter Twenty

Aiden

The Wedding

**B**ec is avoiding me. She couldn't make it any more obvious. We need to have a conversation about last night. We happen to have mutual friends. It doesn't change a thing for me, but Bec's skittish behavior tells me it's messing with her head. She's dancing around me like a magnet, opposing me at every turn, using my movements to drive her own further away in the opposite direction.

"You gonna make a move in this lifetime, or are you just going to keep staring at her?" An unfamiliar voice rings out from my left. One of the bridesmaids I met earlier, Dee, leans against the bar with a shit-eating grin on her face and a beer in hand. "You could try to be a little less obvious. Bec scares easily. Don't get clingy too fast, baseball boy."

"Your friend has a knack for evading me completely. I don't think I could make a move if I wanted to." Which I fucking do. I'm not in the habit of showing my hand to someone who's basically a stranger to me. But hey, Dee's close with Bec, and if she's willing to give me advice, I'll gladly take it.

"I may not know you well, but if Dom trusts you, then I'm willing to go to bat for you too. See? See what I did there?" Dee asks.

I laugh. Dee might be even more ridiculous than Bec.

"But if you tell her I talked to you, I'll deny the entire thing. I swore not to intervene," she says.

"Ah, so she told you," I say.

"I'm the only one she's told. I had to practically drag it out of her. But with you leaving evidence on her neck like a fucking teenager, it was hard to ignore. And I'm very persistent."

"You sure as fuck are." Dylan approaches and puts an arm around Dee's shoulders. "Same as me. Can I get you another drink, Dee?"

"I can get my own drink, Dylan. Go crawl into whatever hole you snuck out of." She pushes him back, and he withdraws with a chuckle, leaning behind her to order another beer from the bartender. "Good luck, Aiden." Dee strides off before I can ask her for more insight on the woman that's held my attention all night.

Dylan claps me on the shoulder. "So Bec told Dee...I'd say that's a good sign. If she wanted to hide you like a dirty little secret, she wouldn't have told any of the girls. They're tight. If Dee's on your side, that'll only work in your favor." I told Dylan about how I met Bec last night, not wanting to bother Dom during his own wedding with my single-life bullshit, but I'm starting to regret telling anyone at all.

"Doesn't seem like it'll do me much good if she's running away from me all night," I grumble in response.

"You heard the boss. Dee told you to back off. Sounds like you should stop chasing her. Let her come to you. You're gonna freak her out, man. Give her a second to breathe."

"Yeah, I can do that. I'm gonna get some fresh air outside, you coming?" I ask.

Shaking his head, he says, "Nah, I'm going to go talk to that blonde that just walked in. Unlike you, I haven't found anyone to keep me busy this weekend. Time to work some magic." Dylan straightens his shoulders, *runs his hand through his hair, and strides away.*

*I make my way outside to clear my head, finding a secluded spot behind a lattice wall. I get comfortable on the L-shaped couch, placing my drink on the table in front of me, which has a low-burning fire pit in the center. The string lights hanging above give off a soft glow. Normally, I'd enjoy the privacy this moment affords me. I'd soak in the peaceful seclusion, knowing that I rarely get time to relax by myself like this during the season. Instead, all I can think about is Bec and what Dee's brief words really mean.*

*I'm not usually a clingy guy. In past relationships, I typically get complaints that I'm too distant, maybe a little too rigid, if anything. So why can't I leave Bec alone after knowing her for only a day? Less than a day. Talk about an inconvenient time to act out of character. When she needs someone more aloof, I'm basically falling over myself to get a chance to talk to her.*

*Leaning forward to rest my elbows on my thighs, I rub my hands over my face, trying to force some sense into my brain, when I hear a small intake of breath. I look up to see Bec standing at the edge of the nook, eyes locked on me.*

*"Hey," I say softly.*

*"Sorry, I didn't mean to interrupt. Seems like you're trying to get some space. I'll leave you to it."*

*"Bec, wait," I call out. I stand but stay where I am. "Please...sit with me?"*

*Is this too clingy? I'm second-guessing every move I make, the exact opposite of the way I felt around her last night. Shit, maybe any chance of us working out is already fucked.*

*She hesitates, but after a moment she sits down a seat away from me, keeping a bit of distance between us. I fucking hate it. She sits there with her perfect body looking like a goddamn dream in that red fucking dress. That dress is going to kill me. I return to my seat, unable to take my eyes off her.*

"You're beautiful," I say. "Red suits you."

She drops her head and smiles. "Oh, Aiden, you're nervous."

"I'm not nervous." Yeah, I'm fucking nervous.

"Well, thank you. I welcome flattery." She laughs, but there's an anxious energy emanating off her that wasn't there last night.

We're both in our heads now. Fuck.

"Call me naive, but not once did I consider that you might be here for the same wedding as me when we met last night," I admit.

"Ha, neither did I. I thought I hit the weekend fling jackpot," she says.

Ouch. Okay, I guess I can't be too hurt by that. Did I expect anything serious to come from an impulsive weekend with a beautiful stranger while visiting another state? Not really. But the more time I spend with Bec, and the more time I spend in the same room as her but not with her, leaves me craving more. I know in my gut that one weekend would lead to every weekend.

"Let me guess, you're not feeling like you won anymore?" It pains me to ask, but I need to know.

She drops her gaze, watching her own fingers twitch and tap on the glass of her drink. I'm not the only one who seems to have misplaced the confidence we both wore last night. Maybe it's the loss of anonymity we had when we were unconnected strangers with an undeniable, unexplainable connection.

"I'm...I'm not sure, Aiden. Doesn't it all seem a little...I don't know, complicated?"

Yes. But for once, I think I'd welcome a little bit of complication into my life if the complication were her.

"I think it's a different opportunity than I originally thought," I say.

She lightly scoffs, her eyebrows raising at me, and I realize that I might have just sounded like a total sleazeball.

"Sorry, that came out wrong. What I mean is that last night, I thought I met a stranger who's intriguing, funny, and sexy as fuck. Instead, I find *out she's also important to people I care a lot about. You being in the same wedding was a shock, but if anything, it makes me want to get to know you more." I take the leap and lay it all out there. Something inside propels me forward, causing me to lean in further instead of retreating, instead of doing what's safe. My stomach is in knots, unsure if risking transparency like this will pay off and get me a real shot at getting to know Bec better.*

*The conversation lulls, and I can feel my heartbeat in my throat. I just met this girl. Why am I so invested in seeing if this goes somewhere? Bec sighs and looks out over at the skyline, avoiding my stare completely.*

*"I can't say I totally disagree with you. But I...I don't think I'm ready for something like this. I mean, we live in different cities. Different states, right? And before, when we didn't realize we were both here for Ellie and Dom, things were different. It'd probably be easier if we didn't push for anything more to happen between us. I don't want to distract at all from Ellie's big day or make anything weird."*

*Does she raise valid points? Sure.*

*Do I still think they're bullshit? Sure fucking do.*

*Because I know Dom, and I'm starting to know Ellie. Not as well as Bec does, but I don't think either of them would have a problem with us exploring this. The distance, sure that's not ideal, but what's the harm in talking more to see if it'd be worth the extra effort? Something tells me Bec would be more than worth it. I can't resist wanting to hold onto the way she makes me feel for as long as she allows.*

*"I understand not wanting to put Ellie and Dom in the middle of anything, especially during a weekend like this. And yeah, I live in Detroit. I'm not looking to trap or trick you into anything. I just..." Feeling frustrated, not able to find the right words to communicate the ache I feel in my gut when I imagine this being as far as things go. Physical connection aside, I just want to see her again. Running my fingers through my hair, I go on. "I don't feel right walking away from you just yet. I know we only met yesterday, but this feels...I don't know, Bec. Does it feel different to*

*you? Is that just me?"*

*She smiles softly at me. Fuck, is that pity in her eyes?*

*"Aiden, I'm sure you're a really great guy. I mean, if things were different, maybe. A different time, different place, different circumstances. I think we're better off if we just focus on Ellie and Dom this weekend and just forget about last night."*

*And there it is. Over before we've even begun. I can only offer a soft smile and a quick nod in response before she quietly walks away. Call me irrational, but I know that this feeling is unlike anything I've ever felt for someone. Do I wish Bec would give me a chance? Of course. But I'll honor her choice and do my best to keep my eyes to myself tomorrow and keep from asking myself...what if?*

*Except that doesn't work. I keep a respectful distance; all of our interactions are surface level and friendly during the wedding. But all the while, my mind races, imagining all that could be between us. When I pack up and leave Columbus on Sunday, I can't fight the hollow feeling that settles in my gut knowing I fucked up something that had the potential to be great with a one-in-a-million woman.*

# Chapter Twenty-One

Aiden

When the doctors first told me my mom had early onset Alzheimer's disease, I was clueless. Her parents, my grandparents, died in a car accident when I was younger, so I never had to watch anyone close to me age. Especially not like this. It started slow at first, nearly unnoticeable forgetfulness and confusion. Mom was increasingly scatterbrained after a long day, but nothing extreme. Eventually the symptoms became more obvious, and we knew something was wrong.

Once Evie and I learned more about her condition, we surrounded Mom with a healthcare team we trusted. We felt confident that we could keep her at home with a few extra services in place. A medication reminder, a home health aide to come over on the days when Evie or I couldn't be with her, and a local support group to help her cope with the changes she was experiencing. We tried our best to create a routine but eventually decided to move her into Evie's apartment permanently. Between Evie's classes and my hectic work schedule, we cared for her the best we could manage. I stayed at their place for the most part, bunking on an air mattress in the living room and only returning to my own apartment after games to shower and grab fresh clothes for my overnight bag. It worked for a while but became more exhausting as time went on and her condition worsened.

As much as I wish we could have avoided my mom living in a care facility, it wasn't possible. That much was clear when she accidentally started a small fire in the kitchen. Evie had run downstairs for a few minutes to get the mail. Thankfully, both Mom and Evie were fine. But getting that call shook me up and reminded me how fragile our situation was and how quickly things can change. We knew that we needed more help, and it gutted me. She's been living here for a few years now, and the staff are great.

My mom is the strongest person I know. A single mom raising two kids? Those are the women who change the world without ever getting the recognition they deserve.

The grief that pounds in my chest on the rare days when she doesn't recognize me is overwhelming. It's stifling. It's suffocating. But it's not as bad as the guilt and the worry. Having her still living in Detroit hasn't been easy. I hate the way it's come about, but I'm grateful she'll be in Columbus with Evie and me soon.

It wasn't long after Evie and I spoke about her worsening condition, that the social worker reached out to us to give us an update and professional recommendation on behalf of the facility staff. Mom needs a higher level of care than they can provide. We were planning the move in a few weeks, but the new facility in Columbus that Evie found has an open bed now and they offered it to Mom. With her comfort and safety in mind, it felt like the sooner the better. I'm here to pick Mom up, drive her to Columbus, and help her settle in her new place. As much as Evie wanted to be here, her rigorous school schedule wouldn't allow her to make the trip. Hopefully, she can meet up with us sometime tomorrow night once we're back in town.

The drive to Detroit goes quickly. I pull into the familiar parking lot, having made countless trips here to visit the woman who is responsible for the man I am today. The exterior of the building is lit up with holiday lights and decorations.

I pause and allow myself one more moment to close my eyes and visualize Bec before I have to face the reality of my situation. The graceful sway of her curves as she moves, her carefree laugh that draws the attention and smiles from everyone in the room, the way her confidence was outdone by her shyness when I left her apartment earlier today. I want to know all the different facets of her personality. Everything I learn about her only makes me more curious, and frankly, more addicted. I crave all the small moments with her. Each one feels stolen after having already struck out years ago.

I wasn't planning on asking Bec to consider being more than friends when I went to drop Hopper off today, but I couldn't stand there for one more second without at least planting the idea in her mind. When we're not together, I wish we were. If she tells me she's not interested, I'll leave her alone and try my best to bury the curiosity she always seems to awaken.

I should have come right out and made it clear that I still wanted her when I first moved back. I should have told her how I've thought about her over the years even though the time we shared was brief. That she captured a piece of me, leaving a hole that aches every time I see her but can't hold her in my arms. All I can see when I look at her, is the potential of something that feels electric.

And fuck me, seeing her vibrator and hearing her confess to using it in the shower...well, that lit up my imagination like a goddamn Christmas tree. I may have been joking in the moment, but the visual has me fighting to keep my attention on where I am and why I'm here and not on the lewd images and fantasies my mind spent most of the drive dreaming up. I couldn't stop picturing Bec in the shower, fucking herself roughly with her hot-pink toy, calling out my name as she made herself come.

Driving with a hard-on is as fucking distracting and uncomfortable as you'd think.

I shake thoughts of Bec away, and the comfort they brought me lingers, making all of this feel slightly easier. That special something I recognized when we first met is still there, beaming from her like a light in the dark. When Mom got her diagnosis, she asked Evie and me to promise that we'd pursue our dreams no matter what. A life with someone like Bec? I can't imagine a better way to describe it than a dream come true.

* * *

**Aiden:** Hey Bec, just got to my hotel. Is Hopper behaving for you?

**Bec:** You tell me...(picture attached)

**Aiden:** Wow, he didn't waste any time getting comfortable. Doesn't look like he left you any room in that bed.

**Bec:** I'm enabling him. I should make him move, but it's more fun to spoil him.

**Aiden:** Says the certified dog trainer. Aren't you supposed to set the gold standard? Enabling him is what I do...what other bad habits should I expect him to come home with?

**Bec:** I'm going to have to sleep twisted up like a pretzel on the edge of the bed tonight. I'm fully expecting to end up kicked to the floor with the way he's moving around. So essentially, you should expect the same spoiled pup to be returned to you. You're welcome.

**Aiden:** I expect nothing less. I'm just glad he didn't destroy any more of your...things.

**Bec:** Can't get your mind out of the gutter I see.

**Aiden:** Nope. My mind will be living in the gutter for the foreseeable future. Consider the moment locked in my brain...on repeat.

**Bec:** Wonderful...if you tell Dom, I swear to god. I'll kick your ass,

Price.

**Aiden:** I wouldn't dare, Miller. Besides, we both know you'll tell Ellie and she'll tell Dom anyway. I just have to wait.

**Bec:** Goddammit, I hate that you're right.

**Aiden:** Can't hear that enough. I'm heading back tomorrow. I can pick up Hopper around 8 if that works?

**Bec:** Yeah, that's perfect...though you might have to peel Hop off the bed by that point.

**Aiden:** Can I bring you dinner? I know it'll be late, but this was a lot to ask. Let me make it up to you. You also still need to tell me how much I owe you for you saving my ass.

**Bec:** Are you kidding? You don't need to make anything up to me, and you really don't need to pay me. I finally have someone to snuggle with. I'm living the dream.

**Aiden:** Then tell Hopper I'm jealous. He's living my dream. You still thinking about what I asked?

**Bec:** Um, yeah...

**Aiden:** Where does that leave us for dinner? Am I having a lonely dinner for one or can I share with the hot dog trainer?

**Bec:** Ha, at first, I read that as hot dog dinner. No hot dogs for dinner please.

**Aiden:** No, those are strictly for cookouts and ball games. I'm thinking something classy, like Antonio's pizza.

**Bec:** Hm, you might know a thing or two about how to make a girl happy, Aiden.

**Aiden:** That's the idea. I'll see you tomorrow, Bec.

**Bec:** Night, Aiden.

# Chapter Twenty-Two

Bec

**Abby:** Okay, what the fuck did I just read?

    **Bec:** You finished? How many times... ;)

    **Abby:** I'm not answering that...but I understand why you told me these books are one-handed reads now.

**Bec:** I told you! So, you're still in for book club tonight at my place?

**Abby:** Count me in. What can I bring?

**Bec:** Just you and your book. We usually order in and the host provides the drinks. I'm making mojitos but I'll have some other options too.

**Bec:** Oh, and any dog treats you wanna share with Hopper. I'm dog sitting for one of my students in training so there will be a rowdy, highly food-motivated puppy here too.

**Abby:** Hopper...you mean that hot baseball player's lab you had in for a makeup class? Since when do you offer dog sitting services?

**Bec:** I don't. Just helping out a friend.

**Abby:** Uh-huh. Sure, Bec. Whatever you need to tell yourself.

**Bec:** I'm going to regret introducing you to my books if you try to turn everything in our real lives into a romance. He just wants to be friends.

**Abby:** He wants to be friends. And what do you want...?

**Abby:** Bec?

**Abby:** The silent treatment, really? Oh, we are so getting into this later. Better get your story straight now.

* * *

"Has anyone tried fucking with a pillow under your hips? I need to know if it's as good as this book makes it sound. Carissa, that's your homework. Be ready to report back next month," Dee demands, shooting finger guns Carissa's way.

Carissa looks around my small kitchen sarcastically, like she's trying to find someone behind her, then back at Dee. "Are you confusing me with someone else? Who do you think I'm going to be practicing this position with? I'm as single as a Pringle," Carissa replies.

"A Pringle is never single. They fit too perfectly together in pairs. Who the hell eats one Pringle at a time?" Dee asks.

"No one," I say. I can't help but encourage Dee sometimes.

"Thank you. At a minimum, you devour two stacked Pringles together and make a mess of yourself with crumbs. That's the rule. You're a hot Pringle, Carissa. It's time to find another Pringle to hop onto...or get under. Better yet, find yourself two Pringles. Turn yourself into a Pringle sandwich." Dee raises her eyebrows at Carissa with a devilish grin on her face. I swear she wears that expression 90 percent of the time and it's warranted. Always fucking up to something.

"Are you reading a why choose romance right now or something?" Carissa asks.

"I am," Dee answers with a smirk. "Why do you ask?"

"Now I really want a Pringle. Help," Ellie whines. "I have breastfeeding munchies."

"On my way," I assure her.

"Can we please change analogies?  It's making me hangry and also giving me weird images of Carissa as a Pringle trying to seduce other Pringles," she implores, calling out from my couch where she's strapped to her breast pump with Hop curled up happily next to her.

Moms deserve a fucking medal. The way her nipples look in those tube things? Yeah, okay, a medal isn't enough. Maybe paid parental leave is a good place to start. Oh, or free ice cream for life. No...maybe endless orgasms from their partners.  I watch the tugging in sync with the little *puff, puff, hmm*...of the machine's motor. Yeah, all three of those combined still aren't enough for me to sign up to use that modern-day torture device. Ellie's a fucking badass.

"Sorry, El.  I don't have Pringles, but I do have potato chips and tacos will be delivered in twenty." I pull a bowl and bag of chips from the pantry and join Ellie and Abby in the living room. Dee and Carissa follow as I set up more snacks on the coffee table in front of Ellie.

Hop follows my every move with his eyes, knowing that at one point or another, there'll be an opportunity for him to steal food from one of us.  He's as ornery as ever, but we've had a good time today. We went to the local dog park and worked on his leash training during two long walks. My hope was that I could exhaust him enough that having guests over wouldn't bother him too much, the need to rest winning out. But he is as well socialized as I suspected, given the history Aiden shared, and he's done amazing.  Sitting while greeting each of the girls as they arrived, he didn't jump on anyone, and he hasn't stolen anyone's shoes...yet.

"Well, if you really need to know, I can vouch for the pillow placement. It's worth the hype," Abby chimes in before taking a sip of her drink.

"I knew I would like you," Dee says. Turning to Carissa, she adds,

"You're off the hook this time, single Pringle. Now, Abby. Tell me *everything*."

"Abby, you don't have to answer her. Dee *promised* she'd be on her best behavior so that you'll want to hang out with us again. Don't scare her away." I do my best to give Dee a chastising look, which is nearly impossible because I kind of hope Abby answers.

Sue me, I'm curious.

"Okay, well, I'll say this. It's good, really good, no matter which way you...flip the Pringle," Abby says.

"I don't get it. Like head to feet?" Carissa asks.

"No, like face up or face down...Pringle style." Abby winces with a crinkled-up smile as she tries to act out the chip-flipping motion with her hands, before giving up. "Sorry, the chip metaphor is really throwing me. On your back or your belly, either way will *not* disappoint. My ex wasn't good for much, but he did introduce me to that, so it wasn't a total loss."

"I bet with the right person it'll be even better. Too bad Ellie's the only one here with one of those," Dee says.

"Are we sure about that? Because Bec owes me an explanation for why there's a furry guest here tonight," Abby says.

"I thought you said Hopper is from one of your training classes. You're helping out the family who couldn't find boarding, right?" Carissa asks.

Okay, so I might have been a little skimpy on the details, conveniently forgetting to mention exactly who that *family* is, but I didn't think Abby would remember to call me out. She's been busy getting her pieces ready for a local art show. I assumed she'd forget my tiny slipup. I've basically begged her to show me her artwork, but she says it's easier to share it with strangers than to show it to her friends. I'm hoping she eventually changes her mind, but I won't push her. If I had any artistic talent, I'd be showing it off.

I act casual, grabbing a handful of chips and joining Ellie on the couch on the other side of Hop. "Uh...he is. Hop is from one of my classes. He's Aiden's dog."

That gets Ellie's attention. Her head snaps up from the candy bowl she's scouring through to find a red Starburst, her favorite. I'm a firm believer that candy is a legitimate appetizer and it should always be included when hosting. I stand by this. I'm always sure to have everyone's favorites on hand. I grabbed Abby's for tonight too. Twix bars. Solid choice. I grab one and shove it in my mouth, hoping I can buy myself some time before I have to answer any questions.

"Aiden is bringing his dog to one of your training classes? How am I just now hearing this? Aiden didn't mention it, and he was just over last week to catch the game." Ellie looks at me with a heavy dose of suspicion. I don't keep anything from Ellie, so I'm sure she's confused why I haven't at least mentioned this until now. Ellie knows me better than anyone. She'll see right through any bullshit I try to throw at her.

I'm done keeping all this weirdness with Aiden secret, anyway. Dee is a great listener, but I need advice from all the girls now more than ever. The problem is, I don't even know where to start.

"I didn't want to mention it before because things with Aiden and I are kind of...strange? I should probably tell you about how I met him," I say.

"At our wedding, right? Am I missing something?" Ellie is sitting on my couch, nips out and I'm the one who feels exposed right now. I feel so dumb explaining my non-history with Aiden, because what is there really to tell? We made out before we realized we were in the same wedding party, and I killed any chance of us going further. Oh, and we definitely would have banged if not for the girls arriving for the bachelorette party earlier than expected.

I look to Dee, the only one who knows the story. To her credit, she's kept my secret for years. I honestly thought she'd last five minutes before blabbing to Ellie and Carissa. She nods with a stern expression, laying a hand over her heart like this is a fucking movie. "It's...time," she says with a poetic pause. I let out a little laugh at her ridiculousness, and it helps. She smiles, and I do too. She always knows how to break the tension.

As awkward as I feel for making a big deal of this, I sigh and dive in, explaining how Aiden and I connected initially and almost took things further. How we'd planned to meet up again after Dom and Ellie's rehearsal dinner before we realized our best friends were getting married. How we decided to call it quits on our weekend fling before it could be...flung? And all that's taken place since he popped back into my orbit two months ago.

Including the audiobook incident in my car and the death of my vibrator. I'm pretty sure my neighbors three floors up could hear the girls laughing. Hysterically. Literally howling at my humiliation. Well, except for Dee, who dramatically wailed as if our friendship was over because we don't have matching vibrators anymore. Yep, my life is a sitcom. Damn Aiden for being right about my big mouth. The girls are going to tease me endlessly.

Yes, it's embarrassing to relive, but it's a huge relief too. I didn't realize how much I needed to talk about this. And these girls right here, they're the best I could ever ask to have sitting around me, helping me figure out what I want. Abby only moved here a couple of months ago, but I knew instantly when we met at work that she's a true friend. A lifer. She's stuck with me now, poor thing.

My cheeks heat as I confess what I'm hesitant to admit. What I've been thinking about since this morning when Aiden left. Considering something *more* with him.

"When Aiden moved back, I thought he just wanted to be friends, but every time I see him, I'm less sure that's the case for either of us.

This morning, he asked me to think about what I want. He didn't say what he wanted, but if I had to guess, he seems like he wants more. I've spent more than three years trying to move on and forget about him, but nothing has even come close to the spark I felt when we first met. It's humiliating to admit that I've thought about him more than a few times over the years. Since he's moved back to Columbus, that...tension I guess you could call it...it's still there. At least it is for me. I can't really explain it. I don't know what to do."

"Babe, that's your answer. You like him. You're curious. Sounds like he is too. Why wouldn't you give it a try?" Ellie asks, genuine confusion written on her face. I'm relieved to hear her question. Not that I thought she wouldn't approve or anything, but because I thought she'd be mad I kept this secret for so long.

"Because I...I don't know. If it doesn't work out, that'll just put you and Dom in an awkward position anytime you want to invite both of us to anything. Plus, he's a legit professional athlete. He could date anyone."

Ellie's expression changes to one of disbelief. "Bec, we're all adults. If it didn't work out, we could figure out how to be in a room together when we need to be. Do you really think Dom and I wouldn't want you to see what's going on between the two of you if after *years* you both are still interested in each other? I wouldn't have minded at all if you guys decided to take it further when you met either. You know I *live* for wedding hookup gossip. Besides, I've known Aiden for a while now...I really don't think you'd have to worry about his career or the attention it gets him. If he wanted to date someone else, he would. He's been in a few relationships since I've known him. I don't think he's the kind of guy to screw you over. Plus, Dom and I would kill him, so there's that."

"Well, okay, but..." I begin to protest, but Ellie isn't done.

"Are you sure this is about Dom and me? Or even Aiden's job? Or are you trying to avoid the possibility of getting hurt again?" I stare back at her, mouth partially open, speechless.

*Is she right?*

"Aiden isn't Josh," Ellie says. "I hate that the relationship made you question how incredible you are. Seriously, Bec. Don't you know you deserve to be loved?"

And for some stupid fucking reason, my eyes water and a few tears fall easily, betraying me and the unaffected face I'm trying to put on. "God, Ellie, I hate you sometimes, you know that?"

Ellie reaches over Hopper to grab my hand, squeezing tight. Her eyes shine as well. I can try to put on a front, use humor or excuses to deflect. Be the funny friend, the quirky friend, the chill friend. As desperately as I try to be what everyone needs, what everyone wants, Ellie sees through it all. She always has. She knows who I am behind any walls I instinctively put up. Maybe this is why for so long I avoided telling her that I like Aiden. Maybe I knew once I told her, she wouldn't let me get away with my usual bullshit. Writing off a nice guy before he can hurt me or I can hurt him.

Relationships and all the risks that come with them, the pain of losing someone, the pain of rejection, haven't seemed worth the risk. Sure, I've dated. Clearly that hasn't worked out. But have I ever given someone all of me? Ever fallen in love? Fuck no. Not even with Josh. Expecting a guy to stick around for the long haul never seemed like a possibility. The fear clawing at the back of my mind always tells me that no matter what I do, I'm not anyone's forever girl.

But what Ellie said...do I really think I don't deserve love? I want to say she's wrong and that I know my worth, but maybe she sees more of me than I'm willing to face myself.

Carissa reaches out to hold my other hand, looking up at me, where she's seated on the floor between the couch and the coffee table. "You shouldn't sabotage a relationship before you even give it a chance. No matter what anyone has made us believe about ourselves, we deserve to be happy. You talk about all the reasons it can't work, shouldn't work, won't work. Are you afraid that if you take a chance with Aiden, it might not work out, or are you afraid that you might find happiness instead? That this might be real."

Dating Josh was like wearing a sweater two sizes too small; restrictive and uncomfortable. Sometimes I wonder why I stayed. Why didn't I end things before he did? I think I kept convincing myself that I was expecting too much out of the relationship, until I shrunk my wants and needs to a size so small I couldn't find them anymore. Settling for whatever we could give each other.

I hid things well enough that the girls didn't see the red flags popping up in our relationship the way we did with Carissa's ex. It wasn't until after Josh broke up with me that I told them how I felt. I don't like to admit when something isn't working. Because what did that say about me? What if I couldn't make it work with anyone, what then?

"I don't want to get attached and have it all fall apart. He seems different. Special. I can't explain it," I whisper as even more tears roll down my cheeks.

"I never want to see you hurt," Ellie says. "But I also want to see you *live*. There are no guarantees. Well, other than a guarantee that I'll fuck up Aiden's life if he's an asshole to you." And that right there has me snorting out a mix of tears and laughter.

"That goes double for me," Dee says. "You say the word, and I'll key whatever fancy car he drives."

I laugh harder, tears rolling down my cheeks. "Dee, no. Please don't get arrested for me. I don't make enough money to bail you out."

"Simple solution. We won't get caught," Carissa adds, shocking me.

"Wow, Carissa. Vandalism, really? I expect better from you," I tease.

"You shouldn't. I can tolerate a lot of shit. But not for my friends. I won't allow that." The seriousness in her voice reminds me that she's still working through her own hurt from her last relationship.

I nod. "I love you guys. Thanks for being supportive and keeping me honest." I turn to Abby, wiping my cheeks dry. "I promise book club isn't normally this emotional. We don't typically talk this much about feelings. Most of our conversations are about fictional dicks and pussies and our jealousy for the lucky characters who get to play with them."

Abby laughs and shakes her head. "I'm sorry I asked about Aiden and started this whole conversation. I didn't know it was a whole secret *thing*. I just thought you were messing around with the hot guy from class. Shit, I was going to congratulate you."

"It was about time I talked it out," I admit. "Who knows, maybe this means I'll get to be the next one to test out the hip pillow position. But tonight, I want to hear what everyone thought about chapter thirty-two because holy fucking hotness."

Dee doesn't hesitate to throw in her two cents about arguably the best spice I've read all year.

A huge weight has fallen off my shoulders after talking this through with everyone, finally relieving Dee of her secret-keeping burden. Thinking of what comes next sends a nervous excitement flowing through me. I know it'll take time to let Aiden in, but I want to believe that the possibility of *us* is worth it and if I give him a small piece of myself, that I can trust him with it.

# Chapter Twenty-Three

Aiden

My stomach is in my throat as I stand in front of Bec's apartment. Thankfully, driving back to Columbus with Mom and helping her get settled in the new facility kept me busy enough that I haven't had a moment for my nerves to catch up with me. Unfortunately, it's all hitting me now.

*Fuck, Aiden, get it together.*

I knock and immediately hear Hopper's frenzied bark. Probably should have warned Bec that Hopper isn't doing well at greeting people without jumping all over them. I'm sure she figured that out quickly.

All of a sudden, there's silence. Not a sound from inside her apartment. For a moment, I'm concerned, wondering what happened, but then Bec opens the door and Hopper is sitting calmly behind her. *What the fuck?*

Of course, that immediately changes once he realizes I'm at the door and he barrels into me nearly knocking me down. His large paws are on my chest, almost sending the pizza I'm holding flying back across the hallway.

"Can I get an assist," I call out, reaching over Hop to hand the pizza to Bec. She laughs, shaking her head, and takes the box into the kitchen. After giving Hopper the attention he deserves—god, I've missed this dog—I close the door behind me and follow him into Bec's apartment. He already seems as comfortable here as he does at my place. Hopper runs and jumps onto Bec's couch before lying down and dangling his long legs over the edge of the cushion, panting and watching Bec move with ease around the kitchen, grabbing plates and napkins.

"I thought I had him there for a minute. It took a few tries, but he's getting better at sitting for greetings. That is, until *you* showed up. He didn't jump on any of the girls last night." Bec gestures to the stool on the other side of her kitchen island. "Grab a seat, and I'll grab us drinks." She turns back to the fridge as I take a seat. I'm so caught up staring at her ass that I miss her question.

"Uh, what was that?" I look up at her face as she turns to look over her shoulder. Busted.

She blushes, smiles, and quickly turns away again. "What would you like? Beer, wine, pop, water..."

"Water would be great, thanks."

"Thanks for bringing this over. I'm starving." She hands me a drink and a plate while taking a seat on the stool next to me.

"I went with a tried and true, four cheese. Hope that's okay."

"Antonio's can do no wrong. I've never met a pizza of theirs that I wouldn't devour." The moan she lets out after her first bite is way more appealing than should be possible, and I have to turn away as she licks her fingers clean.

*What the fuck is wrong with me, drooling over the way she eats pizza?*

"I'll keep that in mind. They're a favorite of mine too." I take a look around her living room quickly, making sure Hop hasn't gotten into anything before taking a slice for myself. "So, what's the damage? Did Hopper help himself to any more of your...things while I was gone?"

"Ugh, I'm never going to live that down. No, other than destroying my self-help assistant, Hopper was a perfect gentleman. We hit the dog park, went on a few walks, and he kept me and the girls company last night during book club. We've decided he's an honorary member and is welcome back anytime. You may have to play him the audiobooks so he knows what we're talking about. Think you can handle that?"

"Are they the same type of books that I heard in your car?" Bec smirks and nods, and I groan. "He's going to have so many questions that I'm not prepared to answer. Never pictured having to give *the talk* this early as a father."

She laughs rich and deep, and I can't stop staring. The way her hair falls off her shoulder as she tilts her head up to the ceiling, eyes squeezed shut, smile beaming. A sexy laugh is my kryptonite, and Bec is going to be the end of me.

Is it sexy because it's sexy, or is it sexy because it's her? I don't know and I don't care.

Bec tells me all about her time with Hopper and shows me a few pictures she took at the dog park of him and his new best friend, Blue, a small Yorkshire Terrier weighing in at about ten pounds with 100 percent more attitude.

We finish our food and Bec offers me another drink. Since she grabs a beer for herself, I join her in having one too. We move to her couch, Hopper between us, soaking up the attention. Every once in a while, our hands touch, grazing one another as we both reach to pet Hop's back. I'd say he's spoiled, but whatever. Dogs deserve to be spoiled.

"So...how about you? Did you have a nice weekend?" Bec asks me, sounding a little apprehensive, which I understand. I haven't offered any details about why I had to leave unexpectedly.

I'd planned to tell Bec about my mom's condition eventually, but it's difficult for me to talk about. I can feel my stomach tying itself into knots. The familiar haze of guilt and frustration at my own helplessness threatens to drown me. I pet Hop softly, and when I catch Bec's uncertain glance in my direction, I know I want to share this with her. I want her to know me. I want her to understand. I breathe out a heavy sigh and relax my shoulders back onto her couch.

"Well, it went about as well as I could have hoped for. My mom...she was still living back in Detroit. My sister and I decided that it was time for her to move here with us. It became the best option after the staff at her assisted living facility recommended that she get more specialized help. She has early onset Alzheimer's disease. They said she'd be safer in a facility that provides memory care services, and a room became available for her here. My sister found a really nice place that can offer the type of care she needs, so we jumped on the opportunity. I picked Mom and her things up, and we moved her into her new place. Evie and I spent the day helping her get settled." I avoid looking at Bec. I don't want to see the surprise, the sympathy, and worst of all, the pity.

I'm surprised by her silence. After a pause, she reaches over, covering my hand that's resting on Hopper's back. I feel her grip my hand in what I imagine is a show of support and meant to bring comfort. It does. When I finally bring myself to look at her, her gaze is thoughtful.

"What can I do? Do you want to rest for a little while and then go back to see her? I can watch Hopper as long as you need."

Her first instinct is to take care of me? My heart pounds tight in my chest at the thought, but I shake my head.

"Evie is still with her. She's going to stay as late as she can tonight, and I'll go back tomorrow morning first thing. We were told to expect a few challenges with this type of transition, so Evie and I want to be around as much as we can."

"And you? How are you feeling now that the move is over?" she asks gently.

I let out a deep breath, surprised at how this conversation feels easier than the other times I've had to talk about it. Maybe it gets easier each time I talk about it, or maybe it's the way Bec is looking at me. With a softness that doesn't make me feel the weight and burden of what I *should* be saying. What a *good* son says in this type of situation. Instead, I can tell her what I'm honestly feeling.

"Relieved, which then makes me feel like a selfish piece of shit. I wanted her to be living in the same city as Evie and me, but wishing for that and having it happen because she's getting worse? It feels hollow." Her grip on my hand tightens slightly, and I turn my hand over to thread my fingers through hers, running my thumb over her knuckle. "I couldn't help the distance when I was traded, and Evie was accepted into a really competitive graduate program. Mom never would have wanted us to pass on those kinds of opportunities. We'd held off on moving her to a new city to avoid making things worse for her by changing her environment, but I wanted her to live closer to Evie and me."

"I'm sure after she works through the initial struggles, it'll be better for her to be closer to you both. It sounds like you're doing all you can, Aiden. You don't have to tell me, really no pressure, but...what's she like?"

I take a second to give her question some thought. "Hm...warm and generous. Insightful and intuitive. I couldn't hide anything from her when I was growing up. She knew the second I stepped out of line or if I was upset and trying to act like I wasn't. She's always been determined and resilient too. My mom left my dad when Evie and I were young. We were better for it, but it took a lot to do what she did."

"I remember you mentioned that when we met."

"Hm...so you *were* listening. That's disappointing. I was hoping my good looks distracted you from my word vomit."

"Turns out I can eat me up some eye candy *and* listen. I'm gifted like that. Queen of multitasking. But I can also catch an attempt at deflection when I hear one. Would you rather not talk about it? That's okay, you know—"

"No, no. I want to tell you." She smiles and turns her body to face me, leaning her side into the back of the couch but keeping her hand in mine. Hop adjusts to rest his head on her knee, and it sends a pulse through my chest seeing them both so comfortable together. Her eyes are attentive, focused on me.

"My mom sacrificed everything for Evie and me. After leaving my dad, raising two kids on her own wasn't easy, though she always made it seem that way. As a kid, I didn't realize how much she must have battled to support my love for baseball. The cost of equipment, camps, travel teams, and tournaments...it's not cheap. Despite the stress I know she carried, plus the multiple jobs she was always working, she never hesitated to tell me and Evie how much she loved us and how proud we made her feel. Not only did she tell us, she showed us. She came to every practice and game she could. She stayed up late helping us with our homework. She welcomed our friends into our modest apartment for dinner with open arms. Mom always gave and never expected anything from anyone in return. When the possibility of playing professionally became a reality, I promised myself that I was going to take care of her and honor all of the sacrifices she made. Now, it feels like I'm letting her down."

"Letting her down? I can't imagine she'd ever feel that way. You and your sister are keeping her safe. I know the change will be difficult, but I'm sure it'll make it easier for all three of you to be living close together again. No matter what, I'm confident your mom feels the love you and Evie show her. When I see Ellie with Luca...I mean, he's only a baby and the bond they have already...that connection can suffer a lot of damage, but it won't break, not if you continue to show up for each other when it counts. You can fill that space with love."

"But this...this is something I can't fix. Something I can't protect my family from. I wish I could do more."

"Of course you do. But sometimes loving the people we care about is the best we can do. They're lucky to have you on their team regardless of what you're facing."

I smile, thinking about what Bec's said. Somehow, her words ease the weight on my shoulders. The constant pressure sitting there, weighing me down, suddenly lighter and not as painful.

"Mom sat me and Evie down for a talk a few months after she got her diagnosis, when she'd had some time to process everything, if that's even possible with news like this. She wouldn't allow either of us to put work or school on hold, even though we discussed our options and offered to drop it all for her several times. I remember her face, sitting at Evie's kitchen table between the two of us, one of our hands in each of hers. Her hair was just starting to gray at the time, and she had it pulled back in the same kind of hair clip she wore my entire childhood. With tears in her eyes, she...thanked us. She sobbed her gratitude for giving her the best years of her life after what she said was a dark and hopeless chapter. My dad...he had a lot of issues. We spent the night looking at old photos, rehashing our favorite memories, laughing until it hurt and all of us were crying." I remember it so clearly. A mix of joy, fear, and love hanging in the air, overpowering everything, making the rest of the world fade away for that brief amount of time. "Mom made Evie and I promise we would live our lives the way we dreamed, no matter what happened in the future. She wanted us to know how much we were loved even if she wouldn't always remember to say it."

A deep, intrusive ache settled in my gut that night. Honestly, it never left. It dulls at times, when things are good and Mom is doing well. And on the really bad days, it roars to life, taking over my mind, plaguing my thoughts with consuming fear and worry. It takes over my body, showing up in different ways but usually a massive headache. Last time Mom had a bad weekend, I was on the road with the team. One of our trainers said he'd never seen my shoulder so tight. All my toxic thoughts were finding their way into the very fiber of my being, spreading through me like poison.

"She sounds incredible, Aiden. And like a total badass." That gets a laugh out of me.

"Yeah, I forgot to mention that. She is a certified badass."

Her laughter, echoing my own, softens into a more thoughtful expression. "It makes sense that you're having conflicting feelings about her moving here. It's not black and white and that's okay. You're allowed to feel more than one thing at a time. It might make you feel better to just let yourself own it. The good and the bad. Don't worry about how you *should* handle things. There isn't a rulebook on this. Try to take it day by day, Aiden. She knows you love her and that's what matters."

I take a deep breath, like it's the first time my lungs have allowed a full breath of air since I moved. Bec's right. Mom will do better here after she settles in.

I rub my thumb over her knuckle again, realizing I'm still holding her hand. I don't want to let go. The feel of her skin on mine is grounding me, dulling the ache I feel from all the heavy shit going on in the last few days. Few years, really.

"I feel like I should be paying you for this session. Where's the funky couch the therapists always have in their office?" I quip.

"You're right, that'll be a thousand dollars. Don't forget to tip. My associate here and I only accept payment in the form of pizza and cold hard cash."

"Dog training, dog sitting, and counseling? You're a triple threat."

"Eh, I'm better at giving advice than receiving it," she replies. "You won't catch me following my own suggestions, that's for sure." Before

I can ask what she means, she quickly shakes the comment off as if she never meant to say it and changes the subject. "If you're ever interested, the Center trains therapy dogs as well. They visit local nursing homes all the time to visit the residents. The staff that work there always tell me it's one of the most popular activities they host. I try to go when I can, especially with our dogs that are newer to the work. I can partner with one of the families to see if they'd be willing to bring their dog to your mom's new place. Once she's settled, you know. Or if she's not a dog person, forget I said anything. You'd probably rather I not intrude, of course. Sorry, I—"

"Bec?" I interrupt her spiral. It's clear she's anxious and already trying to pull back her offer. "Mom loves dogs. So much so that I asked several times if I could bring Hopper to visit her in her last place, but they had a strict policy. Therapy and service dogs only. That's really thoughtful of you."

Her blush burns bright on her cheeks. "Just let me know when. I have a dog in mind, I'll see what her human momma says next time I see her. I bet Hopper could be a great therapy dog someday, too, if you're interested in working on that. He's got the right temperament for it. Once he grows out of the puppy stage, he'll need a bit more training, but then you could bring him with you to visit your mom."

"Mom would love that, and I'm sure Hopper would too."

"What, *this dog?* Enjoying endless attention and affection? You don't say..." We look down at Hopper who has slowly sprawled out as we've been talking, somehow in both of our laps now. She breaks first, both of us laughing.

"I don't know how you did it, but you managed to turn my night around. You're something special, you know that, Bec?"

I can see the doubt in her eyes. She's trying to determine whether I mean what I say. That hesitation, that guardedness wasn't there when we first met. I don't know what happened to make her feel like she can't trust a compliment. Like she can't trust me. But I'm going to prove to her she can, if she'll let me.

"So...did you give it any thought? What I asked yesterday?" I ask her.

"I might have," she replies, looking back down at our hands still locked together.

"And..."

"And, I need some more information," she says.

"Information..."

"You said there were other options that you'd like more than being friends. I want to know what those are."

"You sure you want me to go first, beautiful? You sure you're ready to hear it?" She looks back up at me and nods.

"Good, because I don't want to act like it's enough."

"What do you mean?" she asks, confusion clear on her face, an undertone of hurt in her voice.

"Not what you're thinking." I gently squeeze her hand and rub my thumb over her knuckles again, hoping to reassure her and help fight off any insecurities that she may have about me and what I want. "Being friends with you was never going to be enough for me, Bec. I should have asked you for a chance, a real chance, when we first met. I should have begged you for a shot to show you why we were worth the risks that had you scared to try. And when I moved back, I should have told you the first moment I saw you that I haven't been able to get you out of my head for years."

"There's no way you would have said that to me while I was covered in baby shit."

"As terrifying as that was, you don't know me well enough yet if you think that's what stopped me."

"What stopped you?" she asks.

"I don't want you to be scared, Bec. Not of us. Not of what we could be together. When you said you wanted to be friends, I didn't want to push you on it." I reach out to tuck a curl behind her ear.

"I need you to tell me if what I'm feeling is one sided, if you don't feel anything for me at all, so I can force myself to move on. I don't know how that'll work since I tried while we were apart, and I still couldn't stop thinking about you. But I'll figure it out if you ask me to. If it's not just me, though...if you feel like there's something here too...I'm all in. Being friends was never going to work for me because I want you."

"Me?"

"You, Bec. I want to be with you. I'm sorry I haven't made that clear. I don't want to waste any more time because I think we have the potential to be fucking amazing. My mom made it clear, and I forgot to listen to what she told me. What she made me promise I'd always do. Live out my dreams. I've been playing it scared. I know that means seeing where this leads, with you. Giving us a real chance."

Just when I think I've ruined everything and scared her by running my fucking mouth, she shocks the hell out of me when she stands up, pulling me up with her. She reaches her arms around my neck, steps into me, and presses her lips softly against mine. A brush of her lips that I can barely feel, her breath a whisper against my skin as she pulls away and looks up at me with a look that tells me she's almost as surprised as me.

"I'm sorry, I...I shouldn't have..." but before she can finish, I lower my head to meet her in another kiss, swallowing the soft moan she lets out the instant our lips touch. I wrap my arms around her waist, making sure not to drop my hands too low. *Don't fuck this up, man.*

Her kiss is even better than I remember. After a few minutes of the consuming push and pull, the back and forth, the taking and giving, she pulls back and looks down between us, resting her forehead on my chest. Her breaths are quick, flowing through the fabric on my shirt to warm my skin.

"What's going on in that head of yours, beautiful?" I lean down and kiss the top of her head.

"Too much, but nothing I can seem to put together that makes enough sense to say out loud." She looks up at me through long lashes. Unfiltered emotion shines through her expression in this moment, and she's fucking radiant. "I...I want to try Aiden. Being friends doesn't feel right, but I can't commit to anything serious. I know we met years ago, but in truth, we hardly know each other. What if I'm not what you expect?"

"Bec, I'm counting on it. When we met, I couldn't figure you out. I think that's the thrill of meeting someone really incredible. They surprise you and challenge you and leave you hungry for more. You're worth the wait. There's even more to learn about you now, and I want it all."

"I don't know—"

"One date. One date at a time. That's all I ask. We've had a series of random collisions. I think you called it the universe pushing us together when we met. Shouldn't we see where that goes? Maybe give the universe a break and plan one of our collisions on purpose for a change?"

Her eyes flutter back and forth between mine, trying to get a read on me. I can feel her weighing the truth of what I said. The sincerity. The potential risk. The potential reward. She's not impulsive. She's being cautious. If she ever lets me in, it'll mean I've worked for it. I'll have earned her trust. "One date at a time," she whispers, and my heart thumps so loud I swear it fell out of my chest and onto the floor. "After the New Year. I should warn you, though, despite what almost happened when we met, if you want to try something more serious with me, then you better be prepared to wait. I'm not the kind of girl who jumps into a relationship quickly, and sex will just make this messier while we figure things out."

"Good thing we met years ago. I've had a lot of time to think about what I want to do with you." The reprimand written on her face spurs me on. "Consider me more than prepared to wait. I've had a lot of practice. Tell me, though, does that include this?" I run my hand up her neck and run the pad of my thumb over her jaw. "Can I keep kissing you?"

I get her answer when she leans back into me, her hands holding my waist as she tilts her face back up and kisses me again. I weave my hands through her hair, holding her close to me. Even with her body pressed up against mine, it still doesn't feel close enough.

Before we find a rhythm, I feel her stumble, her body falling to the side breaking our kiss, and I grip her around the waist to help her find her footing again. I look down to see Hop nosing Bec at her knees, begging for her attention. Some wingman he is.

Bec laughs and pulls away from me to reach out and pet Hop. "Thanks for the save, Hop. Don't know what I was thinking letting your dad get away with stealing another kiss tonight."

"Hm...I bet you were thinking I looked irresistible showing up at your door with pizza and thought, yeah, that guy can steal as many kisses as he wants tonight."

"It is good pizza."

"And the kiss?"

"Solid eight out of ten."

"Ouch, eight?"

"Gotta leave room for improvement, don't you think?"

"No, Bec." I run my fingers from her shoulder back down to her hand, watching goose bumps appear. I weave my fingers through hers again, holding her hand, not wanting to break contact just yet. "I don't want to leave any room for doubt in your mind this time. I want you to know I'll give you everything you need. Every time."

"Consider it motivation for the New Year."

"Consider me motivated. I'll get my ten." Bec gave me the rules of the game. One I don't plan on losing this time. One date at a time, and I know just where to start. Batter fucking up.

# Chapter Twenty-Four

Bec

**B**ec: I can never face my neighbor again thanks to you.

**Aiden:** Okay? I'm gonna need a little context here, beautiful.

**Bec:** Don't sweet talk me.

**Bec:** I just had something dropped off at my door.

**Aiden:** Did Santa bring you something? Maybe take it up with the big guy if you don't like it.

**Bec:** Aiden fucking Price, I know you sent this to me.

**Aiden:** Hm, strange. I might have sent you something, but it was only meant to bring...holiday joy. I'm not sensing any holiday joy. I'm sensing Grinch behavior.

**Bec:** If you were here, I swear to god...

**Aiden:** Is that an invitation?

**Bec:** Flirty Aiden doesn't know when he's in trouble. You sent a fucking vibrator to my front door and they delivered it to the 85-year-old woman that lives down the hall!

**Aiden:** You're welcome. Couldn't go another day without replacing Hopper's latest victim. I'd hate for you to get lonely in the shower.

**Bec:** THERE WAS NO DISCREET PACKAGING, YOU DILLHOLE!

**Aiden:** Oh shit, seriously? That's hilarious.

**Aiden:** I mean, that's terrible. An honest mistake, I swear.

**Aiden:** They always send me my stuff in discreet packaging. Did I at least get the right model?

**Bec:** That's beside the point. There's a giant picture of it on the box and a huge red bow on the...tip.

**Bec:** Wait, what do you mean *your* stuff? What did you buy?

**Aiden:** I did select the "holiday packaging" option. I assumed that meant they'd wrap it in Christmas wrapping paper. Guess they decorated the *package* with a well-placed bow instead.

**Aiden:** Enjoy your last year on the nice list. I'm predicting you'll be on the naughty list next year if I have anything to do with it.

**Bec:** You're unreal.

**Bec:** But Merry Christmas you pervert.

**Bec:** And...thank you.

**Aiden:** Merry Christmas, Bec.

* * *

My parents' house at Christmas is chaos exemplified in human form. I fucking love it. I haven't even stepped away from my car after parking in the street, and I can already hear the roar of conversation flooding out while the glow from the windows streams across the snowy front lawn. My family has never known the meaning of "inside voices."

The same twinkling Christmas lights, decorations, and wreaths sparkle against the siding of the two-story colonial home; the wear and tear after years of use go unseen, at least to me. Everything is displayed as it usually is, and the familiarity tugs at my heart, a fresh hit of nostalgia warming me from the inside.

I fill my lungs with a deep breath of cold air as I grab my gift out of my backseat for the Secret Santa gift exchange. My parents, siblings, and

I decided a few years ago that it's more fun to focus our attention on giving one great gift instead of trying to keep up with finding something for everyone. I know my dad is going to put the new fishing gear I found him to good use next summer.

After high school, a lot of my classmates chose to attend an out-of-state college. They wanted space. I guess to distance themselves from who they'd been in high school and figure out if they're someone else entirely when the comfort of their hometown is stripped away. But not me, and thankfully, not Ellie either. I couldn't imagine living anywhere but here. Even now, my apartment is only a thirty-minute drive from my childhood home, which is just outside the city in a quiet neighborhood. Well, as quiet as it can get with us here. I know I'm lucky that I have a wonderful family. Supportive and kind, if a little overbearing at times.

The calm that washes over me every time I find myself on our street, clears away any lingering stress or frustration from the day. The fact that at one time I welcomed Josh into this part of my life still nags at me. He didn't earn a place in my safe space, but I brought him here anyway, assuming that was the next step when you're dating someone. It was only after I brought him home to meet my family, and I could so clearly see the reservations on each of their faces that I realized the seemingly small red flags I thought I saw weren't only visible to me. When he broke up with me this past July, my family seemed relieved, while obviously still worried about me and how I was handling the separation.

A breakup is one thing. Give me time, and I'll move on. But what happened with Josh, and what's been happening in the months since, is what's worn me down. Our relationship wasn't built to last. We weren't a good fit for each other, and that's okay. But on top of that, after he ended things, he started calling me on random Friday or Saturday nights, drunk, asking me if he made a mistake by breaking up with me. *"What if you're supposed to be the one?"* he'd ask me, slurring his words. I'll admit I was lonely, and I'd answer his calls when I wasn't with the girls to talk me out of it.

I don't know if Josh understands the impact of his calls and texts. I'm not even sure how many of our conversations he remembers. To hear from him at night when he's regretful, to have him rehash a breakup *he* initiated, to listen while he weighs the pros and cons of being with me all over again, as if I could give him the answers he needed. As if I could tell him if my faults were too much for him to accept. *He* broke up with *me*. Why am I his sounding board to decide whether he made the right call? Why have I answered? Why have I listened? I don't know. The next day, I don't hear from him at all. Sobering up must remind him of all the reasons why he decided I'm not good enough for him. I never get more than an occasional "I'm sorry" text, usually a day or two later. No explanation. No promises to stop contacting me.

I was going to block his number, but then the frequency of his outreach started to dwindle. I haven't answered a call from him since Aiden moved back. There's only been a few of them to miss anyway. But still, I can feel his lingering presence festering like a splinter that I can't quite dig out, becoming more embedded and painful over time no matter how much I try to ignore it. A wound that no matter how small, is felt and reminds me to be careful who I let in. Reminding me of all the reasons I'm not someone's perfect person. Reminding me of all the reasons I should question what I'm worth.

I didn't used to feel like this. I didn't care what people thought of me. Especially someone who behaves the way Josh does. But I've unintentionally let him rattle my confidence and self-assurance.

I shake off thoughts of Josh and the ugly insecurities he's generated and allow myself a brief moment to imagine what it'd be like to bring Aiden here instead. He'd wear his easy smile and carry himself in that relaxed, collected way he always seems to. My mom and sister would whisper about how handsome he is, and my two brothers would tease me for dating a baseball player when I'm the least athletic person in my family. Sports were never really my thing, but my siblings all managed to excel in at least one. Toby, my oldest brother, would probably have the most to talk to Aiden about, having played baseball in college and being a massive Aviators fan. My dad would welcome him politely but keep a watchful eye on how Aiden interacted with everyone, saving his assessment for my ears only when we have a minute by ourselves, ever the observer. I would watch Aiden with my family and catch his eyes when they drifted back to me like they did at Ellie's party.

I'd feel seen.

How does he have the power to make me feel seen? We're not even really together, are we? No. Agreeing to one date doesn't mean we're official or anything. He doesn't even know me. Who's to say he won't go running for the hills once he gets to know me better or that he won't use my flaws against me like Josh in a running list of reasons why I'm not worth his time?

"Bug's here!" I hear Danny, my older sister, call out from the end of the hall as I step inside and kick the snow off my boots, tugging off my scarf and winter coat, the melting snowflakes already causing my hair to frizz. It takes all of two seconds for her arms to be wrapped around me in a tight hug.

She's the same age as Aiden, but the two years that separate us don't feel like much because we've always been close. Close enough in age that in her toddler talk she squabbled out Bec as *Bug*. Bug sure seems like it should be harder for a toddler to pronounce than Bec, but all the same, the nickname stuck. Danny's lifelong gift to me.

I squeeze Danny right back and watch my brother, Ashton, make his way to us from the kitchen.

"I'll take this off your hands for you, sis. Don't want you hurting yourself doing any heavy lifting," Ashton says with a twinkle in his eye reserved for mischief.

"Ash, don't you dare," I say as I cling my gift bag to my chest. "You'll ruin Secret Santa *again*. No peeking, you impatient child."

"I'm the second oldest. Where'd you learn your manners? Respect your elders and all that, huh?" he replies.

"Oh, you stop that.  She learned her manners from your father and me, same as you, and look how that turned out. You can't teach someone who doesn't want to be taught," Mom jokes and pulls me out of my brother's arms and into hers.

"Hey, Momma," I say into her shoulder.

"Rebecca bear, you haven't been by all month.  I've missed you." Even though all of her children have defaulted to using nicknames, my mom always calls us by our full names.

She releases me and leads us into the kitchen, which overlooks our living room, where my dad and Toby are watching football.

I walk to the Christmas tree, glimmering in the corner of the room, and add my gift to the pile beneath. My gaze roams over the branches, catching on one of the ornaments I made my parents when I was in the second grade, and I smile. The damn thing is so ugly it's terrifying. I've told my parents they don't need to put it up for my sake, but my dad insists on keeping all of the ornaments we've ever made and hanging every single one up each year. The sentiment always makes me melt a little.

After hugging and saying hello to everyone, I settle onto a stool at the kitchen island while Mom and Ash set up a few appetizers on the counter.  Popping the first of what I hope to be about a hundred of Mom's almond cookies into my mouth, the inquisition begins.

"So, what was so important that it kept you from coming to my Christmas cookie exchange?"

"I promise I'll make it next year, Mom. I had something come up last minute for work."

Her expression softens knowing how much I adore my job. While my parents never like to hear any inkling of any of us kids not having a healthy separation between work and our personal lives, they trust us to make the calls on what exceptions we make. Except Toby, they usually beg him every few weeks to make more time for himself.

"More prep for the adoption event you got coming up?" Toby asks from the living room. "I've got a friend from work who is looking for a dog. I asked him to hold off and consider waiting for your event instead."

"Thanks, Toby. I can give you a few fliers to take to your office if you wouldn't mind. Getting the word out is always tough. People lose sight of things like that during the holiday season." I pause and toss another cookie back to buy myself a few seconds to think of how to say this without raising any suspicion. "But, uh...that's not what I meant. I was watching a dog for one of my clients who had to go out of town unexpectedly and couldn't find boarding. I didn't think you'd want a big lab puppy prowling around for cookies during your party."

There. That was perfectly inconspicuous. No need to talk about Aiden. It's nothing serious anyway. Just two adults who might go on a date next month. And who kiss apparently.

Is it hot in here?

"We missed you. Not just us, of course. Mrs. Oakley from two streets down was asking about you again. Her son just graduated from med school, and she finally got his permission to set him up. She told me she's a year away from putting the pressure on him to give her grandkids. What do you think, would you be interested in meeting him?"

"As much fun as that sounds, and as wonderful as it'd be to date someone knowing my future mother-in-law is already trying to put my baby maker to work…"

"Ugh, gross, Bec," Ash groans as he sets out a cheese tray.

"But…I, uh, I'm not looking to meet anyone right now. Maybe Danny and him would get along," I say, hoping to take the focus off me. The glare Danny sends my way tells me my deflection is unappreciated at best. I flash her a megawatt smile.

"Hm…and why is that, I wonder?" Danny grins maniacally. *Shit, does she know?* Maybe she talked to Ellie recently? "Her son sounds like a catch. You should totally get his number. What a cute story to be brought together by Christmas cookie matchmaking. Besides, I just started talking to someone from my gym. Sorry."

"Well, I sort of have a…date. We're not exclusive, nothing serious. I just wouldn't feel right seeing both of them at the same time. I'm not trying to play the field or anything."

That gets everyone's attention. Danny looks genuinely surprised. *Huh, guess Ellie didn't blab.*

"And…? Do we get any more info than that?" Toby asks.

"Who is he?" Ash tacks on.

"When is the date?" Danny beams.

"Okay, everyone give Rebecca a minute. I'm sure she'll tell us all about him over dinner, right, hun?"

I shrug. "Not too much to tell. We met a few years ago at Ellie's wedding and he just moved to town. He asked me to go on a date when he picked up his dog…"

"Wait, he's the client whose dog you were watching?" Danny is way too perceptive for her own damn good. One slip is all it takes. She never misses it.

"Yeah. He had to get out of town for a family thing on short notice, so I offered to help him out. He's a really nice guy, but I was clear that I didn't want to jump into a relationship or anything. I agreed to one date after the holidays."

"You feeling ready for this, Becca boo?" My dad asks with a hint of concern in his eyes.

"Is anyone ever ready?" I counter.

"You take all the time you need, sweetheart. There's no timeline to jump back into dating," Dad says.

"Oh, your father is just being his protective self. You follow that heart of yours, Rebecca. Let it lead you. Trust you'll find its match." My mom smiles at me with such hope. I wish I could steal just a piece of it from her. For every bit of optimism my mom possesses, my dad is every bit the realist. I normally take after my dad, but as much as it scares me, the flicker of hope I have about where things could lead with Aiden only seems to be growing with time. My gut twists in knots as my brain tells my heart to be reasonable. But something about Aiden makes me want to throw all reason away and risk it all.

# Chapter Twenty-Five

## Aiden

Celebrating Christmas in a facility with Evie and my mom isn't exactly how I pictured spending the holiday. We originally wanted to bring Mom home with us for a few days, but after talking it over, we settled on spending as much of Christmas Eve and Christmas Day with Mom as possible. Since Mom is still adjusting to her new environment, we didn't want any interruption to potentially set her back and cause additional confusion or distress.

We brought gifts to exchange, Mom's favorite holiday foods and desserts, and Evie made a playlist with Mom's favorite holiday songs. We had already decorated her room, and the staff decorated the common spaces as well. All in all, it's a cheerful atmosphere and worth it to see the content look on my mother's face as she leans back in her rocker, humming along softly to "Silent Night."

She's been quiet, but I'm relieved to have seen more moments of clarity than I was prepared for during our visit today. We reminisced on a few of our favorite Christmas memories, and she shared memories of her own without us needing to prompt her. It's been a good day.

I look at Evie and catch her observing Mom, a thoughtful expression on her face. My heart aches knowing how difficult it is for her to watch our mom go through this. I would do anything to take away the hurt from the two women I care about most in this world.

When I was old enough to realize the significance of my mom leaving my father, the pressure to protect her and my little sister grew stronger. The anxiety can sometimes cause me to act somewhat overbearing. Growing up watching the way my father treated my mom, and then seeing her break away from him and raise us on her own will do that to a kid, I guess. Everything about our current situation makes a person like me feel out of control, insignificant, and helpless. The solution to our problem isn't something I can give, and it kills me.

"I wish I could freeze this moment in time and come back to it whenever I want," Evie says wistfully.

"You two get together for a picture," I say. "That's one way to do it."

Evie kneels in front of Mom, taking hold of her hands. "What do you say, Mom. Want to take a picture with me?"

"Of course, you look absolutely stunning. We should capture the moment. I wouldn't want to forget it." She smiles adoringly at Evie. When Evie turns to face me, looping her arm around Mom's shoulders, her eyes shine with unshed tears and her soft smile falters for a brief second. I snap a quick picture right before the first tear falls, and Evie acts quickly to wipe it away.

"Well, I think it's time, don't you? I have it right here," Evie says while pulling out a small box with a red bow on top.

Mom started a tradition when we were younger, and we've kept it up every year since. We each take a turn picking a new ornament to add to the tree. Last year, Mom picked an emerald glass ornament with lily of the valley flowers delicately etched onto the sides in silver. It was her year to pick, though we weren't sure if she'd be up for it when we got to the store. When we walked inside, she barely hesitated before she walked straight to the display and pointed, stating she had found the perfect one. "A return to happiness," she whispered softly to herself as Evie gently pulled the ornament from the wall. She wouldn't say much else about it, but it was clearly the perfect pick. I can see the ornament hanging off the artificial tree in the corner of my mom's room.

"Here, Mom, why don't you open it?" Evie places the package on Mom's lap.

Mom gives an enthusiastic "Ooooh" as she lifts the small ornament from the box. "Evelyn, this is stunning." She holds the ornament up in wonder.

"Nice pick, sis." The flat, circular wooden ornament has cutouts in the shape of the city's skyline. As Evie hangs it on a branch, the soft light from the bulbs highlights the intricate outline of each building.

"Thanks. I wanted something to signify the importance of us all being in the same city, together again. I don't care where we live, as long as we're close. It's too painful any other way." Her last words fade quietly. I know the past few months haven't been easy for any of us. She's right. This isn't perfect, either, but it's the right place for us to be. I'm home when I'm with my family, no matter where we may be physically.

"We should probably wrap up the celebrations for tonight. Let you get some rest," I say reluctantly. We had a great day today, but there's always the risk of tomorrow being a bad day. The uncertainty always lingers like an unwelcome guest.

"Yes, I'm tired. It's a good time to call it a day. Oh, and Evie dear, please don't forget to set the timer on the stove on your way out. I don't want to burn dessert again," Mom says.

Evie turns back to Mom, caught off guard. She gives her an appraising once-over, finding nothing amiss. Not physically. "Sure thing, Mom. I'll make sure the timer is set."

My mom doesn't have a stove in her room.

We didn't make dessert.

We clean up, help Mom get comfortable, and notify the staff that we're headed out for the night, thanking them as usual for their care. The staff here have been great, and knowing they're always taking good care of Mom is peace of mind I'd pay any amount to find. When I first saw the cost of residential care that's specifically for adults with cognitive needs, I was reminded to be grateful for my generous salary.

"Well, other than a few hiccups here and there, she had a really good day overall, don't you think?" Evie asks me as we exit the facility and I walk her to her car.

"Yeah, it seems like she's had more good days than bad lately. I was expecting more hiccups while she settles in from the move."

"That doesn't surprise me."

"What do you mean?" I ask.

Evie stops next to her car and reaches into her purse, digging around to find her keys. "When it comes to Mom and me, you're always prepared for the worst. I know you've gotten better at hiding it, but that protective instinct and hypervigilance never fully went away, did it? It makes sense that you're falling back into old habits while we work through this."

"I'll work on it. I know you get annoyed when I do that."

"It's okay to worry, Aiden. I don't think we can help it in this situation. I just don't want it to overwhelm you. You need to take care of yourself too. When you need to lean on me for support, you know you can always call me and talk it through. Like we always have. You, Mom, and me. We don't shut down. We reach out."

I give Evie a quick hug and when I step away, I thank her. "You're right. I know I can count on you. I'm doing okay, but you'll hear from me when I need backup. Promise. I've also been meaning to thank you for your advice."

"All of my advice is golden. What was it about this time?"

"I, uh...I have a date with Bec, Hop's trainer. Well, sort of."

She gives me a look. "Sort of?"

"I talked to her. I was honest with her like you suggested. She doesn't want to jump into anything serious. One date at a time sort of deal. So, I'm going to ask her out after the New Year."

"Well, shit. Look at you, big brother! See what happens when you listen to me? Does this mean you'll take my advice on where to take her for your first date? It's clear you really like this girl, and I don't want to hear you complaining if you fuck this up. You need to get this right. I've been waiting for a sister my whole life and at this rate I'll never get one."

I laugh, because she's not fucking wrong. I need her help.

"Let's get lunch later this week. I'm not going to say no to your help. Bring your A game."

"Okay, but if I'm *gracious* enough to help you, then lunch is obviously your treat."

"Evie, if you can help me plan a first date good enough to convince Bec to say yes to a second, I'll have lunch delivered to you for a week."

"Deal." Evie chuckles.

"And hey, I want you to promise me you'll let me know if you need anything too. I can see it's weighing heavy on you tonight," I say.

She lets out a sigh and glimpses up at the clear, starry sky, keeping her gaze there while she responds. "Sometimes, it doesn't feel real. I feel like this is happening to someone else and I'm just watching. A member of the audience for my own life. When I look at Mom, all I can see is the strong woman who got out of a horrible marriage, raised two headstrong kids, and loved so fiercely. I feel like I lost this huge part of her without really losing her. Like I'm grieving someone who is right in front of me. My mind...my heart can't make sense of it."

I pull her close in another tight hug. I can feel Evie trying to hold it together instead of letting it all go. She doesn't want to fall apart right now and I get it. Sometimes it's too hard to put yourself back together afterward. Straining to keep the pieces together is easier, even if she can't keep it up forever. I hate to see her holding it in, but I don't fault her for it.

"I know, Evie. I know. We'll be okay. The three of us are going to be okay." The pit in my stomach sinks deeper knowing I'm saying words I only believe to be half-true. Because if I'm honest with myself, nothing about this feels like it's okay. It's so far from fucking okay, I could rip my own hair out if I dwell on it for too long, but Evie doesn't need that from me. She needs me to be okay, so I'll keep saying it until it's true.

# Chapter Twenty-Six

## Bec

"I'll never get all this glitter off my tits," Dee shouts over the pulsing music. The club set off glitter bombs and confetti with their midnight balloon drop. We'll get to remember the moment for probably the next week as we pull minuscule glitter remnants from our skin.

"Looks like that guy is willing to help you try," Abby responds, nodding toward the bar as she sways and dips to the music, her medium brown skin glowing underneath the strobing club lights.

"In his fucking dreams," Dee mutters, flipping her short hair back as he approaches. "What are you doing here, Dylan?"

"What a happy accident. Here I am thinking the New Year is off to a shitty start, and then I turn around and here you all are," Dylan says, wrapping an arm around Dee's shoulder, looking down at her and then each of us, showing off his stunning smile and perfectly messy dirty-blond hair. "I don't think we've met yet." He extends his free hand to Abby, who introduces herself.

"Dom left you all on your own tonight, huh? Ellie told us they were staying in with Luca for his first New Year," Carissa says.

"Yeah, Dom may have bailed, but I'm not on my own."

"Happy New Year, everyone." A familiar, deep voice sounds from behind me.

"Hey, Aiden.  How'd this one rope you into playing wingman tonight?" Dee asks.

"Didn't take much. First round was on him, and it beats staying home. Though Hop did try to convince me to stay with him tonight, so I owe him a proper celebration tomorrow."

"Yes, you fucking do!  You take care of that precious baby," Dee shouts, pointing her finger in his face before she gets distracted by the next song and dances her way to Abby and Carissa.

"Happy New Year, Bec," Aiden murmurs in my ear, leaning close as his fingers lightly graze the side of my hip.  I can feel the heat radiating off him as he stands just a few inches away from my bare back where my gold, shimmery dress drops low. The deep tone of his voice resonates down my spine, sending shivers back up to my neck, and my breath catches in my throat. I turn my head to look over my shoulder at him.  It's unfair how sexy he looks tonight in all black, with his top buttons left open, teasing me with a glimpse of his chest. "You look beautiful. Even more so than last year."

"A New Year's Eve joke. You couldn't help yourself, could you?" I laugh.

"Ah-ah. A New Year's *Day* joke. It's after midnight."

"Hm...that's true. Too bad you weren't around for the countdown. I had to find some random guy to kiss."

His easy smile disappears, and he straightens, his gaze raking over the dancing crowd. "Who?" The tease in me loves to hear the jealousy coloring his tone.

"Oh my god, relax. I'm kidding."  I turn my head, wrap my hand around the back of his neck, pull him toward me, and get on my toes to speak into his ear over the music.  "No one here had a vibrator delivered to my door. That kind of chivalry reserved your rights to my first kiss of the New Year. If you step up your game and give me better than an eight out of ten this time, who knows...maybe it'll get you my second kiss too."

Okay, so maybe the last drink or two pushed flirty Bec onto center stage tonight. No turning back now.

The girls are distracted, their focus back on dancing as Dylan heads over to the bar. Aiden tugs my hip to turn me around to face him. Staring up at him, I'm reminded just how tall he is; despite my heels, he still towers over me. He flattens his palm at the base of my spine, setting my bare skin on fire. He slowly leans over and traces my ear with his lips as he asks, "You want to hear my New Year's resolution?" His low voice causes goose bumps to erupt on my skin. Surrounded by a crowd of dancing bodies, there's a natural sway as he holds me.

I wrap my arms around his neck, tugging him down farther so I can respond. "A bit cliché, don't you think?"

"Not with something as important as this. I want to take you on your last first date." He pulls back and smirks down at me. My heart feels like it's going to pound out of my chest as I process what he's saying.

"That confident, huh? This must be some first date."

"What we do doesn't matter so much...if you're there, it'll be everything I've imagined since the moment we met and you sunk your teeth into my skin. What do you say? Next Saturday night, can I take you out?"

I rub my hands down his chest to his waist. *Goddamn, is he built of stone?* "Somebody's eager." I turn away from him and sway my hips to the music with him at my back. I feel his hold on my hips tighten as he stiffens for a moment before he starts to move with me. Emboldened, I reach back and wrap my hand around his neck. I feel him hardening against my ass and my body flushes with heat. The steady beat of the music floods the room, and for a moment I close my eyes and just let this feeling of uninhibited bliss wash over me.

"You're damn right I'm eager." He lightly grabs my chin and turns my head to face him again. "I fucked up when we met, Bec." The seriousness of the look he gives me startles me into stillness. "I let you go without giving you a reason to stay. I don't plan on doing that again."

"But you...you could date anyone. You're successful. You're sweet. You're hot."

"Bec, babe. You're describing yourself. Don't you get it yet? If you give me a second chance, I promise I won't miss this time."

Who the fuck am I to refuse?

"Saturday." I nod. A genuine smile lights up his face, and I can't help but smile back. We dance until the lights come on.

# Chapter Twenty-Seven

## Aiden

Dom may be one of my best friends, but I know better than to ever take him up on his dating advice. I'm sitting in his living room focused on the football game and I brace myself, preparing to disregard everything he says.

"If you're settled on Saturday, I just checked and the jumbotron isn't even that expensive. It'll be worth it. Take her to a hockey game and get a message displayed for her. Then they'll pan to you for the kiss cam, right? She'll love that. Oh, and you should get her a shirt... matching shirts for the game. And I just saw online you can get these candy hearts with personalized messages on them—"

"Ellie, how the hell did you end up on a second date with this guy?" Jake asks with a look of disgust on his face directed at his younger brother as he interrupts him.

"Considering how our first date went, I ask myself that same question all the time," Ellie says from her spot on the floor where she's folding a load of laundry. Jesus Christ, how many miniature socks does this baby need? I swear I've seen at least thirty so far.

"Don't tease him, Jake, it's kind of a cute idea," Chris says, defending Dom's *horrifying* idea. Not cute. Horrifying. If I ever put Bec on a jumbotron, I just know the date would end with her elbowing my gut, using the leverage from the hit to help her make a quick getaway. "At least he's trying to be romantic."

"Is this your not-so-subtle hint that we're overdue for date night?" Jake asks, and Chris smiles and nods. "Okay, Saturday it is, but we are *not* going to a hockey game. I can't trust you if Dom's awful suggestion falls within your idea of romance. Please let me do the planning."

"If you're so much better at planning dates, then what do *you* think Aiden should do?" Dom asks. He rubs Luca's back while he naps on his chest. His sour attitude is clear on his face as he sulks in his chair.

"No way. First, let's hear what Aiden already has planned. I want to know how much thought he's put into this," Ellie says, eyeing me like she's weighing my worth and if I'll meet the standards she's set for her best friend. "The girls and I will be waiting and watching *closely*, Aiden. Bec is my ride or die. Don't even think about hurting her."

I understand the protectiveness, really, I do. Her scrutiny is enough to put me on edge. I'm pretty sure Ellie could kick my ass if she wanted to...or get her husband to help her do it.

"I'm not going to hurt Bec. I know it's weird I never mentioned wanting to date her before, but I've been thinking about getting a shot like this since I met her. I've never met anyone like her. I'm not going to waste the chance she's giving me. I'm not gonna fuck it up this time." She gives me a stern stare before nodding and looking back at Dom as he starts up again. You get this guy talking about romance and matchmaking and he just *goes*. "Also, Dom, I love ya, man, but I didn't ask for suggestions. I promise I got this," I say.

"But you only have a few days left to plan. Are you sure you don't want to steal a few ideas from my first date with Ellie? It was fucking impressive. So first, I mailed her a poem and hand-drawn sketch of us together every day the week beforehand..."

Holy fuck, Ellie is a saint.

Dom goes on to animatedly describe the most cringeworthy first date I've ever heard of in my life. But when I look at Ellie, she's smiling up at Dom and giggling with a look so genuinely happy, it makes me envious. I want Bec to look at me like that someday. Someday when we know each other better, when our lives are fully intertwined and our futures are aligned.

God, I really hope I don't fuck this up.

# Chapter Twenty-Eight

## Bec

**A**bby: You still haven't sent a picture of the final pick, Bec. What are you hiding?

**Bec:** I'm not hiding anything. I'm literally naked. I don't know what to wear, so my birthday suit or towel are looking like my only two options.

**Carissa:** Go with the green dress, it's sexy but still gives him something to wonder about.

**Dee:** No way. Go with the birthday suit and make him wonder how fast he can get you home.

**Ellie:** All the options you sent us earlier look incredible on you. Wear what makes you feel good.

**Bec:** I don't know…maybe this is a sign. I should probably cancel.

* * *

Ellie's photo pops up on the screen as my phone rings. I should have known she wouldn't let me hide behind text messages.

"What's got you second-guessing this?" Ellie asks, skipping greetings altogether.

I'm short on time. Aiden said he'd be here in thirty minutes, so I need to figure out quickly if I'm chickening out on this date.

"Last night...I got a call—" I begin to say.

"From Josh? That fucking asshole," Ellie mutters. "You guys broke up six months ago. What is his problem?"

"We don't know that he was going to be an asshole. He didn't get a chance to say anything. I didn't answer, and he didn't leave a voice mail." *This time.*

"Bec, we both know he was going to be an asshole. What time did he call you?"

I hesitate for a few moments before I answer her, knowing it's as shitty as it sounds. "Two in the morning..."

"Jesus, fuck that guy. Tell him to lose your goddamn number. No, wait, you shouldn't even have to do that. Can we block him or something? I know you were hoping that wouldn't be necessary, but clearly this is getting under your skin. Are you okay?"

I half giggle to keep the hysteria down. "Uh, no. Not really. I didn't want to have to do it, but I did finally block his number this morning when I woke up and saw the call."

"Fuck yeah, girl. I'm proud of you. I know that's not easy."

"I think if I'm being honest with myself, it was easy." My heart doesn't ache anymore when I see the missed calls in the morning. The sting of rejection is muted, though the insecurities it fed still linger. "I don't know why I waited this long. I think I was waiting for him to prove he was still the nice guy I met when we started dating, or maybe I was waiting for validation from him that I was good enough. Anyway, I'm tired of seeing his missed calls and being reminded of everything he claims I'm missing. But what if...what if Aiden feels the same way when he gets to know me better." I hate hearing the self-doubt in my voice.

"First of all, you're not lacking. Josh was too stupid to see how wonderful you are, but that doesn't mean Aiden is anything like him. I don't think it's even a possibility that Aiden will feel the same way about you. He was over the other night with the guys to watch the game, and this date clearly means a lot to him. Of course, I told him if he hurts you, he'll have to watch his fucking back."

"Are we threatening six-foot-three, two-hundred-and-twenty-five-pound professional athletes now?" I tease.

"Nice stats recall, babe. Are we googling the shit out of your crush now?" I can practically hear the shit-eating grin I know she's wearing.

Busted.

"I *might* have looked him up online. For research purposes, obviously."

"*Obviously*," Ellie says with a laugh.

"I didn't understand any of the stats they listed other than his height and weight. Wouldn't he be a better fit with someone who's obsessed with baseball or something? What if he loses interest when the rose-colored glasses of a new fling fade away and he hates what he sees in me?"

"When you talk to Aiden, are you looking for flaws or are you too busy discovering reasons to like him? I think you should stop looking for reasons that this won't work and enjoy yourself. You've gotta stop picking yourself apart."

"Easier said than done."

"I know, babe. But do me a favor and give it a try. One date, right? Give him one date before you decide on the next one. The way he was talking about you the other night when he was over with the guys...I don't know, I can tell this is different. I know it's hard to put yourself out there, but you deserve to be with someone who sees how special you are. Who's to say that guy isn't Aiden? How will you ever know unless you give him a chance?"

"If he's got your approval, then he'll get his chance. You're the best,

Ellie. I mean it. Love you. Green dress it is."

"Good choice. Text me if my intuition is wrong and he's being a douche. If you want to bail, Luca and I will bust you outta there faster than you can believe and we'll go get ice cream."

"Now *that* sounds like a good date."

"Go get ready. Oh...and wear some super-slutty underwear just in case! Okay, loveyoubyyyyye," she rushes out in one breath before she hangs up. I look down at my phone and laugh.

I get dressed quickly and touch up my makeup with just enough time to check my hair in the mirror before I hear the buzzer for my door. Ellie's right. Aiden hasn't given me a reason to look for any issues, but trusting someone is daunting when my attempts at relationships always seem to crash and burn eventually. But if I could take the risk on anyone, my heart knows it wants to take that chance on Aiden.

* * *

We walk hand in hand to a quaint restaurant not far from my apartment and sit at a small table next to floor-to-ceiling windows with a gorgeous view overlooking the river at sunset. The setting is intimate and quiet.

When we get to talking, Aiden doesn't waste any time reminding me of one very good reason I haven't been able to get him out of my head since I met him. Talking to him is effortless.

I don't know why I feel so comfortable with someone I don't know all that much about. Well, other than our few interactions and what the media has said about him, but that's mostly baseball related. I'm not ever admitting to him that I looked him up online, but I'd do it again in a heartbeat to see those pictures of him in his uniform. *Yum.*

His entire demeanor puts me at ease, allowing for the conversation to flow easily. Regardless, it doesn't stop my heart from racing when his gaze roves over my frame, when he reaches out to hold my hand as we walk side by side, or when he places his hand on my waist to guide me to my seat. Each time his skin brushes against mine, my stomach twists with excitement.

We spend dinner talking about how Aiden met Dom and Dylan in college. I share stories from when Ellie and I grew up and how we met Carissa and Dee when we went to the same University, two years after he started there. I'm convinced we had to have run into each other plenty of times and never noticed each other. He vehemently denies this, stating if he ever saw me, he would have proposed on the spot. Dinner has flown by and before I know it, the waitress is asking us about dessert.

"No, thanks. That's our next stop," he says as he pays for our meal, already having shut down my attempt to cover the cost of my meal. He tipped well—my number one green flag on a date.

"Our next stop?" I ask.

"Yeah, how do you feel about walking a little farther in those boots? Will you be warm enough?"

"I should be good."

"Good. If you need it, I could always keep you warm," he says with a wink, standing and reaching for my hand. Renewed confidence flows through me at the way he devours me with his eyes. This right here. *This* is the feeling I've been chasing from the moment I met Aiden Price but could never seem to find it with anyone else, no matter how hard I tried.

There's something electric in his touch, something intoxicating in his stare. I got a taste of him once and nothing has ever satisfied me the same way in all the potential "maybes" I've met since. The lingering hesitation drains from my body, the tension and anxiety replaced with anticipation and excitement. Maybe the right person really can change everything.

# Chapter Twenty-Nine

Bec

The moan coming out of my mouth is unholy. "Oh fuck, this is better than sex. Oh my god, I think I have a new lover."

I open my eyes to find Aiden watching me as I lick my spoon. He quickly looks down at his dessert, coughs into his fist, and adjusts in his seat.

"You're fucking killing me, Miller," he says with a groan.

"I don't know what you're talking about." I sigh and take another bite of my brownie sundae and lick the spoon with a little extra enthusiasm. Dee would be proud.

His eyes lock on my mouth.

"I think you know exactly what I'm talking about. I've never been jealous of a dessert before, but here we fucking are. I'm begging for mercy."

"Can you blame me? You brought me to a build-your-own hot chocolate and brownie sundae bar...*in a bookstore*. This is my new religion. How'd you find this place? I've never even heard of it. The girls are going to be obsessed."

"Evie, my sister, is a bit of a foodie. She's always scoping out local spots. When I mentioned you liked to read, she suggested I bring you here. Well, she demanded it is probably a more accurate statement."

"Ah, so she's the true brains behind the operation."

He laughs then takes a sip from his hot chocolate, licking his lips after. Damn, that shouldn't be so hot, but the guy has great lips. Memories of kissing Aiden while backed against the wall next to a hotel ice machine come rushing back to me, and I feel desire swirl low in my stomach.

"I wanted to get this right." His confession catches me off guard. A flash of vulnerability quickly swept away by a shy smile on his face as he avoids eye contact. "Plus, Evie wasn't willing to risk me ruining our date with subpar dessert. I believe she said I deserve to be single forever if I can't realize how important hot chocolate and brownies are."

"Harsh, but honest. Smart boy for listening. Are you two close?" I ask.

"Yeah, we've always been pretty close. I mean, we had plenty of the typical sibling arguments, especially right after Mom left my dad and we were sharing a small room. Her shit was always everywhere. I wanted to throw away all those tiny shoes she had for her Barbie dolls. She started hiding them in my shit on purpose. She even wrote a threatening note and claimed it was written by one of the dolls after I threw some out. She was a menace." He chuckles, eyes far away in his memories.

"Seems like the punishment fit the crime. You ever throw away my shoes, Price, and you'll get more than a threatening note," I say, waving my spoon at him in warning.

"Trust me, Bec. If I'm lucky enough to find myself in a situation where you're leaving your things around my place, the last thing I'll ever do is throw them out. I'd spend my time convincing you to leave them there indefinitely."

I bite my lip, trying to hold back my grin at his confession. I love how easily he shows affection and is direct about what where he wants things to go between us.

"I'm sure Evie would have appreciated that sentiment when you had no choice but to share a room."

"Evie has her own place now that she can mess up all she wants." Aiden laughs before his smile fades. "I think I felt like it was my job to make sure things were as they should be. I got it in my head that I needed to grow up and take care of Evie and my mom. Of course, Evie wasn't interested in her older brother trying to micromanage anything. I still can get overwhelmed and irritated when things feel out of control, but I'm sure you already figured that out after I word-vomited all my issues on you last month."

"Hey, don't worry about it. I'm glad you felt like you could talk to me."

He reaches over and grips my thigh just above the hem of my dress, giving my leg a gentle squeeze before resting it there, his other arm wrapped around the back of my chair.

"What about you? Don't think I haven't noticed you steering the conversation away from yourself by asking me questions." *Shit, do I do that?* "It's my turn. What's your family like?"

I can't help but smile thinking of my family. "Loud, chaotic, protective, loving. I'm the youngest of four. Two brothers and a sister. Toby's the oldest, takes himself too seriously, always working. Ash is the class clown, lighthearted and fun. Danny is smart and fiery. And then there's me. The perfect baby angel."

"Ah, yes. The youngest sister angel complex. I'm familiar," he says with a groan.

"Rude." I smile and flick his hand on my thigh, which just makes him squeeze again and I can feel my blush hitting my cheeks. "It's not my fault the youngest children are always the best. It's just science or something."

"Or something for sure," he says, grinning back at me. "And your parents?"

"They live about thirty minutes from my apartment in the home I grew up in. They're almost complete opposites in every way except for how they feel about each other and the way they care about us."

A flash of grief passes over Aiden's face so quickly, I question if I even saw it. "They sound awesome, Bec. I'm really glad you have them."

The gravity of all that I'm grateful for weighs on my heart, and I think back to Christmas and how I pictured Aiden fitting in seamlessly with my family. I wonder to myself if he'd love them the same way I do. If he'd feel the same comfort in a home that doesn't make him feel like he has to carry any responsibility or grief. I'm sure that's exhausting.

"I told them about our date," I blurt out before I can think twice that I should be embarrassed about that.

His eyebrows shoot up in surprise before his face lights up with interest. "So you were excited about our date. I'll tell you a secret..." He leans in close to me before whispering, "I was too."

"I mean, I mentioned it was casual. And told them about Hopper."

"Did they have more questions about him or me?" he asks.

"Oh, you, without a doubt. They already love Hop. They've seen the photos from his visit. You on the other hand...ehhhh." I rock my flattened hand back and forth in the air.

Can't have him getting cocky.

He huffs out a laugh. "Really, huh, tough crowd?"

"Eh, about half and half. My mom is a hopeless romantic and wants grandbabies. My brothers love baseball. They'd all be easy to win over. My sister and dad would probably take some convincing, though." I realize the follow up questions are inevitable, but with his hand on my thigh I'm not thinking clearly and I can't seem to think of a response that keeps him from digging any further.

"You did warn me they were protective. Any tips to help win them over?"

"What makes you so confident you'll get to meet them?" I ask with a smirk.

"Call me hopeful. Our date isn't over, and I'm already craving another one." Sincerity and a hint of nervousness bleeds into his tone. Something about him being honest with me makes me want to do the same.

"Dad and Danny, my sister, are more like me. More realistic, less romantic. They wouldn't want me rushing into anything."

"I wouldn't want that either. If you need time, Bec, I can give you that," he says, his tone serious.

I instantly pull back, the feeling of rejection seeping in, which he seems to notice immediately.

"No, wait. Shit. I don't always say things the right way, and I can see you getting lost in your thoughts there. Let me try again," he says as he adjusts his body so he's looking at me with an intensity in his eyes. He moves his hand from my thigh to hold my hand in his. His warm, solid touch drawing my complete focus to him. "I don't say that because I don't want this. I don't say that because I'm walking away from you. Like I've said before, I'm all in. I only said that because if you need to go slow, we'll walk. If you need space, it's yours. I'll give you whatever you need. But make no mistake, when you're ready, I'll be here waiting for you. I want to do what it takes to get it right this time. If I'm coming on strong, it's because the pull I feel toward you is impossible to resist. It feels as natural as breathing. I can't help but lean into it.

"I don't know everything that happened with you and your ex, but I already know he's an idiot. He has to walk around every day knowing he fucked up the best thing that ever happened to him. I know how much that sucks, because I've been doing the same thing since we met and I missed my chance with you. I had to think about how you tasted, how you felt in my arms, how you made me laugh, how you kept me guessing, and know that I couldn't have you because I blew my shot. Those walls you built so high around yourself, Bec, I'm going to tear those down bit by bit until you know that you can trust me."

My heart races, heat pools low in my stomach at his admission. In the entirety of my relationship with Josh, not once had I felt desired like Aiden makes me feel with just his words and his gaze raking over me. And while I'm nervous to let Aiden in, I know he's not like anyone I've ever dated.

"Josh, my ex, we dated for about a year. When we broke up, it was for the best. We didn't make each other happy. By the end, we were constantly arguing. It felt like everything that made me who I am annoyed him. But ever since then, he's had a hard time knowing that he made the right choice. He...uh..." How do I explain this? It sounds so stupid when I say it out loud. I can feel the embarrassment and shame overtaking me as I fumble through an explanation. Aiden waits patiently, his attention solely on me and his hand holding onto mine like a lifeline. "He calls sometimes, and wants to talk about us and whether or not he made a mistake breaking up with me."

"He still calls you," Aiden says, sitting up straighter in his seat with a look of hesitation and confusion on his face.

"We're not together, and I stopped answering his calls, but yes. They weren't really two-sided conversations anyway, so there's no point in answering anyway," I admit. "I actually blocked his number this morning. It was overdue."

"I'm not sure I know what you mean, Bec."

"He calls late, usually while he's drunk, and rambles on about all the reasons we should get back together, or he rehashes all the reasons he broke up with me." All the reasons I wasn't good enough. "It depends on his mood, I guess. Sorry...this is really embarrassing. I have zero interest in getting back together with him, but the whole thing has kind of done a number on my confidence."

"Holy fuck, what a tool. Seriously. That's a dick move, and you don't deserve that. He's the one that should be embarrassed."

"You sound like the girls," I say before taking another sip of my hot chocolate. Not that I need the heat. My face is on fire from the humiliation of having to explain this all to Aiden.

"Hey," he uses two fingers and his thumb on my chin to gently turn my face toward him and for a moment, he just holds my jaw there, a look of concentration on his face. "I can't possibly imagine what kind of shitty, idiotic things that guy made up in his mind as reasons to not be with you, but I don't want you to believe any of them. I'm sure none of that was easy to hear, and clearly the guy never learned how to break up with someone without being a total dick. I'm not going to lie and say I wish he was a better man and that it worked out for you with him, because I selfishly want this chance with you, but not at the expense of your self-esteem."

"Not to sound like the bitter ex-girlfriend, but I'm glad it didn't work out with him either. Even without all the mess after our breakup, we weren't a good fit. Besides, if we never broke up, I never would have gone on this date and found out about this place." I give him a side eye.

"And the company, right?"

"Hm...no complaints yet. But you'll have to do a lot to one-up this brownie."

He laughs, carefree, and he leans back to take a bite of his own dessert. "Brutal, Bec."

"It's a damn good brownie."

"Admit it. It's a damn good date too."

"It's a damn good date, Aiden."

# CHAPTER TWENTY-NINE

"I like to exceed expectations. You ready for our last stop?"

"This isn't the last stop?"

"Saved the best for last. Let's go, beautiful."

# Chapter Thirty

Aiden

"Someone's confident. Bringing me to a hotel on the first date? Hoooooly shit..." Realization dawns on her as I grab Bec's hand in mine and pull her through the lobby toward the bar where we first met.

"I was feeling nostalgic," I say with a wink.

"Should we go straight upstairs and find that ice machine again?" Bec asks with a flirty smile playing at her perfect lips.

"I was thinking of a nightcap, but I like your idea better." She laughs and playfully slaps my chest when I start backing her toward the elevator.

"All right, back it up, caveman. That's on me. Let's go get that drink."

We get drinks from the bar before settling into a booth. Bec gives a thoughtful look around the place, taking in the surroundings, no doubt remembering the last time we were here together years ago. I honestly couldn't tell you shit about what looks the same or different. I barely noticed anything about the space the last time I was here, and I don't care about it now either. The woman across from me has my full attention, and I don't see that changing regardless of where we are.

"I don't know how you did it," I say.

"Did what?" Bec asks.

"How you kept a straight face when I explained to you why I thought you were a dog person. I didn't realize how spot on that guess was when I made it."

Bec laughs, throwing her head back. God, this girl shines. I can't take my eyes off her.

"You remembered." She rests her chin in her hand, leaning on the table, her nearness allowing me to see the dimension of color in her bright eyes as they flicker between my own. The elated look on her face wakes up pieces of my soul I never knew existed.

"I remember every moment of that weekend. Every detail of the time I spent with you." I allow the truth to spill out, unable to pull it back, leaving it hanging suspended in the air between us. I could get lost in her stare. She doesn't respond, but everything about her thoughtful expression makes me feel like she remembers that weekend just as clearly as I do.

Who's to say how things would have turned out if Bec and I tried to make things work before? We either robbed ourselves of time we could have spent together or saved ourselves from a difficult long-distance relationship that wouldn't have lasted. I don't care about any of that now. I hope with every part of my being that she'll take everything I have to offer her this time. It's hers already, whether she knows it or not.

"I was right about another thing too. The night I met you, I discovered I really do have a kink for flirting with a certain gorgeous brunette at this bar."

"That game...it was a creative way to flirt. I'll give you that."

"I'd never played that game with another person before that night. Just something I do in my head when I'm alone. But I had to think of a reason to strike up a conversation with the beautiful woman next to me," I say.

Bec leans back against the booth and tucks her hair behind her ear. "So do all the girls fall for that one or was it just me?"

"I haven't played it since," I respond.

"Oh, come on. Not even once?" she asks, disbelief heavy in her tone.

"I didn't want to ruin it by sharing something that had become special with the wrong person."

# Chapter Thirty-One

## Bec

I'm speechless. All this time, I thought maybe I'd imagined just how much I'd been hooked on him when the night seemed to have left just as much of an impression on him.

"That probably sounds really stupid, forget I said that..." he mumbles.

"Two blondes on the left end of the bar," I say in a challenge.

The grin on his face has me smiling myself. After a thoughtful pause, he asks, "What brought them into the city?"

"They're trying to wifey up with a professional baseball player. They heard one likes to come to this bar," I say, shrugging.

"Is that so?" He rubs the scruff on his chin as he looks over at the women I've called out. "You think I use my job to meet women?"

"I think it'd be difficult not to," I respond, feigning a nonchalance I don't feel.  Picturing Aiden flirting with anyone else makes my stomach turn with discomfort.

"Would being with me bother you given what I do for a living?" he asks the question, and the seriousness of his tone is unmistakable.

"I guess I haven't really thought about it. What would it be like?"

"It's not the easiest lifestyle when it comes to relationships.  Especially for the guys with families. We have an intense schedule during the regular season. Then there's preseason training and games. Postseason depends on how well the team does. There's a shit ton of travel. It's a lot to ask a partner to deal with. I've seen some teammates with great relationships who manage to make it work, while others don't do well and it's enough to break them. Not to mention the media can be a bit invasive at times."

"Sounds like a lot to sign up for," I say, stirring my drink with my straw.

"I don't want to sugarcoat it or lie to you. I'd rather you know up front what it's like, but I don't think I can do it justice trying to explain it. We'll take this slow, as slow as you need."

"Right, one date," I say.

"For now." His gaze is thoughtful as he takes a sip of his drink. "Okay, my turn. A man and a woman, sitting in a booth. She's a knockout in a green dress, and he's...eh, he's all right, I guess."

"Just all right, huh?" I can't hold in my laugh, because in no world would I describe Aiden as "all right" looking. "Okay, where do you think this couple is headed after this?" I ask, knowing I'm pushing for him to tell me how far he wants to take things tonight.

Despite what I said before about wanting to take things slow, I want this. I want him.

"I don't know...any ideas?" he asks, scratching along his jaw, his hooded stare locked on mine.

"Maybe one."

* * *

To end our date, I decide to show Aiden one of my favorite places in the city. In the middle of downtown, the art museum has transformed one of their exterior brick walls into a massive chalkboard community art piece, expanding the length of the large building's side. Every month, an artist comes out to paint a new question along the top of the wall, just above the chalkboard. I try to make it here at least once a month to read the answers people leave. It's as if the city has its own journal, a collection of our unique stories all haphazardly thrown together into something uniquely beautiful. Sometimes, I imagine the strangers I see every day, going about their business, are the people who leave their hearts on this wall, knowing no one would know it was them who wrote it.

"It's been here for about two years. Every month, they change the prompt," I explain.

"And people come out and freeze their asses off to write a response?" Aiden pulls me tighter around the middle, my back against his chest, his head low as a deep laugh rumbles in my ear.

"Yeah, we're fun like that. And now you live here, so you get to be fun like that too." I step away and grab two pieces of chalk from the bucket that hangs off the brick wall.

"This year, I'm going to…" Aiden reads off the top of the mural. "A New Year's resolution. Okay, you write your answer over here. I'm headed to the other side."

"You're too cool to write your answer next to mine?" I yell to his back as he strides away from me with purpose.

"Can't have you cheating, Miller."

"I think you're missing the point, no one is grading this, Price."

I roll my eyes to myself as I turn over the chalk in my hand, thinking for a moment of what to write. I watch out of the corner of my eye as Aiden looks the wall up and down, searching for a place to put his answer, before he kneels and starts writing.

When he's done, he waits for me to finish and step back from the wall before coming over to take the chalk from my hand and return them both to the bin for the next person's confession.

I wander to where I saw him kneeling, but there's so many answers written in this area I can't tell what he wrote.

"Which is yours?" I ask.

"I thought this was anonymous," he says, the side of his mouth tilting up as he shoves his hands into his pockets.

"I'll show you mine if you show me yours," I say with a wink.

His eyebrows shoot up in surprise. I love how easy it is to knock him off balance with just a little flirtation. Aiden points to the wall, not even looking at it as he strides toward me.

"That one's mine. Now show me yours," he demands, his hands grabbing at my lower back to pull me against him before sliding his hands over my ass and kissing me. No one has ever kissed me like Aiden does. My mind shuts off, everything becomes fuzzy, and I feel him everywhere.

I break the connection with a laugh and push him away. He falls back easily, laughing with me. I read his addition on the wall and a slow burn ignites in my chest. I lean into Aiden when he pulls me against his side, one heavy arm across my shoulders.

"This year I'm going to...earn that second date," he says before leaning down to kiss the top of my head.

He has to know that second date is his already.

I turn to bury my face in the warmth of his chest. I sneak my hands into his jacket and wrap them around his waist, soaking up his warmth as we hold each other. He lifts my chin and kisses me slowly before it morphs into something needier. He drops his lips to kiss my neck. I lean my head to the side, giving him access to continue. His strong hands run up my back from the base of my spine to my shoulders, sending chills along my arms. When he speaks again, he keeps his head low, mere inches from the spot he was kissing on my neck, his breath hot on my skin, setting my skin on fire. "Think I'll get my wish?"

I hum, basking in the sensation of Aiden's arms holding me close, the heat radiating off his body and into mine. I lean back and close my eyes, inhaling his cologne. "Brownies, books, and booze. It's gonna be hard to beat, but I'd like to see you try." The look of satisfaction on his face is genuine. "Now read mine," I say.

He takes my hand and we walk side by side to my end of the wall. When I point to my horrible handwriting, he reads aloud. "This year I'm going to...kiss him senseless." I burst out laughing, throwing my head back at the look of confusion on his face.

"What am I going to do with you? I assumed you would take this assignment seriously."

"What?" I shout with mock offense. "It's a sincere goal of mine."

"Well, I think our goals complement each other perfectly," he says.

"Only one way to find out," I tease, pushing him against the wall. I wrap my hand around the back of his neck to pull his mouth toward mine. Our lips meet with equal enthusiasm, his tongue slipping to dance with mine, making me moan. Aiden's kiss is overwhelming. All I can think is that *he's* the one who'll succeed in knocking any sense clear from my head with his kiss.

I tuck my hands back into his jacket, his body warming my cold fingers. I trace the muscled ridges of his abdomen that are distinct through his shirt to the buckle of his belt, dig my fingers into his waistband, and pull him flush against my hips.

He groans into my mouth and pulls back, eyes opening slowly.

"What now, Bec?" he asks, his voice rough with want.

"Now you take me home," I whisper against his lips, stealing another quick kiss from his soft lips.

His expression shifts, and his eyes tell me that he's considering his next words carefully. "I thought you wanted to wait. We can take things slow, Bec. There's no rush."

"I was scared when I said that, but I'm not scared now. I don't want to wait," I say.

"Are you sure?"

"I'm sure, Aiden. Take me home."

# Chapter Thirty-Two

Bec

We walk two blocks to Aiden's apartment and get caught in a storm along the way. The temperature hasn't dropped low enough for snow tonight like we'd expect in January, just enough to chill us to the bone as we get soaked. The freezing rain is an extreme contrast to the way my body is blazing, on fire from within.

We run into Aiden's apartment building out of breath, panting and laughing. He pulls my hand, leading me onto the elevator, just the two of us. He presses the button for the penthouse and enters a code before the elevator begins to rise. Because of course he lives in the fucking penthouse.

I lean back against the wall farthest from him in disbelief. Is this moment real? I want it to be real so damn bad.

The air feels heavy, and I can't slow my breathing. My nerves are on edge with anticipation as I stare down at my feet. I feel him step in front of me, towering over me, before I look up into his heady gaze. His hand drags down my jaw and he swipes his thumb over my bottom lip, brushing away a few rain droplets.

I reach for him with one hand, running my palm up his chest to grip his soaked shirt and pull him flush against me. He comes willingly, putting his free hand against the wall of the elevator to the side of my head, using his other hand to lift my jaw, tilting my head back until I feel it rest against the wall of the elevator as it continues lifting us higher. He leans down, breathing in deeply, and whispers, his low voice causing my thighs to clench, "I've thought about this for over three years, Bec. Wondered what it'd be like to make you mine. To mark you in all the ways I've dreamed of since we first kissed."

"What are you waiting for?" I brush my lips over his then take his bottom lip between my teeth and tug gently.

The hand holding my jaw slides down to my neck and he presses softly against my collarbone. "I'm waiting until I have you in my bed, because once I start, I won't be able to stop. If I start here, it ends here, right in this elevator. Is that what you want?" The gravel in his voice sends shivers down my spine and up my thighs.

*Fuck, maybe I do want that.*

"Maybe it is," I say. His presence overwhelms me, and my mind starts to go hazy. I need Aiden to touch me...now.

"No, I don't think so. I think I need you spread out for me. Somewhere I can take my time with every inch of you." I'm unable to recall a single reason why this could be a bad idea. Any risk of this ending badly. All reason flies out the window, and I'm completely overtaken by lust at his words. I'm so tired of fighting this pull between us.

The elevator doors open, and before I can take a step, Aiden lifts me into his arms, grasping where my thighs meet my ass, his fingers digging into my soft curves. I link my legs around his toned waist. My arms wrap around his broad shoulders and my hands meet at the base of his neck, gripping his hair. He turns, opening the door to his apartment as I bring one hand to his cheek. I look into his eyes, hoping to see what I'm feeling returned in his gaze. He holds my stare and all

I can see is his hunger. I'm sure that's what he sees in mine as well.

"Don't make me wait one more second, Aiden," I whisper.

He doesn't answer me. Instead, he makes a sharp turn and presses me against the wall, and ravages my mouth, kissing me like he owns every piece of me inside and out.  I weave my hands into his hair, tugging hard, and grind my pelvis up against him, feeling him hard beneath me. We tear at each other for a few minutes before he pulls away, leaving me breathless and desperate for more.

"I couldn't wait one more second if I tried. You want this, Bec? You want me?" Aiden rasps out, breathing heavily. Despite what he said about not waiting, he pauses for me. He wants me to be sure. I wait for fear or anxiety to rise up, but there's nothing. Being with him like this feels perfect. He stares into my eyes with an intensity that I wasn't prepared for. It steals my breath away.

"Yes...yeah, Aiden. I want it. I want this. Please, I need you." I pull him back to my mouth, seeking him out frantically, and he meets me with equal fervor. My rational thoughts have abandoned me and all that's left is a starving woman who needs to know what this man is like, completely stripped down, raw and needy.

I feel one of his hands running up my thigh to grip my hip, then my waist, slowly finding its way to my breast. He palms me and pinches my nipple through my dress and lace bralette, sending a jolt between my thighs. I gasp into our kiss, feeling my need intensify. "Oh fuck, Aiden."

Without missing a beat, he continues to tease my nipple, moving his mouth to my neck to suck and kiss, leaving me undone. I could feel embarrassed at the moans he draws from me, but I'm not. This man has edged me like no one else I've ever known, and I'm ready for him to take care of me like I know he will.

Aiden's hand returns to my ass, gripping me tightly while he pulls away from the wall, before carrying me down the hall.  I have no fucking clue what his apartment looks like or where we're going, so enraptured in another kiss of his. I lose all sense of direction as he leads me to what I assume is his bedroom.

But we must pass through his bedroom instead, because when he pulls back and I open my eyes, I find myself in the most luxurious bathroom I've ever seen. White countertops pose a striking difference from the dark tiles on the floor and the walls. The lighting is soft and low, like we've entered a cave. There's a walk-in shower to the side and a huge soaking tub in front of a glass window. Do people with money not care if everyone sees them bathing through their fancy floor-to-ceiling windows? I guess it'd take a lot to see us now, tangled in each other on the top floor of Aiden's building overlooking the twinkling lights of downtown. I'm not sure I'd care either way at this point. If he stopped right now, I'd get on my knees and beg him for more, audience or not.

He walks into the shower still holding me and kissing my neck. We're already soaked from the storm anyway, clothes clinging to our skin. He reaches out, turning on the water, and the steam begins to fill the space, slowly warming my chilled body. Caught up in his kiss and the feel of his hard body, his deep voice surprises me when he speaks against my parted lips. "Strip. I need you naked. Let me see you."

He lowers me gently to stand on my own in the spacious shower, the tenderness of his movements conflicting with the demand in his voice. I step back, my legs feeling weak, shrugging off my coat and then bringing my hands to the hem of my dress. Not breaking eye contact with Aiden, I pull my dress up and toss it onto the built-in bench of the shower with a slap. I rip off my boots and toss them out of the shower onto the tile floor. Left only in my bra and underwear, I revel in the way Aiden's eyes devour me, while he brings a hand to his chin to graze over his stubble.

"Fuck, Bec. I knew you were beautiful, but…wow. Your body is perfect." His arm wraps around my back. He quickly finds the clasp of my bra and releases it, tossing it away to join my dress.

"I'm far from perfect," I say shyly, a bit of insecurity bleeding through at the worst fucking time.

He steps against me, fully dressed, clothes soaked. His shirt is practically see-through, sticking to every inch of his defined abdomen. He lowers himself to one knee and looks up into my eyes as he uses both hands to grip and massage my breasts, teasing me and kneading them before closing his mouth around my nipple. His hands begin to trail down my stomach before he pulls down my underwear. I watch as he places one hand to my center, where he lightly teases my clit, running his fingers along my slit. "I don't want to hear you talk that way about yourself. Like I said…you're fucking perfect."

"Oh fuck." I let out a moan when he continues to tease me, rubbing small, light-pressured circles against my clit. I lean back on the cold tile of the shower wall, tilting my head up toward the ceiling, my eyes closing involuntarily. My entire body lights up under his touch. I glance down to watch him slowly push a finger inside of me, filling me not nearly the way I need. I'm ravenous for him. I can't help but grind against his palm, seeking out more friction, more pressure, which he graciously gives by pressing another finger inside, pumping slowly. Encouraged by my unmistakable agreement, becoming louder every second, his movements intensify.

"Look at you, beautiful. You're riding my fingers like a goddess. Fucking soaking my hand."

Aiden lifts my left leg, hooking my knee over his shoulder, and he lowers his mouth to my center, licking my clit, and I scream out. My hands shoot down to grip him roughly by his wet hair. He devours me, and I give as good as I get, shamelessly grinding myself into his starved mouth, the scratch of his stubble on my inner thighs only heightening the sensation. The warm water from the shower now envelops us in steam and I lose all sense of self, surrendering to the feel of his warm tongue exploring me and his fingers fucking me, making me writhe against him, unable to hold back my moans.

The pressure builds quickly, consuming me. Aiden's other hand digs into my ass, telling me he's not stopping until I give him what he's after, leaving me teetering on the edge. "Aiden, I…I'm gonna…" My mouth drops open and I gasp as I come harder than I ever have in my life. It's impossible to keep his name from my lips. I call it out between moans and expletives, the words almost drowning beneath the hum of the water raining down beside us. He continues licking me, his fingers keeping pace, allowing me to ride out my orgasm until my knees are weak and I'm left staring up at the ceiling.

"Holy fucking shit…" I pant. I look down to see Aiden pull away from me, licking his lips and smirking up at me. If it's even possible, I feel another rush of wetness pool between my thighs at the sight of him like this.

I grip him by the collar of his soaked shirt and pull him to his feet, hastily tearing it off and tossing it to join the growing pile of discarded clothes. His dark eyes are focused on me, his expression unmoving. I tug on his belt, releasing the clasp. Unable to wait any longer, I reach down to palm him through his pants, finding him hard as steel. His breath catches at the contact, and his jaw clenches as his eyes close.

Driven by the need to taste him, I hurry to unbutton and unzip his pants, shoving them to the ground, leaving him in only his black boxer briefs. I stare at him, needing a second to take him in. His body is lean and strong from what I assume is rigorous training. His arms, chest, stomach, and thighs are corded with toned muscle. "Like what you see?" Aiden lets out a small laugh while dropping his briefs to the ground. He steps out of his clothes and kicks them aside. I'm sure I'd laugh at myself too. I'm pretty sure my jaw is hanging open.

"I've never seen a body like yours. You're unreal," I say. "Yeah, I really like what I see, Aiden." I trail my hands along the ridges of his lower abdomen and set my eyes on his as I drop slowly to my knees. "But I want a closer look..."

I watch his chest rise and fall quickly as I lower one hand to the base of his thick shaft. I lightly draw my fingers up and down his impressive length, swiping my thumb underneath the tip, feeling a bead of precum smooth over the head, causing his abs to flex. When I return to his base, I grip him more firmly, looking up to watch him as I wrap my lips around the head of his cock and start to lick and suck, taking more of him into my mouth with each pass. Groaning, one of his hands finds its way to the back of my head, wrapping a section of my wet hair around his fist. Not pushing me but guiding me.

His size makes it difficult, but I close my eyes and work to fit as much of him in my mouth as I can until I feel him hit the back of my throat. I work the rest of him with my hand.

"Shit, Bec. Your fucking mouth..." I look up to find Aiden's heady gaze set on me before shutting my eyes again. "Look at me." I flick my eyes back up to him, not stopping my movements. "So incredible. But fuck, if you don't stop now, this will be over before either of us wants it to be."

Encouraged by his praise, and how fucking powerful and turned on I feel bringing a man like Aiden to his knees for me, I work even harder to fit his length as far as I can, and then I swallow with him at the back of my throat, pushing him closer to the edge. I lower my hand to his balls, running my finger between them. I look up to find his eyes closed and his other hand pressed into the tiled wall behind me in a fist. He groans as he pulls away, releasing himself from my mouth and leaving me breathless. He tips my chin up with his fingers running his thumb over my bottom lip.

"Stand up, beautiful. We're nowhere near finished," he murmurs, turning off the water.

He takes my hand and pulls me to stand. Aiden grabs a towel that's hanging outside the glass shower, wrapping it around me and allowing me a minute to pat myself dry and quickly wring my hair to avoid it dripping all over. He quickly runs the towel over himself as well, hardly taking his eyes off me. When we finish, Aiden tosses the towel aside and wraps his strong, calloused hand around my lower back, pulling me into his solid body. He lowers his forehead to mine and runs his other hand over the back of my head to my neck.

"Tell me I can have you, Bec."

"Fuck me, Aiden," I whisper. I run my fingers through his hair as he smothers me in another passionate kiss. He breaks away suddenly, leading me by our joined hands out of the shower and into his adjoining bedroom.

Having been caught up in his kiss on the way in, I'm just now seeing his room for the first time, though it takes my eyes a minute to adjust. Despite the fact that the lights are off, the room is aglow from the downtown lights filtering through the windows.

Across from where we exit the bathroom, there's a king-size bed with a luxurious black duvet and a stack of pillows across the wrought iron headboard. On one side of the room is another wall of floor-to-ceiling windows. The high ceilings accentuate and magnify the glimmer from the gorgeous skyline, twinkling and winking at us. The night sky is full of pillowing dark gray clouds. The storm continues to rage on, droplets of water running down the windows, blurring the lights below.

The furnishings are minimal but elegant, a dresser topped with a mirror, a small, cushioned ottoman at the foot of the bed, and a plush rug to pull it all together. The corner of the room also has an oversized chair draped in a blanket and a few more pillows. The entire ambience is dark and warm, soft and comfortable. The style feels modern but cozy.

Without a conscious thought to do so, I walk closer to the view, drawn to the beautiful sight below me, and raise my hand to gloss over the cold glass.

Aiden approaches behind me, giving me goose bumps, awareness flowing through my limbs at his proximity. His hand presses mine against the glass, and I'm caught between the scorching heat radiating off his skin and the chill from the window. I feel his breath along my neck, a rush of adrenaline throughout my body, and a tightening in the base of my stomach.

"You're stunning, Bec. Every time I look at you, I find it hard to breathe. I want to give you everything. I want you to have it all."

I reach my free hand behind me to wrap around the back of his neck, the front of his body is pressed against my back, and I turn my face to the side so I can see him. His confession causes desire to strike me low in my belly.

I offer a confession of my own in reply. "I want everything you have to give. Don't hold back." I lean my head back against his strong shoulder and arch my back, pressing my bare ass back into his pelvis, grinding into him firmly.

Aiden lets out a deep groan at the movement, wrapping his free hand around my hip, pulling me back against him harder, his stiff cock resting between my thighs, along my slit. My hips instinctively start to grind back and forth along his length. I can feel my wetness coating his shaft, easing the movements.

"Fuck, Bec, you're dripping. Is this soaked pussy all for me?" His fingers grip my hip harder, driving me to quicken my pace, rotating my hips so my clit hits the head of his cock with each pulse. His filthy words escalate my arousal.

"God yes, it's all for you. Please."

Aiden immediately responds to my plea, pulling away briefly only to turn me around, lift me into his arms, and take several powerful steps away from the window to toss me across his plush bed. My body bounces on impact, and before I have a moment to adjust from the fall, Aiden crawls toward me and covers my body with his, lining up with my center. My knees fall open for him, my body welcoming him to where I've wanted him for so long.

Our lips meet in a starving kiss, surrendering to what we both want. We're a tangled mess of greedy limbs, hands, and tongues. Aiden pulls away quickly, and I go to protest before I realize he's stepping away to grab a condom from his nightstand. He sheaths himself and my mouth waters at the sight of his body.

He returns to bed to lie on top of me and mutters in a gravelly voice, "Eyes on mine, gorgeous. I want to watch you fucking fall apart. I need to see it, and I need to hear you."

I look into Aiden's eyes and gasp as he slowly enters me, stretching me perfectly. He steadily pulses in and out, driving deeper and deeper until he's filling me completely. My moans echo around the high ceilings of his bedroom, and I hear Aiden mutter out an expletive. When he bottoms out, he continues his rhythmic movements while I cling to him. My arms rove over his body, his waist, his back, his chest, his shoulders. I can feel his taut muscles flexing as he works me to the edge again. With each thrust, he rotates his hips, giving my clit the friction it needs. My hips buck up to meet his, matching his movements with equal intensity. I climb higher, and I lose control of my muscles as they twitch and flex, my body frantically seeking release.

Aiden leans on one forearm next to my head as he runs his other calloused hand from my ass, down my thigh, to the back of my knee where he pulls to lift my bent leg higher, pressing it back into my body. The shift allows him to drive even deeper, never relenting the grinding pressure on my clit. "Aiden, right there...just like that...fuck, you're so deep," I cry out.

"Shit," he says with a hiss. "You're so goddamn tight. I want you coming all over my fucking cock." He groans as he relentlessly pounds into me.

"Fuck," I moan. My jaw drops open on a silent scream as my orgasm rips through my stiffening body, every nerve lighting up and tightening before I melt into the mattress. I weakly hold onto Aiden's shoulders as he thrusts into me several more times before he stills, groaning his own release before he collapses, his head falling into the crook of my neck. He holds me close as our breathing calms.

When he pulls back to look at me, he smiles at me so genuinely, so carefree, and chuckles. I can't help but smile and giggle in return.

"Jesus...absolutely everything about you was worth the wait," he murmurs as he lowers his forehead to mine, closing his eyes and breathing deeply. His words break something open inside my heart, leaving room for me to hope, to wish, and to dream. For once, the feelings don't terrify me. Instead, I feel my smile grow.

# Chapter Thirty-Three

Aiden

"So, the answer is no, huh?" I ask.

"Hm, the answer to what?" Bec mumbles, sounding exhausted. I should be tired, too, after everything we've done tonight, but my entire body feels alive, electricity running rampant under my skin from her touch. I could get used to her in my bed, tucked into my side, with her leg wrapped over my thigh while I absentmindedly skim my fingers over the freckles dotting her shoulder.

"You don't have any tattoos after all. All these years I imagined what kind of tattoo you had, assuming, with false confidence, you did in fact have one and wouldn't confess when we met. I believe you said it was 'too personal.'" I give her air quotes, then shrug. "I guessed wrong." Bec giggles and tucks her head into my shoulder, her arm wrapped around my waist, squeezing tightly, making my chest constrict with unexpected emotion at her closeness.

"You weren't wrong. I do have a tattoo. Just a small one." She rests her chin on my chest, her smile easy and content. Something clenches in my chest with how fucking right it feels.

"Bullshit, I would have seen it by now. Where?" I lean back to scan her perfect body, but she pulls away, giggling and covers herself with the sheet, tugging it close to her chest, hiding her perfect tits from me.

"Hold on, I want to know what you imagined. Let's hear it, Price."

I shift, getting comfortable, lifting one hand to place it back behind my head, considering her demand.

"Well, I'm embarrassed to admit I probably couldn't remember all my ideas if I tried. I've given it a lot of thought."

"Oh, *really*? I'm intrigued. Go on." She turns to her stomach, folding her arms beneath her cheek, peering over at me.

As stupid as it sounds, I know I'll tell Bec anything she wants to know. Finding the words to open up has never come this easily to me, but I want her to keep looking at me like this. I want her to share her unfiltered thoughts with me too. I want her to be comfortable around me. I want her to want to be here with me because it makes her happy. It's scaring the shit out of me, but I'm not walking away from this. Not when I finally feel like she might say yes to me this time. She might give us a real shot.

"Well, at first, I pictured you with some kind of flower along your hip. But I know that's not the case after tonight's *thorough* inspection. Then I thought maybe it'd be a quote along your ribs. Or maybe a significant date or some type of constellation. You were talking an awful lot about the universe when we met. Figured you'd love to have a piece of the stars on your skin."

"Wrong. All wrong. Though admittedly your sense of creativity has me insecure about the ingenuity of my tattoo." She buries her head in the pillow before turning her head to peek at me with one eye, her hair a wild mane around her.

God, she's a knockout. I think I like her best like this. Mussed up, carefree, and naked in my bed.

"Then it's my jersey number, *obviously*. Gotta say, Bec. I'm flattered."

"You wish."

"I kinda do. That'd be fuckin hot." She rolls farther away from me and lets out a loud laugh. I let out a chuckle too. "Let me see, Bec. What is it?"

She pauses at my lowered voice, frozen for a moment or two before she gives her head a small shake, spurring her into action.

"Okay, but if you make fun of me, I'm leaving." She sits up, wrapping the white sheet around her body. She pulls her knees to her chest and then shifts to stretch her legs across my thighs, leaning her side against the pillows and looking at me with a sad smile. She wiggles her foot. "Dog prints...up my right ankle. I love all dogs, obviously, but my girl Lucy was special. I got these paw prints about a year after I adopted her. I was a wreck when I lost her. The grief consumed me more than I could've imagined."

I haven't seen Bec quite like this before. She's usually cheerful and upbeat. I can see how much this loss still hurts her in her posture, the way she's curling into the pillows, caving in on herself. This is one of those losses that chips off a piece of your heart. A piece you give away willingly, knowing you'll never get it back. A love that you give to someone knowing they're forever a part of you.

I wrap my hands around her ankles, softly coasting my thumb over where the delicate paw prints wrap around her ankle bone. "It's perfect. Way better than anything I could have dreamed up. Tell me about her."

She smiles softly to herself, her eyes on her hands while she fidgets with the edge of the sheet, lost in thought and memories. "I met her at the shelter I volunteer at. She was older, terrified, and seemed so fragile. In really bad shape after years of neglect. I hate to think about what she survived before she was rescued. I didn't expect to get as many years with her as I did, so I'm really grateful for the time we had together. She had no training of course. I was still working on my certifications." She shrugs, and her smile grows. "I guess she was my first real student, which was lucky for me because she was the most well-behaved dog all on her own. Wasn't too much for me to handle while I was still learning. It took her time to trust me, but when she did, it...it was incredible. She was so gentle, always looking to be pet and doted on. Over time, her energy increased along with her faith in people. She finally showed her playful side. You'd think a dog who had been through a life like she had wouldn't give anyone else a chance, but she just...transformed into this ray of light. She showed me what we can become, no matter what we've been through, when we're given unconditional love. People talk about their soul dog, and Lucy was mine. She understood me intuitively."

"She sounds like a really great dog. I'm glad you found each other." I reach out to grab her hand from her lap, giving a gentle squeeze.

Bec pulls her legs back, dropping her knees to one side and tucking her feet to the other, her free hand gently gliding over the two small paw prints behind her ankle bone. "I miss her. I wasn't kidding when I said I was grateful to dog sit Hopper. It was amazing to have a dog living with me again, even temporarily."

"He was really depressed coming home with me after a weekend with you. I'm pretty sure you're his favorite person in the world."

"Well, it helps that I walk around with treats attached to my hip every time he sees me; he is *unbelievably* food motivated."

"Maybe Hop is my soul dog because I find myself drooling over your hips too."

"Ew, Aiden." She shoves my shoulder playfully and lets out a loud laugh. "I don't know if that was a compliment or just gross."

"Yeah, that one felt weird. I can't seem to filter any of my weirdness when I'm around you."

"Weird-ass compliments aside, I feel the same way. But now it's your turn. Where's your tattoo?"

"I'm not as badass as you, Bec. No ink on me."

"No ink *yet*. Now that's an idea in case I ever win a bet against you or something." She winks at me, and I make a mental note not to ever bet against her because she looks downright devious right now.

"Remind me not to get on your bad side." She giggles and lies back down, her head on my shoulder, body curling up against my side.

We settle into a comfortable silence, but my mind is racing. I have to go for it.

"Bec, can I ask you something?" Sensing my more serious tone, she looks up, propping herself up on one elbow at me, and nods.

"I know you didn't want to pursue anything between us when we met, and I understand why you felt that way. We lived in different cities, and that would have been really difficult. But I gotta be honest, I would have done it for you. I don't want you to feel pressured into anything, but does my living here change anything for you? Because... fuck, Bec, I really want to see where this goes. I want to see where we could go. Everything about tonight felt right. The time I've spent with you since I've moved back, it's meant everything to me."

She looks at me, her eyes piercing straight through me, leaving me feeling all sorts of vulnerable. Bec sighs deeply and I feel myself brace for the embarrassment and disappointment of her rejection...again.

"I wasn't ready for you when we met. I know I mentioned the distance at the time and the weirdness we'd be risking with our friends if things didn't work out, and yeah, that was all a big part of it. Aiden, you scared the shit out of me. At first, our connection felt like a strike of lightning. Intense and spectacular, but dangerous and fleeting. When you showed up at the rehearsal, my gut told me to run. That nothing serious could ever work between us. We live in two different worlds, your career and mine. And with our friends getting married, it just felt so messy. But even as my mind tried to write you off, every other part of me wanted to see where a weekend together with you would lead. I don't want to confuse you, but I normally don't have a lot of optimism when it comes to relationships. The last relationship I was in...it did a number on my self-esteem and my ability to trust people. I'm still working on it. I want to give us a shot, but just know that it'll take me time to let you in. But...yeah, I want to see where this goes too."

I can feel my heart pounding. I snatch Bec into my arms and roll on top of her, pressing her into my bed and kissing her with everything I have, wishing I could erase every memory of her ex with my touch alone. I don't care how long it takes to tear down these walls she's built to protect her heart. I'll wait as long as it takes for them to fall.

I feel her smile against my lips as she wraps her arms around my neck and her legs around my waist, lining our bodies up just right. I feel her roll her hips up into mine and she lets out a soft moan. I can feel her slick against me and my cock throbs, hardening from the feel of her skin on mine, her movements, and her words. I pull back to look at her, lips swollen from kissing and her chest heaving with her quick breathing. "You fucking scared me, too, Bec. You still do. But only because I don't know how to walk away from you. You're a force of gravity that I couldn't fight if I wanted to. Turns out I don't want to anyway. I couldn't stop thinking about you no matter how little time we had spent together. I've never felt like that about someone. I'll give you all the time in the world to build your trust, with me, with us. You're worth it."

Bec pulls me back down to her lips and kisses me once, soft and unhurried. She pulls away slightly, beaming up at me, her lips still brushing against my own when she speaks. "I couldn't stop thinking about you either." She rolls her hips back into me again and I groan. She's hot, wet, and ready for me.

I grab her hand, interlacing our fingers and pinning it to the soft pillows above her head as I grind against her, rubbing my cock along her slit. Her eyes drift close as she gasps at the movement. "I want you to watch while I show you all the ways we could belong to each other. This was inevitable from the moment I met you. I knew we'd be perfect together."

I lower my head to her chest and suck her nipple into my mouth, grazing it gently with my teeth and flicking with my tongue. She moans and, despite my request, closes her eyes and arches her neck and back until she's tilting her chest farther into my mouth. I take what she gives me and lavish my attention on her breasts, licking, sucking, and pinching her nipples until she calls out my name.

"Oh god, Aiden, please. I need more."

"I want to take my time with you."

"No, I can't wait. I need you to fuck me." She reaches down and grabs me, pumping me with her hand while she kisses me deeply, her body writhing beneath me. Any plans I had for what's next immediately disappear and I thrust forward into her grip, groaning at the friction.

I sit back, resting on my heels, and Bec lets out a small whine of protest. Before she can pull me back, I tuck my palm under her sweet ass and flip her over onto her stomach before grabbing her hips and tugging them up into the air.

She gasps as I slowly slide one of my palms up her spine, applying light pressure to her upper back until her elbows hit the mattress, giving me the best view I can imagine. Her plump hips swell below the dimples of her lower back, and I bite back a groan as she stretches her arms out to grab the bottom of the headboard rails, arching her back to press her ass into my dick.

"You want it like this, Bec?" I reach around her side to play with her nipple while I teasingly rub my cock against her. She moans something that sounds like agreement.

"Use your words, gorgeous. I need to hear you."

"Yes, fuck, yes, Aiden. Please."

"Love to hear you begging. Don't move, and I'll take care of you." I step back to pull another condom from my nightstand, toss it on the bed next to her, and climb behind Bec. I can hear her quick breaths and see the rise and fall of her back while she waits for me in the same position I left her in.

"Good girl." I rub my fingers along her entrance, sliding one all the way in, causing her to moan long and loud. She's wet, but I want her drenched before I take her again. I pull my hand back and lie down on my back, my knees bent over the end of my bed, feet on the floor. I push into my heels, driving my face up exactly where I want it, between Bec's thighs, while she's still holding onto the headboard, chest pressed to the mattress.

"What are you doing?" she pants. I reach up to grab her ass cheeks, pulling her down slowly before I taste her perfect pussy.

"Holy shit," Bec yells out. I hold nothing back as I flatten my tongue, making long strokes up to her clit where I then make slow circles. I set a rhythm and keep pace. Bec's hips twitch and she begins to grind on me, straddling my face. I love the feel of her losing control over me, taking her pleasure. I grip her ass harder, pulling her to my mouth, waiting to hear her let go completely, her moans telling me she's close. I push one, then two fingers into her, pulling toward her front wall. I don't have to wait long before she's frantically gyrating and calling out my name, every muscle in her body tensing.

When I feel her relax, I take one more taste before lightly slapping her ass cheek. She giggles and rolls to her side, panting.

"Um, we're going to have to do that again," she says, giggling.

"I plan on it." I crawl up the bed to lie next to her, pulling her into my side to lie together.

But Bec doesn't stay still for long before she sits up to grab the condom. She reaches over and grabs my dick, rolling the condom down to the base.

*Fuck, why is that hot?*

Before I can think about it too closely, Bec straddles me, pushing me down with her hands on my chest. The view is...well, the view is beyond fucking perfect as she leans forward and her elbows squeeze her tits together. I reach up and tease her nipples.

"Some other time. Right now, I need you inside me." In one swift movement, she drops herself onto my cock, and I groan at the perfect pressure of her walls around me.

"Ride me, Bec. I want to see you fucking lose it." I thrust my hips up, driving into her from below to encourage her to move. I'm barely hanging on in anticipation. Her hips grind down while her clit slides over the connection point between our bodies. I trail my hands down past her waist to where her hips meet her ass, and I grip her tight, fingers digging into her soft skin following the rhythm of her movements.

When I look down, the sight of her lifting, dropping, and rocking against me almost has me finishing. "Look at you, claiming every fucking inch like you were meant for me." Her half-lidded eyes find mine and her mouth falls open with a seductive moan as she picks up her pace, chasing her climax.

I sit up, threading my fingers into her hair at the base of her neck and gripping tightly, wrapping my other arm around her side to rest my palm between her shoulders, pressing her chest against mine. Bec doesn't miss a beat with the change in position; she continues to pulse above me and weaves her hands into my hair, tugging without restraint. Our lips graze each other as we work our bodies into a frenzy. I'm lost in the feel of her fingernails digging in and scratching at my skin and the sound of her moaning my name. I feel the familiar tightening begin in my legs, drawing up to my balls.

# CHAPTER THIRTY-THREE

"Fuck, babe, I'm close," I say.

"God, me too. Fuck, I...I'm right there...don't stop." And then I feel her tighten around me. I watch as her mouth drops open, her eyes on me, my name falling from her lips as she tips over the edge again. The sight is so fucking perfect, she pulls me right over the edge with her as she steals my lips in another kiss.

I knew from the moment I met Bec that everything felt different with her. Natural. Instinctual. Chemical. Having her in my arms, smiling at me as we both come down from our collective high, her forehead resting gently against my own, only solidifies the way I feel. I'll do anything to see that smile. I'll do anything to protect this connection between us. Anything to protect her heart so she knows she's safe to share it with me.

My body wants her more than I thought possible, but the shit she's doing to the rest of me? My goddamn soul? She's going to wreck me. All I can think is, I really hope she does. I want her to ruin me for all other women. There won't be a piece of me left that doesn't exist for her. She's it.

* * *

When I wake up, I smile to myself as I take in the view beside me. Bec and I let Hop out of his crate that I keep in my office and into the bedroom after we finished doing things I couldn't in good conscience let him watch. He happily joined us acting like it was no big deal that Bec was here, like she belongs here. *I feel the same, bud.* Hop jumped onto the bed, immediately curling up in a tight ball. Bec wrapped herself around him, and I wrapped myself around her before drifting into a peaceful sleep.

However, after sharing the bed with both of them, I know Bec wasn't lying to me. She's just as bad of a blanket hog as Hop. Looking at them now from the edge of the bed that I've been forced almost off of, Hop is asleep on his back, paws up. He's lying sideways on the bed, practically taking up the space of a full-grown adult. Bec is next to him, laid out like a starfish and completely tangled up in my blankets. I gave her a T-shirt to wear to bed. My shirt swallows her torso, with the exception of her full hips where it sits more snugly, and when she adjusts in her sleep, shifting her leg over the edge of the comforter to lie on her side, it exposes the full length of her leg, tempting me to reach out and run my greedy hands up her thigh again. Seeing her perfect ass hanging out of my underwear she's wearing, my shirt riding up along her waist...the sight has my mouth watering, hungry for another taste.

Instead, I take in the sight of her for a moment more and then quietly make my way to the kitchen to start breakfast. My steps are lighter than they were yesterday, and I know if I don't want to scare Bec, I need to ignore how good this feels for now. It's too soon to come on this strong. I know she's guarding her heart for good reason. I just need to give her a better reason to let me in.

# Chapter Thirty-Four

## Bec

**E**llie: Anyone hear from Bec yet? Dom has spent the entire morning harassing me about how her date with Aiden went. He's gossiping like a preteen. I'm going to chuck my bagel at him if he wakes Luca before I finish my coffee.

**Carissa:** Last I heard, Aiden took her back to the hotel bar where they met before your wedding.

**Dee:** Romance at that level is BJ worthy in my book. It's basic math.

**Carissa:** Kind of a fucked-up math problem if you ask me.

**Ellie:** Dom can't control the volume of his voice. He's whisper-shouting with excitement. Emphasis on shouting.

**Ellie:** Give me something. Anything. Please, I beg you.

**Abby:** Bet that's real close to what Bec was saying to Aiden last night.

**Dee:** Abby, you're my new favorite. Don't ever change.

**Ellie:** His excitement is devolving into panic. My marriage is at stake here.

**Bec:** Tell Dom he needs to get a hobby.

**Abby:** Proof of life received. But that's not what we asked for...we need DETAILS. What happened? Did you get to see his baseballs?

**Dee:** She *strikes* again.

**Ellie:** You know Dom already has a hobby. There are four unfinished puzzles lying around my house. He's working on one right now and it hasn't helped. Answer the question, Miller.

**Bec:** No comment. I plead the fifth. Please direct all media inquiries to my agent. (picture attached)

**Carissa:** Bec...is that Hopper?

**Dee:** Holy shit, are you at his place? Are you playing with his baseballs right now? How big is his bat?!

**Bec:** I hate that I'm even playing into this, but ladies...home fucking run.

**Dee:** THAT'S MY GIRL!

**Abby:** Uh...we're going to need a lot more information.

**Ellie:** I can't even explain the shriek Dom just let out. Dom wants to host the next book club at our house. Fair warning—he's going to eavesdrop when we talk about your date. He said he promises he won't tell Aiden anything.

**Carissa:** I'm so happy for you, Bec. Aiden seems like a really nice guy.

**Dee:** I repeat—how big is his bat?? Bec?!

* * *

"Uh-oh, I've seen that look before. No good comes from a look like that. You causing trouble in here?" Aiden is leaning on the door frame of his bedroom, his arms crossed against his chest, watching me with a smirk on his face.

I smile and raise my hands up in surrender, dropping my phone in my lap onto Aiden's soft comforter. Comfy as fuck bedding. Green flag.

"Busted. The girls are begging for an update on our date. I'd like to say you're off the hook and I'll handle it, but apparently Dom is nosey as fuck, too, so you should prepare yourself for that."

Aiden walks over casually, palming the back of my head and pressing a soft kiss to my forehead before sitting on the edge of his bed, facing me. The simple act sends my heart tumbling, but I ignore it, trying to appear unrattled. "I should have known this was coming," he says. "Dom wouldn't stop texting me before we met up last night. He keeps sending me dating *tips*, which are embarrassing enough it's made me question Ellie's judgment for giving him a second date at all, let alone marrying the guy."

"Trust me, I've heard *all* about their first date. I make Ellie retell the story all the time. Dom always takes over because he is so damn proud of his *moves*, he can't help but try to defend them. It never gets old. But I have to admit, it was a good call to completely ignore his suggestions."

"Does that mean I did okay without them? Do I get to hear your review of our date or is that only for the girls, and Dom, to know and for me to guess?"

"I'm waking up in your clothes, in your bed, with an obnoxious smile on my face. Obviously, it was terrible. Swing and a miss, big guy. I thought you played baseball or something."

"Yep," he says, attempting to hide his smirk and nodding his head. "I had a feeling you were trouble. And now, I find out you're a liar too. I see you, Miller." His hand finds mine and he lightly runs his calloused fingers over the pulse point at my wrist while he stares at the point of contact. "What are your plans for today?"

"I've just got a few things to catch up on for work. A couple errands."

His eyes light up and I'm stuck staring, unable to look away. That inexplicable pull I feel toward him grows stronger every moment we're together. My insides twist, my heart warring with my head— one telling me to slow down, the other telling me to let go, give in, and enjoy whatever this is between us.

"What if I proposed a...first date extension?" Aiden asks.

"Hm...what would that look like?"

"Well, there's breakfast and coffee in the kitchen." He lifts my wrist to his lips and presses a soft kiss there.

"Can't say no to free breakfast from a man in boxer briefs."

"You missed the cooking show, I'm afraid, but you're invited anytime." He continues kissing up my forearm and up to my shoulder, speaking into the crook of my neck. "And after breakfast, I can take you home so you can get what you need from your place for today and tonight."

"Tonight too? A little greedy, don't you think?" I ask, a bit breathless from the way his mouth feels against my skin.

Sitting back to look at me, Aiden asks, "What if I wasn't ready to let you go just yet?"

"What happened to one date at a time?"

"This can be a first date extension or a second date, you decide. Either way, I want you in my bed tonight...if that's what you want. Nothing has to happen, I just...I leave for Spring Training soon. I'm being selfish. I want more time with you before my schedule gets crazy. I'll need a few more memories to distract me when I should be focused on my job," he jokes as he smiles at me. He pauses and lifts his hand to palm my cheek, brushing his thumb over my bottom lip. "I've worn out all the memories I had with you while I was waiting for this second chance." For as confident as he seems, there's an undercurrent of vulnerability too. It's a relief to hear my own uncertainty reflected back to me, to know we're both swimming in unknown waters makes it a little less daunting. I like being on equal footing, and I like that he's asking for what he wants instead of leaving me guessing.

"Last night probably gave you some new material to work with," I say, and we both laugh.

"Yeah, you bet your fine ass every detail is permanently etched in my mind. Let me help you today with work. Give Hop and me a job."

"Well, I've never had an assistant."

With a wink he says, "Look at that, I'll be the best you've ever had."

*He is. No contest.*

"You're ridiculous, you know that? You don't mind tagging along? I have to run to the store and then get a few things prepped at home. It's nothing exciting. You probably have way better things to do with your day."

"Bec, trust me when I say I can't think of a better way to spend my time. I don't care what we do. Just try and bore me, baby. I don't think it's possible. But first things first, breakfast," Aiden says over my lips, stealing a soft kiss as he gently pushes my chest back onto the bed with the weight of his own body. He slowly drags his T-shirt up from my waistline toward my collarbone, exposing me to the cool air. He kisses his way down my stomach, causing my pulse to quicken and heat to trickle up my thighs.

"I thought you said breakfast was in the kitchen," I say in a breathless whisper.

"Your breakfast is, but mine is right here. And I'm fucking starving."

Okay, Aiden isn't just the best I've ever had. He's the best I'll ever have.

# Chapter Thirty-Five

Aiden

"You sure I can just...walk in with him?" I hesitate in the doorway of the hardware store with Hopper at my side as I scan the entrance, waiting to get reprimanded by a passing employee.

Bec strolls leisurely ahead of me, grabbing a large cart. "Yeah, most home improvement stores are dog friendly. Sometimes when dogs in training are having a lot of trouble with socialization, I meet them here with their families to practice leash walking and working through their anxiety. I don't think Hop needs any help there, but it's good practice all the same."

"Then lead the way, Miller. What are we looking for exactly?"

"So, most of the staff at the Center volunteer at New Hope, a local animal shelter. Our organizations have a strong relationship. We partner together often."

"The shelter you got Lucy from, right?"

The look on her face when she quickly turns to face me tells me I've surprised her, which honestly pisses me off, but I keep my expression neutral. She's shocked I remembered that detail she told me just last night. What low bar have the people she's dated been failing to meet that it surprises her that I'd remember something clearly important to her? I have questions, but I won't push her.

"Yeah, I met Lucy girl there. Of course, I have completely professional boundaries and no overly emotional attachments to their work," she jokes.

"Naturally," I flash her a grin as we round the corner of one of the aisles and weave into the next.

"Well, they're hosting one of their biggest events next month, their annual adoption fair and fundraiser. Every February, they rent out the convention center and bring in all of their ready-to-adopt pets to try to offset the influx of animals they take in after the holidays. People who realize too late that the pet they were gifted was too much responsibility for them to take on. New Hope secures a lot of local sponsors in order to organize everything, and the money raised supports the shelter's operations for several months out of the year. At the last meeting, I signed up to create the adoption board that'll be at the entrance. I need supplies to build the frame that I'll secure canvas fabric to, and then I'll attach slots for us to slide the photos into. Since animals can be adopted at any time, we need to be able to update the board quickly. It works better when we can shift things around leading up to and during the event. Last year, we didn't have a centralized place where all of the animals could be seen at a glance. This year the board will give them an idea of what pets are at the event and where to locate them in the convention center. It's one of several things we're updating this year to hopefully make us more efficient and help more animals find their families."

Selfless. This girl is fucking selfless. Her unmistakable passion for helping animals makes me admire her even more. As she explains everything to me, her expressions and gestures become more animated and she talks more quickly as we work our way through the store, gathering the supplies she needs, clearly excited about the project and all the nuanced details that have clearly been given a lot of thought to make this event as successful as possible.

"I gotta say, I'm impressed. The event sounds really cool. When is it?" I ask.

"Oh...no. You don't have to come if you don't want...I'm sure you're busy and you already have a dog and Spring Training is coming up and—"

"Bec..." I turn my body to face hers and place my hand over her abdomen to stop her from walking any farther. She pauses and looks to me as I step beside her. I gently turn her face toward mine with two fingers under her jaw. "I don't think you're hearing me, babe. This is important to you. Which means it's important to me. I *want* to be there, if I can. Don't doubt the truth in what I'm saying, please. Give me a chance to show you that I'm being genuine before you tell yourself that I'm just saying what you want to hear. I'm not that guy."

She stares at me for a moment, measuring the sincerity of my words before I see her sweet smile slowly blossom, the beauty of the moment hitting me in my chest.

"You're not what I expected at all, Aiden."

"That's what I was hoping to hear. I plan on exceeding all of your expectations. Get used to it."

"Valentine's Day. The adoption event is on Valentine's Day."

"It's a date," I say. Then I press my lips to hers because it feels too damn good.

# Chapter Thirty-Six

## Bec

The New Hope adoption event draws a bigger attendee turnout every year. It's desperately needed, since we can count on the number of animal surrenders after the holidays increasing too. Unfortunately, this year is no exception. Part of me understands, no one can fully control their circumstances in life, and if someone chooses to give a pet to a person who isn't prepared to take on the responsibility, it's not a good situation for anyone. Another part of me can't stand the thought of how confusing and traumatic the entire ordeal is for an animal.

The thought makes my heart ache. I feel my body overtaken with the intense need to move, to hurry, to act. A restlessness settles in my bones, and I know the only thing I can do is keep focused on the tasks I agreed to take on in preparation.

The remedy is never simple. The shelter is underfunded, under-staffed, and runs on the fumes of a handful of dedicated, but burned-out, employees and countless volunteers. It's never enough to keep up with the strays and surrendered pets that come through the doors looking for a new home.

I step out of the kennel after returning the puppy I was working with today to his bed. The vet's best guess is he's about six months old. You wouldn't know it by looking at him. His energy is not that of a carefree, fun-loving puppy. His tough beginning stripped him of that silly puppy stage and what's left is a cautious boy who will have a long journey ahead of him before he can trust a human. I've only worked with him for a few weeks, but I'm hoping his future family will bring him to the Center for classes after he's adopted. New Hope always provides our contact information to the families, especially for those who take home the animals that we work with while they're at the shelter.

"See you soon, little one. You get some good rest." I wait until he settles onto the cot, his eyes tracking my movements carefully, always alert, before stepping away.

I catch sight of Abby closing another kennel farther down the aisle.

"Hey, slugger," she says casually as she breezes past me to head toward the main office that's used as a sort of catchall room. We have event planning meetings there, lunch breaks, meetings with families, pretty much anything that requires a decent amount of space. Something New Hope is certainly short on. Every inch of this place is used to its fullest capacity to house animals and the things they need to thrive. This room is what's left as the hub for everything else it takes to keep the place running.

"'Slugger.' That's new," I say.

"You know, since you're hitting home runs now and everything."

"It feels like you and Dee are in a race to make as many baseball references as possible. Maybe you two need to meet Aiden's teammates since you're so into the sport."

"Say no more. Where do I sign up?" Abby asks with a wink. "Hey, are you done for the day? Wanna grab some coffee next door?"

"A million times, yes. I feel dead on my feet," I say.

Abby hesitates for a moment before continuing. "I didn't want to text you and ruin what I can only hope was a good date because you *still* haven't told me much of anything, but you should know, the Kellers pulled their sponsorship for New Hope."

"What? How could they do that? How could they do that *now?*" We have a month left to get ready for the adoption event and the shelter is already at capacity as is. The Keller family owns several massive businesses in Columbus, one of which Dee works for. They notably donate to many local organizations and charities across the city. Why would they pull their support for New Hope? They're our largest sponsor.

This is bad. This is really fucking bad.

We bundle up before walking next door, grabbing coffees, and sitting down in the cozy café as Abby fills me in on the details and the few plans New Hope has scrambled to put together to try to regain some financial footing.

Abby pulls out her laptop to show me a few places she's asking to make a donation, just a few from a list of many that the staff and volunteers are scraping through. Any support we manage to find will be like putting a Band-Aid on a broken leg. As a volunteer, I don't know all the details of New Hope's financial situation, but I have to imagine the Kellers' backing has been a critical reason the organization has kept its doors open.

"I'll reach out to my brother. His company is involved in the community and always donates to New Hope. I'll see if they can dig a little deeper into their pockets this year," I say. It won't be enough, but maybe if we find enough Band-Aids, that will at the very least buy us some time.

# Chapter Thirty-Seven

## Aiden

**A**iden: Are you home?

    **Bec:** I'm about to be, why?

    **Aiden:** I need your help. I have too much food and someone needs to help me eat it.

    **Bec:** Are you trying to spring an impromptu date on me, Price?

    **Aiden:** This isn't a date, this is survival. You need to eat and I do too. It's science.

    **Bec:** I would normally prefer to play hard to get...but I'm starving.

    **Aiden:** Good answer because I'm already here.

    **Bec:** Creep much?

    **Aiden:** You're late for our date. Let's go, Miller.

* * *

"I don't want you to take this the wrong way, because those baseball uniforms are really out there doing the most, but you waiting in front of my apartment with food in hand may be the sexiest you've ever looked," Bec says as she walks up to the entrance to her apartment building. I follow her inside and show her my most confident grin.

"I aim to please." I lean down to whisper in her ear as we step onto the elevator. "Does this mean you're googling me?" I can't help but tease her. She looks cute red with embarrassment.

"Ugh, forget I said anything. I have loose lips when I'm hangry. Let's get upstairs and eat before I stick my foot in my mouth again, please."

"If you keep talking about your lips and your mouth, we might not make it to dinner."

"Tempting, but not tempting enough to distract me from what's in your hands. I need a shit ton of calories to forget about this shit show of a day. Preferably 50 percent of that comes from chocolate. What's in the bag?" she asks while unlocking her door to let us into her apartment. She leads us into the kitchen, and I drop the bags onto the counter.

"Fettuccine alfredo and chocolate eclairs. Does that pass the Bec test?"

"God, you're perfect. Thank you for this," she says as she pulls out plates and utensils, placing them on the counter next to the food.

"Rough day?" I ask, unpacking the take-out containers.

"Yeah," she says with a sigh, running her fingers through her hair and then leaning her palms on the countertop. "New Hope just lost a huge sponsor, so we're scrambling a bit to find replacement funding. It's not just the event. The entire organization's operations will be impacted by this."

"Oh wow, I'm sorry. That's tough," I say, crossing my arms and leaning my hip against the kitchen island.

"The staff are optimistic, or at least they're acting that way. Maybe they're trying to manifest the money with positive affirmations and all that. Or they're too scared to admit the reality of the situation out loud. I don't know...we'll have to secure so many smaller donations to replace the one we lost. It's going to eat up a lot of resources and we're already running thin on coverage to manage the influx of animals. Sorry, I'm rambling." She inhales deeply then lets out a heavy breath, her shoulders dramatically falling with her exhale. "It'll be fine. We'll just keep pushing forward. We'll make it work." I can hear the undercurrent of anxiety in every word she's saying.

"How can I help?" I ask, leaning forward and tucking her hair behind her ear. She turns into my touch, closing her eyes for a few seconds before looking back at me.

"You're sweet, you know that? Keep surprising me with pasta and chocolate, that'll help more than you know."

That's not enough. Not even remotely enough. But I'll let it go for now.

"Not a big fan of cooking?" I ask with a laugh.

"Not unless you want your food burned to a crisp or dangerously undercooked. I'm afraid there is no happy medium with me. You've been warned."

"Noted. Takeout it is."

"You seem to know your way around the kitchen, enough to make breakfast at least."

"My mom loves to cook. Well, she used to. Evie has all of her old recipes. She always included us in some way. Some of my earliest memories are from cooking with her. My dad expected it, and I wanted to help her."

"You don't talk about him much," she says cautiously.

"Yeah, I guess I try not to."

I don't know why I even mentioned my father. As usual, being around Bec causes me to drop any filters I usually use to keep any memory of him buried away.

"I'm sorry. I don't mean to pry," she says, stepping back, giving me space.

"No, really, it's okay. Some people don't deserve to stay in your story. The healthiest thing to do sometimes is to walk away like my mom did. It wasn't easy, but she made it," I say with conviction, stepping toward Bec, removing the space she put between us.

"I wish she didn't have to go through that. I can't imagine how hard that was for her and for you too."

"She's the strongest person I know." The sudden swell of emotion tightens my whole chest. How can I go from teasing and joking around with Bec, to throwing my darkest memories onto the floor in front of her. Talking to her, sharing everything with her is too easy. "Their relationship was toxic. His behavior and their arguments were only escalating. She finally had enough and thankfully found the support she needed to get us away before things got worse. She knew what he was capable of and didn't want to stay to see it."

I feel her arms wrap around my waist before I hear her whisper against my chest, "Aiden, god, I'm so sorry. You were so young. I can't imagine what that was like for you. I'm glad the three of you got out of that situation."

I wrap my arms around her shoulders and rest my chin on her head, squeezing her back. Holding her against me, the relief is indescribable. She's a balm on the burns life's given me. "It's all right."

She pulls away to look up at me, but keeps her body close, holding onto me tightly. "No, it's not. You all didn't deserve to be put in that situation by someone that's supposed to love you. Someone that's supposed to be safe."

"We found our safety with each other. In our new lives without him." I shake off the ache of vulnerability and turn back to the food. I don't want her to see too much. To see how much my past scares me. How it haunts me. How terrified I am of turning out anything like the man who was supposed to be my role model, but turned out to be angry, selfish, and unkind. The man who could let his family walk away with nothing from him but cruel words and bad memories. "I didn't mean to ruin the pasta with all my baggage."

"I'm glad you told me. I don't want you to ever feel like you have to share more than you want to, but I want you to know that I see you. The way you talk about your mom and your sister like they're the roots, the foundation holding you steady. It's really beautiful how the three of you made it through all that and came out stronger together as a family. Don't apologize for your story. Besides, there is nothing you could say to ruin pasta."

With a chuckle, my shoulders drop with relief at the shift in conversation. How does she make that so easy? She manages to take the heavy and make it lighter. It's still there—it'll always be there—but she makes it tolerable. I carry the food and plates while she grabs us drinks, and we settle on her couch, spreading the take-out containers across her coffee table.

"Um, Bec. I gotta ask...what's going on here?" I point back and forth across her window while she spoons food onto our plates.

"Oh, had you not noticed my plant graveyard?"

"I would say I'm shocked I missed it, but you know, Hopper running around with your vibrator like he was in an eight-hundred-meter relay was a little distracting."

"Not my fault you haven't taught your pup manners," she sings.

"As his dog trainer, I would strongly disagree with that," I say with a smirk.

"I've trained a lot of dogs, Aiden...believe me, that was a first. I'm not adding that lesson to the curriculum. Besides, you've been here twice. I can't believe you wouldn't notice."

"Yeah, well, I was distracted during that visit too."

"By what?"

"You. All I could think about was how badly I wanted to kiss you."

She tries to hold back her smile and fails beautifully.

"Listen, I was just trying to add some good energy into my apartment," she says. "I got jealous of all those plant moms online with their earthy vibes and green thumbs. I was told that I was safe to start with a cactus and succulents. I was promised those fuckers were all hard to kill."

"I hate to tell you this, but they are. They're built for neglect."

"Well, apparently I'm an inhospitable roommate to everyone but Hopper."

"You're telling me you can take care of numerous dogs at the Center and New Hope, but the plants in your window can't get an ice cube once a week?"

"I tried," she yells around a mouthful of pasta, pointing at the offending plant remains with her fork. "They ganged up on me. They were all on different schedules. I think I confused them and overwatered some and dehydrated the others."

"Okay...but why are they still there?"

"I'm holding out hope, man. I still put an ice cube in there when I think about it. If they're so hardy, then they can reinvent themselves, have their midmovie makeover, and show up better than ever. What a comeback, right?"

"That would be...something." I eye her skeptically, my voice dripping with sarcasm.

"You just wait. That one on the end there. He hasn't given up yet. I swear that branch is a little greener today."

"Sure, Bec, I'll keep my eye on him. So, what's the plan for the event now with the change in funding?"

She lets her head fall on a groan, before looking back at me. "It'll be a hectic few weeks while we scramble to find donations before the event. Abby and I are going to hit up a few local businesses and basically beg for their support. We'll try to piecemeal this until the staff find a long-term solution. My brother also agreed to increase his company's contributions. Every little bit will help."

"I'd like to chip in too. How much do you need?" I ask, before taking a bite of pasta.

She jerks back, seemingly shocked I would offer at all. "Aiden, no. I can't take your money while...while we're..."

"While we're what, Bec?" I ask, arching an eyebrow in her direction, daring her to admit what we're becoming...what we are to each other already.

"While we're...talking."

"Hmm...that's right...talking. *Conversations* with you are certainly my favorite."

"Aiden, be serious, I can't accept a donation from you—that'd be wrong. I'm not telling you about all this so you'll throw your money at me. Just...just let me work with New Hope. We'll figure this out."

"Why would that be wrong? It's okay to rely on other people sometimes, Bec. You think I'm playing professional ball because I did it all on my own? Fuck no, I had help from more people than I can count. It's more than okay to ask for help. And it's okay to accept an offer when it'll be useful for what we both know is a great cause. Let me help, Bec."

"I don't know. It feels weird. How about you just come to the event and get Hop a sibling? Help in that way."

"As much as I would love that, Hopper needs my full attention right now, especially with my schedule picking back up soon. But I'll be there for whatever else you need."

I didn't expect Bec to draw a line between her professional life and me. There's no reason I wouldn't want to lend a hand to a cause as great as this when I have plenty to give. But a small part of me does feel relieved to know she isn't eager to dive into my wallet. Not that I ever thought she would be—I know Bec isn't that type of person—but after a few dates gone wrong, it's something I steer clear of when it becomes obvious.

"Having you there in a show of support will be more than enough. I...I really appreciate you being such a great listener."

Bec gives me an idea—unintentionally, I'm sure. She doesn't know it yet, but there's nothing I wouldn't do to support her. This is just our beginning.

# Chapter Thirty-Eight

Bec

The morning of the adoption event, the drone of my apartment buzzer startles me, even though I'm already awake. I've been staring at the ceiling of my bedroom, unable to fall back asleep after a fitful night, racked with nerves. I drag myself to the intercom.

Who would buzz me this early? It's seven in the morning.

"Hello?" I call out, voice still groggy.

"Good morning, sunshine. Caffeine delivery to the hottest dog trainer in town."

His voice has me straightening up immediately. "Aiden? What are you doing here?"

He chuckles on the other end of the speaker, and I can practically hear his smirk as he replies slowly, enunciating every syllable, "I repeat. Caffeine delivery. Can Hop and I come up?"

"Uh, yeah, sure. Just give me just a second." I hit the buzzer to open the entrance door and begin to run around in a flurry, trying to find some pants. I settle for a pair of pajama shorts and don't have time to replace my holey, ancient T-shirt before he's knocking at my door. Dammit, why don't I sleep in cuter clothes? I haven't had to worry about this since Josh.

I open the door to find Hopper sitting at Aiden's side, but his paws start to dance with excitement while he tries to restrain himself from leaping on me. Aiden is dressed in joggers, a sweatshirt, and a simple jacket. He shouldn't look that yummy in lazy clothes while I look like something that crawled out from underneath the bed on Halloween.

"Hey, gorgeous," he says. Aiden cues Hop to follow while he walks through the doorway, pressing a light kiss to my forehead as he passes me by. A familiar flutter starts in my stomach at the simple, sweet gesture. The enticing aroma of coffee pulls me into the kitchen, and I join Aiden while he unpacks a drink carrier. "This is for you. They added sugar, but I thought you could use extra...get over here."

He reaches out, wrapping his hand around mine and hauling me into his firm chest. His fingers find their way from my jaw to the back of my neck as he leans down, kissing me with unsatiated hunger. I kiss him back with enthusiasm and use my hands to pull him closer to me by the front of his sweatshirt. A small moan escapes me as he pulls away, both of us breathing each other in.

When I open my eyes, his are still closed. He leans farther into our embrace, tucking my head against his chest. We stay there, in no hurry to separate, and he holds me tightly in his arms. I love a steamy kiss, but you can tell a lot by the way a person hugs too. The feeling of Aiden around me is comforting and exhilarating all at once. His hold on me tightens briefly for a moment before he pulls back.

"I missed you," he says.

"It's only been a few days since I've seen you."

"I've become addicted. A few days feels like a lifetime." He reaches around me to grab my coffee and hand it to me. "Big day today. You ready?"

I sigh and take a sip. "You couldn't have picked a better day to save me with coffee. I couldn't sleep at all last night. I'm exhausted, but

I'm ready."

"You should have called me. I could have come over to help you work through those nerves."

I smile at him over the lid of my drink. "Yeah, I bet you could have. But then, I don't think that would have helped me get any more sleep."

"If I can't exhaust you to the point of sleep, I'm not doing my job, Bec."

"I'd like to see you try."

"Tonight? Come over after the event," he says.

"Okay. Yeah, I'd like that."

"Me too." The grin beaming from his face is infectious as I feel my own blooming. "Okay, well, I'll get out of here and let you get ready. Is this the New Hope uniform? I like it." He teases, tugging on the bottom of my holey T-shirt."

"Smart-ass. Everyone knows the uglier the pajamas, the more comfortable they are."

"Hey, I said I like it and I meant it. Especially the sneak peek I'm getting right here..." I gasp as his fingers graze the side of my left breast through one of the holes in my shirt and he leans down to kiss my neck. "I'll see you soon."

"You're coming?" I pant out. He smirks down at me, chuckling.

"Yeah, babe. I'm coming today. And later tonight, you will be too." He winks at me, calls Hopper over to follow him, and walks to my front door, leaving me breathless in the kitchen. "I'll see you soon." He smiles before closing the door behind him and Hopper, who follows him happily.

When I hear the latch click, I can't keep the dumb grin from igniting on my face or the butterflies from letting loose in my stomach. I hurry around my apartment getting ready. The coffee and food Aiden dropped off do wonders to revive me from my zombielike state.

By the time I reach the event center, my energy is peaking. My heart fills with a sense of pride and anticipation as I walk underneath the large banner on the outside of the building where large, scripted letters will hopefully draw the attention of interested families, *Fall in love with your furever friend – Adopt today.*

I leave my things with the rest of the volunteers' belongings in the back room, and I don't waste any time before jumping into the weeds; I work quickly getting signs posted, directing people where to go, making sure the display board I made for the entrance is up to date with any last-minute changes, checking in with the dogs still in training to see how they're handling the change in environment, and prepping potential adoption paperwork.

Before I realize how much time has gone by, I feel hands squeeze around my waist. "Bitch, this is *amazing.* I'm so fucking proud of you."

"Dee, you made it," I exclaim, turning around to give her a hug.

"Of course, you and Abby have been killing yourselves to get ready for this. I wouldn't miss it. You know I can't take on any pets right now, but I at least wanted to come show my support and make a donation. I still can't believe the Kellers pulled their sponsorship. Total dick move. If I didn't need to suck at the corporate teat to survive, I'd quit my job in protest."

"I promise, that's not necessary. It's been a hectic week, but we'll get through it," I assure her.

"Carissa wanted to make it, but she got called into work last minute. She asked me to tell you how sorry she is and that she's proud of you too."

"You guys are too good to me. It's the same event every year, you don't always need to make the trip."

"Yes, we absolutely do. Look at all of this, it's incredible," Ellie calls out as she bounds over to us, Luca bobbing along on her chest in his baby carrier, Dom following closely behind. She wraps me in a quick hug, Luca drooling slobber onto my shoulder as she pulls away. "This must have taken forever to set up."

"Most of the last two days. Oh, and I know how much you love Golden Retrievers, Ellie. The *cutest* little guy came into New Hope yesterday. He's somewhere along the back wall." I pinch her side and give her a wink.

"I am here for moral support today only," Ellie says. "I can barely keep up with everything we have going on already. Luca just entered some type of sleep regression that everyone on the mommy boards is making a big deal about. I think Luca would need to have some sort of regular sleeping schedule for a *regression* to be possible. We just don't sleep at all. There, problem solved, no regression."

"Ellie, you're a superhero. You know that, right?" I ask. "We should have a girls' night at your place. We'll stay up all night with Luca and binge rom-coms while you and Dom get some sleep."

"I heard binging rom-coms and came running. When is this happening?" Abby asks as she approaches.

"You decide, Ellie. Tell us when you want a night off, and we'll be there with snacks for the night shift," Dee agrees.

Ellie laughs it off, but I can see her eyes welling with tears, and she gently bounces Luca and gives him a soft kiss on the top of his head. "I'll let you guys know." I make a mental note to check on her. My gut's telling me she's not okay.

Dom gives Ellie a look of concern, his eyes briefly meeting mine, and then turns back to her and says, "I love the plan. Luca is definitely a night owl, and we've been struggling. The place looks great this year. Nice work, you two."

We catch up for a few more minutes before Abby and I get pulled away to check on a few dogs getting settled into temporary kennels. Dee, Ellie, and Dom stick around for about an hour before they head out, Luca out of patience and in desperate need of a nap and Dee following their rushed exit. My parents and siblings also visit and shower their praises on me and the other volunteers. My family and my girls and their unwavering support fills me with a surge of gratitude and pride. Being able to share my passion for my work with the Center and New Hope means everything to me. But no matter how hard I try, I don't convince any of them to take home a pet. There's always next year.

As I'm closing up one of the kennels, I hear rumbling of energized chatter from the entrance of the building. I make my way to the front and spot Aiden with several guys that I don't know, all wearing Aviators apparel.

I walk toward him hesitantly, not quite sure what to expect. But when he sees me, his entire face lights up.

"Bec, this is incredible. I was just showing the guys the board you made. It turned out great," he says, pointing his thumb back over his shoulder.

"So, this is Bec?" The guy to his left asks. "I'm Roman, and this grump is Pete, don't mind him. Great to meet you. I was promised there would be puppies here."

"Uh, yeah," I respond, still unsure what's going on. "The youngest dogs are in the back section, over that way. We keep them in that area to make sure that our older animals have a chance to be seen as well."

"I plan to post pictures with a few of the seniors, too, but I gotta get my puppy fix first. See ya later, Price," Roman says with a clap on Aiden's shoulder before striding away eagerly, the guy named Pete following him, shaking his head.

"Uh, what's going on, Aiden?" I ask.

He tugs his hand over the back of his neck a few times before saying, "Please don't be mad. I know you don't want money from me, but there are other ways I can help. I asked a few of the guys on the team to stop by today and post some pictures from the event to help draw a crowd, maybe a few potential fans who may be looking to adopt a pet. They all agreed to link New Hope's website, too, so that people who can't come can still donate." He drops his head back before looking at me and wrapping his strong hands around my shoulders. "Shit, you look mad...I can ask the guys not to post anything if it makes you uncomfortable. I thought...I just thought maybe it could help give you guys the boost you need—"

"Aiden, no," I say to stop him. I place my hand on his chest, looking up into his worried gaze. "It's just—I'm speechless. I don't think anyone's ever done anything like this for me before. Do you realize how helpful that kind of media attention would be for an organization as small as ours? Thank you for thinking of me. I mean...for thinking of New Hope. That was really thoughtful."

His shoulders drop on a deep exhale, like all the weight just fell off him, and he hits me with one of his incredible smiles. I give him one of my own right back. I can't believe he did this. Is this what it feels like to have a partner who supports you?

"I'm happy to help. Now, who should I post on my page."

"I've got just the friend in mind. Follow me," I say as I turn and lead Aiden to one of my favorite dogs. "Meet Charlie, she's a twelve-year-old chihuahua with one eye, no teeth, no attitude, and no worries. She's the biggest sweetheart in the place. All she needs is soft food, a warm bed, and a good snuggle."

Aiden follows me into the kennel we have set up for Charlie, all of which are large enough for two people to visit each animal with a volunteer present. Aiden immediately drops to the floor, sitting next to Charlie. He waits for her to approach him in her own time. Of course, she doesn't wait long before hopping onto his lap and smiling up at him like he's her entire world. Aiden's broad shoulders melt just a little, and he strokes her underneath her chin, gently showing her the affection she so desperately needs. The adorable moment nearly wrecks a piece of me, driving huge cracks through the walls I've built around my heart, the ones I've been clinging to in hopes of keeping some distance between Aiden and me, just in case.

"This girl. Yeah, this girl needs to find a great home today." He smiles up at me, handing me his phone. "Can you take one of us for me to post so people can find her on my page and fall in love like I just did?"

I'm helpless against a man with a dog. Guys tend to think they need a big dog with a tough personality to prove they're tough, too, but they're wrong. Show me a man tenderly holding a tiny, fragile senior dog and my heart is a puddle on the goddamn floor.

I snap a picture and Aiden takes a few minutes to post it on his page with a link to our website for donations and Charlie's adoption information. One of the newer volunteers calls me over to help her with a family who wants to finalize an adoption, and Aiden kisses me on the forehead before returning to his teammates. The flurry of activity that began when they first arrived increases the longer they're at the event. As time goes on, I can't help but notice an influx of people, many of whom are wearing Columbus Aviators gear.

Abby and I meet up to bring out another dog we've been working with due to some hyperactivity. We do our best during the event to make sure the dogs that have needed more intensive training are seen by families as well, walking them around the area and talking through their more specific needs with potential adopters. While it might take us more time to find the right fit for the dogs Abby and I tend to work with, I can't explain how rewarding it is to see it all work out when we get a good match. I'm convinced there's a family out there for every dog, and you can't convince me otherwise. When we get to witness them finding each other, it's simply magical. A moment that I know changes all of their lives forever in the most special way.

I glance up and spot a group of women looking to be in their twenties, walking over to Aiden and his teammates. A flare of jealousy ricochets through my chest, sending sharp pains through my insides. I pause, reminding myself that Aiden has fans approach him all the time. This is nothing new to him, even though it's weird for me to witness. It's clearly something I'll need to get used to if I plan to keep seeing Aiden. Besides, this is what we wanted. The guys' media posts are working, and there are more people at this event than in any year I've seen.

The women wrap up their goodbyes with Aiden and the guys, and then go to the information table. Abby offers to continue walking the dog around, seeing that I can't keep my eyes off Aiden.

As I approach him, I can hear the man Roman introduced as Pete politely declining to sign an autograph for a fan, but offering to do so outside after the event is over. I inwardly thank him for not creating what I'm sure would be a frenzy, and a distraction to the goal of the event. Aiden catches my eye over the head of a fan and shows me a huge smile before he returns his attention to the young boy, telling him about how he had the same jersey number as Aiden last summer while playing in his T-ball league.

"I hope you come back to the adoption fair next year and I get to hear all about your next killer season, little man. Remember to keep your glove down and eye on the ball." The little boy's parents thank Aiden, and head in the direction of our kid's area where we have a few games and activities set up to help the kids learn about taking care of pets.

"Next year, huh? You making plans or something, Price?" I shove his shoulder playfully, ignoring the flutter in my stomach and the way my nerves are buzzing at the implication behind his words.

"Or something." His expression changes, from sarcastic to something a little more thoughtful and serious. "There's no way I'd miss this. It's inspiring what you're doing here. I've seen three families adopt animals today, and it reminds me of when I found Hopper.

Watching someone meet the newest member of their family...that's something special."

"It is, isn't it?" My heart swells knowing he understands just how important all of this is to the animals who are so deserving and ready to find their safe place in this world, and the lucky people whose hearts will grow with every goofy thing their new pet does as they get more comfortable with time. "I look forward to this moment every year." I take a look around the event center, really taking it all in. It's astonishing how full the place is, baseball players mingling with staff, volunteers, and families. The dogs getting more one-on-one attention than we're able to provide at any given point during the year. The hopeful looks on children's faces as they pass each kennel, tugging on their parent's clothes and pointing excitedly.

"What you did today, Aiden...it was unbelievably thoughtful. Tonya, New Hope's director, just pulled me aside to say they've received an overwhelming number of online donations in the last two hours. The relief on her face...I can tell she is going to sleep better knowing she can keep New Hope afloat during this transition period. You made that possible. I don't know how to thank you."

He steps toward me, only a few inches separating us. His voice lowers as he says, "What the guys and I did today wouldn't mean anything without the work you do and the passion you have to help these animals. You're unlike anyone I've ever met." He brings a hand to my jaw, stroking my cheek with his thumb. "I didn't do this so you would thank me. I did it so that you could feel how much I care about you, how much I want to see you succeed, and so that you know you can count on me. I want you to know that beyond any doubt."

"I...I think I'm starting to see that."

"Believe what you see. I'm not going anywhere."

"You make it sound so easy."

"That's because with you, it is."

He brushes my hair back, and then I feel his hand stroke down my arm until his fingers intertwine with mine. The closer I get to Aiden, the more having him at my side feels less like a risk and more like a comfort. Can I trust my heart that wants to fall for everything that he is and everything he says, or should I listen to my head warning me to wait for everything to fall apart? For now, I ignore the negative intrusive thoughts and let my heart race at the feel of his warm hand engulfing mine, and I squeeze his hand back loving the way it feels.

# Chapter Thirty-Nine

Bec

That night, Aiden opens the door to his apartment, and I don't hesitate before wrapping my arms around his neck and my legs around his waist, jumping into his arms, and kissing him deeply. He takes less than a second to respond, gripping me firmly under my ass and groaning into my mouth as I grind against him.

I'm tired of overthinking. I'm tired of having my guard up. I want to go back to being the woman Aiden met at the wedding. The woman who was carefree and confident. Everything with Aiden feels right, and for once, I just want to give into the euphoric feeling of being with him, regardless of where this all ends up between us. I want him to make good on the promises he made to me earlier today. I want to fall asleep worn out and exhausted from everything he can give me.

As if he can hear my thoughts, he walks us to his kitchen counter, placing me on the edge. Through my leggings, the feeling of the cool granite beneath my thighs sends chills up my spine.

"Where's the shirt from this morning?" Aiden asks. "I was looking forward to seeing you in it again. Thought maybe I could tear it off your perfect body before I got to work worshipping it."

"You wouldn't dare. I've worked hard wearing that shirt down to complete distressed perfection," I say through our shared kisses, lightly tugging on his bottom lip with my teeth.

"I've been thinking about you all day. Take off your clothes," he says into our parted lips while they lightly press together.

"You first." I reach down to grip the hem of his shirt and pull it over his head, revealing his muscled torso. I run my hands over his chest to his belt before undoing the clasp, button, and zipper. I push his jeans down with my feet. The buckle of his belt rattles when it hits the floor before he steps out of his pants, leaving him in only his boxer briefs, his erection straining against the fabric. "You made me promises this morning, and I came to see if you can deliver on them."

His stare turns heady under his dark lashes as he smirks at me. He grips my ass and pulls me to the edge of the counter in a show of strength and spreads my legs around his body, lining himself up with my center, slowly grinding against me.

I grip his shoulders and let my head fall back. "Fuck, Aiden."

"Bec, I will deliver on every single promise and then I'll make a hundred more and deliver on every single one of them too. I've been waiting all fucking night to do this. I was so tempted to fuck my fist at the thought of tasting you again, but I wanted to wait for the real thing."

With one hand behind my head and one hand on my chest, he slowly pushes me backward until I'm lying across his kitchen counter, my legs still clinging to his waist as he stands at the edge of the counter.

"Hips up, babe," he commands, and I comply, pressing my palms into the smooth stone counter, raising my hips several inches into the air while he pulls my leggings off and tosses them to the floor. Aiden doesn't look away from my center, covered in a black satin thong. "Tell me, beautiful, have you been awake at night thinking about us? Have you touched yourself imagining it was me instead? Maybe used that pretty pink vibrator you love so much?" He bends down and kisses a trail of wet kisses up my inner thigh, while hitching my knees over his shoulders.

My mind goes blank, my stare locked on the sight of him making his way up my leg, and I can't find the words to answer his question. I close my eyes and run my fingers through his wavy hair, tugging him gently toward where I want his kiss most of all.

"So ready for me," he says, his voice rumbling low as he places a soft kiss on my underwear. He pulls the fabric to the side before running his tongue along my slit. I moan and grip his hair harder, my hips flexing, instinctively seeking more of his touch. He slides his hands beneath my ass, pulling me even closer before he unleashes his mouth on me with a hunger I've never felt in my life.

"Fuck, you taste better than I remember," he mutters before returning his focus to my clit.

"Aiden, fuck me. Please, I need it," I plead. He's already driving my body to the brink of hysteric need and all I want is for him to take me on this counter.

"Fuck, I'll give you whatever you want," he groans. He pulls me off the counter, sliding my body along his until my feet hit the tile flooring. He pulls my shirt over my head and leans down to suck one of my nipples into his mouth through my lace bra. I arch back and give in to the sensations. Aiden's attention to every inch of my body instantly clears my head; the incessant stream of worries that I can never seem to shut off goes silent. He takes me completely out of my thoughts and all I can focus on is the feel of his rough hands on my body, the strength of his movements, the discipline of his touch, never too rough but always firm. He turns me around abruptly to face the counter and I arch my back, rubbing my ass into his groin.

I look over my shoulder at him before I thread my fingers into the lace straps of my thong and drop my panties to the ground. "Now, Aiden."

His stare is locked with mine as he shoves his boxers to join my underwear on the floor. Aiden steps closer, rubbing his erection along my soaking slit and gliding over my clit. "Shit. Hold on, I'll be right back. The condoms are in my room."

"I...got tested after my last relationship, and I'm on birth control. I'm comfortable going without one if you are," I say, desperate to feel him bare inside me.

He wipes a hand over his face. "Shit, Bec. I'm good too. Are you sure?"

"I'm sure. Now, are you going to make me beg or what?"

"I'd love to hear you begging for my cock. But you worked so hard today. I'm going to take such good care of you," the gravel in his voice sends a jolt of electricity to my core as he runs his lips over my bare shoulder. He presses his thick cock into me, slowly entering me bit by bit, his fingers digging into my hips. We melt together, finding our rhythm. Our need for each other building until we're both desperate. The intensity of his thrust strengthens, my breathing quickens, he presses one palm against the base of my neck and the other to my clit where he slowly and firmly circles the pressure point with his steady fingers.

I press my palms into the counter, spreading my legs farther and arching my back to meet his pulsing hips, his length fully entering me with each stroke. My impending climax builds, and I reach my hand back to grab his sculpted ass and I pull at it, a plea for him to go harder. He wordlessly obeys, and I feel him driving into me with more powerful thrusts.

"Being inside you like this feels so fucking perfect. Do you feel how crazy you're making me? How you make me fucking drip for this perfect body of yours. These..." He presses his fingers into my soft hips. One of the places I'm most insecure about if I'm honest with myself. I've always had full hips no matter my weight. "These goddamn hips have me in a fucking chokehold. I never want to come up for air."

"Oh god. Aiden, I...I'm going to come," I say.

"The first of many. Let me hear how much you love this; how much you need this...as bad as I fucking do."

I clench around him, finding my release, my head falling back against his shoulder.  I cry out as my body responds to his words and his touch.

"Atta girl." He slows his movements and pulls out of me, leaving me feeling empty.

He's not finished, and as tired as I am, I desperately want more. He folds his hand around mine and pulls me alongside him into his bedroom.

When we cross the threshold, he wraps an arm around my lower back, the other running along my jaw before weaving into my hair and tugging at the roots. He kisses me slow and sweet. A stark contrast from the out-of-control way he took me just moments ago in the kitchen. This feels so different, like so much more than sex. It feels like an intimacy I've never known. Like a surrender to the unknown. A blind trust in something new. Something that shouldn't feel familiar in my heart, but yet it does. Like he's always been there and is just now showing up to take up a space that's always been his.

He slowly walks me backward until my legs hit his mattress. I fall back and scoot to the center of his bed. His gaze slowly peruses every inch of my body, and he rubs his hand over his chin.

Aiden wrecks every pessimistic belief I've ever had about dating and what it's doomed to be like. With him, I don't feel exposed, I feel safe. I don't feel embarrassed, I feel worshipped. I don't feel insecure, I feel valued. I don't feel timid, I feel emboldened. I don't feel dependent, I feel empowered.

"When I'm with you, it's like my mind can't believe that I'm living this moment. I don't want to blink. I'm afraid I'll wake up and realize you never gave me this chance," Aiden says.

"Is it all a dream, then?" I ask.

"If it is, don't wake me. Let me be with you for a while longer. Let me rest with you in my arms."

"And if I'm not ready to rest?"

"Then open those pretty thighs for me so we can wear each other out," he says as he crawls up the bed. Once he's between my legs, he sits back on his heels, his perfect physique on display in the soft glow of the sun setting through his windows. I feel his fingers softly stroking up my leg from my calves to my thighs before pulling my legs around his waist.

I let out a gasp as he lowers his body against mine and enters me. He holds us there, unmoving, as we both breathe together. His eyes find mine for a quick moment before he's kissing me, his tongue chasing mine. As he begins to rock us into a synchronized rhythm, every touch we give each other, every moan we let out, overwhelms my senses.

Every move our bodies make together sends me higher, racing toward ecstasy. When I find it, Aiden crashes with me, filling me with his release. We cling to each other, breathing each other in, slowly coming back down from the high we found together.

Aiden steps away to grab a warm washcloth and cleans me before climbing into bed beside me. He circles his arms around me and kisses the top of my head before letting out a content sigh. My arms instinctively tangle themselves up in him.

"What happens now?" I ask, unable to keep the anxiety from bleeding into my question.

Aiden releases a heavy breath. "That's up to you, Bec. I know I want you. Do you feel the same?"

I tilt my head back to see his expression, a mix of hope and uncertainty. By the undercurrent of doubt in his tone, I can tell I've been guarding my growing feelings well.

"I feel the same, Aiden. I'm sorry I've been so hesitant, so scared."

"Then, we give this a real shot. If you're ready for that. I leave for Spring Training in a few days. It'll be an adjustment with all the travel, but I want to make this work."

"You make me want more. More of this. More of us."

"I want that too. Every moment I'm away from you, all I can think about is seeing you again. Every time I see you, I want to pull you into my arms and never let you go. I know you're scared. I am too. But this...this is right. I know it."

"I believe you," I mumble, exhaustion finally taking over and sleep pulling me under. Before I can think of anything more to say, I slowly drift into a peaceful sleep wrapped in Aiden's arms.

# Chapter Forty

Bec

**B**ec: Is this another gag gift?

**Aiden:** Another? When have I ever sent you a gag gift?

**Bec:** The vibrator, Aiden. Now this?

**Aiden:** That was not a gag gift. That was a genuine gift I was hoping you'd enjoy using. It's not my fault you can't follow directions and you're gagging yourself with it. There are other toys specifically made for that. Sounds like user error.

**Bec:** I'm choosing to ignore that last text.

**Bec:** I can't believe you'd send me a plant. This poor innocent thing will be dead before you get back. It's doomed to join the others in my windowsill graveyard.

**Aiden:** Look closer, Bec. It's fake. I'm not willing to be an accomplice to murder. Let the real plants live in the wild.

**Bec:** You might be onto something there.

**Aiden:** I'd rather be on you.

**Bec:** Honestly, same.

* * *

It's been almost two weeks since Aiden left for Spring Training. Thankfully, between training classes and my time spent at New Hope, I've been plenty busy. If I wasn't falling into bed exhausted every night from overworking, I might have more time to think about Aiden and how much I miss him. I can't hide from my own feelings forever, and as much as I'd like to avoid getting attached to a new relationship too quickly, I know he's dug in deep already with how often my thoughts are fixated on him in the rare moments of quiet.

Is he thinking about me too? Does he miss me the way I miss him? Is he losing interest with the distance between us?

If I'm not racking my brain with questions fueled by insecurities, then I'm snapping myself out of flashbacks of him looking up at me from between my thighs with a smirk on his lips, or looking down at me with a hooded, hungry stare as his hands wander all over my body. It's enough to distract me, and despite the embarrassingly *very* regular use of my vibrator, I'm still left unsatisfied. After only a few nights together, I'm completely addicted to Aiden Price.

I'm sitting at the front of the training room, my eyes unfocused on the clipboard in my hand, lost again in thoughts of Aiden, while I wait for the next class to arrive. Hopper and Aiden's class. They won't be here of course. I know Aiden made other arrangements for Hopper while he's away, and I'm trying not to take it personally that he didn't ask me to watch him. I really did love having a dog around the apartment again.

When I catch myself in another daydream of what Aiden could be doing at this very moment, I look up to find all of the families and their pets seated and ready to begin. Ten minutes later, we've discussed the new skill for the week and I'm now making my rounds to assist as the attendees work on the cue for the first time.

The door flies open, catching my attention, and I watch as Hopper bounds into the training room, his leash trailing behind on the ground like a snake. He does a large circle and greets two dogs before spotting me and running to lie in front of me, presenting his belly for scratches.

"Please promise not to tell Aiden how much I let Hop get away with while he's gone." I recognize Aiden's sister from the restaurant and immediately feel better knowing he asked her to watch Hopper and he didn't choose a dog boarder over asking me.

"Your secret is safe with me. I'm Bec. Evie, right?" I ask.

"Yep, the most obnoxious dog aunt you'll probably ever meet. And also, the least punctual. Sorry we're late. Hop got a hold of one of my shoes and it turned into an all-out battle in my living room."

"Been there…" I mutter to myself, not thinking.

"He destroyed your shoes too?"

"Uh, yeah, something like that." I nod, tuck my hair behind my ear, and quickly change the subject. Not really a story I want to revisit with Aiden's sister. "No worries about the time, we just got started a little bit ago. I'm glad you and Hopper were able to make it to class today. Aiden didn't mention you'd be in."

"He doesn't know," she says with a devious look on her face. "I couldn't pass up the opportunity to introduce myself and see if you'd be interested in teaming up for a little…surprise."

"What kind of surprise?"

"Want to meet for a coffee later? We can get to scheming." She shoots me a wicked grin, and I know that Aiden isn't ready for whatever Evie has planned.

* * *

An hour later, I'm sitting on the heated patio at the coffee shop next door. Hopper is lying underneath the table between Evie and me, exhausted from his class. I guess ignoring Evie's instructions for an hour zapped the energy right out of him.

"Congrats on the adoption event. Aiden told me it went well. Almost cleared the shelter of all the animals needing homes, right?" Evie asks before sipping her drink.

"He mentioned that?"

"Are you kidding? He went on and on and on about it. He begged me to come and adopt a dog. I'm sorry I couldn't make it. Like I told him, I'm ready for the responsibility of a dog *aunt*, not dog *mom*. He was trying to describe some kind of board or something that you made? He went on for like five minutes before he remembered he took a picture and showed me that instead. Zoomed in on all the details and then spent another five minutes telling me about the dogs he met."

My shock must show on my face hearing how much Aiden has told Evie. Like the day meant as much to him as it does to me. The thought warms me from the inside.

"He and his teammates sure drew a crowd. It wouldn't have been nearly as successful if they hadn't shown up," I say.

"My brother is pretty smitten. And by smitten, I mean he's acting obsessed and driving me nuts."

We both break out into laughter, mine sounding a little nervous and hers genuine and unreserved. I feel my stomach flip at the thought of Aiden driving his sister crazy talking about *us*.

"So, you want to surprise the hell out of him?" Evie asks.

"What'd you have in mind?"

"Come with me to Arizona. Aiden has a preseason game next Saturday. We can take a quick flight out there, stay the night, and fly back the next day."

"I don't know...won't he be annoyed if I show up unannounced and uninvited? Can friends even go to those games?"

"*Friends?* The way he talks about you sounds like a lot more than friends."

"You could say that," I say, unable to keep eye contact with Evie.

My face heats remembering all the ways we are absolutely *more* than friends, but we didn't talk labels before he left, so I'm not exactly sure what to call us at the moment. "I mean...what about Hopper?" I change the subject, looking for an out. Anything to avoid facing the uncertainty of how Aiden would react to an unexpected visit like this. I don't want to come off as needy.

"Way ahead of you. Dom agreed to take him for the night. I guess Aiden has been over there a few times with him already, and Dom said he's great with the baby. It's just for one night too. I told Dom I'd buy him and his wife dinner to pay them back. Plus, the cost of anything Hopper might destroy while he's staying there, but fingers crossed there aren't any destructive incidents."

"I'd need to ask one of my coworkers to cover my classes. You sure it wouldn't be overstepping?"

"Listen, Bec. I don't know you, but I know Aiden. And when he talks about you, he's...happy. I want that for my brother. I want to see him happy." The heartbreak behind her words strikes me. With everything Aiden has told me about his past, I know there's a lot of hurt there. I want happiness for him too. I'm not sure I'm capable of giving it to him, but I hope I am. This growing flame between us feels consuming, reinvigorating. The distance we've had between us for the past two weeks has only helped me realize how strongly I crave being in his presence. His name lighting up my phone has my pulse racing. I hope he feels the same way.

"What makes you think he wasn't happy before?"

"You can't see it, because the change is *you*. Aiden is the best brother I could ever ask for. He's spent the last twenty years trying to take care of our mom and me. I want him to find someone special and make that work. Please don't get freaked out or anything. There are no hard feelings if this is too much, too soon. I just got excited when I heard your date went well and that you two were still talking. I wanted to go to a game to support him, anyway, and I know he'd love to see you. Plus, I thought this would be a fun way to get to know you."

Before I even have a chance to process what she's said, she's already pulling back, rubbing her palms over her face, doubt evident in her posture. "Sorry, this was a dumb idea," she says. "I'm probably coming off all wrong, the annoying younger sister dragging you out to coffee and asking you to hop on a plane to see a guy you just started dating."

"Evie, wait." I shove my nerves down, the ones that make me want to decline her offer. I decide the risk is worth it. Time and time again, Aiden has me pushing past my comfort zone, because I know he's worth it. "I have three older siblings. No offense, but compared to the way they hover, you'd have to try a lot harder to outdo them. I would love to get to know you, and I can't think of a better way to start. When do we leave?"

# Chapter Forty-One

Aiden

"Good game," Roman says as he passes me on his way out of the locker room.

"Yeah, thanks, man. You too," I reply. The high after going four for four and hitting a home run is washed away when I checked my phone. No missed calls or messages. It's unfair for me to expect any after only a few hours, but the distance between Bec and I is becoming painful. I'm craving every taste of her she'll give me.

We haven't been able to talk as much as I'd like with our mismatched schedules in addition to being in different time zones. The random message here and there, her sass, her teasing, her shyness sprinkled with bouts of that familiar confidence, are all that's getting me through until I can see her again. I slide my phone into my back pocket, sling my bag over my shoulder, and head to the parking lot, not looking up as I walk out of the locker room.

"God, does he look depressed or what?"

"Why is he sulking like a baby? Did I black out? I thought they won the game."

Denial hits me first, stopping me from walking any farther. No way. No fucking way those voices belong to the women I imagine they do. Still, I can't help turning back to confirm my head is lying to me, teasing and taunting me because I'm missing Bec and my family.

"Hoooooly shhhit," I drawl. "What...what are you doing here?"

Bec looks up at me, her shoulders curve in the smallest bit, a sheepish look spreading over her face. Her hair is pulled into a messy pile on top of her head. She's wearing cutoff jean shorts, an Aviators jersey, and Chucks. She's the most beautiful woman I've ever seen.

My body is frozen for a moment more before I take three large strides until she's only inches from me. I don't think, my body acts on impulse. I slide my palm along Bec's lower back and pull her toward me. My arms circle her shoulders, hugging her close, eliminating any space between us. Her head fits perfectly in the space between my chin and chest, and as she leans into me, her arms tuck into my chest. Every ounce of tension in my body melts and drifts away and I completely relax with Bec in my arms. I drop a soft kiss on the top of her head, softly whispering, "I can't believe you're here."

"Well, I had to make sure you're a real baseball player. I haven't even seen a trading card. Seemed highly suspicious," she says.

"Had your doubts, did you?"

"Not anymore. You were great."

"How did you get here?" I ask.

"You're welcome," Evie says from down the hall where she's leaning on her elbow with a shit-eating grin on her face. "I couldn't handle another morose phone call from you. Thought you might need some fans in the stands tonight, so I dragged Bec along with me."

"How...how did you two...?" I'm so shocked, my sluggish brain can't even formulate the questions I need answers to in order to figure out how my sister and Bec are together in front of me. I point my finger back and forth between the two of them, hoping my inability to form the question doesn't stop them from giving me answers.

"I gave her a copy of your seventh-grade class picture in exchange for her agreeing to be my travel buddy." The light behind Evie's eyes might as well be a dancing flame. Little sisters...they know exactly how to humble you.

I press my eyes shut, saying a silent prayer to no one that she's lying right now. "Not seventh grade."

"Seventh grade," Bec confirms. "Finally, I get to watch *you* board at the humiliation station. It's about damn time for you to take your turn."

"In my defense—" I sputter.

"In my defense, I was about to sneeze," Evie speaks over me animatedly, dropping her voice low. She winks at Bec. "Told you. That's his excuse every time."

"Because it's the truth! What kind of monster refuses to retake a twelve-year-old kid's photo when they snapped it *midsneeze*," I yell. "That picture haunted me all the way through my senior year of high school."

Bec takes a step back, leaning against the concrete wall beside Evie. The two of them share a look, and my stomach drops. That look can only mean trouble for me.

"What else did you do, Evie?" I ask.

"Nothing you need to worry about right now." Bec pats my chest in a placating gesture. "So, where's good for dinner around here, hotshot?" Bec makes her way down the hall toward the exit, and before Evie can follow her, I step in front of her.

"Evie...what did you do?" I repeat.

"Relax, big brother, we're just messing with you. The picture was the only dirt I shared...for now. But..." Evie leans to the side, looking over my shoulder at Bec and then back at me, her smile softening. "I see why you're so caught up on her. She's really great, Aiden. I can see it in your eyes already. You're wrapped up in this way more than you even realize. Now don't fuck this up, okay? I want to see you happy.

You deserve it."

She pats my shoulder, and a chuckle of disbelief escapes me as I turn to follow them. Evie's wrong, though. I've always known I was in over my head when it came to Bec. Now that I know her better, now that she's given me glimpses behind her defenses to the woman underneath, I'm all too willing to sink into deeper waters, thanking her the entire way down. Her confidence may have suffered a slight setback, but I'm not doing my job if she doesn't realize how damn perfect she is. And how damn perfect she is for me.

* * *

"Aiden, breathe. Evie's a big girl. She can handle herself."

"I'm not watching her." I'm watching Pete, and I swear to god, if I see his hand brush her leg one more time, I'm going to give my own teammate a black eye.

Turns out, Evie and Bec are staying in a hotel nearby and when Evie suggested we go for drinks after dinner, I didn't think twice about it. I should have realized the team would be celebrating, but I was too distracted by Bec's hand in mine and how fucking hot she looks in that jersey with my name across her back. I'm paying for it now, watching my stupid teammates swarm my sister. My blood is boiling, running hot through my veins.

"If it bothers you that much, I think I know how to take your mind off it," she says, running her hand from the nape of my neck down my back to massage between my shoulder blades.

The shift in her tone pulls my attention from the overwhelming urge to play the overprotective brother. The corner of her mouth quirks up when my eyes meet hers.

"There he is," she says confidently. Bec leans in close, her breath hot against my neck as her hand trails up my back again. She tilts her head up toward my ear and whispers, "I wanted to see if I could hit a home run of my own tonight."

Without any warning, she wraps her other hand over my upper thigh, inching toward my dick, which springs to life immediately. I cough and adjust myself, trying to hide how hard she's making me even though she's barely touched me. I'm not easily rattled, but everything about Bec's hands on me muddles my thoughts, and my mind empties completely until all that's left is the compulsion to consume her.

"Come upstairs with me," I say, pulling her closer to me with a strong hand around her waist.

"What about Evie?" she says, leaning into my side, her tits pressed into my rib cage.

I groan. "One second," I say before reluctantly pulling myself out of her grasp.

I adjust myself again before standing up and then stalk over to the bar where Pete and Evie are laughing with one another.

"Well, if it isn't the man in question," Evie taunts.

"You're right, Eves. I can see the hearts in his eyes when he's close like this. Couldn't tell from across the room," Pete says.

I ignore him completely, looking only at Evie. "Evie, Bec and I—" I begin to say.

She holds up her hand, cutting me off. "Don't make this weird, big brother. Go hang with your girlfriend. I'm fine here by myself."

"I'll keep you company," Pete says quickly.

"Matthews, I swear to god, if you even think of trying something with my little sister, I'll—"

"You'll what, Aiden? We've talked about this. You promised. Now, go enjoy your time with your girl. I'll take a cab back to my hotel and text you when I get there."

I know what I promised. After years of scaring off dates and hopeful boyfriends with my overbearing tendencies, Evie had enough. While she was earning her undergraduate degree, she ripped me a new asshole for it. She wouldn't talk to me for three weeks, our longest fight. I know it's not fair to think I can protect her from everything, but the fear of losing control...well, it's not something I handle well when I'm worried about the people I care about.

"Text me when you leave here, and when you get into your room," I demand.

She salutes me before pushing me lightly on the shoulder back toward Bec. "I promise. Now, go. Stop wasting your time worrying. I'm having fun."

"Evie, I...I didn't thank you. For going to meet Bec. For bringing her here."

"No thanks needed, Aiden.  By the way, thanks for covering my bar tab." She winks. "Charged to your room, I figured you wouldn't mind."

I chuckle in response. "I owe you a hell of a lot more than that. I'll look for your text."

Dropping my smile, I look over at Pete to see his dumbass staring at my sister, his eyes lit up with obvious attraction.

"Don't piss me off, Matthews."

"You don't need to worry about me," Pete concedes, chuckling over the rim of his drink. "Have a good night, Price."

* * *

"Hurry up," Bec says, pushing me playfully while I fumble with the key card, dropping it on the floor of my hotel room as Bec backs me up to the wall just past the doorway, her hands forcefully pushing against my chest. When I hit the wall, I let out a small groan as she eagerly kisses and sucks on my neck.

"So demanding," I say.

"And I'll continue to be demanding the rest of the night." She looks up at me smugly as she palms my hard cock through my pants. Wasting no time, Bec pulls my belt buckle loose with her other hand.

"Is that so? Tell me." I grip Bec by her ass, digging my fingers into her cheeks, turning her to pin her against the hotel door, her body encased by mine. "What is it you want? I'm more than happy to give it to you."

"I want the second baseman I watched all day to fuck me so hard I forget about the two weeks I had to spend without him." My rigid dick swells and hardens even more hearing the filthy words coming out of Bec's mouth. It feels amazing to be wanted. But to be wanted by her, to see and hear the way my body craves her is reciprocated only drives my need for her higher.

"I thought I sent you something to take care of yourself while I was gone," I tease.

She pushes me off her unexpectedly, and I stumble backward a few steps, laughing.

"You're right." She shrugs. Her breathlessness and disheveled appearance contradicting the way she's trying to come off as unaffected by the heat between us. "I should get back to my own hotel room and finish myself off since you were so generous to give me a *replacement*."

I drop my chin, all joking forgotten. "Say that again."

"Thank you for pointing out that I *don't* need you." She turns, reaching for the door handle, but I grab her wrist before she can open it and pin her back against the door once again, her hand above her head. I grab her other hand and hold them both firmly against the wood frame before leaning down to whisper in her ear.

"I'm going to show you just how much you fucking need me. Do you know how I know? Because of this," I say, brushing the knuckles of my free hand over her blushing cheeks, her face flush with want. "Because of this." I palm her breast and pinch her tight nipple through her shirt while she gasps, her head dropping into the space between my neck and shoulder. "And because of this." I slip my hand into her shorts, running two of my fingers through her soaked entrance.

"Oh fuck," Bec pants, her head dropping back against the door frame, her eyes shut tight while I take my time exploring every wet inch of her.

"Look at me, Bec." When she does, her eyes are heavy with lust and she bites her lower lip. The sight of her like this sends another bolt of arousal to my groin.

I lift my hand between us and take my fingers coated in her arousal into my mouth, sucking on the taste of her.

"This doesn't taste like someone who doesn't need me. This tastes like you need me as bad as I fucking need you. Every time I think about the look on your face when I'm making you come, I get so goddamn hard. I'm tired of fucking my fist thinking about it, Bec."

"Jesus," Bec moans.

"Our bodies speak a language I didn't know until you. Now tell me you fucking need me so I can fuck that pussy like I've been craving for weeks now."

"Fuck. I need you, Aiden," she whimpers. Bec's hands strain against where I still have them pinned with one hand, her hips grinding against my dick.

I release her and step back, reaching down to pull her shirt—my goddamn jersey—off her perfect body. Her lace bra does nothing to cover her nipples and I bend down to suck one into my mouth, giving it a bite.

Bec gasps and grips my hair, holding me to her, demanding more of the combination of pleasure with a little pain. "Don't stop," she says.

I don't. I suck and lick and grip and taste her tits until she's writhing against the door. She yanks my head back to kiss me fiercely and my body responds to her lust instantly.

I push my pants and briefs to the floor and step out of them while Bec tears off her shorts, thong, and bra. I still can't believe she's here. That she came here for me. Traveled all this way just to be with me for one night. I won't waste a minute of the time we have together. I want her all night.

We collide again in a fit of clumsy limbs and greedy tongues. I lift Bec into my arms and lean us both against the door of my room, pressing the head of my cock to her slit.

"Yes, yes," Bec pants between fierce kisses. Our groans overlap as I pulse into her between her deliciously thick thighs. She wraps them tightly around my waist. When I'm fully seated inside her, I pause and revel in the feel of her walls squeezing my cock like nothing I've ever felt before.

"Fuck, Bec." I sigh, still in disbelief that she's here. That she can be this perfect for me, despite my flaws.

"Make me come, Aiden. I need to come."

The desperation in her voice matches the relentless rhythm of movement taking over between our bodies. She grinds her clit against my pelvis while I drive into her, squeezing her ass cheeks in my palms, her pussy gripping me just as tightly. I know I won't last long.

"God, just like that," she says, her voice shaking. Our breathing is heavy, our movements more uncontrolled, and I feel her body tightening in my arms as she gets closer to coming. When she topples over the edge, my name falls off her lips in between her moans and sends me barreling into my own release as I groan into the space between her neck and shoulder.

We stand for a minute together, our breaths slowing, our bodies still wrapped tightly around each other, her arms linked around my shoulders, my cum spilling from where we're still joined.

I feel her startle in my arms as a firm knock sounds three times on the opposite side of the hotel door. Her eyes lock onto mine, as wide as saucers.

"This is Steve from hotel reception," a male voice rings out. "We got a noise complaint. Can you two keep it down?"

Bec bites her lips between her teeth, stifling a laugh, and I try to do the same.

"Yeah, man. Sorry about that. Had the TV too loud, I think."

"Jesus fucking Christ," I hear my new friend Steve mumble as he walks away.

I pull out of Bec, carry her to the bed, and drop her onto the mattress with a bounce before collapsing beside her. We slowly turn our heads toward each other at the same time...and burst into laughter. A gut-splitting, soul-reviving laughter that blinds me to all the darkest parts of myself and leaves only Bec, only the light that shines from her warming me from the inside out.

# Chapter Forty-Two

Bec

"Barbie has a fucking last name? I don't believe it," Dylan says incredulously from across the table.

"Believe it, bitch. It's Roberts. Now, write it down. We only have forty-five seconds to turn in our answer," Dee responds confidently beside me. Aiden is sitting on my other side, his arm around the back of my chair.

Earlier today, the Aviators walked away from their home opener with a win. The group of us who went to cheer for Aiden met at a bar downtown afterward to celebrate. Once Dee realized the bar was hosting a trivia night, she forced us all to participate. The competitor in her just can't help herself.

For the last hour, she's been working Dylan up with her extensive trivia knowledge while every single one of his guesses has been wrong. I've enjoyed sitting back and watching them go at it. They both bring plenty of fire and stubborn confidence—borderline arrogance—to the table.

"How the fuck do you know that, Dee? For some *weird* reason, I can only imagine you cutting off your Barbies' hair in a fit of rage, thriving in the anarchy of it all," Dylan says.

"And you're not wrong, sweetie pie," Dee retorts. "My dolls all got badass haircuts compliments of yours truly. They looked like damn runway models when I was done with them."

The announcer confirms that Dee's answer is correct, and I swear I hear Dylan muttering curses under his breath before taking a big gulp of his beer. Dee smirks at him while chomping on a crispy fry.

"I'm almost scared to try to answer any of the questions with the encyclopedia sitting next to you," Aiden murmurs in my ear.

"You and I both. With any luck, she'll share her winnings before she realizes how much pain she should be in from carrying all of us on her back to victory," I say quietly enough that only he hears.

"Next round is on us," Dom calls out as he and Ellie rejoin the table with two buckets of beer to share.

"How is Luca doing with your parents tonight, Ellie?" Carissa asks.

"Well, he refused to nap but took a bottle, so I'm calling it a partial win," Ellie responds. "Even if that means bedtime is going to be an absolute shit show," she adds, grimacing.

Ellie has been doing her best adjusting to spending time away from Luca, especially since she's gone back to work. She tries to make time to go out with friends while also making some time for herself, but she always seems more relaxed when she brings Luca with her instead. Lately, all of our get-togethers have been with Luca around, which we all love. But she didn't feel comfortable bringing him to the game today, so to the grandparents he went...with plenty of video chats to check in.

"You be sure to call his favorite uncles over when you're ready for your next break. We'd be happy to take the night shift if you two need some rest," Chris offers, and Ellie leans into his side, wrapping her arms around his waist.

"You really are the best brother-in-law," she says.

"What the fuck, Ellie? I'm sitting right here," Jake yells over the roar of the bar as the trivia MC calls out the next answer, which Dee also guessed correctly.

"Did *you* offer to watch your nephew so I can sleep?" Ellie asks sarcastically, still squeezing Chris tight, and he wraps his arms around her protectively.

"Yeah, did you, Jake?" Chris asks. Ellie and Chris always team up against Jake and Dom. When they met, it was agreed that the married-in siblings have to have each other's backs, and they take one another's side in every disagreement I've ever seen between the four of them.

"No, but we all know if Chris is there, then he's dragging me along too. Whatever, I don't need to be your favorite brother, Ellie. When Luca's old enough to know better, I'll be the favorite uncle. Just give it time. You wait and see," Jake says with a pout.

"Aiden, I was impressed with your pitcher's command of the strike zone tonight," Abby says, grabbing my attention.

"Oh yeah? Big fan I take it?" Aiden asks.

"Eh, I grew up playing softball. I can appreciate a good pitch when I see one," she says with a shrug.

"Abby's trying to teach me the lingo," I say.

Aiden eyes me skeptically, a smirk pulling at the side of his mouth before he asks, "Babe, what are you talking about?"

"Well, I don't know anything about baseball. When the announcers say stuff about you, I want to know what they're talking about," I respond.

"And how did that go today?" he asks, his lips pulling into an uneven smile.

"It could have gone better, but I was distracted by the soft pretzels. Those are delicious by the way," I say.

He leans in close, humming low in my ear. "Almost as delicious as you."

I bump my shoulder into his and take a quick look around the table of our friends, who have broken off into several conversations. It strikes me how much I appreciate being here with Aiden. It helps that he's met everyone before and he's close with Dom and Dylan, but it still feels surprisingly easy having him join me in the group I've known for so long. It's always felt awkward bringing someone I'm dating to hang out with my friends...but not Aiden.

Even with Josh—who was my longest relationship to date—it was always uncomfortable trying to bring him into the larger group. Most of that was probably my fault. I could never really be myself around him. I didn't want to pretend to be someone else around the people who know me best, so I wound up feeling so confused I mostly just kept quiet during those hangouts, keeping to smaller side conversations if anything.

I've always held a piece of me back, thinking that when I met the right person, it'd be easy to let someone in. I'm sure I'm missing some kind of life lesson here, where I should make myself more vulnerable, but being with Aiden has only solidified my belief. Because none of this feels forced. Every moment I spend with him feels genuine. It shines a light on how painfully wrong all my past dating attempts have been. Maybe it really is that natural, that comfortable, with the right person.

I'm still reflecting on this when I excuse myself to the bathroom. I'm so distracted by my own thoughts that I barely catch myself before running headfirst into someone as I exit the restroom.

"Oh shit, sorry. Didn't see you there. Excuse me," I say, keeping my gaze on my phone, stepping to the side to let them pass me.

"Bec?"

*Fuck, I know that voice.*

"Hey, Josh," I say, turning toward him.

"Bec, wow. It's really good to see you," he says with enthusiasm.

"I mean…you look incredible. How have you been?"

I haven't heard anything from him obviously, since I blocked his number. I thought when I did finally see him again, the heartache and embarrassment would come rushing back as if it had never dulled, but I was wrong. Seeing him now, after knowing what it's like to be with Aiden, it's almost laughable how little I feel.

I know without a doubt that Josh was right to end things between us. We could never work. Yes, he's wrong to have strung me along like that after breaking up with me. To keep looking at me as if I could find his soul mate for him, but I recognize that he's probably just feeling lost himself. Holding out hope that somehow, by reaching out to me, he was at least taking action, trying to find his person. He's wrong for the way that he went about it, but I think I understand him a little better now.

It's a relief to know that whatever hold he used to have on my emotions, it's gone now.

"I'm good," I answer. "Doing better than I have in a while."

"Oh, that's great. I've been thinking about you a lot. You haven't answered my calls lately, not sure what that's about, but that's okay, I guess. Maybe we could get a drink sometime. I'm about to call it a night, I'm on a blind date right now, but I can tell she doesn't compare to you."

*Oookay, is he fucking serious right now?*

"No thanks, I'm seeing somebody." As much as I resent the way Josh acted since our breakup, and clearly, he's undeserving of the blind date he's here with tonight, I still hope someday he finds his person. And he gets his head out of his own ass before then. He's got some work to do.

"Already? It can't be serious, right?" His stance changes, and he sounds disgusted.

*Already?*

As if the eight months we've spent apart mean nothing at all and his drunk calls mean everything. As if he deserves for me to wait for him. As if I deserve to feel like shit, shaking my confidence with every repeat rejection he delivers. As if he didn't just admit to being on a date himself?

The overwhelming desire to cry flares as anger floods my veins and I do my best to will it away. Any overwhelming emotion always comes out as tears. So goddamn annoying. Before a single drop can spill onto my cheek, I feel a hand on my lower back, warm and comforting.

"It's serious," Aiden says firmly. His presence alone instantly causes my shoulders to drop in relief. For once, I don't have to face Josh's scrutiny and indecision alone. Instead of embarrassment, I feel safe having Aiden here for this conversation. Like for once, someone is protecting my heart instead of ripping it open to see if the contents meet *their* needs and expectations.

Aiden's never looked at me like he was weighing my worth and what benefit I could bring to the table. He's only looked at me with curiosity, intrigue, passion, and warmth. The contrast between a future with him at my back and my past standing in front of me is stark.

"Aiden Price? As in the Aviators' second baseman? Congrats on the game, man," Josh says, a note of hesitation in his voice. He's still trying to piece together what he sees in front of him.

"Thanks, but I'd be even more appreciative if you'd drop the condescension from your tone when you're speaking to Bec."

*Okay, why the fuck is that so hot?*

"No offense, but Bec and I have a history that you don't need to concern yourself with."

"You're right. Because it's *history*. I suggest you lose her number because she doesn't want to speak to you, in case her not answering your calls wasn't a big enough clue." He dismisses Josh by turning me toward him and running his hand along my jaw to pull my gaze up to his. "You ready to go home, beautiful?"

And the tear that originated from anger melts into something sweeter as it finally topples over onto my cheek. Aiden wipes it away quickly, and I smile and nod. "I'm ready."

# Chapter Forty-Three

## Aiden

After leaving Josh with an irritated look plastered on his face, we say goodbye to our friends and I drive Bec to my place, since she caught a ride to the game with the girls. The ride is mostly quiet, her hand in mine, resting on her thigh, her humming along softly to the music.

When we get to my apartment, we settle on the couch with Hopper between us greedily demanding our attention. God, he's going to kill me if I fuck this up with Bec. When I say he's already attached to her, I mean it. I guess we both are.

Wanting to check in with her after her run-in with Josh, I decide I can't wait any longer to bring it up. "So, that was Josh," I say, trying to keep it low pressure to see if she feels like talking about it.

"That...was Josh." She runs her fingers through her hair, taking a deep breath. "You probably think he's a douche, but it felt different when we first met. It wasn't until things got more serious that it became clear it was never going to work out between us."

From what I overheard of their conversation, Josh is a real tool. Regardless, I don't judge Bec for who she's dated in the past. It's not like any of my brief relationships have worked out either.

You don't really know who anyone is until you see them struggle. Until they're forced to take down their own demons or surrender to them. Until they're fighting through something and have to decide who they want to be on the other side of that battle. Relationships start easy, but when shit hits the fan, I want to know that my partner and I can turn to each other and not against each other. Maybe that's me being judgmental, or maybe that's me projecting my own messed-up bullshit onto everyone else.

"People tend to show us who they really are eventually. How did it feel to see him?" I'm sure Bec can hear the insecurity in my voice, hoping to god she's over him and ready to take things further with me.

She sighs, letting her head fall back on the couch, mindlessly petting Hopper's ears.

"Am I a shitty person if I say I barely felt anything?" she asks, turning to look at me. "Josh and I had fun in the beginning, but things were never perfect. When we'd gone a few days without seeing each other, it didn't feel like he was hungry to see me again. When I reflect on it now, I wasn't missing him during our time apart either. Shouldn't you miss the person you're with? Shouldn't you crave them? And tonight, he acted like I sprinted into another relationship. Like I still owed him something."

"You don't owe him anything, Bec. He called it quits, so he has to live with that choice. He doesn't have any right to make you question your reaction to his decisions. He lost that right when you two broke up. And Bec?"

"Yeah?"

"Don't ever forget how incredible you are. He should never have left you doubting how wanted you were. I got one weekend with you and you left me starving for more. I don't want you to question the way I see you. At every turn, you surprise me in all the best ways."

"You don't have to say that."

"Exactly. I don't have to say that. I said it because it's true. I won't pretend to know what you went through, but I can understand if the way Josh ended things left you confused. Let me be the one to remind you how much he didn't see. Do you trust me?" I ask.

"I want to," she says quietly.

"That's a start." I want to be the type of man who deserves someone like Bec. I don't know that I am, in fact I'm sure I'm far from it, but I sure as shit want to try.

"Do you remember what I told you my biggest fear was when we met?" she asks, her eyes glassy.

"You were afraid of losing yourself," I say softly.

"And I *did*. I let one relationship change the way I see myself. Before that, I felt like I was finally finding my confidence, you know? I knew what I wanted in life and I was just looking for someone to share it with. It's terrifying that one person had the power to shake that all to the ground.

"With Josh, there wasn't any huge wound he ripped open and left hurting. Instead, the relationship left a million small cuts in whatever sense of self I had spent my college years refining, the culmination of too many moments of self-doubt rising to the surface like a scream I had buried and hidden under my so-called confidence and easy-going attitude.

"I kept internalizing things he'd say that made me feel less than, whether it was undermining my career, my appearance, my apartment, not supporting me in front of his family or friends, or teasing at my expense. I'd laugh it all off, because I guess I was embarrassed how much it bothered me. Over time, I ended up giving all this power to the lingering voice in my mind that built up every passive comment to mean more than it did. It festered and morphed into this nagging need to watch what I say and to try to become this version of myself I thought I *should* be, not the version I am.

"I always felt like I needed to say the right things, do the right things. I don't think Josh even noticed that something was wrong. He had no idea who I really was, so how could he know? It's a lesson I think I had to learn. I don't just need firm boundaries to avoid getting hurt, it's also so I don't ever feel like I need to turn myself inside out to reshape myself into this imaginary, perfect version of me."

I take a moment and think about everything Bec's shared. It makes sense the way she's held back with me. It's going to take time for her to trust me and to trust herself with me. All that matters is that she told me she's willing to try. I'm a patient man, and for her, I'd wait a lifetime.

"Sometimes I think it's harder to realize a relationship isn't good for you when there's no huge fight, no final straw," I say. "Then one day, you sit back, and you don't recognize yourself when you're with that person, and you're forced to ask yourself how the fuck did I get here?"

"Exactly. I built this shell of who I thought I should be and used it as a shield to hide who I am. I think I was just tired of being alone, but I found myself feeling alone even when I was with him. When Josh finally ended things, I thought what the fuck was that all for? Why did I spend all that time trying to fit into this box I thought meant more than the version of me I loved, hiding underneath it all," Bec says.

"I don't ever want you to hold back with me. You don't have to tame yourself into some smaller version of who you're meant to be. I want you to shine. I don't want you to doubt your instincts, I want you to listen to them. I don't want some watered-down version of you, Bec. I want it all."

"You're really sweet, you know that, Aiden?" It's a relief to see her smile again.

"You want sweet? I can be sweet. You want spicy? I can be that too."

# CHAPTER FORTY-THREE

I shrug and smirk. "I'll be whatever you want."

"Hm...how spicy?"

"That depends on how much heat you can handle." Watching her blush and laugh it off brings an ease back into the room as the conversation lightens.

Hopper jumps down onto the floor and starts to chew on one of his new bones, allowing me to pull Bec closer into my side where she snuggles in and pulls her feet up and to the side leaning into my shoulder.

"Can I ask you something?" she asks.

"Anything," I reply.

"Back in the fall, when you ran into me at the restaurant where I was leaving what was probably my worst first date ever..."

"God, that fucking idiot. I forgot about him."

"What did you say to him before he left? He looked a little... irritated," she says.

I smile at the memory. "Before I tell you, I need you to know that I would have respected your decision if you asked me to take up a permanent residence in the friend zone." I stroke my fingers lightly over her shoulder.

"Okay?" The little wrinkle in her forehead as she looks up at me is distractingly cute.

"I told him that he shouldn't take another woman on a date until he could recognize how much of an asshole he was to you...then I thanked him."

I can tell that catches her off guard. "You...thanked him."

"I did. I thanked him for fucking up his shot with you so badly he'd never have another chance with you. I thanked him for making the mistake of letting you get away, because you are intelligent, passionate, generous, beautiful...and meant for me."

That day, I promised myself that if I ever convinced Bec to give us a shot, I'd do everything in my power to make her want me as much as I want her. To need me as much as I need her. I know she's not there yet, but dammit if I'm not going to give it my all.

"You wanted this even then?" she asks.

"I've wanted you since the moment I met you. I could never get you off my mind, even when I barely knew you," I say, hoping she can hear the sincerity in my voice.

"I know I'm not coming into this all with the best sense of self-esteem. I don't want you to feel burdened by that."

"Needing validation of what I feel for you is not a burden, Bec. I should've been honest from the start about wanting to be together, but I don't want you to question where I stand. I was addicted to you after one kiss, and every day I want you more."

"I want you, too, and I want you to know that I've moved on. I haven't felt anything for Josh in a long time and tonight only proved that we never would have worked. But with you...things with you feel so different. A part of that scares me, but a bigger part of me knows it's a good thing. The type of good thing I don't think I could really get enough of."

I kiss her and it feels like the only thing grounding me is the pressure of her palms against my chest, her lips pressed softly to mine. Her mouth parts, and our tongues meet, the sweet taste of her making me groan.

I turn slightly to fall back onto the couch, grabbing Bec by her hips and pulling her on top of me so we're both lying on the couch, her legs straddling mine. The tension crackles between us, the electricity unrestrained and potent.

She grinds against me and my hardening cock twitches underneath her. I palm the back of her head with one hand and grip her ass with the other as she continues to roll her hips against mine. I kiss along Bec's neck, moving both hands to squeeze her breasts as she gasps and whispers my name.

She sits up, removing her shirt and bra. I sit up, too, and lick her hard nipples, causing her to moan and arch her back, pushing her chest closer to me, inviting me to continue.

"Stay with me tonight. Stay with me every night. I don't want us to sleep alone when I'm not on the road," I say as I switch my attention from one breast to the other. Bec gasps but doesn't answer me.

"I don't usually beg, Bec, but I will if you ask me to." I'd do anything she asked me to.

"Yes," she pants. She takes my face in between her hands and kisses me, consuming me. "I'll stay."

I lift her and switch our positions so she's lying on her back. I crawl on top of her and Bec draws her legs up the back of my thighs as I slide down her body, pulling her leggings off, leaving her in just her underwear and my head between her thighs. I drape her legs over my shoulders.

"You didn't even let me beg..." I say, my lips skirting along the edge of her black thong. My hands are rough from years of playing ball, but her skin is soft and smooth as I trail my fingers up her outer thighs.

"For good reason," she says. I look up to see her propped up on her elbows, smiling down at me. "I'd rather your mouth was busy doing something else."

"Fuck," I groan into her thigh before looking back up at her. "How are you this perfect?" I slide her panties to the side and give her a long, slow lick up her slit before I devour her.

I don't hold back. I don't want her in her head, doubting what we could have because some asshole made her feel like shit for no goddamn reason. I want her to feel how much I want her. I suck and lick her clit, applying a pulsing pressure before pressing a finger into her as well.

"Oh shit," Bec says, her breathing heavy. "Just like that."

After a few minutes, I press another finger into her soaked pussy and make a pulling motion toward her front wall, causing her to clench tightly around my digits. With my other hand, I press down firmly on her lower stomach.

"God, don't you dare stop," Bec demands.

Her entire body tenses and she clenches around my fingers as she moans my name. I don't stop or slow my movements as I work her through her climax, her words blending into something unintelligible while she bucks her hips, trying to ride my face and my hand, grinding against the hold I have on her stomach.

Her body relaxes into the couch, any lingering tension melting away. When I lift my head from her soaking entrance, I watch the labored rise and fall of her chest as her breathing begins to calm. Her nipples are still hard. I kiss my way up her stomach to suck on one of them and palm the other in my hand. Every part of Bec is stunning—her eyes, her smile, her curves, her thighs, but I could live forever worshipping her tits.

Her hand weakly cups the back of my head. I love seeing her worn out like this for me.

"You're really fucking good at that," Bec says. "My turn."

Before I can register the meaning of her words, she's gripping my hair roughly, pulling my mouth off her breast with a pop. She pushes at my shoulders until I sit up. When she has enough room to crawl off the couch onto the floor, she moves to kneel between my legs.

She runs her hands under my shirt and up my abdomen. I lean forward, allowing her to pull my shirt over my head, and she tosses it carelessly onto the floor behind her. She doesn't make eye contact with me, completely focused on removing my belt buckle and unzipping my pants. It isn't until she has her hands tucked into the top of my jeans that she looks up to me, her eyes gleaming, waiting for me to tilt my hips and help her remove my pants. When I do, she refocuses on undressing me.

My breathing becomes heavy while I watch Bec lick her lips as she pulls the waistband of my boxer briefs down, my cock springing free. She wraps one hand firmly around the base of my shaft before her eyes lock onto mine. She leans down, rubbing her breasts against my inner thighs and running her tongue along the bottom of my cock. I expect her to pull back when she reaches the head, but she doesn't. She closes her eyes, wraps her pretty lips around my dick, and drops as far onto my shaft as she can, humming contently. I squeeze my hands into fists, pressing them into the couch as I fight the reflex to buck my hips.

My vision blurs, and I reach out, gripping Bec's hair, trying to slow her eager movements so I don't finish before I've had a chance to enjoy her perfect mouth on me. She bobs, sucks, and squeezes me, and I can't keep my eyes off her while she works me down her throat.

After a few minutes, her free hand slips into my briefs and she lightly tugs on my balls. I know I can't hold out any longer.

"If you don't want to swallow me down, gorgeous, then you need to pull off now," I manage to choke out. She hums around my cock and doubles down.

I come hard, my breath stuttering as my entire body tenses with pleasure. My orgasm rips through me and I don't want to look away from the sight of Bec on her knees for me, but I can't help closing my eyes as my head falls back against the couch. She feels too fucking good.

Bec doesn't give me any relief, not slowing her movements. "Jesus," I mutter, pulling lightly on her hair where I still have my hand tangled. She pops off my dick and smiles up at me, with mischief in her eyes as she licks her lips.

"You got me beat, babe." I heave out. "If you thought I was good... fuck, you're better."

# Chapter Forty-Four

Bec

"This was a mistake," I say with a sigh.

"You say that like I embarrass you or something," my brother Ash says as he drapes his heavy arm around my shoulders. He radiates a carefree, spontaneous energy no matter where he is or what's going on.

"You *do* embarrass me. Why are you wearing that?" I groan.

"Oh, you mean *this*?" he says as he pulls the bottom edge of his shirt taut so the writing is unmistakable.

"Yes, she means *that*. God, even I'm embarrassed for her," Toby says with a grimace.

"Thanks, Toby," I say.

"Nah, I'm with Ash. That shirt is priceless. You should have told me. I would have ordered my own," Danny says.

"Toby, you're officially my favorite sibling. They're not invited to any more games," I say with a sneer directed at Danny and Ash, who are trying to humiliate me to death.

When Aiden offered tickets for my family to come to one of his games—in really fucking great seats that we would never splurge on ourselves—my first instinct was to say no. But after Ellie let that fun fact slip in front of Danny the other weekend at lunch, she wouldn't stop blowing up our family group chat until I agreed to take Aiden up on his offer. Then my mom decided that we needed to go to an early afternoon game so that Aiden could join us for family dinner at their house afterward. Essentially, everyone not named Bec decided that it was time for Aiden to meet my family.

Aiden seemed all too willing to take my family up on the invite to dinner, so maybe this won't be anything like when Josh met my family. Old Bec wouldn't be so terrified of this step, but when my family met Josh and their negative assessment of our relationship was spot on, it's hard to want to face their judgment again. They know me so well. If Aiden has any red flags that I'm missing, they'll shine a light on them so brightly I'll never be able to unsee them, and well...I don't want to see any red flags with Aiden.

My feelings toward him are stronger than I thought possible. So, I reluctantly agreed to this meeting because if I really do like him, then this moment is inevitable anyway. I want Aiden to know the people who raised me, and I want him to love them like I do. While I know I don't need my family's approval, I still want it. I've always been close with my family. I want the person I spend my life with to love them too. So, yeah. No pressure.

Oh, and this is made infinitely worse because my smart-ass brother decided to special order and wear a shirt that reads *Number 15's Future Brother-in-law.*

*Kill me now.*

"Rebecca, if you really like Aiden, he'll have to get used to Ashton anyway. Might as well not sugarcoat anything here," Mom says with a sigh.

"I don't know whether to be appreciative or offended, dearest mother," Ash says with a grin.

"Offended. The answer is offended," Toby says as the batter strikes out, ending the fifth inning.

Aiden's had a great game. According to Toby, he's made diving stops, laid out for a ball that saved at least one run, and he has two "ribbies." I really need to learn what the fuck this all means.

It still feels surreal to sit in the stands and watch Aiden play and to also know him as the humble, easy-going guy that he is off the field. The way he acts when it's just us always has me forgetting what he does for work. That is until I'm sitting next to a fan who can rattle off his stats that make zero sense to me but are obviously meaningful enough for a stranger to memorize them.

It also helps that he looks really fucking hot excelling at the sport he obviously cares so much about.

"Your boyfriend's got a great arm," Toby comments seriously. "Quick too." He hasn't taken his eyes off the game, his love for the sport evident in his undivided attention. It's no surprise he was the first to agree to come to the game. When I mentioned where we'd be seated, I even got a rare Tobias Miller smile.

"He's not my boyfriend," I say back.

"He's meeting your family...he's your something," Danny mumbles in between bites of her hotdog.

"He's my...I don't know, just don't mention titles tonight. We aren't labeling anything, okay? Please don't make it weird," I plead.

"Was this his idea or yours, Becca boo? The no labels thing," Dad asks, voice tinted with a hint of concern.

"Mine. I wanted to take things slow," I say. Dad nods, seemingly happy with my answer.

"It's unseasonably warm for April. We could probably have dinner outside on the patio tonight, don't you think?" Mom asks with excitement in her eyes. The woman loves to host. She's probably had the house staged for Aiden's arrival for three days, not a dish out of place. She was a bit...excited to hear that Aiden and I were still seeing each other. I'm not saying she's itching at the idea of one of her children being in a relationship in hopes that she finally gets to help plan a wedding, but I'm not *not* saying it.

# Chapter Forty-Five

## Aiden

"You should turn around while you still can," Bec says when she answers the door for me at her parent's home.

"Uh...everything okay, babe? Your eyes are the widest I've ever seen them." She doesn't move out of the doorway. She just stands there, frozen with a look of regret.

"Are you sure...*absolutely sure*...you want to do this?" she asks.

"Of course, Bec. I'm excited to meet your family," I say with a confidence I do *not* feel. My stomach is in my ass and I'm already sweating. I haven't met the family of someone I was seeing since high school. So yeah...you could say excited, or you could say *motherfucking* terrified. Both can be true, right?

"Please ignore everything you see and hear tonight if it in any way makes you want to run away from me screaming," she says, resigned as she steps aside to let me into the house.

I follow Bec down the hallway and into the main living space. When we turn the corner, her family is lined up, standing side by side...and they're all staring at me.

"Welcome to our home, Aiden. I'm Rebecca's mother, but you can call me Denise." The delivery is a bit rehearsed and her smile looks a little stiff, but her eyes are warm and her words are kind.

"And I'm Bec's father. You can call me Mr. Miller." Okay, Bec's dad's greeting is...a little more formal. A little less warm.

Denise elbows Mr. Miller in his side. "Thomas, we talked about this."

He clears his throat. "You can call me Thomas, I guess." He mutters the last part under his breath.

"You guys promised to act natural. Exactly what part of this feels natural to you?" Bec asks with her arms crossed and her hip leaning against the kitchen table.

"Aiden Price...you have the distinct honor of joining us for...*family game night*," a guy in his late twenties sings, cupping his hands around his mouth to amplify the volume of his announcement. "I'll be your host, Ashton Sweet-Cheeks Miller. Meet my cohosts Danny the Devil Darling and Toby the Shit-on-your-party, Buzz-kill Extraordinaire. Now," he claps his hands together, "time to pick teams."

"God fucking dammit," I hear Bec mumble from beside me. When I look over at her for some sign as to what the fuck is going on, her stern expression breaks down into a smile. "Well, I should have expected this. Aiden, are you any good at Pictionary?"

* * *

My family may be small, but the three of us did have family game nights growing up. But nothing...not a single one of our quiet nights playing Monopoly or Scrabble prepared me to play Pictionary with the Millers.

"Blood? A sacrifice! No...water? A baptism!" Denise shouts, hopping up and down with her hands clenched in tight fists at her shoulders while she attempts to guess anything and everything that Bec could possibly be drawing. The guesses fly out of her mouth in a stream of consciousness. I barely have time to process the first guess she shouts before she's yelled out three more in the same breath.

Bec draws two more droplets and a cloud.

"Rain!" Danny screams, jumping to her feet to clasp one of her mom's fists in her hands.

I thought I was competitive...I've had to be to make it this far in my career. That was until I met the women in this family.

Bec points excitedly and beams silently at Danny, signifying she guessed part of the word correctly. She continues to draw, and it takes all of two seconds before I hear Denise scream, "RAINBOW," at the top of her lungs.

"Yes," Bec screams, and the three women celebrate loudly.

When the group settles down, it's my turn to draw while my team, Toby and Thomas, guess the word. I stand and walk to the easel, grabbing a card on the way. I can't remember if I've ever played this game before, and I'm by no means an artist, but how hard can it really be? Guessing has been easy enough. The cards haven't had anything too complex. This should be fine. No, this *will* be fine. I flip the card over so only I can see it.

*Eggplant.*

*You gotta be shitting me.*

I have to draw...an eggplant.

My eyes immediately find Bec's in a silent plea for help. But she misreads my hesitation as weakness in the game. The competitive little shit smirks at me, crosses her arms, and sits back on the couch next to her sister.

"Uh-oh, did superstar Aiden Price get a hard one?" she taunts, her eyebrow hitting her hairline.

*No, babe. I'm sure as shit not hard right now, but what I'm about to draw in front of your fuckin' family might look like it.*

I let out a rough breath that stutters into a labored cough. I think my body is shutting down with preemptive embarrassment. I'm pretty sure that's possible. Yeah, that's a real thing and it's happening right fucking now.

"Aaaaaand...go," Ash shouts, looking at the timer on his phone since he's proclaimed himself the judge and "commissioner" of the game.

*Okay, I can do this. I just have to draw...a vegetable. Not a dick. Don't draw a dick. Draw...a vegetable.*

I can see my hand shaking as I bring the marker to the paper, my back to Bec's family. I let out one more deep breath before I start to draw.

I'm feeling a little relieved as the image takes shape. I even add the stem and leaves to distinguish it more from...you know.

But then I take a step back and turn to face Bec and her family. Ready to hear their guesses.

Except the room is silent.

This house hasn't been silent since I stepped inside hours ago. Not a moment of quiet in introductions, through dinner, or during this game. Bec's family maintains a consistent rumble of side conversations at all times. Enough so that I find myself jumping from conversation to conversation as everyone pulls my attention in a new direction. I don't know if I've finished a full thought tonight or if I just jumped from topic to topic, joining and rejoining different discussions, moving fluidly throughout their group. It's just their natural state of being it seems.

But not now...now, they're all sitting quietly. Staring at me.

Bec's face is pale and her eyes are huge. Her head slowly shakes back and forth. *What...what the fuck does that mean?*

I turn back to my drawing to make sure it looks strictly vegetarian and not...carnivorous. And...okay, maybe it's not as good as I originally thought. Okay, maybe it's terrible.

I steal another glance at the Millers. Bec looks the same as before, her head still shaking in disbelief, her eyes never leaving my drawing. Danny is trying to hide her shit-eating grin behind her hand. Denise's mouth is hanging open. Ash is nodding his head, his lips pursed, one arm crossed against his stomach while his other hand is rubbing his jaw. Toby has his lips pressed together with his teeth, his head tilted and his eyes squinting as if he's trying to convince himself he's not seeing what he's seeing. And Thomas...I can't even look at Bec's father, so I'm just going to pretend he's not here.

Yeah, it's pretty phallic, I guess.

*Shit, the stem and leaves definitely look like pubes.*

*God fucking dammit.*

Finally, someone breaks the silence, but it doesn't bring any relief to my heart that is threatening to pound out of my chest. I'm really sweating now. My palms are slick as they hang at my sides in defeat.

"That's a penis," Bec's dad says. "You wanna tell me why you drew a penis on the family Pictionary board, Aiden?"

I look back at the board, then at him, still trying to find the right words to say next when Ash chimes in. "Yeah, don't you play ball or something? You could have at least added those too?"

"Ashton!" Denise reprimands.

"What? If you're gonna draw a dick at family game night, might as well throw in some balls too," he argues, like this is a completely reasonable assessment of the situation.

"It's an eggplant," I yell way louder than necessary. "I swear it's an eggplant. I can't draw for shit. I'm sorry. Here." I rip the card out of my pocket and desperately hold it out in front of me.

Just when I think it's time to bolt out of the room, through the front door, and into my car to make a quick getaway, Thomas shocks the fuck outta me. The man lets out a cackle so loud, so unhinged, it seems unbelievably out of character for the reserved man I've been getting to know all evening. Everyone joins Bec's dad, laughing at what I know will become a memory I'll never live down.

"Bec, if you keep Aiden around to play Pictionary again, then I demand to be on the other team from here on out. Stick to your day job, Price," Thomas says, standing and clapping me on the back.

"Yes, sir. I think I'll be doing just that."

# Chapter Forty-Six

Aiden

"You need to promise right now. Do it," Bec pleads, her voice maniacal.

"Okay, I promise I won't laugh," I huff. "Can I take the blindfold off now?"

"Not yet, keep them closed while we walk inside." She tugs on my arm, pulling me into her apartment. I feel Hopper rush past me, and I drop his leash as he presumably makes himself at home on Bec's couch.

"I know what this is. Is this the VIP room treatment? Am I about to get a special birthday dance, Bec?

"You wish, perv."

"You bet your perfect ass I do." I reach my arms in front of me, blindly grabbing for Bec, coming up empty until I feel her shoulder brush against me. I find her arm and pull her against my front clumsily, my arm wrapping tightly around her waist.

"You couldn't handle a dance from me, old man."

"Ah right, of course. I'm twenty-eight going on ninety."

"They say you're only as old as you feel."

"And I'm hoping they're wrong. My shoulders are at least three decades older than the rest of me."

"Is that what that fun little popping noise is?" Bec asks. One of the glories from living out my dream of becoming a professional athlete. The body takes a beating.

Escaping my clutches, Bec stumbles out of reach, and I hear rustling around her apartment, the flicking of light switches, and the distinct sound of a match being struck.

"Uh, Bec? This was fun, but I should be on my way...ya know...if you found your way into a pyrotechnic-type hobby."

"Take off your blindfold, smart-ass."

Chuckling to myself, I do as I'm told, relieved to finally see what Bec had deemed a "top secret birthday surprise."

My brain couldn't string two words together right now if I tried. Bec's apartment is dark, the only light emanating from the candles lining the cake Bec's holding, casting shadows around her in flickering rays of light from the flames, her expression soft and unsure. Behind her, the couch is wrecked, torn apart with cushions and pillows on the floor, backed by...backed by moving boxes.

The way the furniture is set up in Bec's living room...it's exactly how I described my eighth birthday, my favorite memory, when I told Bec about it years ago. When Mom and Evie used boxes, blankets, and pillows to make furniture for our family movie night.

"Wh-what is this?" I stammer quietly, almost to myself, but Bec hears me, her face falling.

"You hate it. Shit, this was so dumb..." She hurries to slide the cake onto the counter and runs her hands through her hair in a frenzy. "I'm sorry, this was so weird. Forget it."

I take three steps toward her and pull her body flush with mine, one hand on her lower back and the other on the back of her neck. Our kiss starts hungry and after a minute, melts into something gentler, her hands running up my chest. Slow passes of our lips, shared breaths, and the slip of her sweet tongue against mine. I drop my forehead to rest on hers.

"Is this what I think it is? You did this for me?" She nods with a meek smile. Relief evident on her face. "Are you trying to ruin me?" I ask. I let go of the breath I was holding as I bring her against my chest. Holding her here, it feels like finding a buoy in the center of a storm. Secure and safe. I'm in unknown waters now. The risks threaten to drown me. But I'm not scared. Not with her.

"Thought I'd repay the favor. It feels like I've been ruined since I met you," she whispers against my neck.

"Show me. I want to see everything."

Her face ignites, radiating joy, her smile beaming at me.

"Well, my assistant here is already demonstrating the high-class accommodations we have available for the evening, sir." She walks backward into her living room and does a dramatic sweep of her arm to feature Hopper, who is licking himself on a pile of couch cushions and pillows thrown haphazardly on the floor in front of the coffee table.

"And here you'll find a selection of our finest entertainment sure to have you laughing, crying, soaking in nostalgic bliss, the works." She shimmies to the side while she displays a stack of DVDs like a kid showing off their science project.

"I don't know the last time I watched a DVD. Do you have a player for these?" I ask.

"I had to borrow one from Dom. These are from the library. Only the best on your very special day, of course."

I walk over to inspect the selections she's made, and my chest tightens as I read the titles. A weight drops to the bottom of my throat as I try to find the ability to speak.

"Some may look familiar." She watches my expression carefully, with a smug grin on her face.

My favorite baseball movies from my childhood, the ones I told her about years ago, are stacked on Bec's coffee table. To anyone else, it's a thoughtful gesture, but to me, it's everything. *She* is everything.

"Admittedly, I had to ask Dom to confirm the titles, because I couldn't remember them exactly and I was spiraling in the middle of the library frantically googling every known baseball movie I could find. Kids were starting to stare. It took a minute, but we figured it out. But don't get too excited, we won't be watching any of these first."

"What movie won out over these *impeccable* selections?" I ask.

"You have to watch this first." Bec reaches behind the pile to reveal a worn copy of *A League of Their Own*. "I can't allow you to go one more day without watching this. It's basically a crime that you haven't seen this. It's a classic. You'll never be the same," she says, rocking the DVD from side to side with a small bounce in her knees.

I can't take my eyes off her. I look her up and down, in disbelief that someone like her is even real. "You're right. I could never be the same after this." I stalk after her while she retreats backward, never taking her eyes off me as she circles back into her connected kitchen, putting the island between us.

"But wait, that's not all!" Any nervousness she had from my initial reaction is gone, that lighthearted spontaneity returning. The carefree state I always want to see her in. She may not realize it, but she's trusting me every day, more and more, little by little. She takes the lid off a pot on her stove with an amused expression. "Only the finest sustenance for the celebration."

"Is that mac and cheese?"

She nods and laughs. God, what I wouldn't give to hear that every day for the rest of my life. My eye catches on the counter, the candles still lit from Bec's reveal earlier.

"And, uh...what happened here, hun?" I gesture to the cake, if you can call it that.

She holds up her hands defensively. "Okay, it's been a while since I've made a box cake and I'm not a great cook. Believe it or not even the mac and cheese was a struggle. It's not my fault the cake sort of...cratered in the middle? I stole a taste to make sure it doesn't taste like garbage. I can confirm, the aesthetics are lacking, but the deliciousness is not."

"Get over here," I say, my voice low. She doesn't hesitate and immediately walks into my arms, her chin propped on my chest, eyes on me. "You did this for me?" She answers me with a soft smile.

"Everything you told me about that birthday sounded so perfect. I thought it'd be fun to relive it together."

"No one has ever done anything like this for me before," I say quietly, not trusting the shake in my voice. The ache in my chest is sharp as I realize I don't feel like I deserve it. I don't deserve her. "That memory was from a really great day surrounded by a sea of terrible ones. My family was in the thick of healing."

"Did I mess up? Is this too much?"

"It is most definitely too much. But only because I don't know how I'll ever pay you back for something this genuinely thoughtful."

"Relationships aren't about keeping score, Aiden. They aren't about tallying up what we owe each other. I did this because I care about you, and I wanted you to feel it."

"I want to be the man who's worthy of this...kindness."

*Love.*

*I want to be worthy of Bec's love.*

"You already are," she says quietly, her words soft but sure. Bec loops her hands around my neck and pulls me down for a quick kiss.

"But I do have a confession. I've seen this movie before," I admit.

"What? When we met, you said you hadn't ever—"

"I watched it the day I got home from Dom's wedding. It's a good movie. A great movie. You could've borrowed my copy. I ended up buying it. Even lent it to a few teammates so they could watch it too."

"Why did you...?" Her voice tapers off timidly.

"When we met, you understandably had doubts." I reach up to brush a loose curl behind Bec's ear. "But I knew. I knew I was ready for you, for us. I was clinging to anything that felt like you...any connection to what I wished we could be."

A single tear drops down her cheek.

"Hey, there's no crying in baseball," I say, before wiping the tear off her cheek with my thumb. She breaks out into a fit of laughter and I join her, my heart so full I can feel it trying to break through my chest just to be closer to her. It's hers anyway.

"Did you really just quote *A League of Their Own*?" she asks.

"I really did," I say with a smile. "Can I take you somewhere tomorrow?" I ask. She wipes tears of laughter from her cheeks and nods. "Good. There's someone I want you to meet."

# Chapter Forty-Seven

Bec

When Aiden first told me about his mom's condition, I felt the uncomfortable itch of helplessness crawling over my skin. It was evident how hard all of this has been on his family, and I wanted to take away all of his pain at that moment. When I look at him now, that gnawing feeling rises up again.

While I'm grateful that I don't have experience dealing with something like this, it also makes me feel inadequate as far as helping Aiden with the challenges that he's facing and will continue to face as time goes on. So, I do what I do in any situation where I don't have the answers, when there's no solution, when it's clear that compassion and empathy are the only things needed; I listen. I listen as we drive to the facility and Aiden describes the check-in procedure, his mom's daily routine, how the staff works with her, and how he and Evie handle their visits on both the good days and the bad days.

Aiden estimates we have a fifty-fifty chance of catching her on a good day. Evie agreed to meet us there as well, in hopes that a good day wins out.

While he's trying to appear calm—his voice and his hand resting on my thigh are both steady—I still notice his restless leg, bouncing the entire drive and the tense set of his shoulders. It's clear nothing about this is easy for Aiden.

I'm honored he wants me to meet his mother, and equally terrified about what that means for us. Somewhere along the way, the walls I surrounded myself with out of spite have weakened. I was jaded by the entire premise of love. I was never going to get my own love story. I had accepted that the ones I read about are works of fiction, not fact.

So why does it feel like I can't find the flaw here?

Why don't I see an ending to whatever this is?

Whatever we are to each other, it's become so much more than just one date at a time. He fits into my life easier than I imagined possible. I'm left with a growing sense of hope and optimism that *maybe* this could all work out, if we both let it. I'm surprised to find the thought doesn't scare me like it used to.

Aiden puts the car into park lets out a heavy sigh. My chest aches with how much I'm wishing for this to go well. For his mom, for me, but mostly for him.

"It's not too late to turn around," he says. His voice is laced with indecisiveness.

"I can't wait to meet her." I thread my fingers through his hand that's resting on my leg and give it a reassuring squeeze. "If you're ready for this, I'm ready too."

I'm startled by a hand slapping on Aiden's window.

"Jesus Christ," Aiden mutters, rolling down the window. Evie pops her head in the frame, a goofy grin on her face.

"Hey, lovers. You know this is a parking lot and not the drive-in, right? Aiden, your mother is right inside. Imagine the scandal if she had to explain to Phyllis that you and your girlfriend were canoodling in public the next time she and the girls got together to play bridge. *Think of her reputation.*"

"You're fucking ridiculous," he retorts, but even he can't resist the chuckle breaking through his steely pretense, probably grateful for the break in tension from the weight of the moment.

"I know." She giggles, then slaps her hands on the hood of the car. "Come on, Bec. Mom's going to love you."

* * *

"It wasn't like that." Aiden pouts.

"It was exactly like that," Evie whispers to me, loud enough for her mom and Aiden to hear. We're sitting in a brightly lit corner of the common space in the memory care unit. The couch Aiden and I are sharing has a floral print in earthy color tones, the petals swirling over the curves of the furniture. On the couch along the next wall, sit Evie and Ms. Price, who asked me to call her Judy when she introduced herself. Her smile is warm and her demeanor calm.

Judy turns to look at me and says, "Aiden took his role very seriously. He was so proud he practiced every night at the dinner table for a month. I always said he should pursue acting. He really found his voice in that performance."

"Mom, I had two lines," Aiden grumbles.

"And they were *very* believable. You had the crowd on their feet," Judy replies.

"No, Mom, *you* were on your feet," Aiden says.

"And Evie," she counters proudly.

"Yeah, and me," Evie says. "It's not our fault the rest of the audience didn't follow our lead. That's basic play etiquette. Someone stands, you stand too. They were the best two lines of the whole play. Especially since you were dressed as a jellyfish." She turns to me, gripping my hand in hers, leaning toward me conspiratorially. "Aiden flailed his arms so dramatically that he slapped the kid next to him in the face with one of the tentacles on his costume. The kid hit him back with his crab claw right after he delivered his line. Straight to the jaw. Priceless."

My ribs ache from laughter. "I can picture it now, but man, I wish I could see the real thing," I say.

Evie gets that look on her face that I'm beginning to recognize means she's up to something, most likely something at Aiden's expense. Aiden noticeably straightens, his face paling.

"Evie...you promised," he says quietly.

"I did no such thing," she hisses at him, then turns to me with downright wickedness in her stare. She practically runs every word together, spilling them out in a rush. "We have it. We have it on tape. You need to watch it."

"Mom, please tell me you don't still have it," Aiden pleads.

"How else would I be able to brag about you to my friends here?" Judy asks, the picture of innocence.

"Oh, I don't know, maybe turn on a game? One I get paid to play professionally in?" Aiden replies.

"I do that too. I'm proud of all of your accomplishments."

"Saying two lines in an elementary school play of *The Little Mermaid* isn't exactly an accomplishment," Aiden says.

"Honey, as a mom I get to say this. The big moments and the small moments, they all shine just as bright in my eyes."

Aiden's gaze softens and he says, "Okay, Mom, I'll have to trust you on that."

Without anything needing to be said by Aiden or Evie, I can tell we caught Judy on a good day. It even feels like a great day. I know those are even more rare from what Aiden's told me. She's shown a bit of confusion here and there, but for the most part, she's been alert and oriented with enough clarity to recall and share a few memories of Evie and Aiden from when they were younger and follow along when her children share stories of their own as well.

After introductions and answering some of Judy's questions about myself and how Aiden and I met, I've spent a good part of the last hour laughing at sweet childhood memories told from the lens only a mother can see through. The love in her voice...no amount of memory loss could wipe that clean. It radiates from this woman who sacrificed so much to raise the two adults in front of me.

She's everything Aiden said she was. She has a strong maternal presence, the kind that fills you with reassurance, confidence, and comfort. Having someone like that in your corner means everything. I know because my parents fulfill that role for me. To know that she had to take on the responsibility for herself and their father in his absence, it's incredible. The selflessness and the strength it takes to be a single parent...I can't begin to imagine the tenacity it requires.

Judy's smile fades for a moment, replaced by one less certain. "Uh... did you ask me something, dear? I swear I was just looking here for something." Her gaze is unfocused as she turns toward the stack of magazines on the small table in front of the sitting area.

Aiden looks to Evie, a moment so quick and practiced, communicating more pain and grief than I could ever fathom in less than one second.

Aiden stands and walks to his mom's side, softly squeezing her shoulder. His smile forced.

"Don't worry, Mom. I'll find it for you," he says gently.

"Oh, okay. I think I'll just wait here," she replies. Her attention drifts to the small television in the corner, where a home renovation show is playing on mute.

"Are you okay here for a minute or two while Evie and I check in with her nurse?" Aiden asks me quietly, returning briefly to my side, brushing my hair back behind my ear.

"Of course, we'll be fine," I say, looking up at him with the most reassuring smile I can muster.

I watch Aiden as he and Evie walk away and begin talking with the staff at the nurses' station.

"It's rare to see that, you know?"

"I'm sorry, Judy. Rare to see what exactly?" I ask.

"Don't tell me you don't see it too. I may be getting older, but I've still got my wits about me. That is a man so deep in love it's changed the very fabric of his being. The very bedrock of his reality. You two must be very happy together. Such a rare thing to find. A rare thing to keep. How long have you been married now?" she asks, inclining her head toward Aiden.

"Oh...oh, we're not married...I mean..." I say hesitantly, not sure how she'll respond to me if I contradict her. But I can't just say I'm married to her son, right? Isn't that going to confuse her more? She doesn't know me. Does she even recognize Aiden right now?

"My apologies, my mind isn't what it used to be. Well, it can't be long now before you two tie the knot. Can I give you some advice from one woman to another? Not that you need it when your partner looks at you like that...but be a dear and humor me, will you?"

My heart warms. The sweetness Aiden's spoken of regarding his mother shines through even the cloudy confusion she's battling now. "I'd love some advice."

She reaches out and grabs my hand, placing her other hand to rest on top. She leans toward me. The comfort of a mother emanating from her is like a hug after a long day. A refuge.

"Remember you're playing on the same team. Life will throw a lot at you. It's easy to forget that you're fighting for the same thing sometimes. A life of joy, a life of happiness. It doesn't come easy and it takes work, but it's possible if you remember that you have a partner and not an adversary. Sometimes he'll need more from you, sometimes you'll need more from him. It's never even, but it should always be kind. It has to be selfless, but not sacrificial. Love will take you far, but friendship and respect will make you invincible."

"That's really beautiful," I whisper.

"Oh, the words aren't the beauty of it. The beauty is found within the bond you share. You feel that with him. That kind of love," Judy says matter-of-factly.

It's not a question, as if the look on my face is all the confirmation she needs. But I respond anyway. Even though it's terrifying to say out loud, I let it slip. The secret I haven't even acknowledged myself falls past my lips to the most important woman in Aiden's life, and she may never remember that she heard it first. "Yeah, I think I do. I think I feel that way with him."

"Then don't let go, dear. Be brave together."

In this moment of anonymity, Judy can read my thoughts and emotions more clearly than I can even discern them myself. I smile back at her, my happiness genuine and consuming. I glance back at Aiden briefly to find his stare locked on me. I want to be brave for him. I want that more than I realized.

# Chapter Forty-Eight

Aiden

**B**ec: How am I supposed to pack if I don't know where we're going?

    **Aiden:** Easy. You don't pack anything and this turns into my favorite kind of weekend.

**Bec:** A naked weekend?

**Aiden:** See? You get me.

**Bec:** If you don't tell me how to pack, I'll be forced to exclusively bring granny panties and my grossest, stained oversized T-shirts with more holes than I can count.

**Aiden:** Babe, you can't lay on the dirty talk 30 minutes before the game. How can I play when I'm picturing your shitty shirts on the floor? You got my dick hard.

**Bec:** Get your head in the game.

**Aiden:** Pack the big panties and grungy shirts. Pack whatever you want, Bec. It doesn't matter what you wear since I'll be tearing everything off your body so I can lick every inch of you.

**Aiden:** You there?

**Bec:** Excuse me. My brain is still buffering.

* * *

Bec and I took separate red-eye flights. I left straight from my away game. I couldn't keep the destination secret forever, but I did wait to tell her where we were going until it was time for her to pick up her plane ticket at the airport.

From the look on her face now, her smile beaming from the passenger seat in our rental car, I can tell she's not disappointed.

"I've never been to Colorado. I'm so excited," she says while her eyes flicker over every highway marker we pass. "Where are we headed?"

"We're close now," I answer vaguely.

"So, what brought on this impromptu kidnapping anyway?"

"I'd hardly call sending you a plane ticket kidnapping."

"Semantics. You didn't tell me where I was going until I was already on my way here," Bec says.

"You could have turned around," I argue playfully.

"And leave you all by your lonesome? What would the tabloids have to say about you vacationing alone?"

"We won't need to worry about that here." *Thankfully.*

I've never drawn much attention from the media. I don't give them much to work with. My lacking social life keeps me boring enough to avoid the spotlight, and I like to keep it that way. Though, more has come up since the guys and I promoted the adoption event on social media back in February. Given that it's June, I'm surprised the buzz has lasted this long.

"How mysterious...I'm glad you finally asked Ellie to pack for me. I assume you told her what we're doing while we're here?"

"She knew the basics when she packed your bag. Which by the way, you'll need to change when we get to our first stop."

"Uh...okay? You might be the only guy I would agree to a date with at seven in the morning."

"I wanted to beat the crowd," I say, pulling into the parking lot. "Welcome to Rocky Mountain National Park."

# Chapter Forty-Nine

Bec

The hike to Mills Lake is stunning. At every turn, the rugged landscape takes my breath away. And not a single inch of the trek compares to the view of the lake itself.

Aiden and I take our time on the trails, catching up and laughing. Conversations with Aiden have always flowed easily, and today is no different. Every now and then, I look up from where I'm checking my footing to catch Aiden smiling at me. A look of contentment drawing up the sides of his mouth.

Something about being here with him, the fresh air invigorates the pulse in my veins, breathing life into my lungs. The mountains standing tall in the distance make me feel small, and with that feeling comes an indescribable comfort to my soul. In this quiet, boundless space, all my indecision and anxiety couldn't possibly matter. What significance can any of my stressors hold in a world so wonderfully wild? What problem could matter more than living in the here and now, appreciating the small and large wonders around me?

When we finally stand lakeside, Aiden wraps his arms around my waist, whispering into my ear from behind me, "Was this what you had in mind?"

"What do you mean?" I absentmindedly ask, still enthralled in the view before me: crystal clear waters below snowcapped mountains. I look over the lake, through the trees, unable to fully appreciate the beauty given the overabundance in front of me.

"Your dream vacation..." Aiden says, his voice wavering with a hint of uncertainty.

The memory resurfaces. "Oh my god, Aiden..."

He squeezes me tightly against him, nuzzling into my neck. "You said you wanted an escape. To experience the world more simply, stripped down to the raw elements. Did you find the peace you said it'd bring you? Is it as freeing as you imagined?"

"You chose this spot because...you remembered that I..." I stumble over my words, unable to accept that he is this goddamn perfect.

"I told you; I remember everything about the weekend I met you, Bec. What you said about being in a place like this...how it would make you feel. I wanted to give you that. And I selfishly wanted to feel it with you."

I turn over my shoulder to look at him. "How did I ever think you could be my perfect one-night stand?" I huff out a laugh of disbelief.

"I would have begged for more," he says seriously. "One taste, and I was lost to you. Even the idea of you was enough to hook me forever."

Being lost to Aiden feels like it might be the place I finally find myself. The man I was terrified of getting close to may just be everything I never dreamed could be mine. I run my hands over his arms, which are still wrapped tightly around my stomach, soaking in his affection like the sun's rays on my skin warming me inside and out in this place that makes me feel invincible.

# Chapter Fifty

## Aiden

"Fuck. Shit. Ow," I yell, dropping the pan with a loud clatter on the stove top. Then I hear the smoke detector go off. "Goddammit," I mumble. I jog around waving a spare baking sheet in the air underneath the alarm until it falls silent. The only sound left is my heavy breathing.

"Uh, everything okay over there, chef?" Bec asks from the living room. I turn around to find her watching me, her arm draped over the back of the couch, which faces a wall of windows with a stunning view of the sun setting behind the mountains. I picked this cabin specifically because of how isolated it is and the view she's supposed to be facing now. Instead, she's watching me absolutely destroy dinner with a smirk on her face.

I run my hand through my hair roughly, tugging on the ends knowing I'm fucking up this meal and my dumbass didn't bring a plan B. We're a good distance from the closest grocery store, and since we opted for a late dinner so we could fuck over the rail of the balcony as soon as we got here, the store will be closed before we can make it in time to grab more food. Can't say I regret a thing, though. Watching Bec's ass in her tight leggings throughout the entire hike this morning had me ready to rip her clothes off the second we were alone, and she was just as eager.

Every time I get a taste of Bec, she leaves me starving for more. Even now, all I want is to abandon my hopelessly shitty attempt at a meal, take her into the bedroom, and stay there for the rest of the night, tasting her instead. But she traveled all night and morning to be here and hike with me. I need to make sure she eats something. I stare down at the smoking pan abandoned on the stove top, not sure if the thing is even edible at this point.

"This might be a little...well done. Give me five minutes and it'll be ready." *Jesus, what the fuck am I saying?*

Knowing there's nothing I can do in five minutes to fix this, I coat the dish in more sauce, hoping that will cover the burned edges and dry meat, set the pan on the table, and grab the bottle of wine. Hopefully, more wine will distract her from how awful this dinner is about to be.

I take a desperate swig out of my glass. "All done here. Ready when you are," I say, not making eye contact with Bec.

"Ooookay..." she draws out and walks over to join me at the table.

"More wine?" I immediately offer. She nods, so I top off her glass as she sits down across from me.

"So, what'd you make?" she asks.

"It's, uh, a chicken and pasta dish Eves sent me. She's always sharing new recipes. Figured this was a good time to give it a go."

I'm going to kill Evie when I see her. She said this was one of her "easy, go-to, twenty-minute meals." It took me forty-five minutes to annihilate these ingredients.

"Hmm..." she hums while she pokes and prods the solid mass of slop on the plate in front of her. "Looks...interesting. I'll have to ask her to send me the recipe too," she says with a smile, still not taking a bite.

"Oh, yeah, sure," I say.

*God, I look so fucking dumb right now.*

Bec lifts a forkful to her mouth, and I stop breathing, knowing this is going to be horrible. Should I let her try this? Not alone, I guess. *Fuck it.* I take my own massive bite, because if she likes me enough to try this mess of a meal, then I like her enough to go down with her.

And fuck, it's worse than I thought.

Shutting my eyes and dropping my head down while I muscle through the chewy bite, I hear Bec put down her fork and look up to see her wiping her mouth, humming again softly to herself.

"Yum, wow. That's...um...well, that's great. Really, uh, really different," she says while nodding profusely, before lifting her wine glass to her lips and taking three large gulps.

I narrow my eyes at her.

"Did you just spit that bite into your napkin?"

"Huh? What? Nope, not me. *Noooo*, sir, you are mistaken," she sing-songs to me, avoiding eye contact.

Well, damn, she's cute when she's trying to protect my feelings.

"Let me see, Bec."

She snaps her eyes up to look at me. "What? No, that's...private."

"Your napkin...is private?"

She stares at me, frozen. Her hand hiding her napkin from me, half-tucked under the edge of her plate. It's adorable how guilty she looks. As if it's a greater offense to not eat the shitty food I made for her than for me to feed her shitty food to begin with.

"Yes, okay! I spit it out! Aiden, god I *really* like you but this is...awful. *So awful.* I'm so sorry." And by the end of her apology we're both laughing.

"Shit, I know. Give me your plate. This belongs in the trash. Don't even look at it. I'm afraid the one bite we had will make us both sick for the rest of the trip. We're probably on borrowed time." I gather our plates and walk to the trash, scraping both clean and putting them in the sink. "If this is it for us, just know, I wanted to buy frozen pizza, but Evie said I was a shitty boyfriend if I didn't put in more effort."

She stops laughing, her eyes locking with mine, a shy smile on her face. "Boyfriend, huh?"

Like an idiot, I didn't think twice about using the word even though we've been taking things slow. I'm in no rush to label anything; I want Bec to be ready for that next step, but the word just slipped out, feeling so natural I didn't even realize what I had said until she questioned it.

"How would you feel if I said that's what I wanted you to call me?" I ask, trying to get a feel for her reaction.

She stands up and walks over to me, wrapping her arms around me and leaning her head against my chest. Instinctively, I hold her close, breathing in the smell of her shampoo, her hair still damp from the shower we took together before dinner. Having her in my arms like this calms my nerves. It reminds me that even when I stumble over my words and feel like I'm fucking this all up, this is where I want to be. Whenever my arms are around Bec, my mind completely empties of everything but her.

"Before, I would have said that word wasn't necessary. That we don't need labels. But I think I've been playing it scared. Scared of letting myself have what I want. Scared that I'll lose it like I always do." She looks up at me and my arms tighten around her, wanting her closer even though we're as close as we can be. "I think calling you mine would make me happy, Aiden. But only if you call me yours too."

I run my fingers along her jaw, tilting her chin and kissing her. Holding onto each other tightly, I feel her body melt into mine, and I know that hearing her say that to me is all I've wanted since I met her. Since she first smiled at me. Since she first made me feel like more than my career. More than my past. More than the expectations others hold for me. More than the expectations I hold for myself. She made me feel like I was enough. I don't ever want to stop trying to do the same for her.

*I think I love her.*

The thought hits me, and I shove it away, too thrown off by it to deal with it now.

I pull back from our kiss and look at her. We're both breathing hard, still holding onto each other, and I drop my forehead to hers.

"I'll tell anyone who will listen that we belong to each other. I'm just sorry you can't brag about your boyfriend's cooking skills. As it turns out, they're nonexistent."

"Seems like you're about as good a chef as you are an artist." She yelps and giggles when I slap her ass. "Have no fear boy toy, I never come unprepared." She pulls away from my hold, leaving my arms empty, and I feel the urge to pull her back to me.

"*Boyfriend*, you mean."

"Ah, right. It'll take some time to get that right. I'll have to update your contact info on my phone."

*Smart-ass.*

She walks into the bedroom and returns with her carry-on bag. She drops it onto the counter with a thud. Before I can question it, she tips the bag upside down and a mountain of snacks and a few drinks fall onto the counter.

A small giggle escapes her, and I realize my jaw is hanging open, taking in the vast array of chips, trail mix, and candy in front of me. I have no clue how it all fit into her bag to begin with.

"Uh, Bec? Did you rob an airport vending machine?"

"Okay, as my *boyfriend*, you can't judge me for what you see here. *This* is how I travel. I'm a mood snacker. I never know what I'm going to want on the plane ride, and their on-plane snack options never cut it. Besides, flights make me nervous and the snacks help. So tonight, our dinner options are this or the *lovely* meal you made us. What's it going to be, Price?"

Caught off guard by her reasoning, I pause.

"Wait, you don't like flying? Why didn't you say anything?"

"I haven't flown a ton in the past, and this was admittedly the first time I flew anywhere alone." She shrugs, beginning to pick through the pile to find a snack. "But I wanted to see what you had planned. I wanted to see you."

"You faced your fears for me, only for me to try to poison you. God, I'm the worst." I grab her hand and pull her back into my arms.

"If I have to share my mood snacks with anyone, I'm glad it's you," she whispers seriously into my ear before her laughter lights up the room around me.

# Chapter Fifty-One

Aiden

"Okay, truth," Bec mumbles from behind the rim of her wine glass. She's bundled in a blanket as we sit in a pair of Adirondack chairs on the second story deck just outside the wall of windows of the small cabin. The sky is clear, showcasing the light of the stars and moon from above. We lit the fire pit in the center of the patio table and the warm glow from the flames dances across Bec's skin.

"What's your favorite dessert?"

"Ugh, Aiden. The point of the game is to distract us from being hungry, not make me hungrier," she whines.

We finished her snacks hours ago, and since neither of us is desperate enough to eat the dish I ruined, we've filled up on wine since the snacks ran out.

"I won't know what dish to ruin next if you don't tell me your favorite."

"Didn't you say you used to cook with your mom all the time growing up? I thought you had skills or something."

"I thought I did too," I say with a laugh. "My memory must be fucked. I bet my mom spent more time in the kitchen fixing my mistakes than I realized."

"All right, fine...brownies. All brownies, even the easy box mixes. You can't mess that up at least."

"It's cute that you think that'll make it harder for me to fail. Also, do I need to remind you of what happened to the birthday cake you made me? You know, the one with the crater in the middle. I believe that was also a box mix, right? Those can be just as challenging."

"I have no defense. I was really humbled by that damn cake. On second thought, maybe we need to promise each other we'll only get desserts from a bakery or something."

"Deal," I say in agreement.

"Okay, Price. Truth or Dare?"

"Truth."

"Awe, too scared to dare?" she asks.

"No, too cold to risk anything that requires me to get out from under this blanket. I think my nipples are harder than a mannequin's right now."

"You've gotten comfortable mixing up the dirty talk," she says.

"I like to keep you guessing. Okay, Miller. Hit me with a question."

"I want to put a disclaimer here...you don't have to answer this one if you don't want to. No penalties."

"Ooookay?" I say, confused about the direction she's about to take this conversation.

"Do you...do you speak to your dad?" she asks, hesitation clear on her face.

My face falls. Of all the questions she could ask, I didn't expect one about my father. Pain pulses in my chest at the thought of having to share more about this part of my life, but if I want Bec to be honest with me, I know I need to reciprocate.

"No, I don't." Letting out a heavy sigh, I go on. "It's hard to talk about."

"I'm sorry. You don't need to say anything else. I shouldn't pry. It's just...your mom and sister are so wonderful. And with everything you've told me, I know the three of you have overcome so much. You've managed to be there for each other through it all while still accomplishing so much. I was wondering if he had any place in your life now."

"Hey, it's okay. Don't feel bad about asking, really. It's understandable that you'd have questions." I look away, not sure if I can manage to share all that I want to if I were to watch Bec's reactions, so I just look into the fire instead.

"My father was...angry. He never physically harmed us, but he made people hurt in other ways. I think my mom knew...knew that it was only a matter of time before his emotional outbursts escalated, and she wasn't going to stick around for that. He made it difficult. He limited her access to their finances and refused to cooperate in the divorce process for the longest time. She made huge sacrifices getting us out of that environment, and I've never wanted to go back knowing all that waited for me was pain. I haven't talked to him since I was drafted. That's the last time he reached out. It felt like a convenient time for him to want to reconnect and it was clear from our conversation that he hasn't changed since he and Mom separated."

"I'm sorry. I think it was really strong of you to hold that boundary. It sounds like he hasn't done the work on himself that would warrant more of a relationship to be built between the two of you. Not that you'd owe him that even if he did."

"It's not easy. There's always that small part of me that wishes I knew what it was like to have my dad in my life. Then I felt guilty for missing someone like that. Or maybe it was the idea of someone...who I wished my father could be," I say.

I know there will always be a part of me that wishes my father was the kind of man I wanted to be involved in my life, the kind of father who deserved that recognition and my time, but he isn't, and that's up to him to change, not me.

"When we first left, I was afraid for so long that he'd turn up at our front door. I was young, but when we left home, when we moved out, it all became so real, and even my young mind felt like I needed to take care of Mom and Evie. Mom never wanted that, neither did Evie, and when I pushed for control so that I could feel like I was protecting them, they made it clear that we weren't going to operate like that as a family. So we didn't, but the drive, the impulse to protect the people I care about is still there and it can come across as overbearing. I started to feel like I would turn into him. Like my need to control everything around me was close, too close, to the way he needed to control everyone around him."

"I can understand wanting to protect the people you love from experiencing anymore hurt. But Aiden, I can't imagine you being anything like your father. Not with what you've shown me, not with how you act around your family, or how you act with me."

"It's taken time for the hypervigilance to settle, but the longer we were on our own, the better I felt. The fear of being anything like him...it can be stifling." I shake my head, trying to will away the uncomfortable pit that's settled in my stomach talking about this.

"Hey..." Bec says softly, reaching over the arm of my chair to grasp my hand in hers. "It's okay to be scared. Being afraid only makes you human, and the fact that you even think like that shows that you're not like him at all."

I squeeze her hand and let the feeling of her palm against mine ground me for a moment as I consider what she's saying. I normally try to bury the hurt and fear, afraid that talking about it will make it more real. But giving it a voice tonight didn't make the pain worse like I expected it to. Instead, it feels like the ache in my chest has dulled, just a little.

"Pretty sure I owe you a few truths for that one," Bec says. "That was a weightier answer than my favorite dessert."

I chuckle, relieved by Bec's effortless ability to make life's burdens feel a little lighter.

"I'm holding you to that."

"Really, I'm sorry. I didn't mean to upset you."

"You didn't. I told you before that I want to know all of you, nothing watered down. It wouldn't be fair of me to ask that of you without offering the same. Besides, I think you're right. Spending time in a place like this," I pause to take a deep breath, looking up at the clear sky littered with stars and the light from the moon, "it really does put things into perspective."

I can hear her draw in a deep breath beside me, her gaze lifting to the sky as well before breathing out slowly. "It's beautiful. Aiden, I need to thank you."

Our eyes connect as she stands, pulling me to stand in front of her before wrapping her arms around my waist and resting her chin on my chest.

"For what?" I whisper, letting my hands fall to the base of her spine, pulling her closer.

"For bringing me here. For telling me more about you even though it's difficult. For being you and making it easier to feel like I can be me too."

The impulse to tell Bec that I'm falling for her tugs in my gut, but I push it down, feeling too raw from our conversation. But I still want to show her.

While words come easier than ever before when I'm talking to Bec, the way our bodies connect is effortless. When I tilt her jaw to kiss her, all the negative emotions my memories drudged up fall away, leaving only the feeling of her warm body in my arms and her soft lips pressed to mine.

I pull away long enough to ask her again, "Truth or dare?"

"Dare," she mumbles against my lips before kissing me again.

"I dare you to get naked and wait for me in bed. You have three minutes to get ready while I lock up."

A radiant smile overtakes her face, and I shiver at the loss of her warmth as she pulls away from me and runs inside.

I smile to myself as I turn off the gas fire pit, close up the cabin, and let my imagination take hold while I picture how Bec will look waiting sprawled out for me.

The sight that awaits me when I walk into the bedroom isn't what I expected.

It's so much fucking better.

"You cheated," I say with a mock accusatory tone.

Bec is smirking at me while kneeling in the middle of the king-size bed, her knees spread open as she sits back on her heels, wearing nothing but a black lace lingerie set. The sight alone has me rock hard, and my cock aches, straining against my pants.

She shrugs, the movement knocking one of her bra straps off her shoulder. "I figured you wouldn't mind. I assumed you'd want to unwrap me yourself."

She reaches both hands up and grips her breasts, squeezing them for me, and my mouth waters at the sight of her cleavage and rosy pebbled nipples.

I reach behind my head and rip off my shirt. I take three steps before I'm climbing on top of her, placing one hand between her shoulder blades to cushion her fall.

"You came here with that in your suitcase, knowing how delicious you'd look waiting in this bed for me?"

"No, remember? I didn't pack my bags," she says, before giggling into my neck as I nibble on her earlobe.

"Remind me to send Ellie a thank-you."

"And what about me? What do I get for putting it on?" she asks indignantly.

"Babe, you'll get a *very* different kind of thank you," I say, pulling away from her and standing at the end of the bed. I grip her ankles firmly and pull her in one smooth motion so her ass rests along the end of the bed.

Bec lets out a gasp and the sound echoes off the vaulted ceilings of the bedroom. The lighting is muted, the only source being the two bedside lamps on the nightstands and the gas fireplace in the corner that Bec must have turned on when she came inside. The soft amber haze makes her skin glow, and I run my palms up her calves to hook her legs around my neck.

I grip her thighs, my fingers pressing into her soft curves, pulling her closer to me. I groan at the sight of her perfect pussy wrapped up in black lace crotchless panties.

"You wanna know *my* favorite dessert?"

"I think I already do," Bec says breathlessly, leaning up on her elbows to look down at me with a knowing smirk on her face.

"I'm fucking starving, so I plan on having my fill tonight. Now, lean back and grind this perfect pussy on my face."

I lick her, groaning at the taste of her evident desire. My cock is painfully hard now, pushing against the bottom edge of the mattress. I press another kiss to her soaked entrance before circling her clit with my tongue. Bec moans and grips my hair roughly, her hips tilting up toward me, seeking more contact. I happily give it to her.

"Oh, my god. More, I need more," Bec says, continuing to rock her pelvis against my tongue.

I drive my tongue into her several times before rimming her slit. When I lick her clit again, I release one of her thighs and slowly press one finger into her, making Bec moan louder.

"How do you want it, gorgeous?" I ask, while pressing another finger into her. I can feel her tightening around my hand as I rock the heel of my palm against her clit, and I know she's close.

"Fuck me, please. I need you inside me now," she pleads.

I pull my hand back and stand, which she protests with a small whine. I can't help but grin at her knowing she feels as needy as I do.

I take off my pants as she scoots up the bed, pulling the tops of her bra down to show me her incredible tits. She bites her bottom lip and tugs on her nipples. I palm my cock at the sight of her sprawled before me, her pussy wet from my tongue, her body lighting up with need.

"You're so fucking beautiful. I can't take my eyes off you," I say, unable to mask the raw desire in my voice.

I crawl onto the bed, hungry to taste more of her. I kiss my way up her stomach and take my time sucking and biting her nipples, working my way up her body until I'm kissing her neck. Unable to wait any longer, I kneel between her legs and drive my aching cock into her in one powerful thrust, groaning at the tight feel of her, hot and wet.

We both moan as we find our rhythm together. The passion melting into something soft and gentle.

I grind against her pelvis, applying pressure to her clit with each pulse, and her nails dig into my shoulders where she's gripping me tightly.

Her mouth drops open and her head falls back as I rock into her. When she comes around my cock, the sounds of her moaning my name causes me to follow her into my own orgasm.

I collapse onto my side, pulling her with me, not allowing for any space between us. Our breaths mingle as they slow and she leans into my neck.

After a few minutes, we decide to take a bath together before going to sleep. The feel of her resting her body against mine in the water brings a sense of peace I've never felt before.

When we make our way back to bed, I pull her back against me, drawing small circles on her hip with my thumb. We stay awake for another hour, talking and laughing, soaking up the time together before our schedules separate us again.

I don't remember us making the decision to go to sleep, but when I wake up the next morning with Bec in my arms, I feel more content than I knew was possible. I hold her close and breathe in this moment, grateful for the incredible woman who decided to give me this chance. The woman I was made to love.

# Chapter Fifty-Two

Bec

"Your dad's been gone a long time, Hop. You ready to give him the cold shoulder when you see him?" I look down at Hopper, whose only response is to let his tongue flop out of the side of his mouth and wag his tail back and forth across the kitchen tile. He sits patiently, waiting for scraps to fall from the counter where I'm making breakfast.

Aiden has been gone for several days playing road games, and I convinced him to leave Hopper with me since Evie's schedule was busy and she couldn't be around for him much. He says he doesn't want to overstep and inconvenience me.

Me. A dog trainer.

Inconvenienced by this sweet baby angel of a dog.

The man is *confused*.

I forgot how much having a dog in my space makes it feel like home. Since I lost Lucy, it's been too painful to imagine living with another dog again. Bringing Lucy home was the most special moment I've ever experienced. But while welcoming a dog into your life is incredible, the worst day inevitably follows when you have to say goodbye. It's been too much to imagine going through that again. Thankfully, having

Hop around has slowly started to heal a small piece of my heart.

Hopper hasn't left my side since Aiden dropped him off. He's come to work with me to help demonstrate the skills we cover in my classes, he's sat by my side every night while I binge-read the dark romance we decided on for this month's book club pick, and every night he snuggles into my side to sleep. When I wake up, he's sprawled out, usually with his paws digging into my side. I figure we must be dueling it out for bed space throughout the night while we sleep.

I love having a companion again.

"All right, boy, you ready for a special day today?" I call out to him.

Again, those warm, brown eyes meet mine. His happy wiggles barely contained by his big, furry body.

Dogs. We're just not worthy of their loyal, patient, exuberant love.

* * *

The stadium's family section is crowded. Dogs, kids, and their parents all mill around singing a chorus of happy greetings and excited squeals, interrupted by the occasional playful bark.

When Aiden mentioned that the Aviators host a dog-friendly game every July, I practically begged him to let me bring Hopper. Again, he didn't want to give me the extra work. Again, he is *confused*. This is my Disney World.

Plus, bringing Hopper here is a great opportunity to continue working on his socialization skills, especially if Aiden is serious about wanting him to become a therapy dog. Like I expected, Hopper has done well, enjoyed himself, and greeted both pets and people like a pro. He's the cutest show-off in the stadium today. Well, at least the cutest dog.

Watching Aiden on the field is a huge distraction, but one I welcome.

"Did you know a beer here is like twenty dollars? I think I was just robbed by a college freshman who's pulling a cut while working concessions," Dee says over the buzz of the crowd as she approaches with two beers in her hand. "Little shit didn't even discount it when I told him I know one of the players and I offered to bring him something signed."

"I bet he'll tell all his friends about the crazy lady double fisting beers claiming to know one of the players after his shift. I'm telling you, there's not a version of that story where you come off as the reasonable one," I say.

"Shit, you're probably right. You're buying the next round then. I don't want to look crazy twice," Dee says before handing me my drink. "So, when do you two need to head down there?" she asks.

"After the next inning." Aiden said it was no big deal and all I had to do was meet him to hand off Hopper, but my gut is still twisted up in a giant knot.

When the Aviators' media team heard that Aiden's dog would be in the stadium today, they added him to the list of players who would take their dogs onto the field in between the seventh and eighth inning for some promotional photos.

"Hooooly shhhhit..." I hear Dee draw out as I cue Hopper to sit at my side while a few younger puppies run past us.

"What, what's going..." I look up and I'm rendered speechless.

One half of the giant screen above the bleachers is lit up with the logo for New Hope, while the other screen shows Tonya, New Hope's director, being interviewed by a woman in an Aviators polo. Their voices, ringing out through the stadium speakers, are muffled by the roar of the crowd—that, or I'm in such a state of shock that my ears are ringing—so I can't make out what they're saying. Thankfully, there's closed-captioning on the screen.

Dee reads aloud and it feels like the whole world is spinning around me as I will my brain to keep up and take in everything she's saying, but I can't even manage that.

"Oh my god, did you know about this?" She looks at me, the shock evident in her expression, I'm sure a mirror to my own. "Did...did they just say that a portion of proceeds from today's sales will go to fund the New Hope animal shelter?"

"I–I had no idea," I stutter.

*What the fuck is going on right now?*

Dee whistles. "That dude loves you something fierce."

Her statement snaps me out of my frozen state. "No, no, he doesn't. It's too soon for that. We're still getting to know each other?" I squeak out like a question. "This has to be a crazy coincidence. I haven't talked to Tonya in two weeks or so..."

"Okay, Bec. Okay," Dee says as she pats Hopper's head. "Your momma has gone and lost her mind over your daddy, don't you think, handsome?" she asks Hop, kneeling next to him to scratch under his chin. He soaks up the attention and falls to his side in a plea for more affection.

Meanwhile, I can't seem to form any kind of response. All I can do is stand, holding Hopper's leash in my hand like a lifeline, staring at the screen. And when they cut to a shot of the team standing in the dugout, I catch a glimpse of Aiden watching the interview with a huge smile on his face. I feel my heart trying its best to beat its way out of my chest at the site of him, knowing in my soul that Dee is right and Aiden is responsible for this.

* * *

"Bec, is that you?" Tonya asks as she approaches me. I'm standing in a small room with several of the team's families and their pets, waiting to hand Hopper over to Aiden for the promotional photoshoot.

I feel slightly uncomfortable and out of place realizing that I'm the only one here that doesn't seem to be a family member. Players' wives, kids, and pets mill around the space, and while everyone has been welcoming and kind, I'm still reeling over the shock of the massive amount of donations New Hope is bound to receive today to give my full attention to mingling.

"Tonya, what are you doing here? How did all this happen?" I ask.

She beams at me. "It's incredible, right? A few weeks ago, the team's community outreach liaison called me saying they were looking for a local shelter to partner with for today's game. We made some commitments, and we're setting up a contract to be community partners for the remainder of the season. If things go well, it might extend to next season too. Can you believe that?"

I shake my head, speechless. Because I absolutely can't believe it.

"I can't tell you how relieved I am. I was worried for a while we'd have to start cutting staff and limit the number of animals we brought in. This popped up right in time." There are tears in her eyes as she speaks. My gut twists knowing how much heart Tonya puts into her work at New Hope and how stressed she must have been facing this alone.

"I didn't realize things were hitting that point. Tonya, you could have told us, you didn't have to carry this alone," I say.

"Of course I did. It's my job. I didn't want to alarm anyone until we knew for sure what needed to happen. But no matter, it's behind us now. I'm not going to let yesterday's struggle dull the shine of today's opportunity."

That's the thing about Tonya, nothing ever stops her. A nonprofit like hers is fueled by crappy coffee and the pure determination of her and the team. My heart swells knowing all the good she's going to do with this type of financial stability for her organization.

"Well, I better be off. I'll see you next week." After a quick hug, I watch her prance away to meet with more of the event staff.

"Excuse me, I don't normally do this, but you might be the hottest fan I've ever seen in this stadium. Wanna come home with me later so I can peel these shorts off this perfect ass?" The rumble of Aiden's voice in my ear sends shivers up my spine as he steps behind me and grabs my hips.

I turn to face him and don't bother to correct Hop's behavior when he jumps all over Aiden out of excitement. Aiden laughs and kneels to give Hopper attention. "Always the cock block," Aiden jokes quietly.

"Aiden, did you do this?" I ask, ignoring his playful greeting.

I need to know.

He stands and hugs me close with his hand at the base of my neck. "Do you always look this beautiful when you're surprised? I gotta admit, I like seeing you a little flustered."

"How?"

He shrugs casually. "The team is always looking for local programs to support. All it took was a meeting with our community liaison. It wasn't much, I promise. The guys who came with me to the adoption event vouched for the organization too. It was an easy call for them to make."

"Wh-why?" I managed to whisper.

His smile fades and it takes him a minute to find the words he's looking for.

"You're important to me. New Hope is important to you. I'm in a position to help. Why wouldn't I do this?"

"That simple?"

"That simple," he says.

When he leans down to kiss me, it almost makes me believe him. Maybe it really is that simple. Two people caring for one another, supporting each other. I help take care of Hopper when he's gone. He helps the shelter I adore get the donations it needs.

But maybe it's more.

Maybe I want it to be more.

Does he feel this too? Is he craving my touch like I'm craving his? Is his day starting to revolve around the time we have together like mine is? Is he overthinking every gesture wondering if whatever we have between us is what people spend their lifetime searching for?

"I'm almost scared to ask based on your reaction to the first surprise," he says against my lips when he pulls away from our kiss. "But will you come out on the field with Hopper and me?"

"Oh, isn't that just for families?"

He looks almost hurt for a moment, before he recovers with that easy smile of his.

"Do me a favor and don't overthink it. I want you with us."

"Still that simple?" I tease.

"That simple," he says with a smirk.

The practical part of me knows that neither of us wants to give voice to what's left unsaid between us, both afraid for different reasons. But I don't want to think about that, so I do what Aiden asks. I stop overthinking it. He wants me with them, and I want to be with them. For today, that's enough.

* * *

**Abby:** Since when are the Aviators an official New Hope sponsor?!

**Bec:** I can barely believe it myself. Aiden and his teammates pitched it. I had no idea, but Tonya was all too excited to jump on board.

**Dee:** If that team asked me to jump on board, I'd be willing too.

**Ellie:** I'm starting a new album in my phone to store all these shots of Bec, Aiden, and Hopper together at the game. The media is eating this shit up.

**Carissa:** Seriously, Bec your face is everywhere. How does it feel to be Aiden's hot mystery girl?

**Bec:** Ugh, embarrassing. Why does everyone care?

**Abby:** Probably because he's been keeping his personal life private until now. The last article I read said he barely shares anything online.

**Dee:** Congrats, gorgeous! You popped his publicity cherry!

**Bec:** Dee, you need help.

# Chapter Fifty-Three

Aiden

**D**om: Hey, man, cool pic. Hopper is obviously the star, but you and Bec look nice too.

**Aiden:** Thanks, I guess?

**Dylan:** Yeah, really cool. But what does this mean?

**Aiden:** What the fuck are you talking about?

**Jake:** What's going on with you and Bec?  Last we hear, you're botching a weekend getaway, now you're taking your relationship public?

**Chris:** Is it a botched getaway when they left with official boyfriend/-girlfriend status?

**Jake:** Babe, be on my side.

**Chris:** I'm always on your side.  I'm literally sitting right next to you. But clearly that weekend was a win, and Aiden's got the photos from yesterday's game to prove it.

**Dylan:** Okay, but Jake has a point. How serious are you two?

**Aiden:** Do we have to do this?

**Dom:** Yes, we're doing this. You get to ignore the media's questions but not ours. Do you love her? If you love her and hurt her, Ellie is going to kill you.

**Aiden:** Why does everyone assume I'm going to fuck this up?

**Dom:** I swear I don't think that, but have you seen Ellie mad? You don't want to, I promise.

**Aiden:** I think I can handle it. Besides, it won't come to that.

**Dom:** Godspeed, man.

* * *

Another few away games combined with Bec's work schedule has left us without any real time to talk. A string of texts is all we've been able to fit in for the last few days. I don't regret having Bec join Hopper and me on the field at the game. In fact, having her there with me felt right. It was the first time I didn't hesitate to let the world see a piece of my life outside of baseball. I wanted everyone to see how happy I am and the person responsible for that happiness. But now, I'm worried about what all the media attention has made Bec think. I've had to convince her not to overthink the slow steps we've made forward in our relationship, and I don't want her to worry about what this all means.

While I drive to her place to see her and Hopper, I stress over what a few days could have done to her inner monologue. I hope she doesn't shut me out or shy away from what this is.

Maybe I'm just projecting, because I can't seem to face it either.

When I walk into Bec's apartment with the key she gave me, all of my worries are drowned out by the sound of her belting out what I'm pretty sure is an old My Chemical Romance song at the top of her lungs. Smiling to myself, I look around the corner into her kitchen to spot her facing away from me, singing into her wooden spoon microphone and dancing for a very entertained yellow lab.

I lean against the fridge, watching as she leans forward, bent at the waist, her arm thrown back behind her. She passionately sings along to the song word-for-fucking-word until it ends.

I break the silence with a slow clap for what might be considered the performance of the year.

She turns around suddenly, out of breath. Just when I think she'll act shy and embarrassed, she surprises me, running toward me, jumping into my arms and wrapping herself around me.

"You're back," she exclaims, clinging to me, out of breath from her production.

The weight of worry I was carrying around expecting her to be ruminating over our relationship status and the media's attention on her falls away immediately. Bec doesn't care about any of that. She just cares about me. And the thought warms my entire chest. I pull her in close and kiss her forehead.

"I'm back, beautiful. And you have some explaining to do," I say, smacking her ass then pulling her tighter against me. God, I've missed her body. I've missed *her*. "Since when did you become a rock star?"

"I've always been one," she says smugly. "Twenty-first century emo music is supremely underrated if you ask me. But my concerts are limited to my kitchen, my car, and my shower."

"Where do I buy my ticket? I'm especially interested in the shower venue," I say, turning to press her back against the wall so I can kiss and suck on her neck.

She hums, leaning her head to the side to give me better access. "We might be able to work something out."

I pull away and look down at her. Everything I've ever wanted is right here in my arms, and all I can feel is gratitude. I don't think Bec has any idea how happy she's made me. But I'm going to do everything I can to show her.

# Chapter Fifty-Four

Bec

"Where's your vibrator?" Aiden asks, his voice gruff with desire. He walks us out of my small kitchen and into my bedroom, shutting Hopper out of the room. I only have a brief second to send a wish out to the universe begging that he'll behave himself out there, while also hoping Aiden doesn't behave himself in here with me.

"What?" I ask.

"Where's your vibrator, babe?"

He peppers warm kisses along my collarbone, driving my body crazy with need. It's only been a few days, but every touch of his drives me wild, making it hard to answer his question. I just want him to shut up and keep kissing me like he needs it as much as I do.

"Top drawer of my dresser. Why?" I ask.

"I want to try something. It might seem familiar...lie down on your stomach for me, beautiful."

That gets my attention.

He drops me onto the bed with a bounce, turning toward my dresser. I watch him grab my vibrator and walk back to me with it at his side and a devilish smile on his face and he lifts his eyebrows.

*Holy shit.*

"Did you read my...?"

"Yeah, babe. I read your book." He reaches forward and grabs my ankles, pulling me roughly toward him, his arms running up my legs to grip my outer thighs.

"When?"

He shrugs. "I bought it the day after you drove me home from Dom's holiday party. It piqued my interest."

That book was smutty as fuck.

"Well, what'd you think?" I ask him as he pulls my pants and underwear down my legs slowly, his eyes fixated on my entrance.

"It didn't disappoint. Fucking filthy. Just like us. Do you want to see what I have in mind?"

I nod my head.

*Words? What are words?*

"Turn over, baby. Let me see that perfect ass."

I flip over to lie on my stomach and squeeze my eyes shut. No way. No fucking way is this real. Aiden's ready to act out a scene from my spicy books. *Are you fucking kidding me?*

I'm in heaven—heading straight to hell—and I can't wait. My breathing picks up pace and I feel a slight tremble through my core in anticipation.

"Spread your legs and pull your knees up toward your sides. Pretend my head is between your sweet thighs. Show me how flexible you can be, gorgeous."

*Jesus Christ.*

I know the second I open my legs he'll be able to see how wet I am from where he stands behind me, and that only makes me want to do it more.

I bend my knees, drawing them up to my sides as much as I can, leaving little room between my pussy and the mattress.

"Fuck, Bec. You're so goddamn sexy," he grunts out, his voice hoarse.

I feel him crawl up the bed behind me, his body hovering over mine, his breath behind my ear.

"Don't move, sweetheart."

His hand slides between my stomach and the mattress. He's holding my vibrator, and when he reaches my center, he pulls his hand back, leaving me sitting directly on the toy.

"Do you remember this part, Bec?" His mouth pressing wet kisses lightly along my spine sends a rush up my thighs.

"Yeah," I manage to whisper in response.

"Do you remember the game?"

I couldn't forget it. I've been thinking about it ever since I read it back in the fall. Sometimes you read a scene that you know will never leave your raunchy mind. Forever in the bank to call on when you need it. This is one of those forever scenes for me.

"Yes."

"Tell me," he demands.

*Fuck, why does it feel dirtier to say it out loud than to read it?*

"He...uh..." I swallow loudly. "He fucked her while her vibrator was between her legs and the bed."

He slowly trails his fingers across my shoulders, pulling my hair to one side. "And?" I can hear the smile in his voice as he drags his lips up my shoulder blade to the back of my neck.

"And every time he spanked her, if she made a noise, he turned the setting up to a higher power."

"Hmm...such a good reader. Always paying attention. Do you want to play with me?"

"Fuck yeah, I do," I say, before rocking my hips back so my clit hits the toy and my ass presses into Aiden's groin above me.

"You're amazing, you know that, Bec?" I can hear the break in his confident demeanor, the sweet and thoughtful Aiden making an appearance before the dominant Aiden takes over again. "Say stop and we stop, okay, babe?"

I nod.

"Need to hear it, beautiful. Use your words."

"I understand. I say stop and we stop."

"Good girl. Now lie all the way down and relax for me. I'm going to take care of you."

I feel Aiden pull away and I settle onto the mattress, the toy pressing against my already swollen clit, turning my head to the side and resting my cheek on top of my hands. I peek back over my shoulder to see Aiden staring at my ass as he drops his athletic pants to the ground. He stalks toward me and catches my eye before crawling back onto the bed. His smirk makes desire flare low in my stomach as he grabs my ass cheeks firmly and massages them for a quick second before pulling his hand back and spanking me.

Caught off guard, I gasp and then moan as the sting dissipates. The smack of his hand forces my clit to press against the toy between my thighs and the unexpected pressure makes me even wetter. I couldn't stop myself from crying out even though I saw it coming. I don't think I've ever been this aroused in my life.

Aiden chuckles. "Off to a great start here, Bec." He snakes his hand around my hip to find the toy beneath me, and he turns it on the lowest setting.

"Oh fuck," I pant. He isn't even in me, and I'm already soaking.

I feel Aiden's hard length press against my entrance and barely enter me. He pulses the tip of his cock in and out several times, and it's torture. I want him to fill me. I want to be so full of him I can't breathe. I want him to drive into me again and again until I fall apart.

"You feel incredible. You're drenching me, baby, and we haven't even started. Fuck," he growls.

He finally thrusts farther and farther into me until I can feel his hips hitting flush with my backside. Aiden has one hand pressed into the mattress holding his weight and the other grips me where my neck meets my shoulder, his fingers on my collarbone keeping me steady as he drills into me with more force. With each push, my clit rubs against the vibrator and I'm coming undone from the competing sensations. I can't keep quiet, so I don't stand a chance of doing so when his hand leaves my neck and delivers the second slap against my ass cheek.

I'm moaning, gasping. Holy fuck.

"You know, I think I'm winning this game," Aiden says, his voice rough as he continues to drive all the way into me without slowing his pace.

He reaches around my side again to turn the vibrator up to the next setting. We're both losing control now, driven by need. He's thrusting into me forcefully and I'm alternating between pushing my ass back into him and riding my vibrator. We're both hungry for each other, chasing release.

"Aiden, I can't...I'm going to..."

"Not yet, Bec. I'm not done with you." He pulls out of me and tugs my hips into the air before he presses his face to my center and licks me up the middle.

He laps at my slit and I press back against him, moaning loudly, seeking pressure against my clit, which he delivers. When my orgasm runs hot from my center out over my limbs, I feel a sharp smack against my ass cheek again. The scream that leaves my throat sounds feral and I can't help the way my body thrashes against him.

Aiden grips my hips as my orgasm fades and presses me right back down onto my vibrator. The stimulation is almost too much. Before I can process what's happening, his cock is pounding into me, driving my clit against the toy, sending me barreling into another orgasm.

"Bec, you're gripping me so fucking tight. Fuck." I feel his movements falter and stagger unevenly while he pulses into me.

"Gonna come. *Shit.* Gonna fill you up while I watch your perfect ass ride this vibrator. Give me another one. I want one more, Bec." He manages to turn the toy to the next setting and this one pulses in a staccato rhythm, setting me off again, clenching around him while I fall apart.

I hear Aiden's breathing catch as his movements still, pumping his release into me, doing what he promised and filling me. When he's finished, I lie breathless and reach down to turn off my vibrator, the aftershocks of my orgasms making the sensation too much to handle any longer.

I feel Aiden relax along my back, offset to my side so he doesn't crush me with his weight. He's breathing hard into my shoulder between light kisses on my back.

"I think I like your books, babe," he says.

"I think I have a newfound appreciation for them too," I reply, laughing.

How lucky can a girl get?

# Chapter Fifty-Five

## Aiden

I can't keep them straight. The nurse has been explaining Mom's medication changes to me and Evie for the last ten minutes, but I can't breathe around the knot in my throat, let alone remember any of the goddamn names.

"We're hoping to see some improvement with the changes, but it'll be some time before we can tell if they're having the desired effect," she explains patiently. Evie nods along attentively as she listens to the potential side effects of the drugs they're introducing. There's more talk of treatment plans and expected outcomes. Likelihoods, goals, and timeframes. I hope like hell Eves is absorbing the information better than I am.

"Anything else we should know?" Evie asks, a slight tremble to her voice.

"Not right now. The staff will continue to monitor her and let you know if we continue to see an increase in her symptoms or any reaction to the new meds. We're here anytime you want to call with questions." The young nurse looks sympathetic, and her tone is compassionate. But it doesn't matter. It doesn't make any of this easier to hear.

It's not her fault that her patient isn't doing well. And it's not her fault that the patient is my mother. All I can do is fucking sit here and listen to how this attempt to slow the latest bout of symptoms could go wrong or not help at all.

I can feel my pulse in my temple, and I let out a deep breath while stretching my back over the back of my chair, as if moving can somehow expel the anxiety out of my body and get the weight off my lungs.

I catch a glimpse between the blinds of the small office window and notice Bec walking into the unit with a beast of a St. Bernard waddling next to her with a dopey grin on its face and drool hanging from his panting mouth. I watch as she stops to talk with the staff at the nursing station in the common space. Her smile is warm and bright, a beacon calling to my entire body, making me want to sprint out of this office and into her arms.

The nurse she's speaking with gestures to the office we're in, and Bec glances in my direction, catching my eyes immediately. Even from a distance, with just her eyes on mine, I feel better. Being near her numbs the pain in my soul. The weight of all this helplessness that's about to crush me evaporates and I can fucking breathe again.

How do you ever thank someone for being that kind of light in your life?

Bec returns her attention to the staff member, and I realize the two women in the room with me are looking at me expectantly. I clear my throat and sit up straighter. "Sorry. What was that?"

"We're planning another meeting next month to check in on Mom's progress. When are you free?" Evie says, the wobble in her voice still noticeable.

We settle on a date and time and leave the office to find Mom and Bec huddled together in the large living space. Mom's gaze is a little unfocused, a clear sign to me that she's confused and trying to fit puzzle pieces together like they've been soaking in water, the edges soft and crumbling and too hard to hold or mold together.

Bec's speaking to her softly and petting along the dog's back as it sits between them. Mom reaches out to pet the animal's head, and a smile lights up her face when she gets an appreciative lick on the back of her other hand from the gentle giant.

Mom knows—knew—me better than anyone in the world. Raised me, protected me, loved me. I've seen that familiar expression of joy on her face more times in my lifetime than I could ever count. When I was younger, Evie and I would draw her pictures to hang on the fridge, I would tell her elaborate details from the school field trips I went on, and I would gush over every detail of the big plays when I had a great game. She gave me the same smile then. So why does it feel like seeing it now might shatter my entire fucking heart?

Sometimes, it feels like she'll never smile like that again. As if all the smiles I see from now on are from a woman I know better than anyone even though all I'll be to her is a stranger. She did everything for me. She deserves more. More time than I can give her.

"Before we go over there...Aiden, are you okay? It doesn't feel like you're really *here* right now." Evie stops me, pulling lightly on my shoulder.

I sigh. "No. I can't get out of my head with all this shit going on. But what can we do?"

She drops her hand and shrugs, blinking away the tears I know she's fighting. "What can we do? We love her. We hold her close when we can, and...just hold onto every moment we have together."

I nod at her, unable to find the right words. My thoughts blur together and I can't pull anything helpful from the jumble. Instead, I give my sister a hug, and we walk together to join Mom and Bec.

"Who do we have here?" Evie asks, the uncertainty in her voice gone—I'm sure with great effort—to hide any distress she's feeling from Mom, doing her best to make the most of the time we have today.

"This is Scout. The most handsome coworker I've ever had," Bec answers.

"*Woooow*, no loyalty. Brutal. I'm telling Hopper," Eves jokes.

"Please. Hopper is my most handsome *volunteer*. Scout is working."

"Evie darling, it's been so long. How are you?" Mom asks, reaching out to palm Evie on the cheek.

It hasn't been long. It's been an hour.

"Doing great, Mom. Hey, it's gorgeous outside today. Want to see this dog get into some trouble digging up all the flower beds in the courtyard?"

"Oh, Evelyn. Don't encourage any bad behavior," Mom says.

"Mom, I'm the second child. It's what I live for." Evie laughs as she reaches down to help Mom stand, loops her elbow with hers, and together they walk out of the doors propped open leading out to the enclosed courtyard. Mom's eyes meet mine briefly as she passes me, and I can see the confusion again. The lack of recognition.

She's trying to remember who her first child is. Who I am.

*God, get me the fuck out of here.*

"Hey, hey…Aiden. It's okay," Bec says gently, reaching for my hand and tangling her fingers in mine, stepping closer so she's standing in front of me, only a few inches between us. "Close your eyes and breathe. Same pace as me." She takes a few slow breaths, just loud enough for me to hear. I close my eyes and do as she asks.

I never believed any of that stuff worked. I always assumed traditional "coping techniques" were just buzzwords, made up to give people some semblance of control when everything is far beyond it.

Give me something to do, something to focus on—the pitcher's tendencies, tracking fly balls, diving stops—and I'm good. Ask me to clear my head, remove the distractions, and calm my thoughts? Not in my wheelhouse.

I don't want to stay in this moment. I want to run screaming from this shitty nightmare and find anything that'll help me forget the emptiness in Mom's gaze as she struggled to remember her son. As she struggled to remember *me.*

But surprisingly, breathing along with Bec does help, enough to keep my feet planted and not sprinting out the doors and away from all this.

Maybe it was the breathing, or maybe it was Bec.

I drop my forehead to hers. "This feels like torture. One minute, she's here and the next, she's gone. Somewhere out of reach. I can't...I can't stand to watch this."

"You can. You can until you can't. Then you step back, live your life, and try again tomorrow. Your mom is here, Aiden. She's here and she'll be here for you as much as she can be. It's a bad day, but that doesn't mean tomorrow will be too."

"What happens when all we have left are the bad days?" I immediately hate myself for asking, giving voice to the fear that crawls up my spine and lingers at the base of my skull, pounding throughout my limbs every fucking day.

Bec's eyes flutter back and forth between mine, and her palm finds my chest, stalling right over my heart. Her voice sounding sure, she says, "If that day comes, I'll be here."

Something settles in my heart, the panic temporarily subsiding. The permanence Bec's alluding to strengthens my resolve even though there isn't a solution, only comfort. Comfort she's offering not just today but in the future. It's enough. Having her with me is more than enough.

I pull her close, breathing her in, and decide those breathing exercises aren't bullshit after all.

# Chapter Fifty-Six

Bec

"Our next student may have joined class a little late, but certainly caught up quickly.  Please join me in congratulating our final graduate, Hopper Price," I say as the room sounds with haphazard applause.

I barely contain my laughter when Hopper pulls his leash free from Aiden's grasp, barreling across the space to join me at the front of the training room at the Center. I kneel down to gift him a stuffed diploma, which he tosses in the air, watches it drop to the ground, and begins playfully pouncing on the thing, adding to the incessant chorus of toy squeaks filling the room from the rest of his classmates.

It's the last session of my puppy training course and my favorite day.  At the end of each course, we host an informal get-together at the Center with no lesson plan. Instead, we throw a puppy party and celebrate the dogs—the way life should be if you ask me. Puppy courses are my favorite because the extra excitement usually results in them acting like they haven't learned a goddamn thing in the months we've been working together, but it's cute as shit.

I stand straight and cue Hop to sit, picking up the toy and tossing it to him once he finally listens and plops his butt on the ground, his eyes wide and focused on me. Aiden jogs up beside him, getting control of the leash again and huffing, exasperated at Hop's antics.

"I'm hoping we don't embarrass ourselves when we level up to intermediate next month."

"You two better not embarrass me. Abby is teaching your class and I'll never hear the end of it if she thinks I showed you...*favoritism*." I whisper the last word with a grimace.

Aiden elbows me softly in the side. "It's okay, babe. We know we're your favorites. Your secret is safe with us."

When we wrap up the celebration, I walk with Aiden to his car and he takes Hopper and me to Ellie's house. Dom insisted on throwing a graduation party for Hopper, and when Dee caught wind of his plan, she threw her support to Dom and wouldn't take no for an answer. Slowing the roll on Dom's enthusiasm is nearly impossible once he gets going, and resisting Dee's demands is pointless.

We walk into Ellie's backyard and Hopper runs ahead to greet everyone. I laugh when I see a trifold set up on the outdoor dining table. Mimicking his own grad party, I assume, Dom printed and displayed at least thirty photos of Hopper on this board, completed with *Congrats, Grad!* in bubble letters across the top.

I scan the images, and as silly as the whole thing might seem, it warms my heart to see the memories all at once like this. Unsurprisingly, Hopper is in every photo, but Aiden and I are in most of them too. There are pictures of Hopper as a younger puppy, him sitting with the girls and me at book club, between Dom and Aiden on the couch while they watch football, the three of us on the field from the dog day at the park last month, Hopper with Judy and Evie from their visit to Aiden's apartment a few weeks ago, and even one from when Hop first met Luca.

"What put that pretty smile on your face?" Aiden asks, grabbing both of my shoulders in his hands and massaging my neck for a few beats before dropping his hands to circle my waist.

"Did you already see this?" I ask, with a nod to the board of pictures.

"Dom made me send him at least fifty pictures so he could decide which ones needed to be on display. I gave him a lot of shit about this before I saw it, but looking at this now, I..."

I turn my head to look at him as he struggles to find the words. "What is it?" I ask.

"I don't know. I like seeing it all like this. My family, I guess. I've always had Evie and my mom, and then last year Hopper, but looking at this, I can see there were still pieces missing. Pieces I'm grateful I found." When Aiden looks down at me, I answer his smile with one of my own, clinging tightly to his forearms still wrapped around me.

"If Dom made this kind of collage for my dog, what do you think Luca's baby book will look like?" he asks.

"I have a funny feeling they don't make scrapbooks big enough to house the thousands of photos Dom already has of the little guy," I say.

"They don't. Don't worry, I'm looking into it," Dom says as he comes out of the house and passes us on his way to Hopper, making us both laugh.

Aiden's chin tucks into my neck, his stubble lightly grazing along my skin. He holds me tighter for a moment, and I close my eyes and breathe, taking a second to remember everything about this moment. The feel of Aiden's warm body at my back, his arms secure around me, the sound of our friends talking and laughing around us, the hum of cicadas buzzing in the humid August air, Hopper's excited barks breaking through the chatter, and Luca's sweet coos and giggles ringing through the hum of conversation.

Is this what sharing a life with Aiden would feel like? I let myself wonder what it would be like to fill every day with joyful moments like this, growing old with him at my side. I initially expect it to raise insecurities and anxieties to the surface, but instead, all I feel is this deep longing. The picture loosely forming in my mind isn't perfect, because I'll never be perfect and neither will he, but our lives together could be something beautiful. That feels worth the risk. That feels like the point of everything.

I'm going to tell Aiden I love him.

I'm not the same woman he met years ago, but for all the cracks and bruises he's seen, he's only shown me affection, compassion, and understanding. He hasn't rushed me or pressured me to take this any faster than I was ready for. He makes me feel wanted. He makes me feel seen. He makes me feel.

Aiden brings me back to the present as he lets out a heavy sigh over my head. "Don't look now, but your star student is about to earn a time-out," he says.

I turn to see Hop's snout running along the edge of the food table across the lawn, his tongue slipping out to steal pretzels and whatever else is in reach.

"Hop, leave it," Aiden says with as much authority as he can manage, marching over to try to reign in the eager pup. I laugh as I watch Aiden begin to chase him around the yard when his cues fail. At least this time, it's only pretzels.

# Chapter Fifty-Seven

Aiden

"Unfortunately, we haven't seen any improvement with the new medications," the nurse says calmly, the unspoken apology clear in her tone.

Calm being the exact opposite of what I'm feeling right now, back in the nurse's office with Evie sitting at my side. Frustration, helplessness, anger, and guilt all swirl in my gut, making it hard to breathe. I'm sick of getting bad news. I hate that it brings up all this shit I don't want to feel. I bury it all down, getting control of my emotions before I speak.

"What else can we do?" I ask.

"The doctor will be here tomorrow, and we can ask her about adjusting your mother's medications again, if you're in agreement," she explains.

"Yes, let's keep trying," Evie says with determination. Neither of us want to accept how little we can change what's happening. How quickly Mom continues to slip away from us.

"Okay. I'll call you afterward to update you and we can meet again to plan next steps."

The Aviators' schedule is packed with a double header tomorrow and a road trip after that. I know I won't get time with Mom for a few days.

Evie and I join her in her room, where she's sitting in her chair quietly watching a show.

"Hey, Mom," Evie says softly, sitting in the chair next to her, reaching to hold her hand.

Mom's gaze sweeps over her slowly and a soft smile appears beneath the fog of confusion surrounding her.

"Hi, Mom, what are you watching?" I ask, wanting to keep the topic of conversation neutral since I'm not sure where she's at today.

My voice seems to startle her, and when she turns to look at me, her jaw drops in shock.

"What are you doing here? I told you I was leaving. I'm taking Aiden and Evie with me. We have nothing more to talk about," she yells at me.

When I register her words, I'm left speechless. The room blackens at the edge of my vision.

Does she...does she think I'm him? My father?

If Evie and Mom were the same age, they'd be confused as twins for how much she takes after her.

I'm not as lucky.

I still have the old photos of him. I've looked him up on social media a few times over the years. I'm not stupid. I know I look like him no matter how much I wished that wasn't true. The resentment has festered at how unmistakable the resemblance between us is.

Mom is clearly confused about what year it is and where she is. That disturbing fact is barely able to register in my mind since all I can think about is how she's unable to distinguish me—her own son—from the hurtful man from our past.

*Fuck, I'm gonna be sick.*

I can feel my insides shredding into pieces right before numbness sweeps over me.

My mom continues yelling at me, demanding I leave. She's roaring her grievances fiercely, fighting a nonexistent threat...or at least one that's long since been buried in our past.

I can't make out any more of her words as everything around me blurs. I'm vaguely aware of myself taking several unstable steps backward out of the room and into the hall. I turn and lean my back against the wall outside her door, before my knees give out, and I slide to the floor in a heap.

Staff members rush into Mom's room. I listen as Evie and the nurses try to calm her and reassure her that everything's okay. After a few minutes, my brain isn't able to comprehend anymore. The roaring static in my head drowns the noise around me. I can feel my mind and body shutting down.

I'm not sure how much time passes before Mom eventually falls quiet and Evie steps out into the hall, sitting down next to me.

I think she says my name, but I don't look at her or respond. She hugs me and I feel her tears as they fall onto my shoulder.

I don't cry. I just let Evie hold onto me as my world falls apart around me. I wish her arms were strong enough to hold me together, but that kind of strength doesn't exist.

* * *

I fumble with my keys before finally stumbling into my apartment.

Hopper jumps up to greet me, his paws on my chest, but I don't have the energy to correct his behavior or remind him to sit. I ruffle his head and keep walking, Hopper trailing behind and joining me when I fall to the couch. I lean forward, my elbows on my knees holding my head in my hands.

Evie drove me home, not trusting me to get here safely. Can't blame her. I can't focus on anything right now.

She follows me into my place and sits on the other side of Hopper.

"We should talk about it, Aiden," she says softly.

"That's the last thing we should do," I mumble in response.

"We need to."

"No, Evie. We really don't. This is our life now, right? I just have to fucking deal with it." I feel so goddamn defeated. Everything is out of control, and I'm trying my best to keep my ugly thoughts from spilling out.

Was today only the beginning? One day, will my own mother no longer be able to look at me ever again? Bile threatens to make an appearance, my stomach turning over uncomfortably, and again, I think I'm going to be sick.

"It was one day, Aiden. One horrible, fucked-up day. It's not fair and it's never going to be easy, but she's still here. We can't give up on her."

I stand and step away from Evie, gripping and pulling at my own hair, so frustrated I could punch a wall.

"I'm not giving up on her, Eves," I shout. "You were there today; she had no idea who the fuck I was. I don't want to be the reason for that reaction ever again."

The look on her face is all pity, and I can't handle it.

"Shit, I'm sorry, Evie. I didn't mean to yell." I close my eyes to take a deep breath, dropping my fists to rest on my hips, my head hanging low, guilt swooping in to punch me in the stomach. "Every time I picture Mom's face from today, the anger and fear there...god, it's got me fucked up right now and I don't know how to handle it."

I've always been terrified that, in addition to appearances, my father's flaws would be passed onto me as well. Having my mom look at me like that...like she'd look at him...it feels like it's inevitable. Someday, I'll turn out just like he did. Angry, selfish, bitter, and alone.

"Maybe you should talk to someone, Aiden. Everything about this is unpredictable, and it's dredging up all the messed-up shit from our past. No one would judge you for getting help to deal with it."

"I'll think about it," I say. I hate the idea, but I owe it to Evie and my mom to at least consider it.

"Please do. Because I...I can't do this by myself. I need you there with me...with us..." her voice fades away and I look up to see her as she begins to cry again.

"Hey, I'm sorry. I'm not going anywhere. I'll be right here for you and Mom both. We'll...we'll figure it out."

She stands and we hug before Hop begins to circle around us, distressed from me shouting and now Evie crying. We both reassure him before he calms down again, but he stays close, nudging my hand with his nose every so often, looking for contact.

When Evie leaves and it's just Hop and me in my quiet apartment, he doesn't leave my side. I don't check my phone. Instead, I go to bed at five thirty, skipping dinner, suddenly overwhelmed by exhaustion. I lie down in bed, my mind completely empty, numbness taking the place of everything. Hopper lies against my side, keeping a watchful eye on me. I rest my hand on his back, holding him close and focusing on the rhythmic rise and fall of his chest as he breathes beside me. He might be the only thing keeping my mind from breaking even further before I drift into a fitful sleep.

# Chapter Fifty-Eight

## Bec

I was disappointed when Aiden didn't call after his visit with his mom yesterday, but I understood when he texted me this morning to apologize. He forgot to text me before he went to bed early wanting to get a few extra hours of rest before his doubleheader today.

It was the first night we've spent apart while he's been in town in almost five months. Since I've been watching Hopper while he's away, it was the first night I've been alone in a long time too. Can't say I liked it. Thankfully, I'll be able to see him tonight before he leaves for the next road trip in the morning.

I missed falling asleep in Aiden's arms. I missed waking up with Hopper kicking my back. I missed Aiden joking about how he needs his own bed so Hop and I can battle it out for the blanket without him being pushed to the edge.

Carissa and I are in the stands watching Aiden's second game of the day. The smell of stadium food and the familiar buzz of excited fans fill the air around us. I may not be an expert yet, but it's clear even to me that Aiden's struggling today. Thankfully, whatever is affecting Aiden's game isn't reflected in the score. It looks like the Aviators will win the game.

"Things are getting pretty serious between you two, huh?" Carissa asks, leaning close enough to be heard over the roar of the crowd as one of Aiden's teammates hits a double.

"It feels like it. I think...I think I want to tell him I love him," I say.

She coughs, choking on peanuts. I laugh, patting her back a few times before she takes a sip of her drink.

"Who are you and what have you done with Bec Miller?" she asks me once she catches her breath. "Has he told you he loves you?" Carissa asks.

"No, but I've made it clear that I wanted to take this all at a snail's pace. Even if he isn't there yet, I still want him to know."

The thought should scare me, but it doesn't. Not anymore.

If you asked me when we first started talking if I would confess to loving Aiden before having that validation from him first, I would have vehemently denied it was possible. But since we went on our first date, Aiden has helped me feel confident in myself and our relationship. I'm not hesitant to take this next step with him. I no longer feel like things could fall apart any minute. I know we'll fight to make this relationship work no matter what we face together.

Carissa looks at me thoughtfully for a moment before saying, "I'm really proud of you."

"Why?" I ask.

"It's brave to try again after things don't work out the way you want them to. It takes a special kind of person to risk their feelings again and again with no guarantees. I wish...I wish I was more like you."

"Carissa, you don't need to be like anyone else, okay? You're enough exactly as you are, you know that right? Josh could be an asshole, sure, but he didn't pull the same bullshit Damien did with you. You deserve to be loved, even if it takes you a little longer to feel ready for it. I think our journeys will have one thing in common."

She rolls her eyes at me. "Oh yeah, what's that?"

"They both end with us finding someone who treats us right. We both find our person." The conviction in my voice and in my gut is undeniable.

I believe Aiden and I belong together.

Carissa was always too good for Damien. No part of me doubts that she'll find someone who respects her and protects her heart like she deserves.

"I hope you're right about that," she says with a sigh. "Enough about me, okay? I want to hear how you plan to tell him."

"Spontaneously and with zero prior planning most likely," I say.

Carissa laughs because she knows me well and my guess is probably accurate.

Making elaborate plans to share how I'm feeling with Aiden feels intimidating, so I'll probably end up word-vomiting my feelings all over him at an inconvenient and *very* unromantic time, like while we're brushing our teeth in the morning or something.

Yeah, that feels like me.

* * *

I'm pretty sure a thousand butterflies are having a rave inside my stomach while I wait for Aiden. When he finally opens the door to his apartment, my heart starts racing in anticipation.

Except when I meet his eyes, my anxiety spikes for another reason entirely. I've never seen Aiden look like this. His greeting is more reserved than usual and his body language distant. His shoulders are slack and the tension in his jaw makes it clear something is wrong.

Hopper's behavior is a red flag too. Usually, he's fighting his excitement, trying to remember not to jump on people when they first arrive. Right now, he's stuck to Aiden's side, only a few inches separating them.

All of the certainty I felt seconds ago slips away, and I'm left feeling desperate to understand what's going on.

"Hey, is everything okay?" I ask.

"Yeah. Yeah, of course. Are you good?"

"I'm good," I say, confused. Maybe my instincts are wrong and he's just upset about his performance at the game tonight.

"Good." He nods at me, and I follow him and Hopper into his apartment. We sit on the couch together, but things still feel off. I try to shake off the feeling, but it's not like Aiden to hold back with me like he seems to be doing now.

"Carissa had a good time at the game tonight," I say. "She thinks Pete's cute. First Evie, now Carissa. Does all the attention go to his head?"

"More than you know," he says.

My heart starts to race the longer we sit in silence. Aiden isn't acting like himself at all.

I didn't realize how hard he could be on himself. I know baseball is his job, but they still won the game. They play so often and he has another chance to try again tomorrow. I don't remember him acting this withdrawn even after some of the tougher losses the team's had this season. Then again, I'm not sure I could ever fully understand the pressure he's under to perform well. Maybe since he was traded midseason last year, he's feeling uncertain about his place on this team.

My thoughts are running wild. I'm trying to rationalize what my gut is telling me.

"What time do you have to leave in the morning?" I ask.

"We have an early flight. We leave for Houston at six. I'll do my best not to wake you and Hopper in the morning. You two should sleep in."

Normally, Aiden spoils me with affection and attention. When he has to leave for a few days, I wake up with his head between my thighs... regardless of how early he has to leave to catch his flight. Am I seeing red flags where there aren't any?

Yes, of course I am. That's the old Bec talking. The one responsible for filling my head with doubt. The one who wasn't sure about Aiden. The one who was waiting for Aiden to finally know me well enough to decide I wasn't the one for him. The one who was convinced none of my romantic relationships could last. I'm not going to listen to old Bec anymore. I want this to work and for that to happen, Aiden needs to know how I feel.

"Aiden, I need to tell you something," I say, hearing the shake in my own voice.

"Hm?" Aiden looks at me like he was lost in thought. He probably thinks I'm acting strange. Admittedly, I am. I'm so caught up in overthinking every little thing he's doing and saying, I'm not acting like I normally would.

It feels like my heart is going to beat out of my chest and onto the couch. I can't hold this in anymore. I need to get this out so he knows and we can move on, like with every other big step we've made together. He's always made it easy to do scary things...so I decide to jump, knowing he'll catch me.

"Aiden, I love you."

His lips part as he looks into my eyes.

Aiden doesn't say anything. He just shakes his head. The stoic expression on his face morphs into a look heavy with despair.

"You shouldn't."

The words fall from his lips so quietly, I'm not sure I heard them right.

"Wh-what are you talking about?" I ask. I can feel tears burning the back of my eyes. My head swims and heat ricochets over my skin from embarrassment.

"Something...something happened yesterday while I was visiting Mom." He leans forward, dropping his head into his hands. "Fuck, I'm so sorry, Bec. I should have told you sooner, but I can't get my mind right today. I'm trying to bury everything until I figure out how to handle it. I tried to focus on the games today and couldn't. I wanted to focus on us tonight, but I can't. You deserve better, but I don't know how to be better. What if this is all I'm capable of?"

"Aiden, what are you talking about? I don't understand," I say as the first tear spills over onto my cheek. "Is your mom okay?"

"Physically, yes. But mentally?" He looks at me and all I can see is fear. "Every day, I lose her bit by bit. She didn't recognize me. That's happened before, you've seen it, but this was different. She thought I was *him*. She didn't say his name, but I *know* her. I could see it in the way she was looking at me and the way she was yelling at me."

My stomach drops.

"She mistook you for your dad?"

"Fuck. This is so fucked," he says with a groan, squeezing his eyes shut and shoving one hand into his hair, tugging on the roots.

Fucked is right.

Aiden's terrified of turning out like his dad. Of course, this incident is going to stoke the fire, fueling that idea. But from what Aiden told me about his father, they couldn't be more opposite. Still, fear has the power to twist and warp your thoughts, leaving you with only negativity and insecurity. With all that Aiden's experiencing with his mom's memory loss, on top of everything else, no wonder he can't think straight.

And I just told him I loved him for the first time.

*Holy shit.*

I was right. I definitely picked the most inconvenient and unromantic time to tell him.

God, I need an undo button for my life.

"You know your mom doesn't think of you like that at all, Aiden. She loves you so much. She's confused...but she knows who you are inside," I say, willing him with my entire being to believe me.

"You didn't see her, Bec. It felt so real. Like I was living inside my worst nightmare. What if you stay with me and I hurt you like that? What if I'm capable of treating people like he did?"

"I know that you're not. I have never dated anyone more compassionate, patient, and caring than you. I know you, Aiden. I have faith in you and faith in us. I need you to hear what I'm saying," I say, panic spreading through my limbs. Aiden's always been the steadfast one in our relationship. Hearing his doubt leaves me feeling raw and vulnerable.

He can't possibly believe that his mother would ever speak to him like that when her mind is clear. She had a bad day. It was just a bad day. Why can't he see that?

"I don't ever want to hurt you," Aiden says, the defeat ringing in the space between us, which feels like it's growing each time he shuts down my feeble attempts to talk him through this.

"You're not going to hurt me, Aiden. I was so afraid that you would. I was so scared of that potential hurt that I wouldn't even consider being with you when we met. But you spent the last seven months showing me that's not possible. I shouldn't have said what I said tonight, but it's not because I don't mean it with every pulse of my heart."

The look in his eyes is tortured.

I won't be able to help him find his way out of this. Not tonight. He needs time.

I'm not the same person I was when Aiden came crashing back into my life. I'm not running away from this, from him, from us. While I have no idea how to make things right, I know someone who can help us figure it out.

# Chapter Fifty-Nine

Bec

Aiden and I decided not to spend the night together. He asked for some time to think but reassured me he would call tomorrow. He kissed me desperately before I left. Old Bec tried to convince me to prepare for the inevitable goodbye, but new Bec told her to shut up.

As soon as I got home, I sought out comfort from my old baggy sweatpants, the giant Aviators sweatshirt I stole from Aiden after the first time he made me breakfast, and a tub of brownie fudge ice cream.

Yes, I'm a cliché, but I don't have the energy to give a fuck.

I'm several spoonfuls in when I hear scratching at my door. It only lasts a second before Ellie bursts into my apartment, leaving the door wide open behind her, my spare key still hanging in the lock attached to her keyring. She rushes toward me frantically and wraps me in a hug so tight it knocks the wind out of me. I squeeze her back, tears rising to the surface for the second time tonight.

I want to act like I never said those three idiotic words to Aiden, but I can't ignore what happened if I want our relationship to survive. So I texted Ellie to let her know we have a "Code Red." Both of us have evoked the cry for help several times since we invented it in middle school. It's our emergency signal to drop everything and deliver a hug as quickly as possible. Ellie was the last one to call it in once she was allowed visitors after Luca was born. I ran to the hospital and held her while she cried in my arms. I'm not even sure how much she remembers from our conversation because she was so overwhelmed at the time.

"It just kind of slipped out, Ellie. This is such a fucking mess," I say, still caught in her hug.

"Slow down. What slipped out? Start from the beginning." She pulls away, hands still resting on my shoulders to look me over in case the damage is physical. Once assured I'm okay, she steps back to grab her keys and close the door to my apartment. "Let's sit."

We settle on the couch and Ellie holds my hand, listening patiently as I recall all that happened tonight.

"I can't imagine how helpless Aiden must be feeling right now," she says. "I think you two did the right thing taking the night apart to give him some time to work through this on his own. Everything you said in response was great, but it doesn't sound like he's in the right headspace to take any of that in right now. Do you know if he can take a few days off work or something?"

"I asked, but he said he'd rather keep playing. I think he's trying to pretend like the whole thing never happened and baseball is going to help him do that. I think he'd rather do anything other than think about how this is making him feel."

Ellie nods. "I don't blame him. I'm sure finding an escape would be easier than talking through it."

Our conversation is interrupted by a knock on my door.

"Did you call the girls for reinforcements?" I ask Ellie.

"No, I wanted to wait until I knew what was going on," she says.

Confused, I open my door to find Evie waiting.

"Bec, I'm so sorry. I just got off the phone with Aiden. I should have called you last night, but I wasn't thinking about anything other than Mom and Aiden. I was up so late crying and it wasn't until I reached out to him after the game today that I realized I should have given you a heads-up on everything that happened."

"Evie, it's okay. You don't need to worry about me. What about you? Are you okay? I know yesterday was awful for both of you."

She falls into my arms in tears.

"It's too much," she sobs quietly.

"I know. It's going to be okay," I promise, even though it feels hollow.

Evie joins Ellie and me on the couch before sharing what happened yesterday from her perspective. All three of us are crying by the time she's finished.

"Should I let Dom know? Maybe it would help Aiden to hear from him," Ellie offers.

"I think it would. Thank you," Evie says. "Aiden spends so much time worrying about everyone else. I don't think he knows how to ask for what he needs. I don't want him to pretend everything's fine and that he doesn't need to talk about this."

"I think in time, he'll reach out. But until then, let's all stay in touch and make sure we try to give him whatever support he needs. How's your mom doing?" Ellie asks.

"She's okay...calm at least. There haven't been any more outbursts since we left. She was asking about Aiden and I and whether or not we were going to visit her today. The nurses are keeping me updated, but I'm going to wait another day or two before I go see her. I need to be able to keep my composure when I see her to avoid causing her any distress. I don't think I could manage that right now."

"That's a good idea. She's lucky to have both of you," I say.

"And Aiden's lucky to have you. He didn't want to tell me what happened between you two tonight. Do you want to talk about it?"

Evie asks.

"I'm pretty sure I made everything worse. I thought something weird was going on when I first got to his place, but I figured I was just doing what I always do...assuming the worst and making something out of nothing. God, I'm so stupid. I knew something was wrong. I should have trusted my gut and kept my mouth shut. Aiden did not need me piling on when he's distraught over your mom's condition."

"What do you mean, piling on?" Evie asks.

"I sort of...told Aiden I love him." The look of shock on Evie's face would be comical if not for everything else going on.

"I knew it," Evie screams. "Oh my god, Bec. That's amazing. I've always wanted a sister." She grabs my hand, holding tight.

"I think you might have missed the part where I told him this *tonight*. Probably the worst time to make that confession. He has enough going on right now, he doesn't need to worry about me. Besides, I have no idea how he feels," I say.

"Please don't let my saying this scare you, but it's clear you both have love for each other. Anyone who spends time with you can see there's nothing surface level about your relationship. It's obvious how consumed by each other you are. You guys should talk once he's had a chance to work through everything with Mom. Please don't give up on him," Evie pleads.

"Seriously, Bec. I know it would be easy to believe the worst right now, but what Aiden's struggling with has nothing to do with how he feels about you," Ellie says. "Don't internalize it."

"He may not have told me he loves me, but everything he's done for me has *shown* me that he cares. I'm not going to ruin everything we have with self-doubt," I say.

They both smile at me in response and Ellie reaches out to hold my free hand, the other still clasped in Evie's tight grip.

Aiden might not be ready to talk yet, but when he is, I know our friends and family will show up in ways he never expected, just like they have for me.

# Chapter Sixty

## Aiden

"What do you need, Dom?" I ask over my shoulder after letting him into my apartment.

He didn't leave me much choice. He's been hitting the buzzer for almost ten minutes and sending me threatening texts. Some were creative enough that I know he had Ellie's help writing them.

He follows me into the kitchen and closes the fridge, even though I just opened it. He waits until I make eye contact before responding.

"I need you to come with me. I mean, with *us*." He gestures to Luca strapped to his chest in some kind of pouch with at least fifty buckles on it. Kid is *secure*.

"Eh, I'm good. I was about to take a nap. Maybe we can catch up some other time," I say, brushing off whatever this is he's trying to do by showing up unannounced.

"Aiden, it's been a week and you haven't talked to anyone. Even if you don't want to talk about it today, you need to at least get out of your apartment. Evie said you haven't left the place for anything other than practice or games. That's not healthy."

I've been ignoring Dom's texts the past few days...and Evie's...and

Bec's. I mean, not completely. I've let them know I'm okay but also that I'm not ready to talk. My plan might be shit, though, because I feel just as bad as I did the day Mom didn't recognize me. I might feel worse.

Dom grabs Hopper's leash from the hook on the wall and gives him a pet before hooking it onto his collar.

"Bring the boss. He could use the fresh air too," Dom says.

Hopper looks up at me with more excitement than I've seen since I got home from my visit with Mom last week. Guilt hits me hard. I haven't even taken him on a walk. He's been by my side while I alternate between rotting in bed and staring into my empty fridge. Bec still wanted to watch him while I was away—because she's perfect and handling all this shit better than I deserve. Hopefully, he had a better time staying with her since I'm terrible company right now.

"Listen, man, I'm not dragging a bunch of Luca's baby shit over to your apartment to do this. You gotta come with me. I've got beer at home and we're ordering pizza. Don't make this any harder than it needs to be."

I still don't know what to say. Should I dig in my heels or just give in and let Dom attempt to help, even though I don't think that's possible?

At my silence, Dom lets out a deep breath.

"Okay, I didn't want to do this, but if you don't come with me, someone scary will show up next."

"Dylan isn't scary."

"Not Dylan."

"Neither are Jake or Chris," I add.

"Not them either."

"Who the fuck are you talking about, Dom?"

"Ellie. If you don't come with me now, Ellie will show up next."

I don't need to hear anymore before I'm putting on my shoes and cap, then taking Hopper's leash as Dom hands it to me.

"Thought so," he says, smug as all hell. "See, Luca? We don't fuck with Mommy, do we?"

The four of us step onto the elevator and Dom holds Luca's arm up to force his infant to give him a high five. "Mission accomplished, little man."

I let out a chuckle for the first time in days, but the relief is short lived at the reminder of what a great dad Dom is. I don't expect anything less from Dom, or want anything less for Luca, but the jealousy and pain at not having that same relationship with my own father cuts deep any time I think too hard about it. It's all I can seem to do lately.

Talking about this is going to suck.

* * *

Three hours, two beers, and one pizza later, Dom turns off the TV, leaving us in silence.

Well, almost silence. Hopper is snoring loudly at my feet while Luca plays with a soft toy in his spot on the couch next to Dom.

"Do we have to do this?" I ask.

"Yeah, Aiden. We really do," he says.

I slump back into the couch, shutting my eyes. It was nice to hangout and talk sports for a couple hours. It was the best distraction from my thoughts I've had all week.

"Look, I wouldn't push you on this if I knew you were talking to *someone*. Evie, Bec, Dylan...anyone. Evie told us what happened with your mom," Dom says.

I shoot him an irritated look.

Did I expect Evie to keep this a secret? Of course not. But the thought of them talking about this behind my back annoys me all the same. All I can picture are varying looks of pity and judgment. Are they wondering what I did to warrant Mom's reaction? Do they know I wasn't acting like my piece of shit father or do they all assume the apple doesn't fall far from the tree?

He puts his palms up defensively. "Don't get mad at the people who care about you for worrying about you. You wanted space, so we agreed to give you space. But a week is long enough. You've had time to try to work through this on your own. It's clear as fucking day that didn't help. It's our turn now. At least let us try, okay?"

I've known Dom for close to ten years now. He knows about my family's past, but ever since I first told him everything years ago, I don't bring it up and he doesn't ask questions.

"I can't stop seeing the look Mom gave me. I keep reliving that moment. I don't ever want her to look at me like that ever again. She was so...angry, but there was also this fear bleeding through. This desperation to get as far away from me as possible."

"Your mom is sick. This isn't her fault and it isn't yours either. You're seeing a connection that isn't there. When her mind is clear and she's lucid, she would never look at you like that."

"Mom knows I'm going to turn out just like him. She finally saw it for herself and that's fucking terrifying," I say. The ache in my chest is burning.

"That's bullshit and you know it. Your DNA doesn't make you an asshole, your choices do," he says. "Do you honestly think she'd be capable of raising you to be anyone other than *her* son? *He* didn't raise you and that's on him. It's an insult to your mom to act like everything she did for you had no impact on the person you are now. She didn't sacrifice everything so you could pretend you're not worth anything. Your dad missed out on the greatest gift fatherhood has to offer: time with our children. So no, Aiden, he doesn't get to pass on his mistakes to you. Your mom knows that. Don't hold this against her or yourself. She can't control her disease, just like you can't control who your father is.

"I'm not saying it's fair what you're all going through, but you don't want to miss the time you have left with her. Isn't it worth risking a bad day to spend even just one more good day with her and Evie? All we have is time. I don't want you to throw it away because you're scared."

"Scared doesn't even begin to cover it. I'm fucking *haunted*. I have no idea what to do."

"You get help, Aiden. Real help. I didn't realize you were internalizing everything that happened with your dad. I would have given this to you when you moved back if I had known. Here," he says, handing me a business card.

"What's this?" I ask.

"This is who I talk to. I've been in therapy since Luca was born," Dom says.

"What? I didn't know. Are you good?"

"Getting there," Dom says with a shrug. "Becoming parents is the best and fucking hardest thing Ellie and I are ever going to do. I needed help figuring that shit out. Everything about our life changed in a second. No matter how prepared I thought I was, I was wrong."

I had no idea. Dom hadn't mentioned anything about talking to a professional since Luca was born last fall.

"Shit, I feel bad. I had no idea. Has it helped?"

"It's not easy, but talking about it helps more than I thought it would. I couldn't be the husband or father I want to be without an outlet like this. I didn't say anything because at first, I was embarrassed. It felt like I was admitting my own failure. But I don't regret it. I plan to go as long as I need to. I owe it to Ellie, Luca, and myself."

"I'm really glad it's working for you. I'm sorry, I didn't know you were having a hard time," I say.

"It's difficult to talk about, same as you, I bet. I promise I'll clue you in next time I need a friend, if you promise to do the same. I don't want to see you like this again."

I look down, turning the card over in my hand. Dom always seems happy and unbelievably grateful. Even when he and Ellie talk about how hard it can be taking care of Luca, he never seems to be struggling. He's made the adjustment seem effortless. I didn't realize how well he could hide how hard this has been for him mentally. But didn't I do the same thing? At least until the most recent incident ignited my baggage like fucking kindling.

"I'll call them," I decide.

"Really?" He sounds surprised. Maybe he thought I'd put up more of a fight, but Dom sharing this with me tells me he really wants to see me give it a shot. If it helped him, maybe it could help me too. He huffs out a heavy breath. "Happy to hear it." He turns to Luca and prompts him to give him another high five. "We got another win, Luca. Look at us, killing it on boys' day."

"Speaking of, where is Ellie?"

"She won't be back until later, her and the girls..." his voice trails off when we hear the garage door opening and a moment later Ellie walks in, seemingly in a good mood, until she spots me.

"Aiden, run! She'll kill you," Dom yells, running over to Ellie to block her from me. He all but throws Luca into her arms. "Murder is a felony, babe. Think of your son."

Ellie doesn't say a word. She takes Luca, lifting him into the air and smiling at him before blowing a raspberry on his stomach then sitting him on her hip. Her gaze locks with mine and the smile drops from her face.

"Aiden, do you remember what I told you would happen if you hurt my girl?"

Over the last week, the only interruption from the horrible memory of what happened when I last saw Mom has been the memory of Bec's face falling after she told me she loved me...and I didn't say it back.

I was so messed up from everything else going on, I couldn't process that Bec was telling me she loves me—that she loves me like I love her. She needed to take our relationship at her own pace, something I've been happy to do. Hearing her admit to loving me should have been the best day of my life. Instead, it was overshadowed by all the fucked-up shit from the day before. I should have told her what happened with Mom sooner. We could have worked through it together, but instead I fucked everything up.

I wish I could have told Bec how much I love her. How my days begin and end with her on my mind. How I want to hold her in my arms every night. How I want us to move in together. How badly I want to marry her. How I picture building a family with her. How I've been hers since the day we met.

I was so trapped in fucked-up memories and my stupid fear that I couldn't accept what she was saying. Ellie is right to be pissed at me. I deserve what's coming.

"I know I fucked up...but I love her," I say quietly.

She sits on the coffee table in front of me, moving Luca into her lap, where he starts playing with her hair. She stares me down with a look so cold I wait for my heart to freeze.

"I know you do. I'm truly sorry about what happened with your mom," she says. The look she gives me is heartfelt. Fuck, it tears my insides up even more than they already are. "So how are we going to fix this?"

A few feet away, I watch Dom's shoulders fall with relief. Turns out we both thought Ellie was more prepared to hurt me than help me.

"Don't look so surprised, Price. I'm asking you again. *How* are we going to fix this?" she asks impatiently.

"Why are you willing to help me? I hurt her," I say, willing my voice to stay calm.

"Tell me. If she told you she loved you on any other day, would you have reacted the same way?" Ellie asks.

"No. *Fuck no.* I would have told her that I love her too...that she's everything to me," I answer.

"*That's* why I'm helping you. My best friend is your girlfriend, and your best friend is my husband. That puts us on the same team. Life's messy and you were dealt a really shitty hand. You're a good guy, Aiden. Bec loves you, and we both know that you feel the same way about her. So, what's our plan?"

"You don't think it's too late?" I ask. It's what I've been scared of since Bec left my apartment after I told her what happened. I asked her to date me, to give me a chance no matter how badly she wanted to avoid letting me in. She was hesitant because she didn't want to get hurt, and when she risked it all telling me she loved me, I shut her down.

How could she still love me now?

"No matter what happened, Bec's not the type of person to care about everything being perfect, she just wants it to be real. She wasn't expecting your response because she didn't realize what you were going through at the time. But she loves you and wants you to be okay. Don't throw away a good thing because you can't tell the difference between your fears and the reality around you. She's waiting for you to be ready to talk to her. Everyone has been waiting for you to be ready," Ellie says.

After the divorce, I felt responsible for Mom and Evie.

It's been just us ever since.

I'm realizing I have more support now than I've ever been able to hope for. For the first time in a week, a glimmer of hope flickers in my chest.

"I'm calling this number," I say, looking down at the card in my hand. "When I figure out how to talk about everything...then I'm calling Bec and making this right."

I look up at Ellie and Dom, his arm wrapping around her shoulder as he comes to stand beside her and Luca. The approval, relief, and genuine joy I see from them makes that speck of hope inside me grow stronger.

I talk about my family being small, feeling like the absence of my father somehow makes it less than what others have. But the family that raised me, the family of friends I've found in Columbus, and the idea of the family I want to build with Bec makes me realize there isn't a missing piece. Everyone I need is here with me, wanting the best for me, and I'm not ever going to let them doubt the love I have for them in return again.

# Chapter Sixty-One

Bec

Three weeks. It's been three weeks since I've seen Aiden.

We still text every day, and I go over to his place to pick up and drop off Hopper when he has to travel for away games. Aiden's never there.

I miss him.

Last night when I picked up Hopper, before we left to go back to my place, I snuck into Aiden's bed and ended up napping for an hour. I wanted to feel close to him, and the comfort of being in his space, along with the scent of his bodywash on the sheets, lulled me into a restful sleep. It was the best I've slept since I told him I loved him...and he told me I shouldn't.

I can't force him to see himself the way I do. I can't rush him to be ready to talk about how he feels about our relationship. I want him to have the time he needs to work through his thoughts so we can figure out where to go from here. It's hard to be patient, though.

"Team's looking great. Playoff talk is circulating the closer we get to the end of the season. Aiden's looking better tonight too. Haven't seen a big play like that from him in a while," Toby says.

I hum in agreement, keeping my response brief and my eyes on the

TV. My family doesn't know the details of everything that's going on. They know Aiden and I are working through some things, but that it's taking a backseat while he focuses on his Mom's health.

I'm not trying to lie or hide things from my family, but at a certain point it feels like this is Aiden's story. When he's ready for my family to know about his past and the way it's affecting his present, then they will. I don't want to overshare and shed a spotlight on something so vulnerable. The type of hurt he's experiencing right now, it's extremely personal. If I want Aiden in my life forever, it's important to me that his relationship with my family is built slowly over time, genuinely with trust on both sides. I explained all of this when they initially asked for more information, and they instantly backed off, understanding and empathy overtaking their curiosity. Probably a first for my family since we are all nosey as hell when it comes to each other's personal lives.

"Any word on how Aiden's mom is doing, hun? Is she feeling better?" Mom asks from her spot next to Dad on the couch. She's tucked into his side, his arm around her shoulder, her head resting on his shoulder.

"Evie and I talked earlier today. She had a really good visit with her yesterday. Overall, Judy's had a great week," I say.

Evie cried when she told me about her first visit to see Judy after everything happened. The relief in her tone was clear. It really was just a horrible day, but that isn't all that's left.

I hope Aiden can see that and he finds the strength to face the uncertainty each day brings. I hope he finds comfort knowing how loved he is by his mom, even when her condition forces her to forget.

"That's great news. I'm sure that's why he's looking a little more like himself on the field," Danny adds.

"When does he come home?" Dad asks.

"He flies in tomorrow night. He'll be back for a few days before he has to travel again," I say.

I'm hoping with every piece of me that Aiden will be ready to see me before he has to leave again. Otherwise, I'll be waiting another week. A whole fucking month.

Like I said, patience isn't my specialty. I'm trying my best not to clue him into that when we're texting, but it's difficult.

Danny's in the recliner behind me, playing with my hair while I sit on the floor, Hop snuggled into my side. I pet Hop and he snuggles closer against me, kicking his legs out to the side getting comfortable.

"What am I, chopped liver?" Ashton asks from Hopper's other side when the dog shoves a paw into his leg, forcing him to scoot away. The second Ashton stops petting his stomach, though, Hopper shoots him a look like, *What the fuck, man—who said you could quit with the massage?*

We sit together in my parent's living room, watching the Aviators win four to two. Toby talks about work as usual. Danny tells us about her upcoming girls' trip to Denver. Ash gives us a rundown on why he and his roommates think they have a chance of becoming professional skateboarders at their age when none of them have gotten closer to the sport than an old video game they used to play in middle school. Mom and Dad update us on neighborhood gossip. Hopper moves from person to person, trying to find out which one of us is the most suitable to snuggle with. *Traitor.*

When the game is over and I'm getting ready to head home for the night, I pop my head out of the back door to find my dad sitting on the deck.

"I'm headed out, Dad," I say.

"Got a minute before you go?" he asks.

I huff out a breath as I plop onto one of the chairs. "Yeah, what's up?"

"I want to talk about Aiden."

"What about him?" I ask.

"I've been thinking about what you said before, and I heard you. I'm not asking for details that are Aiden's to share when he's ready. Besides, I don't need them to know that he's dealing with something pretty heavy right now. What I do need to know is how it's affecting you. Are *you* okay?"

This is what Aiden deserves. I wish more than anything that he could have a father who treats him the same way as mine. The errant thought makes tears pool in the corner of my eyes.

"Thanks for checking in. I promise, I'm good. I just wish there was a way for me to make things easier for him. I didn't know what he was dealing with right away, and I wish I had. I'm afraid I unintentionally made things harder for him, but I'm hoping to talk to him about it soon."

He sits with what I've said for a minute before responding, considering his next words carefully like my dad always does, forever the practical voice of reason.

"I have a feeling I already know the answer to this, but go ahead and spare me the suspense. Is Aiden my future son-in-law?"

The question does me in, and the tears that were threatening to fall earlier finally do.

"I hope so," I whisper.

"Then you two will figure it out. Any man who's willing to show his face here after how things went the first time we met, isn't afraid of much."

I laugh, because he's not wrong. I can picture Aiden's cheeks flush with embarrassment and the memory, however ridiculous, warms my heart. Aiden's Pictionary debut will haunt Aiden at every single family gathering that he attends until further notice, and he's taken it all in stride.

"He's different from the men you've dated before. You two are good for each other," he says.

"Thanks, Dad. I'm sorry I haven't been more transparent about everything that's going on."

"Now, don't you apologize for that. It's clear that Aiden is a man who takes care of his family. I like knowing that's important to him."

"Can I ask you something?"

"Of course," he says.

"How did you know you wanted to live your life with Mom?"

He hums thoughtfully, sitting back and looking up at the sky for a minute. "If you asked me when I was young, I'd tell you it was because she was the most beautiful woman I'd ever seen with an even more beautiful heart. She made me feel like we could take on anything life threw at us, like we were invincible. But now I see that while those were important reasons, it wasn't that complicated."

"How could deciding to spend forever with someone not be compli-cated?" I question.

"Because your mother was the person who made me feel alive. She lights my world with color. I became a better man, living a better life with her at my side. She made every struggle easier, every success shine brighter, every dream more magical. Look at you, for instance. Our family...it's the greatest gift I've ever been given and it's all thanks to her. Sharing a life with your mother is the most beautiful thing I'll experience."

The look in my dad's eyes gives me hope. Maybe it really is that simple.

# Chapter Sixty-Two

## Aiden

"You fly home later tonight. Is that right?" David asks.

"That's right," I confirm.

"And are you still planning to see Bec?"

"I haven't asked her yet, but I plan on it."

My stomach is tied into one giant fucking knot thinking about seeing her again, the rush of conflicting emotions is overwhelming. She hasn't sounded angry with me in our text messages these past few weeks, but how could she not be? I've taken forever to get my head on straight and I'm still not certain I'll be able to talk to her without fucking everything up.

I know I need to do two things: I need to see Bec and I need to see my mom.

I have to make sure Bec knows that I love her. All I can do is hope she forgives me for not saying it sooner and for how I acted when she confessed to loving me first.

Evie has been to visit Mom several times, but I haven't gone with her. I've been too terrified to face the possibility of repeating history. I feel so goddamn selfish. My family needs me and I've been too much of a coward to be with them.

But Dom was right. Today is only my second time talking with David, his therapist—and I guess mine now too—and I know he was right to suggest I make an appointment. David has explained that it'll take some time before we can dig into the root of what I'm struggling with, but he's helped me talk about what's going on right now in a way that doesn't make me want to shut down. He asked me what I want my life to look like and helped me plan what my next few steps will need to be to help make that happen. It's not a quick fix, but he seems like a nice guy, and I think this could be good for me.

David summarizes everything we talked about today and we schedule another appointment for next week before ending the virtual session. I pack up my shit, head from the hotel to the airport, and run through what I want to say to Bec probably a hundred times on the flight home.

When I get back to my apartment, Hopper is there to greet me, but just like every other time I've come home these past few weeks, Bec's not with him. I want this to be the last time I come home to find that she's not here too.

I never told her not to be here, but after that first night we decided to spend the night apart, she texted me to tell me she understood that I needed time, that she'd be waiting for me when I was ready to talk, and that I can tell her when I'm ready to have that conversation.

This woman is too fucking perfect to be real.

I've wanted to call her and beg her to see me, to sit with me and let me hold her without saying anything. But that's not fair to her. I owe her an explanation. I need to be able to talk about this shit. She deserves more than I've had to give. I'm going to dig deep and try my best and hope that she still loves me despite everything I still need to figure out.

"It's time we got our girl back," I say to Hop, who wags his tail in agreement. I crouch low and wrap my arms around my faithful companion, mumbling a soft thank-you into his fur. God, I love this dog. "Wish me luck," I say with a pet on his head before I head out to hopefully bring Bec home with me for good.

* * *

I heave a heavy breath out in an attempt to calm my racing heart as I stand in front of Bec's apartment.

I didn't text her. I was too scared she'd say not to come over.

I need to see her...even if she turns me away.

I give myself another ten seconds before I knock on her door. All the effort I made to temper my nerves is shot when I hear the soft patter of her feet approaching.

I keep my head down, bracing for rejection. I know she's probably peeking through her door to see who could be knocking this late. I wouldn't blame her if she didn't open the door at all.

After a few more seconds, relief flows through me as she opens the door and my entire body reacts to her nearness.

Bec is always beautiful, but when she's like this...hair a mess of curls falling out of a knot at the top of her head, her faded, holey T-shirt hanging halfway down her thick thighs, and pajama shorts that just barely meet the same length as her shirt, her perfect legs on display looking so good I want to drape them over my shoulders and down my back...this is exactly what I want to come home to every day for the rest of my life.

"Aiden," she says quietly.

"Can I come in?" I ask, barely able to make eye contact.

*Please say yes.*

She doesn't say anything. She doesn't move to let me in. One second, she's frozen, standing in the doorway, holding onto the frame for support, and the next, she's launching herself into my arms, wrapping her arms tightly around my shoulders, her head tucked into the base of my neck.

I immediately wrap my arms around her, holding her tightly against me.

"You're here," she whispers, disbelief in her tone.

"I'm sorry. I'm so fucking sorry it took me so long." I don't trust the shake in my voice as emotions wash over me and fluctuate too quickly for me to name.

All I can make out is this overwhelming feeling of comfort...like I'm taking my first full breath in weeks...like I'm finally coming home.

"Let's not do this here." She pulls away and takes my hand, tugging me into her apartment after her. "Come in."

I take off my backpack, and we sit on her couch in awkward silence, but she's still holding my hand as she faces me, one leg tucked underneath herself. I drape one arm along the back of her couch, playing with one of her loose curls with my free hand.

"I have so much I want to say. It's hard to know where to start," I say.

"Take your time," she says.

"When we met, you asked about my favorite memory. I shocked myself when I told you about my birthday like that. I hadn't thought about that day in so long. It was painful to think about that time in my life. Even though it was a great day, the memory always felt tainted by the other shit that was going on at the time. But then you asked...and it just spilled out. You have this way of drawing things out of me that I wish I could bury. The day my mom forgot who I was...I wanted to bury that memory so deep it couldn't ever hurt again. I didn't want to talk about it. I didn't want to face it."

"It's okay," she says softly, squeezing my hand. When I look up, she's crying quietly. Tears slowly falling. Then I realize, I'm crying too.

"It's okay," she repeats, nodding for me to go on.

"I didn't want to face it. But then you were there, telling me you love me. Something I've only dreamed you could feel about me. I'm so fucking sorry I couldn't say it back. I couldn't process what was happening.  I panicked and all I could feel was this...dread.  This needling fear that maybe I really am my father's son, and one day I would hurt everyone around me. You don't deserve that. I couldn't hear you tell me you loved me when in that moment, all I could feel was how much I hated myself and who I was afraid I could become.

"You have no idea how much it means to me, knowing you love... knowing you loved me.  I wish with my entire fucking body that I could take back what I said to you. I wish I was able to talk about this right then and there. I...I'm talking to someone now, a therapist. I'm getting help because I need it...because I want to be a better man. Bec, when I do finally tell you how I feel about you, I want to be someone who deserves to say those words to you."

"Aiden, I'm happy for you, and I'm incredibly proud of you for getting help. Everything you've gone through, it'd be a lot for anyone to take on. I want to support you with whatever you need. As far as you deserving to say those words...and to hear those words from me...I want you to know that I don't need you to be perfect to love you. I'm never going to be perfect either. I think what matters is that we're perfect for each other. The fact that you know how scared I've been of getting hurt and that you were worried about me enough to pull away when you were scared that you were going to be the one to hurt me, I appreciate that more than you know."

"I felt out of control, and I was terrified I was going to turn out to be just like him," I say.

"I don't think you're capable of making the same mistakes as him, but I understand why you'd have that fear. We'll work through it."

"You still want to be with me? I didn't know if I had taken too long to figure out what I needed to do," I say meekly.

"I trust you, Aiden. When you asked for time, I knew you needed it. I knew I wanted to be here for you when you were ready. If our relationship has taught me anything, it's that I know I can count on you."

"I promise it won't be like this again," I say, my voice steady. "I hope with everything that I have, that there won't be a next time with Mom like this, but if there is, I'll learn how to handle it better. I won't shut everyone out like that."

"You had us all worried," she admits, empathy clear in the way she's thumbing the back of my hand and watching me with understanding.

"I'm sorry," I say.

"Don't be. You're here now."

"I am, and I'm not going anywhere. Except to get you this." I grab my backpack and bring it over to her. "I brought you something." When I dump the contents of my backpack onto her small coffee table, she bursts out laughing.

"Aiden, what the hell is this?" she asks, holding up one of the bags of chips.

"I didn't know what my mood snacker would want, so I bought one of everything at the airport for her. Well, I stopped when I couldn't fit anymore."

"And you thought you weren't perfect," she jokes, grabbing a Twix from the pile.

After talking for a while longer, I ask Bec to come home with me to stay the night. To my relief, she's ecstatic and runs to her room to grab her stuff. As much as I've missed her in my bed, I missed being with her more. We spend the night holding each other. Occasionally waking to talk more about everything we've struggled with both in the last few weeks and beyond; how we want to work on our own issues together, the things we missed in each other's lives over the last few weeks, and sometimes just pulling each other closer and lying in comfortable silence. It's everything I needed, and the way Bec relaxes against me and tucks her head in closer to me at every opportunity gives me hope that maybe it's what she needs too.

The next morning, she offers to come with me to visit my mom. I cling to her like a lifeline as we check in at the front desk.

I don't know what'll happen when Mom sees me today, but I know that with Bec by my side, I'm stronger.

The office staff recognize both of us instantly and offer us a warm greeting. When I look at Bec, confused because she hasn't been here often enough to warrant that kind of response, she shrugs sheepishly. She confesses to having visited Mom several times a week while I was unable to, often bringing one of the Center's certified therapy dogs with her.

It takes every shred of self-control I have not to blurt out right then and there how fucking gone I am for Bec. How she's worked herself into every bone and muscle in my body. How I love her more than I ever knew was possible.

But I have other plans for that confession.

Bec gave me exactly what I needed to get through one of the worst fucking times of my life. She showed me more compassion, patience, and love than I could ever ask for. I want her to grasp the depth of what I feel for her just as strongly when I finally tell her.

She holds my hand as we step into Mom's room to find her reading in her rocker.

Mom's eyes lock with mine and her eyes light up brightly with recognition.

"Aiden, sweetheart. I've missed you," she says with so much love, my heart nearly bursts out of my chest.

"I missed you, too, Mom," I choke out as tears threaten to roll down my face. She stands, hugs me close, and I fall apart in my mother's arms.

# Chapter Sixty-Three

## Bec

Two weeks go by, and Aiden and I have fallen back into our normal routine. Since he came back to me after taking the time he needed, we haven't spent another night apart, aside from his away games.

When he showed up at my door unexpectedly after weeks of not seeing each other, it was as if my entire body could relax, finally having him near me again.

He's talking with his therapist once a week, and I'm so glad he decided to take this step. It's clear that it's become a positive outlet, and he seems more confident that it's helping every time he has an appointment, even though he admits it's difficult talking about his past.

Judy hasn't had any more traumatic flashbacks or serious instances of confusion since Aiden started visiting with her again. I can feel the relief emanating off him when we arrive for our visits to discover she's having mostly good days.

I haven't told Aiden that I love him since my first confession, and he hasn't told me how he feels either. I'm not in any rush to push the conversation.

In my heart, I completely understand why he couldn't say those words to me before and I don't want to put any pressure on him to define our relationship status now. I want him to focus on getting himself to a good place. Besides, I know how I feel about him, and he shows me every day how much he cares about me. That's all I need.

I roll over to find Aiden's side of his bed empty.

Well...his edge of the bed, since I woke up spread out in the middle and Hopper is stretched along the rest of the available space. How Aiden never falls off the side of his own bed when he shares it with the two of us is something I'll never understand.

I reach my fingers over the sheets and give my legs a quick stretch, noting a familiar soreness between my legs. Memories of last night bring a dopey smile to my face. I shut my eyes, letting the images flash through my mind.

"What are you thinking about, beautiful? That face is making me want to crawl back into bed with you and never let you leave," Aiden says.

I open my eyes to soak in the sight of him shirtless and in low-slung sweatpants, leaning against the door frame of his bedroom, reminding me of the first night I slept here.

"Would it inflate your ego too much to say I was thinking of you?" I ask. I laugh when he launches himself onto the bed with me. With so little room to spare, he ends up on top of me, trapping me between his body and the mattress. He trails kisses from my jaw to my shoulder.

"Hm...it might, but I promise to use it as motivation. I'll give you more reasons to make that face."

"And what face is that exactly?"

"Like you're happy here. Are you?" He lifts up to look at me with a hopeful expression. I watch as his eyes roam over me looking for any hint he could be right.

"I've never been happier than I am now," I say with confidence.

Aiden was the missing piece I never allowed myself to look for. I used to let my own fears keep me from going after the things I wanted but couldn't dream of finding. But not now. Not now that I know I've found that with Aiden.

"What if I told you breakfast is ready in the kitchen," he mumbles into my neck before nibbling my skin softly between his teeth.

"Had to one-up yourself, huh?" I laugh when he pins me to the bed with his full body weight, his head turned to the side and resting on my chest just below my chin. I place a kiss on the top of his head before running my fingers through his hair.

"Figured you'd need to refuel after last night," he says.

"Hmm...are there pancakes?"

"Of course," he says, looking up at me with a smirk. He pushes up on his forearms, relieving me of his weight, and kisses me lightly on the lips. "Let's go, Miller. Before everything gets cold."

He stands and reaches for my hand. I take it and stand in front of him, stopping him when he starts to lead us to the kitchen.

"And you?" I ask. "Are you happy?"

I would have been afraid to hear the answer from anyone other than Aiden. I wouldn't have asked in fear that the answer would be no, so sure that I couldn't make anyone happy. But with Aiden, I don't have to question if he's happy being with me. He shows me all the time. When I ask him if he's happy, I just want to know that he's okay.

He slides his palm around the side of my neck, his thumb resting along the edge of my jaw. "I used to think I was happy. I tried to bury the shit I never wanted to deal with so deep even I didn't know it was rotting away somewhere in there. Now that I'm trying to work on myself, digging that all up and clearing it all out feels overwhelming sometimes. Mom's illness is still difficult for me to handle. But Bec, you make all of that easier. You make me want more. You give me hope that today will be better than yesterday, and even if it's hard, having you with me makes it easier. I'm so fucking happy with you. Happy doesn't even begin to describe it."

* * *

When Aiden asked me to take a walk with him after we had dinner at one of our favorite spots downtown, I didn't expect to find myself outside of the art museum.

"What are we doing here, Aiden?"

"Didn't you say you try to come here at least once a month?" he asks. He walks backward toward the building, pulling me along in front of him to get closer to the chalkboard wall.

"Someone was paying attention."

"I wonder if you'll be able to find what I wrote," he says.

"You already answered? When?"

"When I got back two weeks ago. Before I came to talk to you and bring you home," he says.

"You wrote your answer two weeks ago, and waited until now to bring me? Let's see it."

"See if you can spot it yourself."

I smile, loving to hear the playfulness in his tone. Life has felt so serious lately, I love when we get moments like this to enjoy being together and having fun without responsibilities or expectations.

The prompt at the top of the chalkboard wall reads, *I'm finally going to...* written in swirling calligraphy. The artist who wrote the prompt used a stunning blend of blue, green, and purple hues in the text and the area surrounding it. I begin to read the phrases strangers left behind, and as always, it evokes a sense of belonging within me.

*I'm finally going to call my sister. I'm finally going to quit my job. I'm finally going to take that vacation. I'm finally going to break up with him. I'm finally going to write a song. I'm finally going to have a place to call home. I'm finally going to move on. I'm finally going to live for myself. I'm finally going to ask them out. I'm finally going to...*

Hearing the voices of so many people feeling, desiring, and overcoming similar things encapsulates what it means to be perfectly imperfect. That our lives could look so different from the outside, but inside...what we feel is etched into our collective humanity, a beautiful goddamn mess.

I scan the wall but don't see anything that *feels* like Aiden.

"I can't find it. Are you sure it didn't get erased?" I ask.

"I'm sure," he says confidently.

I walk closer to the wall then turn back to face him.

"Am I getting warm?"

"Freezing." He chuckles.

I take a gigantic step to the side. "And now?"

"Warmer..." He smiles, shoving his hands in his pockets.

Another step.

"Warmer..."

Another.

"On fire. Smoking hot," he says.

I look at the board behind me, planning to give the area a quick scan to see if I can find something written in his handwriting. But there it is. Right in front of me.

*I'm finally going to tell her I love her.*

My mouth drops open and a small squeak comes out. I turn around to find Aiden waiting for me. He pulls me close and I revel in the feel of his arms locked securely around me.

"I love you, Bec," he says with a look of pure joy.

His words send my heart racing. I know with all that Aiden has been through, he wouldn't say those words to me unless he was ready, unless he meant them. Hearing him say that he loves me sends a wave of relief through me at the realization that he has come out on the other side of what happened before. I hate that his past has caused him to feel so uncertain...uncertain that he deserves to find his own happiness.

I used to question if that kind of happiness was meant for me too. But Aiden has shown me that we deserve to find it together.

"I love you too," I say with a smile just as bright as his beaming on my face.

He rests his forehead against mine, holds my face in his hands, and presses his lips softly against mine. It's not enough. I loop my arms around his neck and pull him toward me so I can deepen our kiss. When our lips pull apart, we stand there for a few minutes while he holds me close in his arms.

"My place is closer. How fast can you get us there?" I ask.

He arches an eyebrow at me. "Only one way to find out." He turns around and brings his arms out to his sides. "Hop on."

"I was kidding, Aiden. We can walk," I say with a laugh.

"Or we can do it my way. Now wrap those pretty legs around me. Let's go, love." That little word. That little, huge word. Hearing it from Aiden sends my stomach tumbling over itself. I step closer and Aiden lowers himself so I can hop onto his back. He carries me all the way back to my apartment faster than should be possible, and I can't help the grin I wear as I cling to his body and laugh the entire way home.

* * *

If I thought carrying me all the way to my apartment on his back was enough to tire Aiden out, I was wrong. Maybe we're both riding the high of telling each other how we feel, but when we finally get through my front door, Aiden drops me to my feet and backs me against the wall in my living room before I can say a word. He holds my head in his hands, his eyes searching mine. With one look, he strips me bare. This man knows every part of my head, my heart, and my body, and the thought doesn't scare me. It fills me with warmth. It fills me with a sense of belonging.

"Every day, Bec. I'm going to tell you *every fucking day* for the rest of my life how much I love you," he says before attacking my mouth with a kiss so hungry, so fierce it takes my breath away.

"I love you too," I say when he moves to kiss my neck. "So much." With one hand, he threads his fingers into my scalp and he tightens his grip just enough to draw a moan from me. His other hand palms my breast. My clit is pulsing in anticipation.

"Off," I demand, tugging at his pants and kicking off my shoes.

Aiden laughs. "Hands up, beautiful."

I lift my hands without hesitation and he rips my shirt off before pinning my hands above my head against the wall. He leans down, his voice rumbling in my ear. "Turn around."

Aiden's grip on my wrists is loose enough to allow me to turn toward the wall. I turn my head, resting my cheek against the cool surface. "Stay still," he says, running his hands from my wrists down to my waist, before snaking them to the front of my stomach. He undoes my pants and pulls them and my thong down my thighs slowly before having me step out of them. I can feel my chest rising and falling. I'm already breathless, panting and turned the fuck on.

I yelp in surprise when I feel him kissing my ass while gripping and squeezing my cheeks where they meet the tops of my thighs. I tilt my head to rest my temple against the wall, my skin buzzing with tension. Aiden returns to stand behind me and undoes the clasp on my bra without any trouble.

I'm completely naked, my bra only hanging on from the straps. Losing my last shred of patience, I whirl away from the wall and toss my bra to the side. I run my hands under his shirt, up his muscled abdomen and chest before tugging his shirt over his head and onto the floor. Aiden seems to run out of patience as well because he doesn't wait for me to help him before taking off the rest of his clothes. The sight of his hard body ignites my arousal into an uncontrolled fire.

I press my palms against his chest and push him backward until he falls onto my couch. I straddle his thighs and suck his bottom lip into my mouth, biting it and running my hands from the sides of his neck into the hair at the base of his skull. He groans into our kiss. His rough hands grip my thighs tightly before he squeezes my ass and pulls my center against him.

"Fuck, Bec. I love you so much."

"Show me," I whisper against his lips as I sink down onto his thick cock, causing us both to moan. We lock eyes and hold each other close as our bodies melt together. I've never felt this close to him. I know I'm exactly where I want to be...exactly where I'm meant to be.

Aiden pulses up into me as I drop onto him, matching his rhythm. I rotate my hips to grind against him. His thickness causes the perfect stretch. When he sucks my nipple into his mouth, I let my head drop back, looking up to the ceiling. He runs his hands up my back and grips my shoulders, pulling me down onto him harder.

"Oh fuck, Aiden. That feels so good."

He hugs me tightly against his chest and somehow lowers himself off the couch to kneel on the floor. I cling to him as he lowers my body to lie on the living room rug, all the while his cock is still hard and pulsing inside of me. He hovers his body above me before thrusting into me, working us both into a needy push and pull. He drives against my clit and my orgasm races up my thighs before exploding through my veins. He follows me over the edge, calling out my name. When he falls to my side, he pulls me alongside him, no space between us. We lie there together, in a heap on the floor of my small apartment. Secluded in our own little bubble of the world together.

Both imperfect but growing together every day into the people we want to be. For the first time, it feels like the person at my side is going to help me be the person I want to be rather than hinder that progress. Aiden makes me better and I hope to do the same for him by holding each other when we need support, challenging each other when we need the push, and loving each other through it all.

Our breathing slows and I hear him taking a deep breath, breathing in before kissing my forehead.

"Thank you, Bec. For taking a chance on me. For not giving up on me. For loving me."

"Like you said, Aiden. I'm going to love you every day. I want them all," I say. He places a light kiss on my nose.

"Since the first day I met you, Bec, all my days have been yours."

# Epilogue

## Aiden

"Merry Christmas, Judy. We'll see you later tonight," the nurse says to Mom, who waves in return as we exit the memory care unit.

Mom hasn't shown improvement over the last few months, but her condition hasn't worsened either. There are still bad days—though none as bad as that horrible day this past August. Thankfully, therapy is helping me learn to deal with Mom's memory loss in a healthier way. Having Bec with me makes everything easier too.

The Aviators made it to the playoffs this season, losing in the semifinal series. As much as I wish we'd made it further, having the extra time to spend with my family this fall, Bec included, is something I'll appreciate for the rest of my life.

Next year, the team has its sight set on the World Series, but for now I'm grateful for the real win—solidifying a seven-year contract with the Aviators with a no-trade clause, securing my place on this team and in Columbus. It's the type of stability I need for Mom and the type I want to be able to offer Bec too. Her family, friends, and career are here. We both love this city, and we want to live our lives here together.

When she told me her lease was ending and she needed to renew, I asked her to move in with me. Well, with me and Hopper. Did I employ my best boy to tug on Bec's heartstrings? I sure fucking did.

No regrets, well, except that now I practically get kicked out of bed every night while the two of them spread out like starfish. Hop was ecstatic when I walked into our place holding a box of her belongings, like he knew from the start that she belonged with us permanently.

The new contract also gave Bec and I the reassurance we needed to start looking for a new place together. Bec and I have talked about our options, and we both want a yard for Hopper, so we're looking at a few neighborhoods near Ellie and Dom.

I help Mom to my car, Hopper trotting along cheerfully on my other side, officially a certified therapy dog approved to visit Mom and the other residents, thanks to Bec and Abby's training over the last year. The show-off has been soaking up all the attention he could garner for the last hour while we got Mom ready for a visit to the Miller's for Christmas lunch.

Denise and Thomas were kind enough to extend the invitation to Mom, Evie, and me for the holiday this year, and Bec's elated expression hearing me accept the offer assured me I'd made the right call. It'll be the first time we have our families together, and I can't explain what it does to my insides to feel like my small family is growing like this. It feels right.

Evie is meeting us there and will bring Mom back for the night when she's tired. She's having a good day today and even remembered what gifts we bought for Bec's parents when we went shopping together last week.

Mom hums along to the Christmas carol on the radio as she pets Hop's head while he rests on the center console between us.

Bec greets us at the door, and after my mom calls her by name, she pulls Bec in for a long hug. Bec smiles at me over Mom's shoulder as she reciprocates the gesture, circling her arms around her as well. Seeing Bec glow with the same joy I do when I realize Mom's head is clear fills my chest with gratitude. It means as much to her as it does to me.

The celebration passes in a haze of good food, drinks, and conversation. The buzz of chatter, laughter, and the occasional bark from Hop is the perfect soundtrack for our colliding worlds. I never imagined I could experience this type of contentment. Denise, Danny, and Mom spend a good chunk of the evening bonding over Mom's favorite home renovation show, turns out it's Denise's favorite too. Evie and Ash are battling it out for biggest smart-ass in the room as they launch quips at each other, much to the amusement of Tom and Toby.

I'm shaking the snow off my shoulders as I follow Hopper back inside after his quick bathroom break. He bounds into the room at breakneck speed, nearly slipping on his ass as he rounds the corner to find a cozy spot on the couch next to Denise. Scanning the room as I remove my boots, I catch Bec standing at the edge of the festivities, observing our families as they mingle together. I step behind her and wrap my arms around her stomach, her palms warm the back of my hands as she threads her fingers through mine. I drop a soft kiss to her temple and relax when I feel her body melt against mine.

"Thank you, Aiden," she whispers, angling her head to the side and leaving room for me to drop my forehead to her shoulder.

"What could you possibly be thanking me for, beautiful. You haven't opened your Christmas gift yet. Maybe if you're lucky it'll vibrate like your gift from last year." She gasps and smacks the back of my hand. I sneak a quick nibble of her neck before placing a kiss over the same spot.

"I'm trying to be serious, Aiden Price."

"And I'm trying to seduce you, Bec Miller," I say quietly.

"Relentless," she huffs in a laugh.

Bec turns in my arms, her chest pressing against mine, and laces her hands together at the base of my neck. "I said thank you *because* Christmas gift or not, you've given me everything I could have ever wanted this year." Her eyes glitter as they stare into my own.

"Do you remember how things were between us last year? I can't believe you'd ever think that I gave you anything that could ever rival what you've given me. You gave me a chance. You risked everything to let me love you. I'll never be able to explain how desperately I wanted that...how much I appreciate how far we've come since then. How much we've both grown."

The woman in front of me astounds me every goddamn day. Discovering every piece of who she is makes me fall more in love with her. If she lets me, I'll be old and gray and still learning new things about who Bec is, and loving her more with every passing minute.

We hold each other close, stuck in our own bubble momentarily before Ash and Evie start throwing stuffed snowmen decorations at us, demanding that we get a room.

*Later.* I mentally promise Bec when she gives me that look. The smirk she gives me in return tells me she got the message.

We've almost finished exchanging gifts when I turn to Mom and Evie and hand them the ornament I chose for this year. I can hear Bec quietly explaining our tradition to her family, who observe with polite interest. Mom slowly unwraps the small box and I hear her gasp before she lifts her fingers to place them over her mouth.

Evie looks over at me, eyes glistening with emotion. "I love it."

Mom gave everything she had to make sure Evie and I were able to find joy after walking away from the heartache of her divorce. I wanted to honor that new beginning. Mom rubs her thumb back and forth over the photo in the frame—the three of us the day we moved into our first apartment on our own. A fuzzy, low-quality, disposable camera picture that Evie made us take. In the photo, Evie's giggling, holding bunny ears over my head while I stick my tongue out at her. Mom is looking at us both with pride and love and relief.

I used to think that I needed to bury the happy memories from my childhood along with the painful ones. We took this picture during one of the most difficult times of our lives. A lot of healing needed to happen for all of us afterward, and we're still not done. But like when Bec surprised me for my birthday, I'm finding that revisiting the memories from that time in our lives doesn't feel as dark or confusing as it did before. I'm learning to take the good with the bad. I can appreciate the struggles for helping to make me the man I am today, just as much as the good times. Those perfect moments sprinkled in between the hardships make everything we endured fade into the background.

"What a beautiful life you two have given me," she says, her voice thick with emotion.

"What a beautiful life you gave us," I say back to her. Her eyes meet mine before the first tear falls and the three of us spend a few minutes honoring the moment, the Millers quietly giving us some privacy as they move to the kitchen to get dessert ready.

"I love you, Mom," Evie says before enveloping her in a hug so tight it looks painful. I'm about to pull her off, but Mom just giggles.

"And I love you, sweet girl. I love you both so very much."

Mom and Evie take off after dessert, leaving me with Bec and her family for the rest of the night.

Ashton waits about...oh, I don't know...all of thirty seconds before asking, "So...Aiden, you up for a game of Pictionary?"

I'll be hearing this joke for the rest of my life, which I have no problem with. That'll mean I'm lucky enough for Bec to keep me around, and really that's all I want for Christmas this year and every year after that.

* * *

After I fail miserably at Pictionary with the Millers again, thankfully with less embarrassment this time, Bec, Hop, and I head home for the night.

I follow them into our apartment. The merging of our belongings in a hodgepodge fashion is comforting...with the exception of the dead plant graveyard Bec insisted on keeping when she moved in. I have a soft spot for her relentless optimism. And hey, that one plant she had her eye on does look a little greener in the daylight. Sort of. Well, that's what she says, so I agree with her.

I make us a drink and the three of us move into the living room to exchange presents. Of course, Hopper goes first. When Bec gives him the cue, he tears into the wrapping paper, shredding it to get to his new bone and stuffed reindeer. His tail flops loudly on the floor, making his appreciation and excitement known.

"You first, babe," I say, handing over her gift. She doesn't hesitate, tearing into the packaging almost as eagerly as Hop did before pulling out the comforter I bought.

"New bedding? You know how important it is to me to have the perfect comforter. Thank you, Aiden," she says, feeling the fabric in her hands.

"That's *your* new bedding. Part of your gift is that Hopper got his own identical blanket for the bed. You both deserve to be comfortable and I can't mediate the blanket battles anymore. You both get your own from now on."

Bec laughs and crawls into my lap to kiss me, still giggling softly against my lips.

"That's so very thoughtful and selfish of you at the same time," she jokes.

"It feels like a win for everyone," I say with a smirk.

"Uh-huh. Sure, hun," she says.

Bec stands and grabs an envelope from one of the stockings and hands it to me. "This is your gift," she says a little quieter, an undertone of anxiousness in her voice.

I open the envelope and read each word carefully...twice.

My heart beats wildly, pounding so loud I swear I can hear it. My eyes burn and a quiet choking sound escapes my throat when I try to speak. I cough to clear it.

"I hope this is okay," she says hesitantly.

"Bec, what is this?" I ask in disbelief.

"I spoke with the Aviators' community liaison—the same person you worked with to orchestrate the partnership with New Hope—and we're working on finalizing the details with another organization. Next season, the team will be an official partner of the local Alzheimer's Family Resource Center. The Aviators will be supporting the organization and the work they do to help families who need assistance accessing care for their loved ones."

I'm speechless, unable to even look at her. I keep staring at the paper and the words all blur together.

"I didn't know what to get the man who can afford anything. Did I overstep? I'm sor—"

I drop the paper and pull Bec into my arms, both of us kneeling on the floor next to our tree and our dog. I can't stop the tears from falling.

"It's the most thoughtful thing anyone's ever done for me. You're incredible, babe. I love you so fucking much. It doesn't feel possible to love you more...then you go and do something like this." I devour her in a hungry kiss that leaves us both panting when we part, and I hold her head in my hands. "Thank you, Bec."

She's crying, too, holding her palms over my hands as I stroke my thumbs over her cheeks, wiping her tears away after they fall.

"I love you too." She presses another soft kiss to my lips. "Oh, and I also wanted to give you something small to unwrap," she says before standing to grab the last gift under the tree, wiping the last of her tears away with the back of her hand.

"I don't know how you could top that…" Words fail me as I tear the wrapping paper open to find a pair of boxer briefs…with eggplants on them.

Bec bursts out cackling. When she catches my arched eyebrow, she hurries to her feet and flies down the hallway, running away from me, her maniacal laughter ricocheting off the walls and her bare feet slapping against the floor.

I give her a head start, waiting to chase after her, and scratch Hop's head as he plops onto the couch snuggling with his new toy.

When I find Bec, she's already stripped down to some red lace thing with straps down her thighs, laid back on our bed. I rip my shirt over my head, throwing it to the floor, wasting no time before she's coming on my tongue and on my cock, moaning my name.

When we're both spent, we get into the bath, her body resting between my legs, leaning her back against my chest. The lights are off, but I can see her perfect curves in the glow from the cityscape outside our window and from Bec's candles flickering on the bathroom counter.

We sit in comfortable silence. Bec trails her fingertips up and down my forearms, resting her head in the crook of my neck, her cheek against my chest. My thoughts meander, but they keep coming back to one thing. One unsettling, missing piece that I can't wait to put into place…soon.

"One more game of Pictionary?" I ask.

She looks up at me, confused. "Now?"

"Yeah, now. Turn around, give me your back." She turns in my lap, facing me and wrapping her arms around my shoulders and her legs around my waist. I know how this ends…with us going for round two while water splashes over the edge of the tub, making a mess…but not yet. I want to do this first.

# CHAPTER SIXTY-THREE

"This isn't how Pictionary works," she says with a wry smile.

"Humor me. Now, I need you to pay attention, baby," I say as I start drawing on her back with the pad of my pointer finger.

"God, with you drawing? I'm afraid no one is winning here."

I give her ass a light slap under the water with my free hand, making her smile. Despite her dig, she closes her eyes and focuses her attention on the feel of my hand on her back, tracing over her skin, drawing the picture I can't get out of my mind.

"Uhh...is it a Christmas tree?"

I nibble her neck, causing her to arch and gasp. I start over, tracing the picture onto her skin a second time.

"Try again," I say.

"I don't know...a house?" she guesses.

*Closer, but no.*

"Wrong," I say, before leaning down to suck her nipple into my mouth. She threads her hands into my hair, tugging me closer to her chest, encouraging me to keep going. So, I do, all the while tracing my mind's picture onto her back.

"A bed?"

"Sorry, Bec. Three strikes, you're out," I say before pulling her down and thrusting up into her, making her moan before she starts to ride me.

I laugh to myself, focusing all my attention on the beautiful woman in my arms. I guess Bec will have to wait until she sees the ring herself. Until then, I'm going to focus on loving her the best I can until she agrees to let me do just that for the rest of our lives.

# Acknowledgments

To you, the reader. *Thank you, thank you, thank you* for giving my characters and me a chance. I hope you enjoyed reading Bec and Aiden's story as much as I enjoyed writing it. It took a while to feel like I got it right, but I guess that's life. We learn and grow as we go, and that's definitely what this writing adventure was all about for me. I know how precious your time is, and I'm incredibly grateful you chose to use it reading *Winning the Nightcap.* I plan to dream up additional novels in the future, exploring some of the stories introduced in this group of friends, or maybe something completely different. Feel free to find me on social media and tell me what you want to see next! Until then, you have my sincerest gratitude for sharing this experience with me. Cheers to your next good book.

To my husband. My number one boyfriend isn't a professional baseball player. He's the guy who played baseball growing up and let me pester him with a million questions about the sport he loves because I know *so* very little. He's the guy who consistently encouraged me to pursue this farfetched dream of publishing a *spicy* book. He's the guy who stubbornly refuses to get a piercing...for research purposes. He's the guy who wanted a "cowriter" acknowledgment because he helped me work through so many questions, ideas, and instances of writer's block that I lost count. Sorry, I couldn't fit your suggested term "meat bat" anywhere. You're one in a million, and I'd marry you again tomorrow. I love our little family, and I have you to thank for this dream coming true. Thank you for always believing in me. Now, let's write another book.

To my son. So much of our journey as mother and son inspired how I view and write about motherhood and life. The challenges, the transformation, the growth, the hilarity, the joy, the love. Being your mom is the greatest thing I'll ever experience. I'm not perfect, but you should know that I love you infinitely. You light up my heart and my world.

To my dogs. One of you inspired the idea of Lucy, and one of you inspired the idea of Hopper, but you both inspired me to write characters like Bec and Aiden who know humans are not worthy of a dog's love. It is too pure. Thank you for the endless snuggles and welcome distractions.

To my family. I hope you all read the dedication page and then skipped immediately to the acknowledgments. I'd like to keep holidays from becoming awkward. All the same, I love you endlessly. My home is with all of you. Wherever we are together always feels like the safest place in the world—full of understanding, laughter, and kindness. Thank you for lifting me up and showing me unconditional love.

To my best friend. Your thirty-plus years of friendship has been a dependable lifeline throughout all the ups and downs we've faced together. Thank you for setting the bar sky high for what a healthy friendship should look like. You shaped what friendship means to me, fueling my writing in a way I appreciate more than I can describe.

To Paisley McNab of Perfectly Write Editing Services. Putting this story into someone else's hands was a daunting step, but you made it incredibly easy. I cannot thank you enough for your support through each step of the process. Before I saw any of your edits, you were already helping me find the right words. I appreciate you for helping me achieve something I used to only dream about, and for making it better than I ever could have hoped.

To the beta reading team at E&A Editing Services. You were the first (besides my husband) to read this book, and your feedback was incredibly helpful as I tried to make this story the best that it could be. Thank you for sharing your time and suggestions so that I can grow as a writer.

To Acacia of Ever After Cover Design. I cannot thank you enough for sharing your talent and creating a beautiful cover for this novel. The end result is just perfect.

To romance authors everywhere. Reading saved me in a way I can't explain. Like so many others, I rediscovered a love for reading as an adult after a years-long hiatus. My unexpected love for books with delicious spice brought me back to life and even inspired me to take a stab at writing myself. I never expected to love it as much as I do. Thank you for sharing your stories with the world.

To the book community. Thank you for the smuttiest recommendations I never knew I needed. I found a sense of belonging reading alongside strangers, and I haven't been the same since. Please keep those spicy recommendations coming!

# About the Author

Jane Hayes is a new author of sweet and spicy contemporary romance. In her work, you can count on finding witty banter, strong friendships, found family, comedic relief, heart-warming connections, and of course, a happily ever after.

When she's not writing, Jane's chasing her toddler and two dogs, oversharing very descriptive details from her latest alien or dark romance read with her husband, working part time at the local bookstore, or devouring another romance novel.

Instagram: @authorjanehayes

TikTok: @author.jane.hayes

Email: authorjanehayes@gmail.com